# BABY BLUE

## SECOND BOOK OF THE CORRINGTON BROTHERS

## LEESA WRIGHT

Copyright © 2021 by Leesa Wright

All rights reserved. No part of this book may be reproduced or used in any manner without written permission of the copyright owner except for the use of quotations in a book review. For more information, address: leesawright.author@gmail.com

FIRST EDITION

Editing, Formatting, and Publishing Assistance
by Chell Reads Publishing, Michelle Morrow

Cover by Ashley Byland

*To the women and families left behind waiting for their loved ones to come home.
To the families of those who paid the ultimate sacrifice.
Your pain and sacrifice is not forgotten.*

## CONTENTS

| | |
|---|---|
| Prologue Early February-1969 | 1 |
| Chapter 1 | 3 |
| Chapter 2 | 19 |
| Chapter 3 | 25 |
| Chapter 4 | 32 |
| Chapter 5 | 40 |
| Chapter 6 | 49 |
| Chapter 7 | 58 |
| Chapter 8 | 68 |
| Chapter 9 | 85 |
| Chapter 10 | 91 |
| Chapter 11 | 102 |
| Chapter 12 | 110 |
| Chapter 13 | 116 |
| Chapter 14 | 121 |
| Chapter 15 | 126 |
| Chapter 16 | 146 |
| Chapter 17 | 156 |
| Chapter 18 | 164 |
| Chapter 19 | 171 |
| Chapter 20 | 181 |
| Chapter 21 | 189 |
| Chapter 22 | 200 |
| Chapter 23 | 207 |
| Chapter 24 | 215 |
| Chapter 25 | 222 |
| Chapter 26 | 228 |
| Chapter 27 | 235 |
| Chapter 28 | 242 |

| | |
|---|---|
| Chapter 29 | 248 |
| Chapter 30 | 255 |
| Chapter 31 | 265 |
| Chapter 32 | 274 |
| Chapter 33 | 283 |
| Chapter 34 | 293 |
| Chapter 35 | 302 |
| Chapter 36 | 312 |
| Chapter 37 | 321 |
| Chapter 38 | 331 |
| Chapter 39 | 340 |
| Chapter 40 | 350 |
| Chapter 41 | 358 |
| Chapter 42 | 369 |
| Chapter 43 | 381 |
| Chapter 44 | 390 |
| Chapter 45 | 397 |
| Chapter 46 | 406 |
| Chapter 47 | 417 |
| Chapter 48 | 424 |
| Chapter 49 | 435 |
| Chapter 50 | 445 |
| Chapter 51 | 453 |
| Epilogue | 468 |
| Max's Funny Words List | 470 |
| Glossary | 472 |
| Also by Leesa Wright | 473 |
| Operation Amethyst 1st Chapter | 474 |
| *Acknowledgments* | 485 |
| *About the Author* | 487 |

# BABY BLUE

## PROLOGUE EARLY FEBRUARY-1969

Elijah Corrington sat on his front porch, exhausted from his day of labor, building a bigger home for his small family. The easy sway of the squeaky swing as it moved back and forth lulled him into closing his eyes for a moment. Hearing the slam of a car door, he bolted upright. He stiffened as he watched the man walk through Elyse's small garden gate and stop at the bottom of the steps.

"Elijah Corrington?"

"Yes."

"Sir, I have a telegram for you," the man said as he handed the telegram to Elijah.

Elyse cradled her infant son to her breast as she rose from the rocker. Gently laying the sleeping babe in his crib, she covered him with his blanket. Tiptoeing from the room, quietly pulling the door shut, she walked into the kitchen and stopped to grab a bottle of wine and two glasses from the small kitchen table, passing through the living room to the front porch where Elijah waited for her.

She stepped onto the porch to see Elijah reading a telegram. His face had lost all color and looked drawn and grief-stricken.

"What's wrong?" Elyse asked.

The anguish clear as his eyes rose to meet hers. He searched for the words, licking his suddenly dry lips.

"Donall. Donall's plane was shot down. He's MIA."

The wine bottle and glasses hit the floor with a thud shattering into a thousand pieces. She looked at the red wine pooled like blood at her feet.

"No," she whispered.

# CHAPTER 1

EARLY JUNE-1969

Anablue Baker padded barefoot along the dock on the San Francisco bay, her long blonde hair blowing in the breeze beneath her floppy straw hat. Her arms full, she struggled with her bulky load. A lollypop in her mouth, an easel slung precariously over one shoulder. She held a large tackle box in one hand, a blank canvas tucked under her other arm. A small three-legged stool held tightly in her grasp.

The dock swelled with the incoming waves and gently rocked the walkway as she teetered, fighting for her balance. She passed sailboats rocking in their slips in the small marina, their whimsical names painted on the bows of the boats, sails appropriately held in place on their tall white masts.

Her mind on the day ahead, her goal now was the coveted

area at the far end of the dock. Her favorite spot to sit, feel the ocean breeze on her face, and paint to her heart's content.

A LONE SAILBOAT pulled into its slip. The boat, old and dilapidated, was in desperate need of loving repair. Its new owner leaped from the boat, kneeling on the dock behind Anablue to tie the rope to its mooring pole.

The first thing he saw was her toenails painted a bright shiny red. His lingering gaze drifted to her slim ankles, to well-shaped calves, up to the edge of her knee-length yellow floral, ruffled skirt. The skirt was molded by the wind against her thighs and curvy bottom. The long blonde hair waved and curled to ringlets against the pale pink of a long cotton shirt covered in brightly colored paint splotches. His eyes moved slowly up her back to her straw hat with fresh-cut pink flowers sticking in the side of the blue-ribbon band. He inhaled as he caught the scent of lemon from her hair.

Intrigued by the shapely woman he stood to stand tall at his full six-foot-two frame. His blue, unbuttoned shirt showed a trim waist and well-defined abs.

Someone called out, "Anablue. You forgot Bart's lunch."

The man glanced to the dock to see a young boy of ten or so, running, holding a white paper bag in his hand.

ANABLUE SWUNG around the easel on her shoulder, missing the man standing behind her as he ducked to avoid being hit.

"Bumfuzzle. Again," she muttered. She swung back, and the man ducked again, but this time, losing his balance, he plunged into the water. Anablue looked around at the sudden sound of the splash. Not seeing anything out of the ordinary, she riveted her gaze back to the boy running down the dock towards her.

The boy handed her the white bag. "Ma said you'd forget your head if it wasn't glued on."

Pulling the lollypop from her mouth, sighing deeply. "I'm sorry Boedy. Thank you for bringing it to me," she replied.

"Do you need help getting your stuff to your spot?"

"No, I'm good. Go on back to the fish market. Your mom needs your help."

Anablue watched Boedy, a smile lighting her face, as he left on the run, racing back along the dock with youthful exuberance.

THE MAN, using his arms, pulled himself out of the water and onto the dock. Shaking his head, the water droplets spraying as he stood. Feeling the spray on her face, turning quickly, she barreled right into him, her cumbersome burdens landed with thumps onto the dock. Her hands splayed against his chest as he gripped her waist, trying to steady her as a wave hit the dock, and they both toppled into the Bay.

Donall Corrington surfaced the water again. Looking for the woman, he didn't see her on the dock or emerging from the cold water of the Bay.

"Son of a…." he dove underwater. He found her by a sheer stroke of luck. Her hair brushed his arm. Grabbing her by her hair, he pulled her body to his, and he pulled her to the surface.

Once they surfaced, she swept her hair from her face. Pulling her along, his arm wrapped securely around her neck. Swimming to the pier, he plucked her out of the water to set her on the dock.

Donall stared into the bluest eyes he'd ever seen. His eyes roamed the exquisite face of the woman: creamy skin, a pert nose. Perfectly plump lips tinged with a hint of blue as she shivered in the cold June wind. Pulling himself out of the water. He raced to his old boat, jumping into the boat. He exited a moment later with a blanket. Settling it on her shoulders, he helped her to her feet.

"Are you alright, Miss?" he asked.

"Anablue," she replied.

"Miss Blue, are you alright?"

"No, Anablue, my name is Anablue Baker," she corrected him. "And you are?"

"Donall Corrington."

"Hello, Donald."

"It's Donall, with two L's," he replied.

"Okay, Donall, with two L's, do you make a habit of knocking girls into the water to drown?"

He regarded her with amusement. "Pretty girls should learn to swim before sitting on the dock of the bay," Donall said.

She scowled, crinkling her nose in annoyance at him.

Anablue looked down at her feet. The tackle box open, its contents of paintbrushes and tubes of brightly colored oil paints littered the pier. She spotted her straw hat floating in the water close to the dock.

"My hat," she cried.

Donall groaned. He dove back into the water, swimming with strong strokes. He retrieved the hat and returned to the dock. Climbing back up, he placed the soggy hat upon her head. With a wide grin, he spotted a soggy flower lying at her feet. He leaned and plucked the bloom from the dock and handed it to her.

"There you go, Baby Blue."

"I'm not a baby," she replied, clearly irritated.

His lips curled into a devastatingly irresistible smile. "No, but I bet you're somebody's baby?" he said.

A delicate frown creased her brow as she worried her lower lip. "You're fresh for someone I just met."

Another wicked grin split his face. Spotting a paint tube on the ground at his feet, he bent to retrieve the tube before he stepped on it. Slowly his eyes drifted upwards. Her wet skirt molded against curvy hips, a trim waist, her yellow cotton shirt plastered to perfect perky breasts beneath the unbuttoned pink paint shirt and blanket. His gaze swept to her throat and the faint beating of her pulse, coming to rest in her annoyed blue eyes.

"Take a picture. It lasts longer," she snapped.

EMBARRASSED at her own sharp words, not waiting for a reply. Anablue dropped to her knees, gathered her paints and brushes into a pile, and tossed them into the toolbox. She was surprised to see him bend and scoop the tubes toward her. He picked up the canvas and stool. Anablue pulled the lollypop from her mouth, her eyes wide as she looked into the face of the man. Water dripped from his wavy black hair on the top of his head, the regulation haircut trimmed short and tight on the side. A strong jawline framed a strikingly handsome face. His sparkling brown eyes, the width of his shoulders, his bare chest, visible beneath his unbuttoned shirt. Feeling her skin flush, realizing she was staring at his furry belly. Raising her eyes to meet his amused expression, her thick lashes fluttered as she lowered her eyes.

Clicking the toolbox shut, securing the clip, he stood. Looking up at him, he offered her his hand and pulled her to her feet as he handed her the canvas to tuck under one arm.

"May I assist you further?" he asked.

"No, I'm good," she replied as she turned away.

Turning back to face him. "I'm not, you know," she stated.

"Not what?"

"Somebody's baby."

Watching his eyes as his gaze as he swept her body. "You should be," he replied.

Blushing profusely, she walked away, a big smile lighting her face.

Donall, hands on his hips, watched her as she made her way to the far end of the dock. Hearing laughter behind him, he turned. Spying an older man sitting in a sailboat, two slips down from his boat, tied to the mooring.

"I saw the whole damn thing," the man chuckled.

Donall grinned as the man stood and offered his hand. "Welcome to the neighborhood. You can call me Capt. Jack, everyone else does."

Shaking his hand. "Donall Corrington."

Capt. Jack moved his hand to indicate another chair. "Have a seat." Reaching into a cooler at his feet, he handed Donall a beer. Nodding his thanks, his gaze drifted to the far end of the dock.

"That Anablue, she's something else," Capt. Jack said.

"Beautiful," Donall replied.

"Pretty girl, I watch out for her down here," Capt. Jack said. "Whatever she's running from, the sun and sea air have brought a glow to her face. "

"You think she's running?" Donall asked.

"I know she is," replied Capt. Jack. "Just don't know why."

Intrigued, Donall raised an eyebrow.

"I see you've got your work cut out for you with that old sailboat," Capt. Jack said.

Donall grinned. "Bought it in an estate sale. It's been in dry-dock for ten years. I spent the last two weeks sanding and re-painting the hull."

"Looking at you, I'm guessing you're a Navy man through and through," Capt. Jack said.

"Donall chuckled, "Looking at you, I'm guessing the same."

"USS Papago, Captain-ed her for twenty years before I retired six months ago. Now I own a little bar up on the corner, Two-belly Jacks."

"Papago, I've heard of her. Salvage ship out of Norfolk."

"Yeah, salvage, towing. Not a glamorous job, but a great ship. I still miss her. "

"Doesn't matter the ship. Once you've been to sea, it's in your blood," Donall replied.

"What ship do you hail from?" Capt. Jack asked.

"The Tico."

"The USS Ticonderoga. A mighty fine *bird farm. A friend of mine said she's at San Diego now."

"Yeah, she returned from deployment. They'll move her to Long Beach for maintenance shortly," Donall replied.

"What do you do on the Tico?" Capt. Jack asked.

"Fighter pilot."

"Bombing the VC and NVA?"

"Giving them hell," Donall replied.

"You out now?" Capt. Jack asked.

"Haven't decided," Donall said as he stood to leave. "Thanks for the beer."

"Wait a minute. It's almost time."

Capt. Jack stood and hollered. "Eight bells, Anablue."

Anablue looked up and waved. Gathering her supplies, she neatly filled the toolbox. She folded her easel, sitting primly upon her stool. White bag in hand, she waited.

"WHAT'S SHE WAITING FOR?" Donall asked.

"Give it a minute, you'll see. He's never late."

One minute later, an enormous seal launched himself out of the water and onto the dock, knocking Anablue off of her stool, practically lying on top of her.

"Holy shit!" Donall said, leaping to his feet. Capt. Jack chuckled and grabbed his arm.

"It's Bart. He won't hurt her."

"That's a wild animal," Donall replied.

"Just watch. I don't think he's that wild. Someone's pet they released into the Bay. The circus or the zoo? Don't know for sure," Capt. Jack said.

"How do you know it's the same one?"

"See the big scar on his back? Something got ahold of

him once. But he's a crafty one, escaped with some scars and his life."

"More than a few of us can say that as well," Donall replied.

Capt. Jack gave him a long look and nodded his head. "Yeah, a few."

Anablue squealed with delight and clapped her hands as Bart clapped his fins. Reaching into the bag, she pulled out the last small fish. Holding the fish above Bart's head, "Okay Bart, this is it. Give me a kiss and be on your way." She kissed the seal on the snout and gave him his fish, which he swallowed in one bite. "See you tomorrow." The seal barked, clapped his fins, and was gone back into the bay in the blink of an eye. Wiping her hands on her shirt, she sniffed the air. *I smell like a fishwife, only for you, Bart.*

Looking up, she spied Donall watching her. Shaking his head, his face lit up in amusement. Gathering her supplies, she walked slowly, stopping in front of Donall and Capt. Jack.

"Do you have yesterday's painting? Capt. Jack," she asked as she handed him the new painting. "It should be dry by now."

"I sure do, darlin'. Let me get it for you," he replied as he handed the new painting to Donall to hold.

Capt. Jack went inside the cabin and returned a moment later with another canvas. Handing it to her. "it's dry along the edges and tacky in the center. Be careful, darling."

"I will," she replied.

"Do you need help?" Donall asked.

"No, I'm good. I've got a prime parking spot on a side street pretty close to here," she said.

"You're sure?" Donall said.

"Of course. I've been on my own for a while now. I'm used to this." Looking at the bay and the angle of the sun in the sky. "Damn, I going to be late for work. I've got to run, thanks, Capt. Jack, I'll see you tomorrow," she said. Looking at Donall. "Goodbye, Donall, with two L's, I'll see you around."

"Baby Blue, I'll be watching for you."

Donall watched as her cheeks pinken, and she turned and strolled away. He watched the swing of her skirt as it sashayed back and forth until she was disappeared into the crowd of tourists on the pier.

Remembering the painting he still held in his hands, he held it up to look at it. A grin split his face as he looked up at the majesty of the Golden gate bridge in the distance. The bay dotted with sailboats, their sails catching the chilly wind as they propelled across the water.

*Sitting on the dock of the San Francisco Bay, she doesn't paint bridges. She paints…. flowers.*

Anablue opened the trunk of her car, setting her things inside. Removing her paint shirt, her thoughts traveled to the handsome man she had met. His sparkling brown eyes and the way his mouth crinkled in the corners when he smiled, but he was much too fresh for her. Though the way he looked at her, she did feel warm and melty inside.

It had been a long time since a man had sparked her interest. Maybe high school, and that was Randy Porter, and he had never glanced her way. Sure, she had dated a bit after high school and never while overseas. Things had never been the same for her since she lost Brian.

Brian, what he would say about the choices she had made. Leaving home and everything she held near and dear to come here to live alone. They had always planned to do it together, to leave their small town, and live by the bay in the city of lights. They would sit on the dock of the bay, and he would play his guitar for her while she painted. It was never to be, all of their dreams and schemes. She had lost him, in a war, in a far-away place, Vietnam.

Even now, six months later, her heart still ached. Or Gram, she had lost her eight months ago. Her mother had passed five years prior, and her father? Who knew where he was now? There was also an uncle somewhere. Seeing no reason to stay, she had packed her things, covered the furniture, and left town to make her way in the world.

Climbing into the driver's seat, she cranked the key, and the engine roared to life. Frank Sinatra crooned Silent Night from the eight-track player. The engine rumbled as she pulled away from the curb.

SHE PARKED on a side street close to the City Lights bookstore where she worked. She loved the job. The co-workers and the owner were pretty cool. The customers and regulars were an eclectic group of poets, artists, beatniks, musicians, and free thinkers, all vying to be heard. Somewhat shy, she spent some of her breaks in the store's basement, sitting in the corner, listening to their passionate discussions on current issues near and dear to their hearts.

Placing her purse under the front counter, she signed in on her timesheet. Looking around the store at work needing to be done, she grabbed a stack of books to be returned to the shelves.

"Hey, Maude. I'm here."

"Morning, kiddo," Maude called down from the office. "Or is afternoon already?"

Anablue climbed the ladder, placing a book on the top shelf. Hearing the tinkling bells at the door as a customer entered the store, climbing down the ladder, she rounded the corner. Not seeing anyone, she turned in confusion as a man's hands grabbed her by the waist and turned her to pull her close to his chest.

"Hey Anablue, how about a kiss?"

Pushing against his chest, she let out a small scream. "Let go of me, Gary. What have I told you about sneaking up behind me?" she said. The man was ordinary-looking—about five-six, a slender build, with shoulder-length greasy brown hair.

"Ah, come on, you're always putting me off. Come out with me tonight. There's a new band playing at Bad Louie's."

"How often do I have to tell you that I'm not interested in dating right now," she replied." Besides, isn't Jane your girlfriend or something?"

"Plain Jane? Nah, she's nothing to me, not when I got someone like you in my sights."

"Well, get me out of your sights. I'm not interested," she replied.

The bells on the door chimed again as a young redheaded woman entered the store pushing a baby boy of six months or so in a stroller.

Gary eyed the woman, "Look at her. Nice tits. Too bad she's got a snotty-nosed brat."

"You're disgusting, Gary. Leave me alone, and don't talk about women and babies like that," Anablue said.

"Fine, for now. Has Marcus come by yet?" Gary asked.

"No idea, maybe he's downstairs," Anablue replied.

Gary's eyes swept the tiny red-headed woman again. From the short black and white gingham minidress covering her curvy hips and slim waist, up her body in a slow insolent manner. Pausing on her breasts before he raised his head to stare into her amethyst-colored eyes. He gave her an insolent smile. She coldly returned his gaze as her eyes hardened. Unnerved by the woman, Gary headed toward the back of the store.

Anablue turned to the woman. "I'm so sorry."

"It's alright, it's not your fault. I'm Elyse Corrington. Has the book I ordered come in yet?"

"Let me check," Anablue replied as she moved to the counter to open the ledgers. "Not yet, possibly tomorrow."

The baby started to cry, and Elyse bent to adjust his blanket, handing him his rattle as she softly cooed to him. Still fussing, she lifted the baby out of his stroller.

"He's so adorable. Get a load of those black curls on his head," Anablue said.

Elyse kissed the baby's head, burying her face in his curls. "Baby smell, I love how he smells."

"What's his name?" Anablue asked.

"Bunker. Well, Andrew, but we call him Bunker," Elyse replied.

"That's an unusual nickname."

"It's a long story," Elyse replied.

Not wanting to pry, Anablue smiled. "I can call you when your book comes in."

"No. I'll stop in on my way to the studio in a couple of days. Speaking of names, what's yours?"

"Anablue."

"What a lovely name."

'Thank you," Anablue replied.

Elyse put the baby back in the stroller. Handing him his blanket and rattle, she maneuvered the stroller out the door.

"You okay, Anablue?" Maude called down.

Crossing the store to stand next to the polished wood staircase spiraling up to the second-floor manager's office. "I'm fine,"

"You let me know if Gary gets out of hand, and I'll take care of that little prick," Maude said.

"Don't you worry about me. I can handle him," Anablue replied.

## CHAPTER 2

*Tied to a pole, hearing rough guttural laughter and the swish of the fan belt, the pain screamed across his back.*

Donall woke a start, bathed in sweat, the nightmare so real. He rolled to the edge of the bed and climbed from the bunk. He strode through the tiny galley kitchen, past the small bathroom, and out the cabin door of the sailboat.

One foot upon the bench, he breathed in the salt air—the night breeze cooling the sweat on his back and brow. The lights of Sausalito in the distance and the reflection of the Golden Gate bridge on the bay below calmed the turmoil in his chest. He watched a heavy layer of fog rolling in. Troubled by the dream, his mind wandered back to his short time in captivity, fourteen days to be exact.

The Viet Cong had been cruel and depraved. Precisely what he had been trained to expect of them. He had survived.

He, along with his *wizzo, Hart, had eventually escaped. He was lucky, knowing men who had been held for years and probably still captive to this day.

Shaking his head to clear his thoughts, his eyes came to rest on the far side of the dock. The woman, just thinking about Anablue, she was such a beautiful girl. It had been a long time since a woman had lit a fire inside of him, and this one was perfection. He sighed deeply. He had to focus on his healing. The average woman wouldn't want anything to do with a troubled man.

Knowing sleep was beyond him for now, he looked at his watch, a few minutes past midnight, the bar would still be open. A quick stroll to Two-Belly Jacks and a cold beer was in order.

He went inside, pulled his jeans on, and slipped his feet into canvas shoes. Throwing his shirt over his shoulder, he left the cabin, jumping out of the boat and onto the dock. Whistling, he made his way to the bar.

Pulling the heavy door open. The noise of the bar hit him, people talking, laughing, the music from the jukebox. A couple of men played pool in the back of the bar, while an amorous couple danced shoulder to shoulder to a slow seductive song on the jukebox. The woman leaning her head on the man's shoulder, laughed at something whispered into her ear.

The bar itself was high polished mahogany. Row upon row of glass shelving filled with liquor bottles glowed from the lights above the bar.

Spotting an empty stool, Donall pulled up a seat, waving

to Capt. Jack at the far end. A smile lit Capt. Jack's face as he gave the finishing wipe to a glass with his towel.

Watching him move toward Donall with a rolling gait brought a smile to Donall's face. *He walks like a pirate too long at sea.*

"Donall, welcome to Two-Belly Jacks."

"Nice little bar you got here," Donall replied.

"Little bar to fill my nights, sailboat to fill my days. Living the dream. What will you have?"

"A cold beer sounds good."

Capt. Jack set a pint in front of him and pushed a bowl of popcorn toward him as he turned away to help another customer. Donall popped some kernels in his mouth and sipped his beer.

A SONG CAME on the jukebox, and Donall stopped to listen. The last time he heard this song, a beautiful ballerina danced to it on the deck of the Tico. His mind traveled back to the last day he had seen Elyse and his twin brother, Elijah, right after their wedding at Vung Tau. Had it really been a year since he had seen them? He had been putting it off, traveling the hour or so north to see them, meet his new nephew, and seeing his father. It probably was time. He knew he was going to a tongue lashing from Elyse for waiting so long, but he needed time to sort things out.

He was brought from his thoughts by Capt. Jack. "Haven't seen you around lately."

"Yeah, I went to San Diego for a couple of days," Donall said.

"You resigned your commission?"

"Yeah, I didn't pass the physical. The doctors submitted the paperwork. I'll be out on a medical," Donall replied, as a look of sorrow crossed his handsome face.

"You ever want to talk about it. I'm all ears," Capt. Jack said.

"Thanks."

A MAN SLID into the open barstool next to Donall. "Evening," he said.

"Evening Gary, none of that radical, political talk tonight," Capt. Jack warned. "You scare away the customers with your talk of revolution."

"Maybe it's talk they need to hear, old man. Give me a beer," Gary replied.

"I mean it, Gary. Not tonight," Capt. Jack said as he slid a pint toward him. "Where's that tall, pretty wife of yours?"

"Jane? That old hag is at home where she belongs," Gary sneered.

Gary's eyes touched on Donall, giving him the once over, his contempt visible. Donall returned his look, cool and hard. Gary's eyes slithered away. *This guy's seen some shit.* Spotting a woman at the jukebox, "Well, well, there's Lori, she ain't Anablue, but she'll do for the night." He slid from the barstool, beer in hand, and approached a young blonde woman. Sliding his arm over her shoulder, pulling her close.

"Hey, Lori, where you been? How about a kiss."

The woman wrapped her arms around his neck. "I've been waiting by the phone all week. You said you would call," Lori replied.

"Then why the fuck ain't you home right now waiting by the phone?"

"I got bored," she pouted.

Capt. Jack watched Gary with a look of disgust. Turning back to Donall. "The world takes all kinds, but he's trouble. The Navy kicked him out on a dishonorable discharge. You watch your back around him. Grow your hair out. Try to blend in a little. They can be ruthless with the men returning from Nam."

Donall nodded. "What's a guy like that want with Anablue?"

"Nothing more than another conquest under his belt."

"How does he know her?"

"She works over at the bookstore on Columbus. From what I hear, a lot of those hippies hang around there. Not saying their views are right or wrong, just different. Then again, can't say I'll ever understand this hippy generation," Capt. Jack replied.

Donall grinned. "Why am I not surprised she works at a bookstore?"

"Intrigued?" Capt. Jack asked with a smile.

Donall smiled, winked, and slapped a dollar bill on the bar. "Good night. Thanks for the beer. Keep the change."

# CHAPTER 3

Anablue rolled over in her bed, shivering in the cold. Burying her head under her covers, she counted the estimated number of steps to the space heater, then to the chair to grab her bathrobe. She stuck one foot out and gingerly tested the floor, yanking her foot back inside at the touch of icy cold floorboards. *I need a rug.*

Brian had never told her San Francisco was cold in the middle of summer. These overnight temperatures felt more like a cold winter day in December at home, not June. Steeling her resolve, she flipped back the covers and raced for the space heater, flipping the switch on while grabbing her robe from the chair. *Will I ever learn to leave it on the bed?*

Wrapping the robe around herself while diving for the bed, grabbing her heavy socks off the floor as she went. She burrowed under the covers giving the space heater ample time to heat the room. Mrs. Wang didn't appreciate it if she left the heater on all night.

Wrapping herself in a blanket, she climbed out of bed. Turning the heating plate on to heat the water in the tea kettle, she opened one of the double doors to wander out to the widow's walk, pulling the door shut to capture the heat in the room.

*Foggy again, I won't see the sun until late morning.* Looking down from the top of the massive Victorian rooming house she called home, she could barely make out the outline of her car parked in the driveway. Brian's car.

She could remember the day of his funeral. They had buried him in the old church cemetery. She would forever be haunted by Amazing Grace played on bagpipes. She had left soon after, driving his car here to start a new life.

Her closest neighbors had tried talking her out of her decision to leave, and at the last minute, Mrs. Wu had given her the name of a relative. Mrs. Wang ran a clean, safe rooming house in San Francisco.

The whistling of the tea kettle brought her from her thoughts. Sighing deeply, she went back into her room to have a cup of tea. Payday today. She could pay her rent for July early, gas up the car, buy a book, paint supplies, and if anything was left, food. Grabbing her towel and bath supplies, she headed downstairs to the shared bathroom to shower.

Donall woke to the forlorn wail of the foghorn in the distance. The chill in the air sinking through his blankets. After the heat and humidity of Vietnam, he welcomed the cold of the morning. His mind wandering to the woman, Anablue. She was beautiful. Those eyes, so blue, they fit her name. They reminded him of the sky on the clearest day from the cockpit of his jet. Had it been since February since he had last sat in a cockpit? He remembered the awe he felt, then terror, as he looked out over the earth and the blue of the sky as his parachute floated downward into hell.

His thoughts returned to Anablue. Maybe it was time to go buy a book.

Anablue climbed back up the ladder to return a small stack of books to what she called the naughty shelf. Erotica. She held a basket on her arm. She found that climbing the ladder if she put the books in the basket made the climb much more manageable. Setting some of the books in her basket as she straightened the other books on the shelf first. Maude must have been up here again. She looked at a risqué book cover. Curious, she opened the book.

*The gentleman pirate slid his knife through her corset, slowly teasing, cutting one string at a time. With each cut, Antoinette gasped, breathing heavy, as more and more of her creamy smooth breasts were exposed to his hungry gaze.*

Anablue sharply inhaled. *Bumfuzzle! This book is a bodice ripper.*

Hearing the chimes at the door, she called out. "I'll be right with you."

DONALL WAITED by the cash register for a minute before following her voice to the first aisle. She was up on a ladder reading a book. He stopped, looking at her well-shaped calves. His eyes followed their natural path to look up her short plaid skirt. Grinning, *Damn, she's wearing shorts under her skirt.*

Clearing his throat to get her attention. "Ah-hem."

Anablue slammed the book shut, threw it in her basket, and scrambled down the ladder. Stopping at eye level. A guilty frown furrowed her brow. "Donall with two L's, were you looking up my skirt?"

"Me? Nah!" Donall replied innocently.

She gave him a "yeah right" look. "They're reasons girls wear shorts under their skirts," she gently chided.

Her obvious deflection amused him. He nodded his head. "Yes, I suppose there is," he replied.

"What can I help you with?"

"A book, I need a book."

"You need to be a little more specific," she said, a soft smile curving her pink lips.

"Poetry. French."

Looking at the basket she held in the crook of her arm,

he reached in pulled a book out. *A Pirates Plunder.* Raising his eyebrows, his sparkling brown eyes danced with amusement. Placing the book back in her basket, he didn't say one word.

ANABLUE LOOKED at the basket as the heat rose in her face. *I'm standing here talking to a man with a basket full of….. naughty books. And he must have seen me reading. Oh God,* clearing her throat, embarrassed, she moved to hide the basket behind her back.

"We have a lovely selection of French poetry," Anablue said. "Do you have a specific poet in mind?" she asked.

"Eluard, or de Lorris, de Moun," Donall replied.

"I have a book we received this morning. It has a culmination of many French poet's works. Do you want the English version? "

"French, please," Donall replied.

"You're in luck. I have a few customers who have been waiting for its arrival. We ordered extra copies," Anablue said.

She stepped from the ladder and moved behind the counter. She set the basket temporarily on the counter by the cash register. Looking below, she found three copies of the book. Setting the book in front of Donall as he pulled out his wallet to pay for the book.

"I haven't seen you at the Marina lately," Donall said.

"I was there. You weren't. Except for today, Capt. Jack feeds Bart for me on the days I can't make it."

She handed him his purchase along with his change. "Have a nice day, Donall."

He stood for a minute, contemplating her. "Do you like grilled cheese?"

She nodded. "Two slices of cheese."

He smiled a slow smile. "Guilty pleasures, huh. Okay, have lunch with me tomorrow after you've finished painting. I'll make you a grilled cheese with not one but two slices of cheese."

She gave him a breathtakingly beautiful smile. "Okay. Since I have tomorrow off. I'll have lunch with you."

"Till then, Baby Blue."

"Till then."

SHE WATCHED him through the window as he trotted across the street—what *a gorgeous man. I wonder how he kisses, how he tastes?*. Rousing herself from her dangerous thoughts. Turning to see both her co-workers, Maude and Renaldo standing behind her with surprised looks on their faces. Her cheeks burned with embarrassment.

"What?" Anablue asked.

"Did we hear that correctly? You're having lunch with dark Adonis?" Maude asked.

"His name is Donall. He's not a Greek god, but a flesh and blood man," Anablue replied.

"Oh, but the flesh and muscle on that man," Maude said as she sucked in her breath.

Anablue rolled her eyes. "I'm going to the diner for my lunch break now. You two can cool it. It's not like I've never been on a date before."

"It's the first one we know of," replied Renaldo.

Anablue grabbed her big purse from under the counter. Stopping at the door, she turned around.

"He makes grilled cheese. Other than dill pickles to go along with it, what else could a girl ask for?"

# CHAPTER 4

Elyse wiped the strained peas off her face. "I know you don't like the peas, little man, but please don't spit them at mama." Grabbing another napkin, she wiped at her chest. Looking up, she spotted Anablue coming in the door of the diner.

"Anablue, over here," she called.

Anablue walked the length of the diner, stopping in front of Elyse.

"Hello again," she said.

"Please, sit with me. Are you on your lunch break?" Elyse asked.

"Yes," Anablue said as she slid into the booth.

"I hope you don't mind. It's nice to have another woman my age to chat with," Elyse said.

"Not a bit. I don't have many friends here. So yeah, it's nice," Anablue replied.

The waitress stopped at the table, placing a basket of French fries in front of Elyse and refilling her coffee cup.

"What will you have Anablue," the waitress asked.

"Please, a cup of hot water, Hazel," Anablue said, her eyes sliding to the pile of fries and back to her purse as she dug inside for a teabag.

---

*She's hungry.* Elyse looked to Hazel. "Why don't you bring an extra plate. There's no way I can eat all of these fries, and you know what, I'm dying for one of those California burgers. The one with the lettuce and tomatoes and lots of pickles." Hazel nodded, smiled, and left to place the order.

"They're so big here, I can't eat a whole burger," Elyse said.

"You don't need to feed me," Anablue replied.

"I know, but I've been alone and hungry before, and it's not fun. Besides, you can help me distract Bunker. He needs to eat his peas before he gets his bananas, and he's not happy about it."

---

They both turned to look at Bunker, sitting in his highchair. His little cherub face, hands, and hair were covered in peas as he happily sucked his thumb while playing with the curls on top of his head.

"You're a mess. I have to get you fed before daddy gets here," Elyse said.

"Oh, then I should leave before your husband arrives," Anablue said.

"No. No, you stay right here. It's going to be another 30 minutes or so."

"Tuesdays are rough. I have Karate lessons in the morning, then I have to be at the studio for ballet class and then practice for July's performance. I bring Bunker with me to Karate. My husband usually has meetings with contractors here in the city and meets me afterward to take Bunker home. Lucky for me, the Karate instructor has a playpen I use.

"You're in Karate and Ballet? Anablue asked.

"I'm a blackbelt and a Prima ballerina," Elyse said as she slipped a spoonful of peas into Bunker's mouth. Covering his mouth with her hand as he started to spit it out.

"Andrew Finn Corrington, stop that."

"I wish I could remember where I heard that last name before.," Anablue said.

"Well, trust me. There's plenty of them out there," Elyse replied.

Hazel stopped at the table delivering the hamburger, extra plate, and a cup of hot water.

"Eat it while it's hot, ladies," she said, moving on to the next booth.

"Look at the size of this thing," Elyse said as she cut the burger in half. Placing half of the burger on the plate and sliding it toward Anablue.

"I had my first hamburger a couple of months ago, and I haven't been able to stop eating them."

"Your first?" Anablue said, surprised.

"I didn't grow up here. Well, I was born here, but I was raised in South Vietnam."

"You lived in Vietnam, in the middle of a war?"

Elyse nodded her head." But in all fairness, I lived in Saigon at the embassy and Huế City in a protected compound. It wasn't until my last year there that I lived the war."

Sorrow crossed Anablue's face as her eyes teared, and she looked away.

Elyse reached out, placing her hand over Anablue's. Not wanting to pry, silence fell.

"I lost Brian off the coast of Vietnam. It was a shipboard accident," Anablue said.

"Your husband? Boyfriend?" Elyse asked.

"No." Anablue whispered, "My twin brother."

"I'm so sorry. I did not mean to bring you pain."

"It's been six months. Some days I'm okay. Other days it comes in giant waves," Anablue replied.

"I'd like to say it gets easier, but we both know it takes time," Elyse said.

"You lost someone too?"

"A dear friend. Andy, amongst many others," Elyse replied.

Anablue glanced at the baby. "Yes, we named Bunker after him," Elyse said as she spooned bananas into the baby's mouth.

"My husband surprised me with it. His name was going to be Finn, but in the end, this was better and a way for us to honor Johnson."

"Johnson?" Anablue asked.

"That was Andy's last name," Elyse said. "He was part of the team who protected me during my last year in Vietnam. Someday, I'll tell you all about them."

"I have a date tomorrow," Anablue said, changing the subject.

Elyse's eyes lit up. "Do tell."

"He's tall, dark, and handsome. And he's going to make me grilled cheese on his sailboat," Anablue said.

"Romantic,' Elyse breathed. "My husband makes killer grilled cheese too, but don't be fooled. It's all he knows how to make. I shouldn't be so mean. I don't know how many times I've set the kitchen on fire."

"I love to cook, but all I have in my room is a heating plate to make tea," Anablue replied.

Anablue glanced at her watch. "Oh geez, I'm late. I have to get back to work."

"I've really enjoyed your company. Let's do this again," Elyse said.

"Okay, but next time. I pay my way. Thank you," Anablue said. "By the way, your book is in."

"I'll get it tomorrow," Elyse replied.

Anablue left in a rush as Elyse pulled Bunker out of the highchair.

"Little Andrew. Johnson would be tickled pink," Elyse said as she discreetly bared her breast to feed her son. Covering herself and the baby with his blanket. She smiled as he greedily fed.

---

ANABLUE WALKED INTO THE BOOKSTORE, calling up to Maude. "Sorry, I'm late, Maude."

"It's okay, kiddo," Maude said. "Let Renaldo know your back so he can leave."

Anablue walked to the back of the store looking for Renaldo as Gary came bounding up the stairs from the basement.

"There you are. I've been looking for you," Gary said.

"Why?" Anablue asked.

Gary put one arm up, leaning on the bookshelf next to her. "Why to give you a kiss," he replied as he leaned in. Anablue grimaced, turning her head in revulsion. "Knock it off."

He put up his other arm to box her in. Renaldo appeared at her side. "Let her go, Gary."

Anablue ducked beneath Gary's arm and went to stand by Renaldo.

"Someday, you'll beg for my kisses," Gary sneered.

"Highly unlikely," Anablue replied.

Gary stormed off, knocking into Renaldo's shoulder as he went back downstairs.

"Watch out for him, sweetie. He's a letch and married," Renaldo said.

"He's married to Jane. What a disgusting pig," Anablue replied. "He's just icky."

"By the way. You naughty, naughty girl," Renaldo said.

"What did I do?" she asked.

"Putting the erotica books in a basket by the register. We sold three copies while you were at lunch."

Mortified, her cheeks burned. "No. No, no, no. That was a mistake. I did not mean to leave them there."

"Sure, you didn't, sweetie. Your mind must have been filled with Dark Adonis and dirty deeds."

She opened her mouth and snapped it shut as she narrowed her eyes at him. "Don't you have somewhere to go?"

"Yeah. I've got to run before I'm late for my doctor's appointment. I've got this nasty pain in my side. See you later, sweetie. Enjoy your date tomorrow. Don't do anything I wouldn't do," Renaldo said.

"You're incorrigible," Anablue replied with a smile.

---

Renaldo left the store, crossing the street. He ambled by the diner, looking inside the windows at the customers as he went by. He stopped cold. Breathing deeply. Wondering how he was going to tell Anablue. That guy, the dark Adonis, was inside the diner kissing a beautiful red-headed woman while holding a baby in his arms, and Anablue had a date with the two-timing scum tomorrow.

# CHAPTER 5

Elijah slid into the last booth next to his wife. Baby in his arms, his back to the wall. Always on guard, it was the only way he was comfortable in public places. Noting the dirty dishes on the table.

"You already ate?" Elijah asked.

"I've met the sweetest little blonde. She works at the bookstore across the street. Anyway, she was just going to have tea for lunch, so I split a hamburger with her."

" You said you weren't going to eat burgers anymore?" Elijah said.

"I shouldn't. I still have seven pounds to go," Elyse replied.

"You look good the way you are,"

"My ballet partners still need to lift me. I need to get back to ninety-eight pounds."

"One hundred and five pounds and still full of sass," he replied as he lovingly brushed a tendril from her eyes.

"Any news on Donall yet?" she asked.

"Father called a friend he knows. Donall submitted his paperwork for a medical discharge and disappeared,"

"Try not to worry. He's been through a lot," Elyse said.

"You're worried. He'll show whenever he's ready," Elijah replied.

Elyse sighed deeply. "We have to find him a girl. Anablue would be perfect for him."

"Donall can find his own girl," Elijah growled.

Elyse rolled her eyes. "Oh, don't growl at me Marine, I'm just thinking out loud."

"You should eat before you go home," Elyse said.

"Nah, I'll wait. I want to stop at the music store before Bunker gets tired," Elijah said.

"More sheet music? You should probably finish building the house so we can get the piano out of storage and delivered first," Elyse said with a smile.

---

Gary left the bookstore, walking towards his van parked on the other side of the street. Passing the diner, he glanced inside. Spotting that same dude from Two-belly Jacks the other night. Meeting the dude's eyes, he sneered at him. His eyes rested on the baby and then on Elyse. He shot the guy a look of contempt, stuffing his hands into his pockets. He crossed mid-street to his van.

---

"Let's get out of here. That's the second time some strange guy walking by has sneered at me," Elijah said.

"You've got military written all over you. We both know they are not nice to our returning troops," Elyse said, a shimmer of tears in her eyes.

"Yeah," Elijah gruffly replied. "Any little piss-ant that spits at me will find himself pounded into a puddle."

Concern in her eyes, "Elijah. Please. They have no clue what our troops go through."

Elijah nodded his head. "Lets' go before Bunker falls asleep."

"Yes, I need to get to class," Elyse replied.

"Be careful driving home afterward, brat. It's a long drive."

"I'm sorry you have to adjust your schedule and drive down here so often," Elyse said.

"Don't be silly. This is what we both wanted," Elijah replied.

Kissing his wife goodbye, Elijah watched the swing of Elyse's hips as she walked down the sidewalk toward the dance studio a few blocks away. Looking at Bunker. "Let's go pick up your hot mama's birthday present, then go get some sheet music."

A plain young woman named Kim was at the cash register as Elijah went into the bookstore. He asked for his French poetry book on order. She called down an aisle to a co-worker, asking where the copy had been placed. Another youthful-sounding woman called back; it was under the register. Paying for his book, he left and headed up the street to the music store.

Once inside the store, Elijah headed for the sheet music section. Flipping through the composers, not looking for anything in particular. An aroma drifted up, and he looked down at Bunker. "Oh no, not here, buddy." Pulling back the diaper so he could peek inside. Coughing and gagging, he looked around for the head. He didn't see it, so he went up front. A hippy worked the register, his shoulder-length long brown hair swinging back and forth as he moved his arms to clear the air.

"Dude, your kid stinks," the hippy said.

"Where's the head?" Elijah asked.

Confused. "What's a head?" the hippy asked.

"The men's room," Elijah growled.

"Oh, go through those double doors in the back, the last door on the left."

Elijah pushed the stroller into the head. Lifting Bunker out of the stroller, holding the baby up. "Next time, save it for mama. And that's an order." The baby gurgled and laughed, flopping his chubby little arms while kicking his feet.

"Just so you know. A full diaper is considered insubordination," Elijah said, smiling as he looked into his son's amethyst-colored eyes. Looking at the black curls covering Bunkers head.

"You need a haircut soon. But first, let's figure out how to clean you up."

He stripped the baby's cloth diaper and plastic pants off, throwing them both in the trash.

He miraculously cleaned and diapered the tiny tot, lathering him with diaper cream. Holding the baby up. "I have had hundreds of troops under my command. Crawled through mud and swill, I've been waist-deep in a leech-filled swamp and lived through the worst possible conditions. And none of those experiences come in any way close to the mess you just made." The baby gave him a sweet half-smile, and Elijah's heart melted as it had a thousand times before. "You have your mama's guilty as charged smile."

DECIDING on a whim to stop and buy an album. Donall pulled into the spot directly in front of the music store. Backing up his motorcycle in front of a shiny, sixty-nine red Camaro. Climbing off his bike, he admired the car. *Elijah would dig this car.*

Donall paused in the doorway, taking it all in. Janice Joplin crooned over the speaker system. Black light posters, electric and acoustic guitars adorned the walls. He spotted the large album and 45's records section. Eight-track cartridge tapes sat in neat bins, along with eight-track players and speakers in another area. In the far corner, sheet music. Stacks of candles and boxes of incense, and various black lights filled the end caps.

Donall crinkled his nose as the competing scent of incense and shit hit him. He passed the clerk, who didn't bother looking up from the magazine he was looking at. Going over to the records section, facing the wall, he thumbed through the albums looking for something Anablue might like.

*What goes with grilled cheese and sailboats?*

ELIJAH PUSHED the stroller out of the restroom, Bunker still in his arms. He went to the sheet music section. Grabbing the music that he had picked out earlier. Not paying any attention to other customers in the store, he headed to the cash register.

Elijah cleared his throat to get the clerk's attention. He pulled his wallet from his back pocket as he eyed the area behind the clerk. Bongs, stacks of papers for rolling joints, and men's magazines filled the space. Raising his eyebrows, he placed Bunker back in his stroller.

"It still stinks in here, man," the hippy clerk said.

Elijah nodded his head. Spotting tiny bottles in a basket by the register, he picked up a bottle of strawberry oil. Opening the bottle to sniff its contents, he smiled. *Elyse would love this.* He added the bottle to his purchase.

"Chicks dig that shit, and the patchouli oil too," the hippy said. "A buddy of mine said patchouli oil on men drives chicks wild. Turns them into nymphos."

"It's the other way around. It's men who like it on women," replied Elijah, as he picked up a bottle of patchouli, looked at it, and placed it back in the basket.

"You're not going to buy some for your old lady?'

"My wife is not old, and trust me, she doesn't need it," Elijah replied.

"Dude. You've got white crap all over your shirt."

Elijah scowled at the diaper cream on his blue shirt, wiping at it with his free hand.

Nodding to the clerk. "Thanks, man," taking his bag, he left the store.

Opening the door of his Camaro parked right front, he placed Bunker in his metal seat, buckling him in. He put the stroller in the trunk. Crossing in front of the car, he stopped to admire the motorcycle parked in front of him. *A Harley, Donall would love this bike. I should get a babysitter and take Elyse for a motorcycle ride this weekend.*

---

DONALL FLIPPED THROUGH THE ALBUMS. Stopping, he shook his head. *Idiot, you don't have electricity on the boat. The stereo system and new albums will have to wait for a house someday.* He went over to the portable eight-track players. He chose a shiny red one with the speaker on the front. He turned to the cartridges, picking two out. He took his picks to the register.

The hippy clerk turned and looked at him. "You forget something, dude?" he said.

"No, I have everything I wanted," Donall replied.

"Where's the kid?"

"What kid?"

"The little shitty one." The hippy said.

"I don't have a kid, shitty or otherwise," Donall replied.

The hippy looked at him, then leaned over the counter to look at the floor.

"Same blue shirt, no kid," he mumbled. "You're sure?"

"Yeah, I'm sure," Donall replied as he picked up a bottle of strawberry oil, opened it, and sniffed the fragrance.

The hippy, a little wild-eyed now. "And the patchouli oil for your old lady?"

"She's not old, and trust me, she doesn't need it," Donall replied.

The hippy scratched his head and gave him a strange look. "That's exactly what you said before."

"You okay, man?" Looking at his name tag. "You been sniffing glue on break, Mike?" Donall asked.

"Wow, this is far out, man. Maybe I dropped too much acid last night," Mike replied.

Donall nodded his head, "Yeah. You might want to consider saving some brain cells, dude." and he turned to leave.

"Peace out, man, power to the people," Mike said as he raised his hand and gave him the peace sign.

"Yeah, peace," Donall replied.

Donall noted the red Camaro was gone. He climbed on his bike, revving the engine. He pulled away from the curb. *Maybe I should take Anablue on a bike ride this weekend. We'll see how tomorrow goes.*

## CHAPTER 6

The pile of abandoned clothes on Anablue's bed grew higher as she searched for the perfect outfit. "What does a girl wear on a sailboat?" She rummaged through her drawer, pulling out white shorts and a matching tank top. "My blue overshirt will go perfect." The clothes on the bed moved, and a beautiful Siamese cat emerged from the pile. She blinked twice at Anablue, gave her a look of disdain, jumped off the bed, and sauntered out the door to the widow's walk. Anablue shut the door behind her. *Darn neighbor cat. She makes herself at home on my bed and then is insulted if I disturb her beauty sleep.*

Looking in the mirror, as she dressed, she contemplated her looks. At five-foot-two, she acknowledged she was on the small side. The hip-hugger shorts accentuated her hips and tiny waist.

She pulled on a mid-riff halter top. Biting her lip, she

stared at the bare expanse of her belly and her breasts, not small or large. "I'm just right," she murmured to herself. *But this shirt? Bra-less? Yes? No? Maybe....I don't know.* "There's plenty of women who go bra-less. You can do it. No, I can't. And you're talking to yourself, again."

She pulled the halter top off. Opting for a white midriff shirt lined with pale blue lace edging on the bottom and a bra. *Bouncing boobs...not okay.* With her straw hat, large gold hooped earrings, and a gold hooped belt. A touch of mascara and some blush on her cheeks. Finally, she was ready.

"Blue shirt? It's a lot of bare belly to show off, Anablue," she said to herself. "Just go. You'll be late."

She grabbed her purse. Pulling the door shut, she made it to the end of the hall and down one flight of stairs before she stopped with second thoughts.

Anablue's bedroom door flew open. In a rush, she grabbed the blue shirt, threw it on, and tied it mid-waist.

---

A SIX-BEDROOM HOUSE, the other four rooms all rented out to Chinese men. Anablue was the only female roomer in the house. Mrs. Wang, the landlady, took it upon herself to guard Anablue's honor.

Anablue tip-toed down the final flight of stairs and to the hallway to the foyer. She didn't need Mrs. Wang's mother-hen questioning today. She spotted one of the roomers, Li Wei, in the hallway. Holding her finger to her lips. "Shhhhhh." As she nodded her head towards the back of the house where Mrs. Wang worked in the kitchen. Li Wei smiled, nodding his head. Watching for Mrs. Wang, he gestured to Anablue to cross the foyer while he covered for her. Anablue blew him a kiss, quietly slipped out the door. Anablue waved to Mr. Wang in the garden. A dear old man. He spent his time hiding from his wife in his vegetable garden.

She opened her car door, gently pulling the car door shut; she pulled the emergency brake and ever so quietly rolled down the high slant of the driveway and onto the street before she popped the clutch and started the car a good block away.

Parking her car nearby, Anablue stopped at the fish market. Waving to Boedy, she waited patiently at the counter for his mother, Alice, the proprietress, as she waited on an elderly gray-haired customer. Finishing with the old man, she turned to Anablue.

"You're all gussied up today. What's the occasion?" Alice asked.

"I have a lunch date," Anablue said.

"Please tell me it's a date with someone other than Bart."

Anablue laughed. "It's a man."

"How exciting. Tell me all about him," Alice said.

"Sparkling brown eyes that crinkle when he laughs. A killer smile," Anablue said. "Tall, dark, and handsome."

"Sounds gorgeous."

Anablue nodded. "He is. He has a sailboat down at the marina."

"Oh! Girl. A rich man?"

"I have no idea."

"A pirate, perhaps?" Alice said.

"A gentleman pirate," Anablue replied. Blushing, she remembered the passage of the book Donall had caught her browsing through. *Oh lord. He looks just like what I imagined.*

Mortified at her thoughts. "Fish. Bart's lunch, please."

Alice eyed Anablue. "Hmm, you're blushing, girl."

Anablue handed Alice a dollar bill.

"No charge, sweetie. I can't wait to meet this gentleman pirate," Alice said.

"We'll see," Anablue replied as she headed towards the door.

"Anablue." Alice held up the bag with Bart's lunch.

Anablue sighed. *Damn.* "Thank you, Alice."

Leaving the fish market, she headed toward the marina. She passed a street florist. The young man called out. "Hey, Anablue. I've got a pretty flower for you today."

Anablue stopped. "Johnny, you're going to get in trouble if you keep giving me flowers."

"We have this same argument every day," Johnny said. "Besides, this is San Francisco. You're supposed to have flowers in your hair."

She gave him a thoughtful frown. "So, what do you have for me?" Anablue said.

John pulled butter-colored Chrysanthemum from behind his back.

'Oh Johnny, it's beautiful," she said.

"It will look perfect on your hat."

"I may have to paint yellow Chrysanthemums today," Anablue said.

"Enjoy your day, Anablue."

"You too. Thank you for brightening my day," she said with a brilliant smile.

"Nah, you're the one who brightens mine," Johnny said.

DONALL GLANCED up towards the pier waiting for Anablue to make her appearance. He had been working on the boat all morning and had finished cleaning up and showered.

The crowd parted, and she appeared like a breath of fresh air. He watched in amazement as she walked across the street, a yellow flower in the blue band of her straw hat. She moved with the curves and confidence of a woman who knew exactly who she was.

Enthralled and astonished at his reaction, he watched as she approached him with a smile that lit up her face, and in turn, his. At a jog, he closed the distance between them.

"Good morning, Baby Blue."

Looking into each other's eyes, they shared a smile. "Good morning," Anablue replied.

Taking the tackle box from her hands. "Let me carry that," Donall said.

"You couldn't ask for a more beautiful day," Anablue said, with a sudden case of butterflies in her stomach.

They walked side-by-side down the dock. Stopping in front of Capt. Jack, who lounged in his boat.

Anablue gave him a mischievous grin. "Morning, Capt. Jack."

"Morning, Anablue. You're like a ray of sunshine on a stormy day."

"I believe they call those rainbows," Anablue said, laughter in her voice.

Donall laughed, moving on to his slip.

WATCHING DONALL WALK AHEAD. "We have a date today," she said.

"I know. He told me over coffee this morning," Capt. Jack replied. "You give me a holler if you need anything."

"No worries. I feel safe with him," Anablue replied.

"Enjoy your day, sweetheart," Capt. Jack said.

"You too."

Anablue followed after Donall. His tan-colored shorts accentuated his long legs and trim waist. A short-sleeved green polo shirt fit his broad shoulders. His muscular back rippled beneath the shirt. Green tennis shoes complimented his outfit, and she inhaled sharply at the vision of the man before her. *Dark Adonis, indeed.*

DONALL TURNED AROUND. Anablue's eyes were almost stormy blue. Her long dark lashes flickered, and they returned to sky blue. A delicate blush stained her cheeks as she looked away from his intense stare.

"Do you want this at the end of the dock?" he asked. Indicating her tackle box.

"Yes, if you don't mind," she replied.

She followed him to the end of the dock and set the rest of her things down. He watched her as she set up her easel and supplies.

"Do you like music?" Donall asked.

"I love it," she replied.

"I'm surprised you don't have a transistor radio," Donall said

"I do have a radio here. It's lying about four feet out that way," she said as she pointed out toward the water. "Bart knocked it in the bay my first time here," she explained.

"And that's why you put your things away before he arrives?" Donall asked.

"It only took me two-three times to learn that lesson," she said, with an impish grin.

Donall grinned, "I'll leave you to your painting. You let me know when you're ready for lunch."

"What are you going to be doing while I paint?"

"I have a book I've meant to read."

"The French poetry?" she asked.

"No, that's a birthday gift for someone," Donall replied. "I'll leave you to it."

Donall turned on his new eight-track player and settled into a chair, his feet up on the bench.

Unable to focus on the book, he watched her as she worked. Immersed in her work, she sang along to the tunes and danced where she sat on the little stool. Eventually, he settled into his book and was surprised when Capt. Jack called out, "Eight bells, Anablue."

She stood and stretched, arms above her head. Donall's breath caught in his throat at the bare expanse of belly and curves. Her long blonde hair fell in soft curls around her mid-back and the curve of her breasts. Tan legs, though not long, were in perfect proportion to her body as she stretched again, flipping her hair over her shoulder as she turned. He watched her hair swing around to settle against her back, but not before he caught a glimpse of Venus dimples above the curve of her bottom.

She glanced over to see him watching her. Placing her hands on her hips, she gave him a sassy smile before kneeling. She picked up her supplies. He was out of the boat in a heartbeat. His stride, long and cat-like. Kneeling at her side, he looked deep into her eyes.

"Did you enjoy the music?" Donall asked.

"Oh yes," she breathed. "I hadn't realized how much I had missed it."

Donall laughed. "Good. I enjoyed your stool dancing."

Anablue blushed. Nose to nose now. They were drawn to each other like magnets.

"I forgot you were sitting there. Can I tell you a secret?"

"Of course," Donall replied.

"I can't dance. I have two left feet," Anablue whispered. "The most I can do is chair dance."

Donall smiled, standing up. He pulled her to her feet.

"It's easy. You just need a strong lead." He pulled her into his arms into a slow waltz to the music playing.

"No one ever took you dancing before?" he asked.

She shook her head. "No. The boys I dated back home. Their idea of a date was a six-pack of beer and head for the hills. I had long walk's home alone back then."

"You've never been wined and dined?"

"No. I'm more of grilled cheese and dancing on the dock type of girl," she said.

Donall smiled. Yeah, I think… Donall looked up as a massive black creature hurled itself onto the dock. Slipping and sliding his way. Bart knocked them both off of the dock and into the bay.

# CHAPTER 7

Donall surfaced, pulling Anablue up with him.

"Are you alright?"

Clinging to his shoulders, her face lit up as she started to laugh. "We forgot about Bart."

Donall laughed, a deep rich timber as he pulled her closer. They stared into each other's eyes, and his lips descended onto hers.

Her lips were soft, plump, and sweet. She returned his kisses, hesitant at first, then with a passion that left them both trembling. Bart's bark from the dock broke the kiss. He looked into her eyes. Passion-filled, dark blue, and stormy. She shivered in his arms, and he realized how cold the water was.

"Put your arms around my neck and hang on," Donall said. He swam with her to the dock, lifting her out and climbing to sit beside her. She giggled as Bart nuzzled at her neck from behind. "Okay, okay. Give me a minute," she laughed at Bart's impatience.

"Come meet Bart. He's quite sweet," Anablue said.

"Donall laughed. "Yeah, knock us into the bay, sweet."

She stood and picked up the bag of fish. Bart barked and clapped his fins.

Handing Donall a fish. "Come on, don't be shy."

Taking the fish offered. Holding it over Bart's head. Laughing at the seal's exuberance, Donall was in awe of the massive size of the seal and how gently he took the fish from his hand.

Shaking his head. "Where did he come from?" he asked, as Bart barked once more and dove off the deck.

"I don't know. He just showed up one day," Anablue said.

"How do you know it's a "He,"" Donall asked, a glimmer of laughter in his eyes.

She narrowed her eyes at him." He isn't wearing a pink bikini," she playfully responded.

"Pink, huh? Do you have a pink bikini?"

"I have lots of bikinis."

"So, what we have here is a girl with lots of bikinis who can't swim."

"I will learn. Someday."

"I am going to teach you how to swim."

"You don't need to know how to swim if you're laying in the sun."

"But you do if you're sitting on the dock."

"In all fairness. Every time I've been knocked into the drink, I've been with you."

"Same here. I'm still going to teach you to swim,"

"Okay. On one condition."

"What's that?"

"Please make it warm water. This bay is freezing."

He threw back his head and laughed. "Deal. Warm water. Are you hungry?"

She gave him a sassy sideways glance. "Starving."

"Let's get you dry clothes and the tastiest grilled cheese sandwich you've ever had."

---

ANABLUE STEPPED FROM THE CABIN. Sheepishly, she caught his eye and gave him a shy smile. "I feel silly in your boxers and dress shirt," she said.

"You look beautiful. And trust me, it's been done before."

"So, you've had girls on your boat wearing your boxers before?" she asked.

"No. My sister-in-law, wearing my brother's," Donall replied.

Donall waved to a small table and chairs. "I figured you'd be more comfortable eating out here. I've hung a clothesline for you."

Anablue shyly nodded her head. "Thank you," she said as she spread her things over the clothesline to dry.

He watched as she sat at the table. The blue of the shirt she wore made her eyes even bluer. Barefoot now, her hair starting to dry in blonde wisps. His shirt, a few buttons unbuttoned, showed the slightest hint of creamy cleavage. His mind wandered back to that kiss and her stormy passion-filled eyes.

"Daydreaming?" she asked.

Pulled from his thoughts, he smiled as he sat next to her and pulled her, chair and all, directly in front of him.

Smiling, "Yes, I was wondering if I saw what I thought I saw."

"And what was that?"

He leaned in, cupped her face, and kissed her again. "Yup, just as I thought. Your eyes go stormy when I kiss you."

"That's codswallop."

He laughed out loud. "What is codswallop?"

"Nonsense," she replied with a brilliant smile as he shook with laughter.

"You really are something else," he said.

"Is that bad?"

"No. That is very good."

She gave him a coquettish smile. "Your coals are ready."

Looking over to the portable grill in the corner. "So they are," he replied.

Donall went inside and returned a few minutes later with a tray with all the fixings for grilled cheese, a pitcher of iced tea, and a jar of pickles.

"I originally pegged you as a sweet gherkins girl, but I had second thoughts. I bet you're a dill pickle girl.

Anablue grinned. "Absolutely perfect."

"Me, or the pickles?"

"Both." Her eyelashes fluttered as she blushed.

"I don't think I've ever seen grilled cheese made on a grill," she said.

"No? It's easy. All you need is a cast-iron skillet. The stove inside doesn't work yet. I can make pretty much anything on that little grill," he replied.

"It must be a lot of work refurbishing a sailboat."

"It will be worth it once I'm finished," he replied. "Have you ever been sailing?"

She shook her head. "I've been in a rowboat."

He laughed. "Not the same. The wind as you lean into it, the spray on your face, taste the salt on your lips. The sea is majestic and terrifying."

"So, I've heard," she replied.

"Who did you hear that from?" he asked.

"Brian… you're going to burn your grilled cheese," she cried.

Donall jumped up, quickly flipping the sandwich. He gave her a boyish grin.

"Just in the nick of time," he said.

A minute later, it was ready, and he placed it on her plate.

"There you go, Baby Blue. The best-grilled cheese on the planet."

She cut the sandwich diagonally into four quarters. Her

eyes rolled at how good the sandwich was. Donall sat down with his sandwich.

"Good?"

"Scrumptious," Anablue replied.

"Question: Why do you call me that?" she asked.

"It's those sky-blue eyes," he replied. "My turn. Why Anablue?" Donall asked.

"My mother wanted Annabelle. My father wanted Anablue for the color of the sky the day I was born. They tossed a coin; my father won."

"Why Donall?" Anablue said.

"My mother was Irish. She chose Irish names for all but my younger brother. My father chose his name."

"How many in your family?" she asked.

"Five boys and my father. My mother passed when I was young. And you?"

"There's no one now." A hint of sadness in her eyes.

"You're all alone?"

"Well, my father is out there somewhere." She nodded toward the sea.

Sensing her shutting down, he nodded.

"Show me what you painted today," Donall said.

Anablue grabbed the painting. Handing it to Donall.

"Yellow flowers."

"Chrysanthemums," she said.

"Chrysanthemums? Is that another made-up word like codswhapple?"

"It's codswallop. It's a real word. Can I tell you a secret?" Anablue said.

"Another one?" he said.

"Yes, when I was a baby, they called me chrysanthemum because my hair stood straight up all over my head."

He chuckled. So, tell me chrysanthemum."

"I thought my name was Baby Blue?"

"Baby Blue chrysanthemum."

"There's no such thing as blue chrysanthemums," she said.

He narrowed his eyes at her. "You're a trouble-maker."

She smiled a wicked smile. "So I've been told."

"Tell me why you paint flowers and not bridges?"

A look of anguish shimmered in her eyes. "I'm not ready to paint bridges," she whispered.

*She's grieving, for whom?* He brushed the hair from her face and gently cupped her chin as he leaned and kissed her again.

His finger stroked the bracelet on her wrist. "What's this?"

"It's a POW/MIA bracelet."

"What is it for?"

"They're new. It gives the name of the man, date captured or missing in Vietnam. I'll wear it until he's found and brought home. One way or the other."

"Where did you get it?" Donall asked, his voice a deep, pained whisper. *Is there one out there with my name on it?*

"College girls came into the bookstore one day. We all bought one from them to show our support," Anablue said.

Donall's mind wandered. *He was in a cage again, deep in*

*swamp water. His hands gripped the bars above as he held his head above water to avoid drowning.*

---

Alarmed at the haunted expression in his eyes and on his face. "Donall. Are you okay? You look like you're a thousand miles away," she said.

"More like eight thousand," he replied, his voice strained and distant.

"Are you sure you're alright?" *He's shaking.* Laying a calming hand on his arm, concern in her eyes.

Her gentle touch brought him back to reality. "I'm fine," he said.

"I have to go soon. Mrs. Wang will be worried."

"Who's Mrs. Wang?" Donall asked.

"My landlady. She watches me like a hawk."

"I want to see you again," Donall said.

Anablue nodded her head. "I would like that very much."

"We'll take a ride up the coast this weekend. You ever been on a motorcycle?"

"No, but that sounds fun. I have to work on Saturday."

"Then Sunday it is. I'll pick you up at noon," he said.

"Okay, let me help you clean up here, and then I have to go."

"No, I'll get this later. I'll walk you to your car," Donall said.

They walked up the dock, to the pier, then up another block.

Anablue stopped in front of her car. "This is it."

※

Donall looked at the car. Then up at her and back to the car in shock. He walked around the car.

"You drive this?" Donall asked.

She held the keys up and dangled them.

A shiny black sixty-six Chevelle. A muscle car.

"You drive a muscle car?"

She raised her eyebrows, amused at his reaction. She bit her lip and nodded her head.

"I had you pegged with one of those love bugs for a car," Donall said.

Anablue laughed out loud.

Donall stuck his head inside the car window. Phone books, bucket seats, suicide knob on the steering wheel, furry hanging dice, dog tags.

Shaking his head in disbelief.

"What's in it?"

"A 396. I keep it pristine," Anablue said.

"Can you even see over the steering wheel? Or reach the pedals?" He laughed.

"As you can see, I have phone books to sit on."

"Please tell me you don't drag race," Donall said.

She gave him a look of pure mischief. "Not here."

She popped the trunk, placing her painting supplies inside.

"Amongst other things. Girls can and do drive muscle cars."

Donall grinned. "Of that, I have no doubt."

He pulled her into his arms. Kissing her sweet lips. "I'll see you on Sunday."

Getting in the car, she started the engine, and the horses thundered under the hood. "I'll see you then. Thank you again for the best-grilled cheese on the planet," she said.

Donall watched her rumble away. Shaking his head, he could swear he heard the song Jingle Bells coming from her car.

*Did she say she kept the engine pristine? Nah!*

Chuckling to himself, he headed back to the marina.

# CHAPTER 8

Elyse looked out her front window and watched the car pull into the driveway.

Holding Bunker in her arms, "Guess who's here, sweetie?" as she placed a kiss on his soft cheek.

Calling over her shoulder to Elijah in the kitchen. "They're here."

Elijah strode over and looked out the window watching his father and father-in-law exit the car.

"You ever figure out which one is Gramps and which one is Pops?" Elijah asked.

A smile split her face. "I thought you knew?" Elyse replied.

"Every time I think I have it right. I'm wrong," he said.

"You're sure they're up for this?" Elyse sighed. "Bunker

couldn't have two more doting grandfathers, but some of their methods leave me wondering."

"He adores them both. They will all be fine," Elijah said.

The front door opened, and Pops and Gramps made their loud entrance. Bunkers arms waved in excitement at seeing them.

They exclaimed as one, "There's our boy." As their arms reached for the baby. Elyse held on to Bunker a moment longer before giving him to Elijah's father.

Giving them both a stern look, she began.

"Okay, rules of engagement;

You both must share. Take turns.

I just fed him. If he gets hungry, the baby bottles are in the fridge. Remember not too hot.

I made you a pot of coffee. Do not use the milk in the baby bottles for creamer again. It's breast milk.

If you must march up and down the street singing cadence as lullabies, please stop when the neighbors drive by, they already think we are crazy.

We will only be gone for a few hours. If, by chance, you need something, call my neighbor Maxine down the road. Her number is on the fridge, along with the doctor and hospital's phone numbers.

Also, the *party line on the telephone. Absolutely NO more listening in on the neighbor's conversations.

Try to remember he's a baby, not a Marine.

Do not give Soup treats. He's getting fat.

And last but not least, have fun."

Elyse's father turned to Elijah, who stood trying to contain his laughter.

"That's quite the little Drill Sargent you have there, Elijah."

"Elijah snorted. "More like a General. I'm going to pull the bike out." Looking at his wife. "Five minutes."

※

DONALL DROVE up the driveway and sat looking at the gray Victorian. Spotting a Siamese cat as it crossed the meticulous front lawn to climb the massive Blue Gum eucalyptus tree in the front yard. It jumped from the tree and landed on the railing on the widow's walk surrounding an octagon-shaped room at the top of the house. Anablue was on the widow's walk waving. He waved back.

Walking up the cobblestone walkway, he admired the Rhododendron shrubs beneath the windows. Large flowerpots overflowing with bright, colorful foliage graced either side of the shiny red front door. Ringing the doorbell, he waited a moment before the door opened, and a tiny elderly Chinese woman stood in the doorway, pointing her broom at him. Donall's eyebrows raised at the woman's stance as she demanded in Chinese to know who he was and what he wanted.

Donall bowed, gave her a devastatingly brilliant smile, and in a perfect Chinese, he replied, "Good afternoon, Mrs.

Wang. My name is Donall Corrington. I am here to pick up Anablue."

Watching her reaction, knowing he had her at her raised eyebrows and nod of approval. Smiling, she directed him to wait in the large sitting room to the left of the foyer.

---

Anablue crawled under her bed, searching for an elusive left moccasin. "For Pete's sake, Anablue, clean your room. Then maybe you can find your things." Finding the shoe, she pulled it on. "Now, where's my jean jacket?" Spotting the jacket hanging on a chair, checking her look in the mirror, she grabbed her jacket, was out the door, and running down the stairs.

Slowing her descent to make a somewhat ladylike entrance, she walked into the sitting room and stopped cold.

Donall held a teacup in hand as Mrs. Wang poured more tea into his cup. They chatted in Chinese, and Anablue could only stand there in amazement.

*He speaks Chinese, and Mrs. Wang is actually fawning over him.*

---

Donall looked up to see Anablue in the doorway, with a wink and a wicked grin to Anablue. Standing, he bowed again to Mrs. Wang.

"Thank you for the tea and delightful conversation."

Turning to Anablue, his eyes caressed her where she stood. The soft pink tinge of her cheeks at his perusal matched perfectly with the pale pink of her shirt under a waist-length jean jacket. Hip-hugger bell-bottomed jeans clung to the curve of her hips, and a wide brown suede belt tied her outfit together. Her long blonde hair was braided into a thick braid and hung over one shoulder.

*Breathtaking.*

"Are you ready?" Donall asked, tamping down his sudden desire to loosen her hair and see her naked in his arms. Anablue nodded.

She walked ahead of him. That cute little red heart embroidered on the back pocket of her jeans was enough to drive him wild as he watched the swing of her hips down the sidewalk. She stopped at the bike and turned to look at him.

"How did you do it? Did you put a spell on her? Shoot magic from your fingertips or something? I've never seen Mrs. Wang act like that over anyone," she laughed.

Donall flashed her a smile. He took her hand, lifted it to his lips, and placed a light kiss that was more of a caress on her wrist. Turning her hand over, he kissed the tips of her fingers. "I have no more magic in my fingertips than you have in these brightly painted orange nails."

"So, you sweet-talked her?" she said.

"Hmmm, maybe," he replied.

Anablue shook her head in disbelief. "You're dangerous."

He pulled her into his arms. "Very much so," he replied.

She stepped back, wagging her finger. "Mrs. Wang is watching from the window," she said with a smile.

Donall chuckled. "So she is. Let's go."

He handed her a silver helmet with a visor. "Put this on." Then he put his black helmet on and climbed on the bike. Anablue climbed on. Unsure what to do with her hands at first, she shyly wrapped her arms around his trim waist as he pulled out of the driveway.

Mrs. Wang thoughtfully watched them from the window as they left. She walked into her kitchen, looking at a phone number on her corkboard. She dialed the number. "Captain Baker, please. It's Mrs. Wang."

Elyse pulled her silver helmet on and climbed on the back of the motorcycle, waving to her father and father-in-law, holding the baby. She slid her hands under her husband's jacket, then his shirt, lightly raking her nails across his chest. Elijah smiled, grabbing a hand to kiss her pink fingernails before pulling out of their driveway. He headed south towards the coastal highway.

They drove for an hour or so before Elyse pointed to a gas station at the halfway point they often stopped at. Pulling into the station, Elijah decided to gas up the motorcycle.

Donall sat on his bike waiting for Anablue in the restroom on the other side of the building. Elyse entered the restroom and went into an empty stall. Anablue came out of the other stall and washed her hands. Waving to the clerk as she left the gas station. She went out and climbed on the back of the bike.

Elyse came out of the gas station, spotting Elijah on the other side of the building. She went over and climbed on the back of his bike, and he pulled away.

DONALL LOOKED DOWN at the pink fingernails, lightly raking his thighs. Then her hands reached in and untucked his shirt, raking her nails across his chest. *Jesus.* Glancing over his shoulder, he couldn't see her face as her hands roamed his chest inside his shirt. When she pulled up the back of his jacket and shirt and pressed her bare breasts against his back, he almost dumped the bike.

He pulled into a rest area a short distance up the road. Taken by surprise, he fully intended to have a conversation about their relationship and where it was quickly heading. He scooped her off the bike and strode over, setting her on a picnic table. Pulling his helmet off, he waited while she pulled hers off.

Riotous red curls spilled out, and he found himself staring into amethyst eyes.

"Elyse?"

"Elijah, what the hell are you……Donall?"

Dumbstruck, they stared at each other. Confused, Donall stared down the road in the direction they had come from.

"How?" he said.

"Yeah, how did I end up here with you? And where is Elijah?" Elyse said.

"The gas station," Donall said as they both burst into laughter.

"Obviously, I took the wrong girl," Donall said as he wiped at his eyes.

"Okay, Donall, all humor aside. How do we fix this? Wait. What girl?" Elyse asked.

"Don't you go getting all nosey on me," Donall said.

"Well, you've got to tell me who's with my husband and what she might be doing to him," Elyse indignantly huffed.

Donall raised an elegant eyebrow. "It's our second date. I seriously doubt she'd be doing what you did."

Elyse looked over to the bike as comprehension dawned on her. Her mouth opened into a round O as she inhaled sharply.

"Oh my God…I. Oh my God."

Donall grinned, giving her a wink. "Best back massage I've had in a while."

She smacked his arm. "Stop that. We need to figure out how to fix this."

"Who is she?" Elyse asked.

"I'm not telling you."

"Not fair. I want details," Elyse said. "So, tell me. Why did you stop here?"

Donall gave her a look of chagrin. "Never mind," he growled.

A glimpse of glee crossed her face. "Donall Corrington, you thought she was making the first move, and it unsettled you."

He pointed his finger at her. "You, butt out."

"It's nineteen-sixty-nine. Haven't you heard of the sexual revolution?" Elyse said.

"Yes, I've heard of it."

"Ah, I think you're a little old-fashioned, like Elijah."

He narrowed his eyes. "I am not old-fashioned," he growled.

Elyse gave him a devasting smile. "Whatever you say." Turning serious. "When are you coming home? Elijah misses you."

"I miss him too and my father, but I'm not ready yet."

"There's nothing but love and support at home," Elyse said.

"Elyse, I would think you of all people would understand," Donall said.

"Yes. While I was held captive for a few days, I was never touched. Frightened, yes. Afraid for mine and Bunker's life, yes. If not for the love and support of family and my baby." Shaking her head. "Donall, both Elijah and I have our dark days and nights. Anyone who was in Vietnam does, but we take comfort in each other. You've lost weight, and I felt the scars on your back. Were you tortured?"

Donall nodded his head. "Yes."

"I can't even begin to know the inner turmoil you're going through, but I do know your brother and your father are here for you. Along with me, of course."

"I know you are. I need time."

"That's a pile of crap. Avoiding family is just going to make it worse."

"You don't pull your punches, do you?"

"And you're as stubborn and annoying as your brother."

"Family trait," Donall replied.

"By the way, where are you staying?" she asked.

"I bought an old sailboat. I'm living on it while I refurbish it."

Elyse smiled. "So, now you have your pirate ship and your wench. You're still missing the scarf and gold earring."

Donall gave her a brilliant smile. "I'm supposed to be on a date with that wench. Jesus, I hope she's not sitting at the gas station thinking I abandoned her."

"No, they were already gone before we left, Elyse said. So, what's the plan here?"

"Were you heading south?" Donall asked.

Elyse nodded.

"We're going north," Donall said.

"We always stop at the same gas station on the way back," Elyse replied.

"Okay, let's get back to the gas station. Then make the switch. However, I don't want Elijah to see me yet. I don't want you to tell him that you saw me."

"You're killing me. How am I going to keep a secret like

this from Elijah?" Elyse sighed. "Okay, on one condition. Don't ever mention that back massage to another soul."

Donall chuckled. "Deal. It won't be long before I'm knocking at your door."

"Good. There's someone else you need to meet," Elyse said wistfully.

"I'm looking forward to meeting Bunker. Why do you call him Bunker?" Donall asked.

"Ask his father."

"No shit, you got pregnant in a bunker," Donall laughed outright. "You ready? Let's go."

He handed her the helmet. Giving her a wicked smile. "Behave."

"Not funny," Elyse replied.

DONALL PULLED into the gas station and pulled off his helmet. Elyse climbed off of his bike, lifted her visor, and stood looking at him.

"How can we reach you if need be?" Elyse said.

"There's a little bar about a block off the pier. It's called Two-belly Jacks. You can leave a message with Capt. Jack."

ELIJAH PULLED into the gas station. He watched as she climbed off his bike and headed inside. Admiring the swing of her hips and the red heart patch sewn on the back pocket of her jeans. He shook his head, something was off, but he couldn't quite put his finger on it. She had been almost timid, not at all her herself during the ride today. Still watching the swing of her hips. A beautiful ass.... but not Elyse's. What the fuck?

He took off his helmet and waited patiently for her to exit the gas station.

Five minutes later, Elyse exited the gas station. She pulled off her helmet as she walked towards him. Stopping in front of him, she ruffled his hair and leaned into him. "Have I told you today how much I love you?"

Elijah wrapped his arms around her waist and pulled her closer. "Yes, but you can tell me again," Elijah replied.

"I love you."

"I love you too, brat. Spin around for me." She pirouetted for him and curtsied—no heart on her ass.

He pulled her back into his arms. He lifted her hand to kiss her fingertips—pink, not orange. "Now you can tell me who that was on the back of my bike for the past hour," Elijah growled.

Elyse's eyes widened, and she groaned. "Damn."

---

Donall pulled Anablue into his arms. He pulled off her helmet, beautiful blue eyes stared back at him.

"There you are Baby Blue. Are you enjoying the ride?"

"Yes, but why you keep driving up and down the same stretch of the coastal highway."

*Smart girl.* He kissed her long enough and deep enough to silence her question.

"I have a surprise for you."

"What is it?" Anablue asked.

Donall chuckled. "You'll see. Get on."

Donall headed north toward a secluded beach he knew very well. Parking the bike, Donall grabbed a satchel off the back of the bike. They walked down to the beach, where Donall took a beach towel out and spread it on the sand. He pulled crackers and cheese, fresh Italian Soppressata salami, a small bag of red grapes, and a bottle of red wine, along with two paper cups.

"I thought you might enjoy a small picnic on the beach," Donall said.

"Oh, you do know the way to a girl's heart, don't you?"

Donall grinned. "Hopeless romantic here."

"Okay, Mister hopeless romantic, how are you going to cut that meat and cheese and open the wine?"

Donall smiled and pulled out his swiss knife. "Never doubt the abilities of a man trying to impress a pretty girl."

"A renaissance man, as well," she stated.

They ate their small picnic lunch, and when finished, Donall pulled her to her feet. Shoes and jackets abandoned, barefoot, hand in hand, dodging the surf, they ran and played in the waves.

"Dance with me," Donall said.

"There's no music."

"Sure, there is. Listen to the surf and the cries of the seagulls," he said, pulling her into his arms. A slow waltz, he dipped her. Lost in her eyes, he never saw the incoming wave until it hit, drenching them both.

Laughing, they ran from the waves. Anablue stopped, squealing in delight. "Look, beach flowers."

Donall followed along, admiring the pretty flowers she pointed out. "See, Purple Sea Thrift. Over there, Pink Rock Roses…and." She blushed.

"And the little blue ones?" Donall asked.

She gave him an impish look. "Those are called Baby Blue Eyes."

Donall's smile was a slow and easy caress. "You've got a flower named after you."

She reached down to gently cup a delicate bloom, inhaling its sweet fragrance.

"You're not going to pick it?" he asked.

"You shouldn't pick wildflowers. Leave them for the next person who comes along to enjoy. However, you can gather seeds to plant elsewhere."

She plucked a spent seed head and delicately rolled it between her fingers until soft seeds fluttered to the ground.

Donall gathered her into his arms as his lips found hers. He deepened his kiss as he lifted her into his arms. Carrying her to the beach towel, he gently laid her down. She melted against him as his lips nuzzled her neck and ear lobes. He pulled the binder freeing her braid. Her hair tumbled into soft waves as he ran his hands through, feeling the silky texture of her hair. His hands slid sensuously along her arm to follow the smooth curves of her back and waist as she moaned softly. *Slow…slow down.* He pulled himself away from her lips with a groan.

Anablue reached up and caressed his lips with her finger. "I'm not sure I'm ready for this yet."

He reached out and stroked her cheek with his thumb, and she shivered as her body tingled from the tips of her toes to her crown.

"We'll slow down," Donall said. "Tell me about you. Where's home?"

"Home is a couple of hours east of here. In the middle of nowhere, surrounded by cattle and sheep ranches. Where the Tuolumne river winds through the foothills of the Sierra's. It's where I can see the snow caps on the mountains from the front porch and the stars. I miss the stars. At home, the stars go from one end of the sky to the other. And at night, it's so dark you can't see your hand in front of your face. If I close my eyes, I can still smell the pine trees."

"You speak poetically of your home. Are you homesick?" Donall asked.

"Sometimes. But this where I need to be for now," she replied. "There isn't much to do there. It's an old town from the gold rush days. You know, the kind with a church, a school, bar, and a country store. Small but quaint. Brian used to call it a one-horse town. Our ranch has been in my father's family for generations, but Gram sold parts of it off when my grandfather died."

"How big is your ranch?"

"I don't know, maybe seventy-five acres. Small in comparison to most."

"And now you're living in San Francisco," Donall said.

"This is where Brian and I planned on living. For a little while. Anyway, there's nothing, and no one left for me at home."

Donall frowned. "Who's Brian?"

"Halloo!" Donall and Anablue looked toward the road to see an elderly woman and her little dog standing near his bike. The woman waved, and they waved back.

"She probably saw us canoodling," Anablue said.

Donall let out a guffaw. "What is canoodling?"

Anablue leaned in and placed a soft kiss on his lips. "Kissing, cuddling."

"Hmm, I rather like that word," Donall replied. Showering kisses along her lips and jaw.

"Me too. I should get back. I don't like to worry Mrs. Wang." Anablue said.

"I want to see you again. I want to keep seeing you," Donall said. His thumb caressed her lips, and he lowered his head to place another kiss on her lips.

Anablue gazed into his beautiful brown eyes and nodded her head. "I would like that very much. That old woman is still up by your bike, and she appears to be scowling at us. Is this beach private property?"

"It is private property, but you're sitting with the owner," Donall replied with a chuckle.

"You own this beach?"

"Yes, and three acres behind it. My brothers and I each bought land here a few years back. My father also lives in town. One of my brothers lives a mile or so up the road with his wife and baby. Let's get you home, or Mrs. Wang will chase me around with that wicked-looking broom of hers," Donall said, with an exaggerated eye roll.

Anablue giggled. "Be grateful it's just a broom."

---

Donall stood at her door and placed a sedate kiss on her lips. I'll see you at the Marina tomorrow."

"I'll be there," Anablue replied. Looking up at the sky. "Shoot, now it looks like it's going to rain. I have to run and roll up my car windows."

"I'll do it. You go on inside. See you tomorrow."

"Good night Donall. I had a lovely time today. Thank you."

He reached out to stroke her lips. "I did too."

Donall ran down the sidewalk to Anablue's car parked in the driveway. Opening the car door and he sat down, rolling up the driver's side window. He leaned over, rolling up the other window. His hand brushed against the furry dice and the dog tags. Holding the dog tags in his hand, he read the name Brian Baker, Navy. Glancing at the house. *She's a widow?*

## CHAPTER 9

Maxine Marshall stopped at the front gate of her closest neighbor's home. Hesitant if she should speak up or not.

*If it was me, I would want to know.*

Elyse meandered down the pathway with Soup on her heels. Spotting Maxine at the gate.

"Hi! Maxine. How are you?"

"Elyse. I wanted to speak to you. I just saw your husband on the beach with another woman."

"Do tell. What did she look like?"

"The hussy was small, like you, and blonde. Aren't you upset?"

"What? Oh no. Elijah has been with me all day. You saw Donall, Elijah's twin." Elyse leaned in. "Truthfully, the curiosity about who he's dating is killing me."

"I'm so relieved. You have no idea how horrible I felt.

You're such a lovely young family," Maxine said. "I will tell you that he was all over her, and they appeared to be having a picnic."

"Ooooh, sounds romantic. Thank you for the information," Elyse said. Smiling, she reached over the gate to pet Rosie, Maxine's little dog, while the dogs sniffed at each other through the slats.

---

Elijah looked up from feeding Bunker his dinner as Elyse walked into the kitchen. Soup sat under the highchair in his prime begging spot.

"Have you tasted this garbage?" Elijah said.

"They're called peas, not garbage. Bunker is supposed to be eating them, not you."

Pointing at the baby in his highchair. "I kind of feel sorry for him. They're worse than C-rations."

"You made me eat nasty C-rations."

"It's all we had," Elijah replied.

"I know. Still nasty. Georgia said to try mixing the peas with the bananas."

Elijah grinned. "More garden gate gossip?"

"It is funny how the neighbors stop by to gossip. I just listen. But get this, Maxine was at the gate. She stopped to tell me that she saw you with a little blonde at the beach."

Elijah grunted. "Blonde, huh. Thanks to Donall, I have more fun in other people's minds."

Elyse snorted.

"Seriously, I have my hands full with you. I couldn't handle another woman," Elijah said.

"Well, finish feeding Bunker, then I'll give him his bath, and you can read him his bedtime story. Then I'll show you how full your hands are."

Elijah gave her a slow wolfish smile. "Hmmm, full moon tonight."

"Bonfire on the beach?" Elyse asked.

"And wine," Elijah replied.

"Sounds like a perfect date to me."

AT THE END of the dock, Donall settled himself into a lawn chair, music case in his lap. He stroked his nameplate on the lid. He had dreamt of this instrument and this moment during his time in captivity. Playing the music over and over again in his mind. Each note, each key, every song he had ever learned. It was what had saved his sanity. Some men remembered wives and children or a special girl at home. For him, it had been the music.

Taking a deep breath, he opened the case and pulled out his flute. His hands shook as he assembled the instrument. Lifting the flute to his lips, he played. The music sweet and melancholy, a piece he had often played with Elijah on the piano.

The tears ran down his cheeks as he reclaimed his power,

rejoicing that he had proven his captors wrong and had survived. It was a small victory, but a victory, nonetheless.

※

ANABLUE OPENED the door and wandered out to the widow's walk to sit for a bit. Pulling her blanket closer to block the chill of the night. Miss. Priss, what she called the neighbor's fat cat, jumped down from the railing and settled herself on her lap. A full moon tonight. The bay was peaceful and serene. The cat softly purring. Thoughts of Donall entered her mind as the far-off sound of music floated through the night. A flute, perhaps, resonating across the bay. Music so sweet it moved her to tears. Her heart ached for the person playing such a sad song. As the forlorn piece ended, for the first time in a long while, peace surrounded her.

※

DONALL WAS out for his early morning run. Jogging along the pier, he rounded the corner by the fish market. He spotted a young boy throwing a baseball up in the air and catching it in his mitt. It was the boy who had brought Bart's lunch down to Anablue. He smiled at the kid as he ran by him.

"Hey, Mister,"

Donall stopped and turned around. "Yeah."

"You're the one I saw kissing Anablue."

Donall lifted one eyebrow. "Yeah."

"I was delivering fish for my mom, and I saw you kissing her from the pier."

"What's your name?"

"Boedy."

Donall spotted another baseball glove on the ground, so he picked it up. Boedy threw the baseball to him.

"You're pretty good, Mister," Boedy said as he caught the ball.

"United States Naval Academy, collegiate baseball team," Donall replied, throwing the ball back.

"No kidding. You're in the Navy?" Boedy asked.

"I was."

"So, what's it like?"

"What?" Donall asked.

"To kiss a girl?"

"Isn't that something you should be asking your dad?"

"Can't. He died in Vietnam when I was little," Boedy replied.

"I'm sorry to hear that," Donall said.

"So, what's it like?"

"Kissing a girl. It's nice."

"And you're not afraid of girl germs?"

Donall chuckled. "No, I am not afraid of girl germs."

"Not even a little?"

"Nope, not even a little," Donall replied.

Donall looked up as a woman in her late twenties came out of the market.

Chiding the boy, "Boedy, are you stopping people on the street to play catch with you," she said.

Donall replied. "No, I started it." introducing himself. "Donall Corrington."

"Alice Reid," she replied. "And this is my son, Boedy. I was coming out to play catch with him before the market opens."

Donall shook the boy's hand." That's a good arm you've got there, Boedy. Make sure you sign up for little league this year."

Boedy nodded. "I will."

"Good. I've got to go now. I often run this way in the morning. If you're out here, I'll play catch again."

Boedy smiled.

Donall took off at a slow jog. Alice watched him appreciatively as he jogged up the street.

"Mom. Mom," Boedy said, trying to get her attention.

"Hmmm," she replied.

"That's him. I saw him kissing Anablue."

She looked down at her son. "Oh my."

Looking up the street, she could still see him a block away. *Wow! That's Anablue's pirate.*

## CHAPTER 10

Elyse pulled the heavy door of the Two-Belly Jack's open. Struggling, she maneuvered the stroller inside. *There has got to be a better way.* She waited for her eyes to adjust to dim light. Then, spotting the elderly man behind the bar, she moved toward him.

"Hello," Elyse said.

"Hello, darling'. What can I get for you?"

"Oh, nothing for me. I'm looking for Capt. Jack."

"I'm Capt. Jack," he replied.

"I was told I could leave a message with you for Donall Corrington," Elyse said.

"And who are you, sweetheart?"

"Elyse Corrington," she replied.

Capt. Jack paled. He looked over the bar at the baby in the stroller and the wedding ring on her hand.

"His wife?" he barked.

Elyse shook her head. "No. Sister-in-law."

"I'm relieved. I worry about my… the sweet little girl he's seeing." He shook his head.

Elyse smiled. "You know who she is? Tell me. Who is she?"

A flash of humor crossed his face. "No."

She narrowed her eyes at him. "Seriously."

"Nope, I'm detecting a bit of a stinker in you. If he wants you to know, he'll tell you."

She gave him a look of pure exasperation. "That's what my husband, Elijah said."

Capt. Jack grinned. "The stinker part, or he'll tell you part?"

"Both," she replied. "Fine. Can you please give Donall this envelope?"

"I sure will. That's a handsome little fella you got there."

A beautiful smile lit her face. "This is Bunker."

"Don't take this the wrong way, but he looks like Donall."

"Of course. Donall and Elijah are identical twins," she replied.

THE NEXT MORNING, Donall had returned from his morning run. Sitting with Capt. Jack, his hands wrapped around a steaming cup of coffee.

"Did you hear about the marina?" Capt. Jack asked.

"No. What's going on?" Donall replied.

"It's up for sale. Some yacht club is interested in purchasing the property."

"We may lose our live-aboard status. That means you can only stay on board three nights per week. I'm okay with it since I own the building Two-Belly Jacks is in. I've got four apartments above the bar. I have one. One is empty now, and one other, well, my tenant is planning on moving. The building is clean. Rent is cheap, and the apartment furnished. If you're interested, it's yours."

"I might have to take you up on that offer. My Sailboat isn't seaworthy yet, or I would take it out and anchor off-shore somewhere."

"Damn cold in the winter months. These old bones of mine can't take winter on my boat," Capt. Jack said.

Donall grunted. "It's cold now, and it's July."

"You going to see Anablue on the fourth?"

"I thought she might like to go with me to my brother's place for a barbeque, I can deal with the fireworks displays. However, I'm not sure about the firecrackers," Donall said.

"Speaking of firecrackers. Almost forgot." Capt. Jack pulled an envelope out of his shirt pocket. "This is for you."

Donall took the envelope offered and opened it. Grinning as he looked inside. "You're right about Elyse being a firecracker. The little shit knows me well."

"What is it?"

"Two tickets to her ballet performance," Donall said.

"Ballet?" Capt. Jack asked.

"Elyse is the guest prima ballerina for the Bay Area Ballet Company," Donall said.

"Prima Ballerina? Her husband allows her to work with a child?"

"It's a strong woman who can juggle both," Donall replied.

"It's unusual nowadays, but more power to her if she can swing it," Capt. Jack said.

Donall smiled. "I can't wait to introduce Anablue to Elyse. They are similar in many ways."

Capt. Jack raised an eyebrow. "Anablue is a shy little thing."

"A bit, but we all know you have to watch the quiet ones."

"You seem taken with her," Capt. Jack said.

Donall nodded his head. "She's quirky, sweet, and beautiful. She also has a repertoire of funny words, like codswhapple."

"It's codswallop," Capt. Jack whispered, his voice shaking. A far-away look in his eyes. "I haven't heard that word in years."

Donall looked at his coffee. *What's that all about?*

"I'm going to give Elyse her wish and ask Anablue if she wants to go to the ballet," Donall said.

Brought back to the present, Capt. Jack shook his head. "Anablue would enjoy that. I'm off to Two-bellies. Have to meet with my tenant. Let me know if you're interested in the apartment."

"I'll save you some time and say yes now," Donall said.

"Great," Capt. Jack replied, standing to leave. "I'll see you later."

Closing his eyes, the warmth of the sun on his face. His thoughts were consumed by Anablue. He had found himself on his run this morning outside of her house. He had seen her up on the widow's walk. She had appeared to be reading. Watching her for a few minutes, observing the cat again, climbing the tree to sit upon the railing.

She stood and stretched; her blanket slipping to the floor. Inhaling sharply, the pink baby doll pajamas she wore hugged each soft curve of her breasts. Her blonde hair draped down her back as she lifted the cat from the railing. Picking the blanket up, she pulled the cat close to snuggle under her blanket, and she sat down. Looking around the neighborhood, he grimaced. *Dude. You're spying on her. It's a little creepy.* Turning around, he jogged the mile or so back to the marina.

Shaking his head. He had to admit he had been blindsided by Anablue. Planning to spend this time healing his body and soul. Buying and renovating the boat before he decided what he wanted to do with his life. He had nothing to offer her. Not even a home. Two-hundred square feet of a broken-down old sailboat was fine for a bachelor but didn't qualify as a home to offer a woman. The boat itself often left him wondering if he'd wake up in the morning at the bottom of the bay.

He didn't even have a job yet. Elijah had once asked him to go into business with him building houses. He did like working with his hands, but his shoulder injuries from his time as a POW may hamper that. Maybe a pilot for an airline. It was a similar lifestyle to a fighter pilot. Shaking his head. Jet-setting around the world? He wanted to sleep in his own bed, to settle down, find that special pepper pot, and raise a family. That was it… He just wanted to settle down. It was too soon to know if Anablue was the one. But damn, he was more than willing to find out. Rising from his seat. Sighing deeply, *that fucking engine isn't gonna repair itself.*

---

ANABLUE STOOD on the dock next to Donall's sailboat. The string of profanity coming from inside the cabin burnt her ears. A cloud of choking, acrid, diesel exhaust poured from the galley as Donall stumbled from the cabin, coughing, choking, while waving his arms to clear the air. Finally, he stopped, his loud and descriptive curse dying on his lips.

Her eyes wide, and a half-smile on her face. She bit her lip. "Hmmm. Engine trouble?" she ventured. Donall's frustration was apparent as he snarled, pointing inside the cabin. "That beast. That beast should be taken out, shot, burnt, and sunk to the bottom of the bay."

"Well. Let me look at it first," she said.

"You? You want to take a shot at it? A girl."

"You doubt me?" she asked.

Nodding his head, regarding her with amused skepticism. "Okay, Baby Blue. Take your best shot."

Anablue set her things down. Then, buttoning up her pink painting shirt, she climbed down onto the deck of the boat.

Pulling her hair back and tying it into a messy bun. Then, taking the wrench from his hand, she walked into the cabin with a sassy 'watch me' swing to her hips.

The engine was tucked under the floorboards of the cabin. Lying next to him on her tummy on the floor, she worked while he handed her the various tools she needed.

"I didn't know sailboats had engines," she said. "Kind of odd, don't you think?"

"I think the previous owner added it. You need one if you end up adrift somewhere. I would hate to have to paddle back to port," Donall said.

"Oh yeah. That would not be fun."

"So, tell me how a girl like you knows how to fix an engine?" Donall asked.

"It goes back a while. First, it's time for a secret."

Donall chuckled. "Tell away."

"I'm afraid of horses," she said. "They're big and intimidating. Mind you, I lived on a ranch. I never quite mastered the art of horseback riding like my brother, and just about everyone else did. For me, getting on the horse was like a clown show, let alone getting the horse to go where I wanted it to go.

"Your secret is safe with me," Donall said.

"Anyhow, when I was fourteen, I was always tinkering on my Gram's old tractor, along with old engines in the pole barn. I used it as an excuse not to ride. I was too busy. Eventually, I talked the old mechanic, Bud, into hiring me to work at the gas station in town."

A wide grin split his face. "A mechanic, you're a mechanic."

"Don't laugh. I started out pumping gas and changing oil. Bud finally let me help him work on cars and trucks. He was getting old, so he retired and sold the gas station. The new owner didn't want a girl working for him. I lost my job. So, you see, I've been dealing with sexism for a very long time."

Donall nodded. "You're right. I was out of line. I am sorry."

She nodded her head. "It hurt at the time, but then I was off to "see the world" with a new job. After a couple of years, Gram got sick, and I couldn't leave her alone, so I had to go home. Even after she died, I never went back. Being a woman mechanic, they didn't want me back. I was a bit of an embarrassment for them. I am, however, a certified mechanic."

"How did you manage that?"

"In high school, I took night classes. I stuffed my hair up into a hat and wore my brother's baggy clothes. They thought I was a boy."

"They had to be blind. Even covered in grease, I can see you're a girl."

"My dream when I was growing up was to own that little gas station."

"And now?" Donall asked.

"I don't know right now. The funny thing is, dreams change," Anablue replied.

Donall reached over and ran his finger down her cheekbone to her neck. Snuggling into her, he placed soft kisses on her neck.

"No canoodling the mechanic," she said with a shiver.

Donall's muffled laughter as he nuzzled her neck sent desire coursing through her body. She dropped the wrench and turned to him. He pulled her into his arms as his lips found hers. Tasting, exploring, he plundered her mouth and her neck, moving to the hint of cleavage at the V of her shirt. His hands roamed her body from the curve of her back to her waist and up to cup her breasts. She returned his fervent kisses, lost in his touch. An unknown need grew inside of her.

"Eight bells, Anablue." Capt. Jack's call brought her out of her passion-filled trance. Sitting up, she traced his lips with her finger, leaving a trail of grease.

"You're a dangerous man, Donall, with two L's." She rose to her feet and left the cabin.

Donall ran his hands through his hair. He calmed his breathing to cool his lust. Adjusting himself, he followed her out of the cabin. He climbed up onto the deck in time to see Bart make his grand entrance, slipping and sliding across the dock to stop in front of Anablue.

Donall's eyes widened, and he rushed over to her. "Take off your shirt," he said.

"Why?" she asked.

"Turn around and face the bay. Take off your paint shirt."

He looked at her breasts, and she followed his gaze. She inhaled sharply—two large grease handprints on her breasts.

"You marked me. Here, feed Bart."

He took the white bag for her and gave Bart a fish while she took off her shirt.

"Turn around, Donall." He did as she asked, and she giggled.

"I marked you as well. You should change your shirt."

He handed her the bag. "I'll be right back."

He returned a few minutes later. Anablue gave Bart his last fish, giggling as Bart planted a wet kiss on her face. He jumped back into the bay and swam away.

Sighing, she turned to Donall. "I prefer your canoodles."

Donall grinned. "I would hope so."

"So now that we've marked each other, where do we go from here?" she asked.

"We can go slow and let nature take its course. It's all up to you, Baby Blue."

"I like you very much. But I need you to understand that I need to mean something to you, and you to me, or I can't let anything else happen."

"I know that. How about we start by agreeing not to see other people?" Donall said.

"Have you been seeing other people?"

"No," he replied.

"Me neither. I'm good with that agreement if you are?"

He leaned in to kiss her. "Of course."

She pointed her finger at him. "I said, no canoodling the mechanic. I need to finish the job."

Donall chuckled. "I love that word."

---

ANABLUE FINISHED WORKING on the engine. She bade Donall start it up. It roared to life.

"Old Bud used to say keep your engines and women purring like kittens. I don't think he meant to tell me that, and truthfully, I'm not sure what he meant by it," Anablue said.

Donall roared with delight. "You are definitely a pepper pot."

"What's a pepper pot?"

Running his long greasy finger down the length of her nose. "A keeper."

## CHAPTER 11

Almost Four o'clock, Anablue was excited. She was off work at four and meeting Elyse for dinner and a movie. It had been another busy day.

Renaldo had called again.

Feeling guilty, she had missed his call. With Renaldo still out sick after an emergency appendectomy, she had made a pot of chicken soup that Maude had delivered for her. Busy covering her shifts, but some of his as well. She had no time to make a personal call from work.

Finally, her shift was over. Grabbing her purse and sweater, she made a mad dash for the door, calling out her goodbyes to Maude and Kim.

Walking four blocks toward downtown, she spotted Elyse waiting outside the movie theatre.

Waving, she quickly covered the remaining distance

between them.

"Hey, you. How are you? Long time, no see," Elyse said, hugging Anablue.

"I'm good, and you?"

"Wonderful, it feels good to have a break from the baby and Elijah and not be working," Elyse said.

Looking up at the marquee lights of the theatre." What's the movie about?" Anablue asked.

"I don't know, but the title was interesting."

Anablue shrugged. "Okay, by me. I haven't been to the movie theatre since high school."

"I've never been, so I'm excited," Elyse replied.

They stepped up to the ticket booth. A grizzled old man with a cigar dangling from his mouth looked up at them.

"Yeah, what do you want?" he said.

"Two tickets, please," Elyse said.

He looked them both up and down. "You know this is an adult movie?" he asked.

"We're both adults," Anablue said.

The old man chuckled. "Okay, ladies, a buck-fifty each." As he slid the tickets through the window to them.

"Thank you, Sir," they chimed in. Elyse hooked her arm through Anablue's, and giggling with excitement, they entered the theatre lobby.

Elyse looked around. "Where's the popcorn?"

Spotting a janitor, she approached him. "Excuse me. Where's the popcorn and soda?"

The janitor scanned their innocent faces. Laughing. "There ain't no popcorn or soda here, honey."

Well, it would ruin our dinner anyway," Elyse said, her disappointment clear. They opened the door and went inside the theatre, choosing seats halfway down the worn red-carpeted aisle. Looking around the small theatre. Two other patrons sat at the back of the theatre. A man and woman came in and sat in the front row.

Anablue and Elyse looked at each other. "Did that woman look like a prostitute to you?" Anablue asked.

"Yeah, I'm not sure about this place," Elyse replied, as the lights dimmed, and the movie started.

THE JANITOR LOOKED at his watch and strolled outside to chat with the old man in the ticket booth.

"I give them ten minutes," he said with a smirk.

The old man snorted. "A buck says eight."

"You're on." The janitor replied.

EIGHT MINUTES LATER, right on cue, the doors of the theatre burst open as Anablue and Elyse raced out and up the street, arm in arm. Two blocks later, they stopped, out of breath and hysterical. Their faces beet red with embarrassment.

"Oh my God," Elyse said, placing her hands on her cheeks to cool them.

"Did you see that? Did you see what they were doing?" Anablue asked.

"On film. For the entire world to see," Elyse said, trying to draw in a breath.

"I didn't know that men and women did that kind of stuff," Anablue said.

Elyse stopped laughing. "Oh, sweetheart. Are you a virgin?"

Anablue nodded her head. "And after seeing that, I'm staying one," she said.

"No. No. Don't let that movie warp your ideas about sex. The right man will come along and show you. It's not like that with someone you care about. It's beautiful and special."

"I'm pretty sure I've already met that someone," Anablue said.

"Grilled cheese guy?"

Anablue nodded. "Yeah, grilled cheese guy."

"I have to figure out if I should tell my husband about this. He's going to kill me. He always says I'm naïve about some things. I guess he's right."

"Don't be so hard on yourself. You've only been stateside for what six months. And me. I grew up on a ranch. We're both a little naïve. Now we know. Come on, let's go to dinner," Anablue said.

"We should pick a place we're familiar with," Elyse said.

"The diner?"

"Good idea," Elyse said.

"I'm still wondering what that couple down in the front row were doing," Anablue said.

Elyse rolled her eyes. "No, you don't want to know."

---

Elyse and Anablue slid into the booth. Pulling the menus from behind the tabletop jukebox, Elyse handed one to Anablue. "I'm still discovering American food. A lot of this is strange to me," Elyse said.

"Well, you like hamburgers and French fries. What else have you tried?" Anablue asked.

"We're on a first-name basis with the pizza delivery guy. I eat lots of fruit, vegetables, salads and such, anything I don't have to cook, but that gets boring."

"Mashed potatoes? They have a killer meatloaf dinner here." Anablue said.

"I'm not sure what that is, but I'm game," replied Elyse.

"Let's split a plate," Anablue said.

"Agreed."

They placed their order with Hazel. Anablue searched the bottom of her purse, finding a quarter. She slipped it into the coin slot of the jukebox. They flipped through the song list, looking for tunes to play.

"They've got oldies but goodies on here," Elyse said.

"Yes, and the newer bands too."

Anablue leaned forward. "I have a secret. Well, more of a

question, I guess."

Elyse's eyes lit up. "Okay?"

"I am a little more curious now. Did you see the size of that thing?"

They burst into laughter. "Okay, now I have to start all over to get that movie out of my head," Elyse said.

"I mean. I get that a man lies on top of you, but what do you do with your feet? Do they just lay there?" Anablue said.

Elyse bubbled with laughter. "You won't be worried about your feet. Um, the best I can say is to wrap your legs around his back and hang on."

They giggled, only stopping when Hazel delivered their meal.

"Seriously, how am I going to explain this?" Elyse said with a deep sigh.

Both women flinched as two men slid into their booth.

"What are you doing, Gary? Get out of here," Anablue said.

"Hey, baby. How about a kiss? Haven't you missed me?" Gary said as he leaned into Anablue, touching her hair, running his hand down her arm.

Anablue jerked away from his hand. Looking over to Elyse in horror, Marcus, a tall thin man with greasy black hair, slid his arm to rest on her shoulders.

"Baby, you are hot. How about a little action? Let's cut out, go back to my pad, have a little party." Marcus said. Shaking his long hair, brushing it against Elyse's shoulder.

Elyse shuddered. "I broke the nose of the last man who

touched me without my permission. Remove your arm," Elyse said.

"Oooooh. A little spitfire. I like a little fight in my women," Marcus said.

"Marcus, get your hands off her. Gary, you're disgusting, kiss-off." Pushing Gary away. "I've told you to leave me alone. Quit following me," Anablue said.

A flash of a switchblade and Anablue's eyes widened as Elyse held a knife at Marcus' ribs.

"I once had this knife buried to the hilt in a man's chest," Elyse said, as Marcus held his hands up.

"Get out of our booth. Both of you. Now!" Elyse ordered.

"Don't be a drag, baby. We're just looking for some fun," Gary said.

"Out." Elyse and Anablue both said.

Both men slid out of the booth. "Fucking skanks. You'll pay for this," Gary sneered as he smashed his fist into their plate of meatloaf. The plate shattered as meatloaf, mashed potatoes, and gravy splattered in every direction.

Gary looked over to see the cook, a big, beefy, bald man armed with a baseball bat, and Hazel with a broom quickly approaching.

"Let's split, man. This scene is a drag," Marcus snarled.

The cook called to their hastily exiting backs. "Don't come back in here."

"You ladies alright?" Hazel asked. "Let me clean this up and get you a fresh plate. I'll throw in some cherry pie on the house."

"That would be nice," Elyse said.

Anablue covered her face with her hands and shook as her eyes filled with tears. Elyse quickly moved over to her side of the booth and wrapped her arms around her.

"Can we please get a glass of water, Hazel?" Elyse said.

Hazel nodded. "Sure thing."

Anablue sobbed, "That creep ruined the night. He's been getting worse and now violent. Always coming up behind me. Standing outside whenever I leave work. Touching me, my hair, trying to kiss me. I'm frightened," Anablue cried.

"Have you told anyone?" Elyse asked.

"No, I thought he would give up. He stinks. I'm almost positive they were both wasted."

Elyse sighed. "I will talk to my husband. He will know what to do."

"It scared me when you pulled that knife," Anablue said.

"I know. I'm sorry. I know how to protect myself."

Elyse dabbed a napkin in the glass of water Hazel placed on the table. "Hold still. You have meatloaf on your face.

Anablue laughed. "You have mashed potatoes in your hair."

Elyse gave her an exasperated look. "It's usually peas. Come on, we'll eat and salvage the evening."

"Maybe I should mention this whole thing to Donall," Anablue said.

Elyse's eyes widened. A beautiful smile curved her mouth. "Did you just say Donall?"

## CHAPTER 12

Elyse quietly shut the front door behind her. Placing her keys in the basket and her purse on the small table. She glanced over at the couch. Her heart swelled with love. Elijah was spread out asleep, with Bunker soundly sleeping on his chest. The dog curled up at his feet. God, I am so blessed with these three.

She moved to pick up the baby, and Elijah opened his eyes.

"Hey," he whispered.

"Hey. I didn't mean to wake you," she whispered back.

"I heard you pull into the driveway. What time is it?"

"It's about ten o'clock," she replied. "Let me put him to bed."

After laying the baby in his crib, ordering the dog to stay with the baby, she returned to the living room. Curling into

Elijah, where he sat on the couch, she wrapped her arms around his neck.

"I missed you," she said.

"I missed you too. How was the movie and dinner with Anablue?"

"The movie was not worth mentioning, and I had meatloaf for dinner," she replied.

He nuzzled her neck, placing soft kisses as he went. "Meatloaf? I haven't had meatloaf since Aunt Meg made it when I was home on a break from college. Was it any good?"

"Hmmm, too good," she said as a shiver from his kisses took over her senses.

"What did you eat?" she asked.

"Leftover pizza," he replied as he unbuttoned her blouse. His hands slid inside her shirt, searching for that ripe fruit he craved.

"You're going to have pizza coming out of your ears. You eat so much of it," she said as she climbed onto his lap. Pulling her blouse off, she reached and pulled his shirt off over his head. Placing kisses on his neck and chest. "We need to hire a cook," she said.

"Probably. Eventually." He unhooked her lacy bra. Pulling it off her shoulders, he flung it away.

"And a nanny," he said.

She stopped, and tears filled her eyes as she looked into his. "A nanny?" she whispered.

"It's not what you're thinking, brat. It's not days on end, just someone to help us out once in a while for a few hours.

Neither one of us is capable of doing it all. Your career is important to both of us, and I don't want you to give it up. And I have a business to build. Bunker is only going to stay in a playpen for so long before he's going to want to run and play."

He cupped her face. Looking into her shimmering eyes. "Think about it. It's not a judgment on you or me."

"We have a four-room shack. Where would we put both a cook and a nanny?" she asked.

"If we were smart, we'd find someone who can both cook and watch the baby," Elijah replied as he reclaimed her lips, slowly sliding his hands up her thighs and under her skirt.

Elyse shivered with desire and gave into his exploration. "Maybe you should add a small apartment on top of the big fancy garage you're building."

"Hmmm, good idea," Elijah replied as he pushed her onto her back on the couch.

---

Elyse rose before dawn. Putting a pot of coffee on the stove to brew, grabbing her beach blanket from the back porch, she headed to the shoreline. High tide at this time of day. The beach would be completely underwater. Sitting close to the house with Soup cuddled up in her lap. Inhaling the sweet fragrance of the beach, roses lining the shore. The sun was rising, warming her back as she watched the twinkling stars over the Pacific disappear.

She exhaled. The tears formed and rolled down her face. Pulling a knife on a man. She had overreacted. Shame coursed through her veins, and she sobbed her misery. She didn't hear him come up behind her until he sat next to her on the blanket and pulled her into his arms.

"Why the tears, brat?" Elijah asked.

"Oh, Elijah. I did something terrible," she cried.

"You? Tell me about it."

"We were eating dinner, and two men came in and sat with us. One man has been following and threatening Anablue lately. I pulled my knife on one after he put his arm around my shoulders."

"Did they leave?"

"Yes."

"It's a perfectly normal reaction after what you've been through."

"I've been through nothing compared to you," she replied.

"I'm a well-trained Marine. You aren't. Don't downplay what happened to you in Nam," he growled.

"Elijah, the same goes for you. We agreed we would talk this through if we had had issues. I know you're having nightmares again."

"So are you," he replied.

"I can't get his eyes out of my mind."

"Whose eyes?"

"The gunner, from when my chopper crashed. I keep waking up to see his eyes. I don't even know his name. He saved me, and I don't know his name, she cried.

He cupped her face in his hands, wiping her tears with his thumbs. "Why didn't you tell me this before?" Elijah asked.

"It's been bothering me for a long time," she sniffled.

"Don't cry, brat. I'll see what I can do to bring you peace of mind," Elijah replied. "As for me, I do talk to my father and you. I'm okay."

"Now, do you know who these assholes are?" Elijah asked.

"Just that the one harassing Anablue is Gary, and the one I pulled my knife on is Marcus," she said.

"I'll see what I can do on that as well."

"There's more," Elyse said.

"What else?"

"I know who Donall is seeing. It's Anablue."

"Donall is grilled cheese guy?" Laughing, "I'll be damned. Does Donall know about this jerk harassing Anablue?"

"No," Elyse replied, shaking her head. "I'm feeling a little guilty. I didn't tell Anablue that Donall is your twin."

"Well. He did tell you to butt out."

The baby's cries from the house interrupted their conversation.

"It's your turn," growled Elijah.

Elyse flashed him a beautiful smile as she rose to her feet. "I missed him last night."

"I turned the coffee off. It boiled over again," Elijah said.

Elyse delicately furrowed her brows. "I can't wait to find a cook."

Elijah snorted. "Me too. Getting sick of pizza, and there's nothing but rabbit food in the fridge."

"Ha," she called back to him on her way into the house. "Admit it. You were born with a piece of pizza in each hand."

Elijah grinned. *Probably.*

---

Elijah strolled up to the house. Completing his daily morning perimeter check, he followed the cobblestone path through the garden to the front of the house, with Soup at his feet. Spotting an old yellow van parked within view of the house on the other side of the street. When he approached the garden gate, the van started up, did a U-turn, and headed south toward town.

With no neighbors within a mile in either direction, his brow furrowed with worry. He walked up the steps and crossed the porch and through the front door. Elyse stood on the other side of the living room. Bunker on the floor on his blanket was up on all fours, rocking back and forth.

"Oh, Elijah, do you see our baby?" she whispered with awe.

Elijah smiled, "Yes, I do." He reached over and locked the front door.

*I need to find Donall…*

## CHAPTER 13

Fourth of July. Anablue handed a customer his change. Wishing him a happy fourth, she picked up a stack of newly released books and walked to the back of the store to place them on the shelf. The store was closing early today. That would be enough time to go home and change before Donall picked her up for the fireworks celebrations.

Picking up her dusting cloth and polish, she made her way to a small sitting area near the front of the store. Bending to dust the coffee table, she screamed as hands grabbed her by the hips, and the man behind her ground himself into her bottom. Twisting around, she smacked him upside the head with her can of furniture polish. He, in turn, backhanded her, sending her flying into a bookshelf.

Anablue slid to the floor in shock. *Gary, again.* She watched in a daze as Maude and the store owner, Jonathan, rushed to the front of the store. Making short work of Gary, Jonathan picked him up and threw him out the door to land in a heap on the sidewalk.

"I've told you before. Stay out, Gary," Jonathan yelled out the door. Cursing under his breath, both he and Maude rushed to Anablue's side.

"Anablue, are you okay?" Maude cried as Anablue tried to get up off the floor.

"No, sit for a bit," Jonathan said. Spotting Kim, Anablue's co-worker standing off to the side.

"Kim, run across the street to the diner and get some ice from Hazel," he ordered.

Kim raced out the door and across the street. Breathless, she held onto the diner counter while she caught her breath.

"Hazel," she stammered. "We need ice. A customer hit Anablue," Kim said.

Hazel's eyes bulged. "What? Who would hit a sweet girl like Anablue?" Hazel asked.

"Gary," Kim replied.

"That creep was in here bothering her last night," Hazel said, handing her a bowl of ice and a towel.

"Let me know if you need anything else."

Kim ran back to the bookstore, dodging cars and pedestrians along the way. She made it inside, handing the bowl of ice to Maude. Wrapping the ice in the towel, Maude placed it on Anablue's cheekbone. Anablue winced in pain, rubbing the back of her head.

"I hit my head," Anablue said.

"Hazel said Gary was bothering Anablue in the diner last night," Kim said as she knelt next to Maude.

Turning to Anablue. "Why didn't you tell me?" Maude said.

"Well… I," Anablue stuttered.

"Ah, never mind. Jonathan threw Gary and Marcus out of here the other night. I guess the discussions downstairs were quite… um, contentious, to say the least. Gary hit Martin, and Gary, well Gary is a loser. He's dangerous, and so is Marcus," Maude said. "You need to be careful."

Anablue scowled. "I will. I'm fine. Please let me up."

"You are going to go home and rest. You might have a concussion. You should get checked out by a doctor," Maude mused.

"No doctor," Anablue said.

Maude gave her a motherly frown as she helped her up to sit in the chair.

"I'm fine, Maude. Maybe a little gob-smacked at why Gary is doing this, but I'm fine," Anablue said.

"You and your funny words. Should we call someone?" Jonathan asked.

"Donall lives on a boat at the marina. He doesn't have a telephone," Anablue replied.

"I'll have Kim drive you home, as to Gary, who the hell knows," Maude said.

"I can drive myself."

"No." Jonathan, who still hovered close by, Maude and Kim all shouted at once.

---

Anablue closed the front door. Turning around, Mrs. Wang stood in the foyer behind her.

"Anablue. What happened? Why is your face bruised?" Mrs. Wang said.

"Oh, Mrs. Wang, I was attacked at work. Other than a screaming headache, I'm fine. Do you have any aspirin?"

Mrs. Wang guided her to the couch. "Sit. I will look for the aspirin."

Anablue sat as directed. She really wanted to go to bed and lie down. Listening to Mrs. Wang in the kitchen as she searched for the aspirin. Almost certain the old woman was swearing in Chinese, she grimaced.

Her head throbbed as she eyed the wide staircase in the foyer. "Damn, why is my room on the fourth floor," she mumbled. Standing up, a wave of dizziness hit her; sinking back into the couch. She rubbed her temples. Maybe in a couple of minutes.

Mrs. Wang walked into the sitting room in time to see Anablue sink back down. She rushed to her side. Giving her water. Once she was finished, "Now, lie down," she ordered.

"I have started the water for tea instead of aspirin." Anablue nodded, curling back into the couch. Mrs. Wang put a throw pillow under her head and covered her with a throw blanket.

"Do not go to sleep, Anablue. Just lie here quietly."

## CHAPTER 14

Elijah pulled up in front of Two-Belly Jack's bar. Jumping out of his car, he ran up to the door, pulling on the handle. *Closed?* Looking at his watch, he pounded on the door, hoping someone was inside. Finally giving up, he stood for a moment —*the bookstore. Anablue works at the bookstore*. Getting back in his car, the tires squealed as he pulled out to merge into traffic.

Striding into the bookstore, Elijah looked at the middle-aged woman at the register. He purposefully walked toward her.

The woman looked up. "Oh, Donall. Thank god. I've been trying to figure out how to reach you," she said.

Taken aback for a moment, Elijah blinked. "I'm not Donall. I'm Elijah, his twin brother. I'm looking for Donall," Elijah said.

Maude's mouth dropped open. "Two dark Adonis'?" she

said. Shaking her head. "I'm sorry. I… we're looking for him as well," she rushed on. "Anablue was attacked by Gary, earlier today."

"Is she alright?" Elijah barked.

"Well, she's bruised, and I'm betting she has a concussion," Maude replied.

"Did she see a doctor?"

"No. She refused. We took her home," Maude replied.

"Do you have any idea what marina Donall has his boat moored at?" Elijah asked.

"No. But now that I think about it. The fish market. Anablue has told me before that they have brought Bart's fish down to her at the dock where she paints. Donall's sailboat is at that same marina. They would know."

"This Gary. What kind of car does he drive?" Elijah asked.

"A van, yellow, I believe."

"I live an hour north of here. There was a yellow van parked outside of my house early this morning. If it was Gary, he probably followed my wife home."

"I heard about what happened at the diner. Your wife needs to be careful. Both Gary and Marcus are deranged, and I'm not sure why," Maude said.

"Thank you, Maude, you've been very helpful. If, by chance, Donall comes in. Please tell him I'm looking for him."

"And if you see this Gary or Marcus. I'm looking for them too," he growled.

Maude softly gasped as his demeanor changed, and a dangerous aura surrounded him. "Okay," she whispered.

---

Elijah strode down the pier in the direction of the marina. Spotting it, his heart raced in excitement, and he quickened his pace. His rugged good looks and relentless pace left more than one woman admiring him as he passed them by. Stopping at the dock, he scanned the area, looking for that familiar form. Not seeing him, he walked down the dock, looking at the sailboats moored to their slips. Stopping, hands on his hips, disappointment filled him.

"You sink the boat?" a man's voice called to him. Turning to the man, Elijah smiled, closing the distance between them. He held out his hand.

"Elijah Corrington. I'm looking for Donall."

"Donall took the sailboat to the pump house. He should be back shortly. Hell, there's his boat coming in right now."

Elijah turned to see an old sailboat pulling into a slip. Closing the distance, he stood front and center of the boat.

---

Donall looked up to see Elijah standing on the dock in front of him. Pure joy filled him at the sight of his brother. He hopped out of the boat, throwing the rope around the mooring, and hugged his twin.

The two clung together, feeling the weight of each other's pain of separation and joy at being reunited. They patted each other on the back, speaking in low tones. Finally, they separated and walked together to the end of the dock, deep in conversation.

"I would have given you the time you needed, but we have a problem," Elijah said.

Noting the seriousness of Elijah's tone. "What is it?" Donall asked.

"I understand you're dating a cute little blonde."

"Yeah, Anablue Baker."

"Anablue and Elyse are friends," Elijah continued.

Donall lifted one eyebrow. "How did Elyse manage this one? I never told her who I was seeing."

"She's good. Real good. But even Elyse did not know until last night. Now listen. Elyse and Anablue were harassed last night during their dinner out. Early this morning, I had a van parked outside of my house. Probably the same men. And Anablue was attacked at work this morning by one of those men."

Donall stopped, panic in his voice. "Where is she? Is she alright?"

"She's at home resting. Donall, they are after our women. I don't know if they're trying to scare them or if they mean to do them harm. I have a baby at home I need to worry about as well. We need to find these guys and put an end to this bullshit." Elijah said.

Donall nodded. "If they followed Elyse all the way home, that means they already know where Anablue lives."

Elijah nodded in agreement.

"I need to see Anablue to make sure she's okay," Donall said.

Elijah looked down at his shirt and up at Donall's shirt. Both red. "Damn it. Twenty-seven years, and you still wear the same color shirt as me every day."

"Like I would have known what color of shirt you put on today," Donall snarled.

"It's your turn to change," Elijah snarled back.

"Gladly," Donall said as he pulled his shirt off and turned to jump down into the boat.

Elijah sucked in his breath. His eyes teared at the sight of his brother's back.

"Holy shit. What did they do to you?"

"I don't need your pity," Donall called back to him.

"No. Just my support. Change your fucking shirt."

## CHAPTER 15

Laying on the couch listening to Mrs. Wang drone on about everything and anything she could think of to keep Anablue awake. Anablue stifled her annoyance, understanding that the woman did not want her to go to sleep. The throbbing in her head was intense. Right now, she just wanted Mrs. Wang to stop talking.

The insistent knocking on the front door brought Anablue out of her fog. Hearing whispers in the foyer and the scrape of a chair directly in front of her. Curiosity forced her to open her eyes to look into Donall's concerned eyes.

She gave him a small smile. "I suppose you're here to annoy me as well."

Donall smiled, reaching out to brush a blonde curl from her face. His thumb gently circling the developing black eye and purple bruise on her cheekbone. "Yeah, something like that. How are you feeling?" he softly whispered.

"I'm okay. I have a little bump on my head, and my cheek hurts." She licked her lips, her eyes tearing. "I'm scared. What if he comes after me again?"

"Don't you worry about that," Donall said.

"Will you help me upstairs. Mrs. Wang is an angel, but she's not strong enough."

"Yeah." He stood and scooped her up into his arms.

"I meant walking. It's four flights up," Anablue said as she wrapped her arms around his neck.

"What, and rob me of the chance to hold you in my arms?" Donall said.

"Don't be fooled, Donall, with two L's. I love you holding me in your arms," she whispered.

Donall looked deep into her eyes, nodding in agreement. "The feeling is mutual."

---

Donall shifted her weight in his arms as he eyed the last flight of stairs. Twenty steep stairs almost straight up. *Are you fucking kidding me?*

She giggled in his arms. "Seriously. Put me down. These stairs are a bitch."

"How many times a day do you go up and down all four flights?" he asked.

"Multiple times. It's how I stay in shape," she quipped.

"Be easier to climb the tree out front," he responded with a wicked smile.

"I've often thought so myself," she replied. " It's also faster to slide down the banisters if you're in a hurry."

Donald's mouth dropped open. "Please don't tell me you do that."

"Okay. I won't tell you" she replied, mischief twinkling in her eyes.

He set her on her feet. "I'm putting you down. Only because I'm afraid, we will both fall."

Anablue rolled her eyes at him. "No need to be a macho man."

Donall chuckled, pointing toward the stairs. "Up. Now."

"Cool your jets. I'm going," she replied.

He followed her up the steep stairwell. She stopped as a wave of dizziness hit, pausing for a moment. Right behind her, he steadied her with his hands on her waist.

"You alright? Sit down, if you need to," he said.

"I'm okay… really… I am," she said over her shoulder.

She got to the very top. Groaned and sat on the top stair. Giving him a look of pure annoyance.

"What's wrong," he asked.

"The key."

"And where is the key?"

"In my purse. Downstairs," she said.

"Of course, it is. Don't move. I'll be right back."

"You're awfully bossy."

"And you're sassy. Now I mean it. Don't move, or else."

"Or else what?"

"Do you really want to know?"

"No."

"Good girl," he replied.

---

HE MADE it downstairs in record time without sliding down the banisters. Finding her purse on the floor by the couch. Picking it up, he wondered if it was packed with bricks. It was so heavy. Shaking his head, "It's got to weigh half her body weight," he mumbled to himself as he stopped to scoop up her shoes.

With a few words to Mrs. Wang in the foyer. He eyed the first flight of stairs and the banisters. Shaking his head in disbelief, he bound back up the stairs. He was loath to admit his shoulders ached from the effort of carrying her up three flights of stairs, and this purse wasn't helping.

He made it up all three flights and stood at the bottom of the last flight, looking up at her. Sitting on the top stair, leaning against the doorjamb, she gave him a weak smile.

"You made it," she said.

"I run five miles a day. I spend an hour every day working out, but all these stairs are killers," Donall replied. Climbing the remaining twenty, he handed her the purse.

She dug around in her purse. "Here they are," she said as she pulled out a massive ring of keys.

Donall raised one eyebrow.

"What?" she asked." Shuffling through the keys, she found the key she wanted.

"I don't comment on massive keyrings or purses filled with bricks," he replied.

She handed him the key. Eyeing the small door to her room, he reached up over her to unlock the door.

"And naturally, we have a munchkin door at the entrance to the tower," he said.

Anablue snorted. "Tower, indeed."

Donall stepped above her, ducking down as he opened the door. Turning, he lifted her back up into his arms.

---

"I RATHER LIKE you carrying me to bed," Anablue said. Her cheeks burned, mortified at what she said.

His eyes smoldered. "Have no doubt, Baby blue. Someday, I will carry you to bed, cover your body with my own, and love you the way a man loves a woman."

Somewhat surprised at his words and slightly shocked, a shiver ran through her body. A soft gasp escaped her as she realized she would like that very much.

Carrying her over, laying her on the bed in the center of the room.

"But today is not that day," Donall said. "You need to rest and heal. The doctor will be here shortly."

Scrunching up her nose. "Doctor. What doctor?" Anablue said.

"The doctor I asked Mrs. Wang to call," Donall replied.

Anablue glared at him.

"No arguments," Donall said.

She opened her mouth and snapped it shut. Flouncing to the center of the bed, she winced as her head throbbed anew. Punching a pillow, grumbling to herself. "I'm perfectly fine."

---

Donall watched her as she pummeled her pillow. He had always known that she had a rebellious streak. The quiet ones usually did, and she hid it well. She was pouting, and it was adorable. He wanted nothing more than to kiss those full lips. That floral minidress she was wearing had scooted further up her hips, and he inwardly groaned. To pull those white fishnet tights from her thighs and down each silken leg. He shook his head to clear his thoughts.

"You might want to change before he gets here," Donall said.

"Oh, you're right," she said as she scooted off the bed. Going to her small dresser, pulling out a pair of warm, fuzzy pajamas.

Turning to him, she nodded her head towards the doorway to the widow's walk.

"Um. Yah," Donall said as he headed out to the widow's walk.

The view was stunning. San Francisco Bay, the skyline of the city on the other side. Homes with their gabled roofs covered with clay tiles lined the neighborhood, their streets laid out like steps down to the bay. He walked along the whole circular walkway, admiring the occasional roof-top garden and swimming pool.

He spotted her reflection in the full-length mirror through the window. Quickly turning his back, he tried to focus on the skyline. Giving in to his base instincts, he peeked over his shoulder.

She was breathtakingly lovely. Her long blonde hair curled invitingly over one shoulder. White lace panties accentuated the curve of her bottom and hips, while pink nipples peeked through the lace of her bra.

"She's killing me." He groaned to himself as he again tried to focus on the view.

Serves you right for peeking—you horny bastard.

MRS. WANG KNOCKED on the door. Dressed now, Anablue called for them to enter as she climbed back onto the bed. Mrs. Wang stood in the doorway with an elderly man in tow.

"Anablue. This is Dr. Markham," Mrs. Wang said.

Anablue shot another glare to Donall, watching from the doorway to the widow's walk. He smiled back at her as if she were a small, misbehaving child. She crinkled her nose at him, sorely tempted to stick out her tongue and prove him right.

Remembering her manners. "Hello, Dr. Markham. This is unnecessary," Anablue said. "I'm fine."

"Hmmm, let me be the judge of that," he kindly replied as he sat on the edge of the bed and opened his black bag.

Mrs. Wang stepped out to stroll with Donall, the widow's walk.

"This man who attacked Anablue. Who is he?" Mrs. Wang asked.

"From what I've been told, he was a regular at the bookstore. He's been stalking her. He, along with a friend of his, has been following my sister-in-law Elyse, as well. He's driving a yellow van…."

"You mean like that one parked up the street?" Mrs. Wang said.

Donall's eyes pivoted to the street below. Spotting the van, he leaped from the balcony onto the tree. He was down the tree, swinging from branch to branch until he landed like a feral cat; racing across the front lawn, he pounded up the street.

Mrs. Wang was speechless as she watched his cat-like movement down the tree. In all her years, she had never seen a man move the way that man did.

He raced up the street, right toward the van. The van, moving in reverse, squealed its tires up the street; spinning around, the van sped away. Donall, chasing after it, stopped, picked up a baseball-sized rock from the side of the road and launched it at the van. It crashed through the back window of the van.

---

Donall's rage formed an icy knot in the pit of his stomach as he watched the van speeding away, feeling a sense of satisfaction at hitting his mark and breaking the window. His fear for Anablue was gut-wrenching, and his worry for her safety was growing by the minute.

Pausing to catch his breath. Rubbing his aching shoulder, he looked up to Mrs. Wang on the widow's walk. Eyeing the tree, he didn't want to climb back up in front of Mrs. Wang, but it was that, or four flights of stairs again. Sighing deeply, he headed for the front door. *Fucking steps.*

A couple of minutes later, Donall knocked on Anablue's bedroom door. Mrs. Wang opened the door.

"Good shot," she whispered.

"I would have felt better if it hit one of them," Donall replied.

Anablue looked up as he came through the door. Confusion flashed across her face as she looked out to the widow's walk and back to the bedroom door.

"She has a mild concussion, and she's bruised," Dr. Markham said. "Keep her awake for a while longer. Then let her sleep. But you must wake her every two hours throughout the night. Give her aspirin if she needs it. Otherwise, she'll be fine in a few days."

Donall and Mrs. Wang nodded at the doctor's instructions as Anablue groaned and laid back down.

"Damn," Anablue grumbled.

"I'm going to see Dr. Markham out. Then I'm going to finish making the tea and start some soup for Anablue," Mrs. Wang said.

Anablue groaned again, throwing her blanket over her head. Donall grinned, pulling up a chair next to her bed.

Tugging on the blanket, he pulled the covers off her face. "You have to stay awake for a while," he said.

"Is all of this necessary? I mean, the tea and soup are fine, but I don't want anyone to make a fuss over me."

"Isn't it time for a secret?" Donall asked.

"You know. I've told you lots of my secrets, but I have heard none of yours."

She patted the spot next to her on the bed. Donall sat on the bed, leaning against the brass headboard. He pulled her into his arms. Anablue settled her head on his broad chest, listening to his steady heartbeat. She sighed in contentment.

"Hmm. Secrets. Let's see—one Thanksgiving or the night before. My brother, Aiden and I, stole an apple pie my Aunt Meg had cooled on the back porch. Aiden snuck into the house and took some forks. We demolished that pie in five minutes. Then my other brothers. Elijah, Colin, and Brendan stole another one. My aunt found the pie tins a few days later.

She was mad as hell. She had thought a wild animal had taken the pies until she found the forks," Donall said.

"So, family secrets," Anablue replied, the corners of her mouth curling into a mischievous smile.

"Pretty much."

"Tell me more," she drowsily replied.

"Open your eyes, Anablue. I need you to stay awake for a while longer."

"I'm awake," she replied as her heavy eyelashes floated downwards.

"I think a change in scenery would help," Donall said.

Climbing off the bed, lifting her into his arms. He made his way out to the widow's walk to settle into the chair outside the door.

He looked up as Mrs. Wang appeared with a tray filled with a steaming pot of tea and two teacups. She set the tray down on the small table next to the chair.

"Drink some tea, Anablue. It's much better than aspirin for your headache," Mrs. Wang said as she poured the tea, handing the cup to Anablue.

Anablue obediently sat up, taking the cup offered. The aroma of peppermint and fresh ginger floated in the air as she sipped the hot brew. She finished the cup of tea under Mrs. Wang's watchful eye and laid her head back on Donall's chest.

Mrs. Wang nodded her approval. "I will be back as soon as the soup is ready," she said.

DONALL SHIFTED her weight in his arms. Twilight was falling. The smell of spent fireworks drifted through the air. A year ago, he had spent the fourth of July bombing the NVA along the Ho Chi Minh trail. Today, he had sat here most of the day with Anablue snuggled against his chest. The small slice of Americana had reminded him of why he had enlisted and what he had been fighting for.

From this vantage point, he watched the Fourth of July sailboat regatta races in the bay. The boat's brightly colored sails were decorated with flags as they skimmed across the water. Maybe next year, if his boat was seaworthy, he'd join in the races.

He had watched the neighbors with their backyard barbeques and the block party feel of the neighborhood. Excited children lined up below for a bike parade up and down the street. Their bikes were decorated with flags and streamers of red, white, and blue.

Parents with their tiny tots sat curbside with slices of watermelon, the juice dribbling down their chins, as they waved their miniature American flags urging them on. Afterward, families piled into station wagons. The neighborhood leaving in mass headed for a larger parade and the fireworks display over the bay.

Donall flinched at the occasional string of firecrackers and bottle rockets as Anablue stirred in his arms.

"We're supposed to be on a date today," Anablue murmured.

Donall chuckled softly. "Who said we aren't on a date?"

Anablue sighed, "Well, I would like to at least stay awake for it."

"That egg-sized bump on your head says otherwise," Donall replied.

She reached up, touching the bump on her head. "It's gone down already. I'm feeling much better."

"I'm sure it's the fish soup Mrs. Wang brought you for dinner."

"I would have preferred some of that watermelon the children were eating." Anablue crinkling her nose.

"I didn't realize you were awake then," Donall said.

"I wouldn't have missed the bike parade for the world. That, and the children's noisy excitement woke me up," Anablue replied with a wide smile.

The sky lit up with a spectacular display of fireworks over the San Francisco Bay.

"Look how beautiful they are," Anablue said. "Oh. I bought something for us to celebrate with. Let me up."

Anablue returned a moment later. Settling herself back onto Donall's lap, he tucked the blanket around her.

She opened a small, oblong box and pulled out sparklers. She handed a lighter to Donall, and he lit the end of two sparklers. Holding them at arms-length, they both laughed as the sparks flew in every direction. Anablue took her sparkler and made the shape of a heart. Looking deep into Donall's eyes, he pulled her in for a soft kiss. The sparklers sputtered out, and Anablue laid her head on his broad chest.

"The flute. No flute tonight," Anablue sleepily murmured.

Donall was stunned.

When he could finally find his voice. "You hear a flute?"

"Late at night. It carries on the wind from the bay. It's beautiful. Melancholy and sweet. It's like love songs that caress my soul. Sometimes. I like to think he's serenading me," she whispered. "My favorite is when he plays Moon River."

A sense of peace settled over Donall's heart. Smiling, he placed a soft kiss on top of her head. "I'm sure he is," he replied. "Moon River is my favorite too."

---

ELYSE BRUSHED the sand off the beach blanket. The baby rolled to and fro in front of her, babbling and cooing to the rubber giraffe he held in his chubby hands. He rolled to his tummy and was up on all fours, rocking back and forth.

She looked over as her father sat down on the blanket next to her.

"Look at him, Daddy. Up on all fours," Elyse said.

"He'll be crawling before you know it."

"He's already rolling across the floor," she replied.

They watched as Elijah and the Colonel made their way down the beach toward them.

"It's been a rough day for Elijah and his father," the Ambassador said.

"I know. I had hoped we lived far enough from town that they wouldn't hear all the firecrackers."

"It's the bottle rockets. The ones that whistle. They sound like incoming missiles," he said.

"Elijah knocked both Bunker and me to the floor this morning, thinking it was incoming. Afterward, the baby was crying," Elyse said. "I've been knocked into more trenches than I can count. We were fine, but Elijah felt terrible."

"It's going to take time for them to get past the war. It took me a while, but eventually, I was able to."

"I wish there was a quiet place we could go. A place where we can avoid the fireworks tonight," Elyse said.

"There is," he replied.

"Where?"

"The movie theatre. True Grit is playing," he said.

"Is that an adult movie?"

"Yes. I guess so," he replied.

Elyse's mind raced as dread filled her. She wasn't going to go through that again—just the thought of what she and Anablue saw left her shuddering with revulsion.

"I can't take Bunker to a movie like that," she said. "You go with them. I'll stay here with the baby."

Elijah and the colonel sat down on the blanket. Bunker rolled to his father, and Elijah picked the baby up. Tugging on his ear, the baby fussed as he reached for his mama.

"We have an idea. The three of you should go into town and see a movie. It's quiet in there. You won't hear any of the fireworks outside," Elyse said.

"It's not a bad idea. But, I won't go without you," Elijah replied.

"No. I prefer to stay here," Elyse said, her anxiety about going to the movies clear. Elijah narrowed his eyes at his mate.

"What have you done?"

"Nothing. We both know Bunker wouldn't last through a movie. Besides, he's tugging on his ear again, and he's cutting teeth. I'll be just fine here," Elyse said.

"If that van shows up again? I don't know..." Elijah's voice trailed off.

"I'll stay with Elyse and the baby. You two go to the movies," the Ambassador replied. The Ambassador reached for the baby.

"Come to Gramps."

The baby allowed his mother to give him over to the ambassador.

"An hour ago, you said that you were Pops?" Elijah barked.

"No. Your father is Pops." Elyse said.

Looking at both of the elderly men. "I think the two of you are playing games. Who is Pops, and who is Gramps?" Elijah snarled.

The ambassador and the colonel laughed.

"So, it's settled. You and your father go to the movies. My father and I stay here with Bunker," Elyse said.

"I'm game," the colonel said.

"What's playing?" Elijah asked.

"True Grit is still playing," the colonel replied.

"A western. Haven't seen a good western in a while," Elijah said.

Elyse smiled. "You both need this. You've been on edge all day. We will be fine here."

---

Elijah settled himself into the seat in the deserted theatre, a large soda and popcorn in hand. His father sat one seat away from him.

Another man came in behind them and sat two rows back.

"Life has many twists, Elijah. Where were you at a year ago?"

"On the Fourth of July? Let me see. I believe I was chasing Elyse out of trouble at Tan Son Nhat," Elijah chuckled.

A voice behind them spoke up. "Tan Son Nhat. I was there in Sixty-Seven."

Both Elijah and the colonel turned to look at the man.

"You're a Vietnam vet?" Elijah asked.

"For what it's worth. Yeah," he replied. "Name's John King, formerly known as Lance Corporal King, United States Marine Corps."

"Well, come on down and sit with some fellow Marines, son," the colonel said.

John slid into the seat, one down from Elijah.

"I figured we'd be the only ones in here today," Elijah said.

"There are a couple more guys who live in town in here last year on the fourth," John replied. "Good place to hide out from the world. Can't find a job. No one wants to hire a Vietnam vet. My girl dumped me. Said she didn't want to be with some baby-killer. Shit. I love kids. Twenty-one years old, and I have nothing to look forward to."

Elijah nodded his head. "What do you do for a living?"

"When I can find work, a carpenter," John replied.

"No shit," Elijah replied. "I could use a good carpenter."

The lights dimmed as John handed Elijah a bottle of whiskey. "Pour some in your soda. We'll get through this day together."

"Ooo-rah," Elijah and the colonel replied.

THEY MADE it halfway through the movie before the film got stuck. Overheating, the projector melted the film. They waited fifteen minutes before it was fixed, then it melted again. Smoke filled the projection room, billowing out the projection window. The usher, a young kid of sixteen, appeared at the end of their row.

"Ummm, the projectionist said that True Grit is out for the night, but he can put in another movie he hasn't sent back to distribution yet.

"What's the movie?" Elijah asked.

"The Love Bug," the kid replied.

"What's your name, kid?" The Colonel asked.

"Joey."

"Well, Joey, I guess we don't care. We're in here until the

fireworks are over." He handed Joey a twenty-dollar bill. "Run down the block to the liquor store. Grab us as many bottles of whiskey as you can get with that twenty. There's a big tip in it when you return. Tell Roger, the owner, you're picking it up for me if he gives you any grief," the Colonel said. "And let us know when the fireworks are over."

THE NEXT MORNING. Elyse rolled over in bed. Elijah and his father had made a loud drunken entrance after midnight. She tip-toed out of the bedroom. Past her father sleeping in the recliner, and the colonel, snoring loudly, passed out on the couch. She stopped to put on a pot of coffee and went out to the back porch.

Seeing a man spread out flat on her porch floor, she quietly slipped back inside, locking the screen door. Rushing to the bedroom, she shook Elijah.

"Elijah. Wake up. A strange man is sleeping on our back porch. Elijah. Wake up."

Elijah groaned. "That's no stranger. That's my new employee, John." He rolled over onto his stomach, grabbing her pillow to jam over his head. "Go away and let me die in peace."

"Ha. I guess the honeymoon is over."

Elijah peeked one red-eye out from under the pillow. His arm snaked out, grabbed her by the waist, and pulled her into bed.

She squealed with laughter. Cupping his face. "Poor baby. Do you want some aspirin?"

"What I want is to make love to my wife."

"We have company in our living room. A man sleeping on our porch, and our son is…. standing in his crib, watching us. Oh, my God. How is he standing? He isn't even crawling yet."

Elijah laughed. "He's a strong little Devil pup."

"Don't be in such a rush, Elijah. The day will come when you see the man standing in front of you, all while wondering what happened to the baby. Time goes by fast."

"I know it does. We need to talk about his hair. He looks like a little girl."

"What! No," she said, glaring at him. "I love his curls."

"Not right now, but you need to prepare yourself for his first haircut. We also have to let a baby grow up and let a little boy be a little boy."

Elyse's lowered lip quivered as she nodded, "Okay."

## CHAPTER 16

Donall parked his motorcycle on the street in front of Anablue's house. Walking up the driveway, stopping when he got to the top of the steep incline.

Anablue's car was sitting outside of the garage, not where he had parked it yesterday. The hood was up, and he spied two tiny feet sticking out from under the front end. *What the fuck.*

Cool anger simmered beneath the surface as he reached down and gave the hardwood dolly a yank, pulling her out from beneath the car. He stood over her. His stance was wide and intimidating. Looking down into surprised blue eyes.

"What do you think you are doing?" he demanded.

ANABLUE YELPED as he suddenly pulled her dolly from under the car. Shielding her eyes from the bright sunlight, she lay in his shadow. She looked at his long legs straddling the dolly and up to his bulging crotch. Further up to his hands on his hips, to his stern face and intense brown eyes. *Damn.* She had expected she might get busted by Mrs. Wang, but not by Donall.

"I'm changing my oil," she timidly ventured.

"You are supposed to be resting in bed," he growled, heavily enunciating each word.

"Well. I... It's on my calendar to change my oil and rotate the tires today," she replied. Pushing away from him, she slid back under the car.

He pulled her out again. "Not today." He ground the words out between clenched teeth.

She defiantly narrowed her eyes at him. "Yes. Today."

She moved to roll back under the car and found the dolly blocked from moving as he set his foot upon it. Donall picked her up like she was a rag doll; throwing her over his shoulder, he headed for the house.

"No. No, no, no. Put me down," she cried.

"No arguing. You are going back to bed," Donall said, his voice dangerously low.

He slammed the front door open, surprising Mr. and Mrs. Wang, standing in the foyer. Seeing Anablue slung over Donall's shoulder, their mouths dropped open.

"Anablue. What is the meaning of this? You should be in bed," Mrs. Wang said.

"She was outside, working on her car," Donall growled.

"Anablue." Mrs. Wang chided.

They watched as Donall carried Anablue up the stairs. Mrs. Wang moved to follow them. Mr. Wang stopped her with a gentle hand on her arm.

"Has it been so long, old woman? That you do not remember when we were young lovers amid an argument? Leave them be. Come. Sit with me on the back porch."

Mrs. Wang looked into her husband's eyes. "Old indeed. I look at you and still see the strong, handsome man of our youth."

"And I, in you as well," he replied, as he reached out, sweetly cupping her face in his gnarled hands.

"But, Anablue?"

"She will be fine. She needs a husband to end her suffering. We have both seen how they look at each other. Give them the time they need to work this through in private."

Taking her by the hand, he led her through the kitchen and out to the back porch.

Donall dumped her unceremoniously on the bed. "Pajamas. Now," he demanded.

She came to her knees, crawling off the bed. "I can't believe you did that," Anablue said.

"Did what?"

"Manhandling me like that. Throwing me over your shoulder and hauling me up here like I'm a child. This is not the seventeenth century, you know."

"If this was the seventeenth century, I'd be hauling you over my knee as well," he snarled.

Anablue stomped over to her dresser, ripping open the drawer. She pulled out her pajamas. Without thinking, she pulled her t-shirt off.

"Seriously. Now you're threatening me?"

He strode over to stand in front of her. "There can be consequences for every action, Baby blue. Both good and bad."

She looked up at him and froze at the heat in his eyes. A burning whisper scorching deep down, caressing every inch of her body and soul. Anger was forgotten, her eyes softening to a stormy blue in response.

"You tempt a man beyond control," Donall said, his voice low and seductive.

Clutching her shirt to her chest, she moistened her dry lips. Holding his gaze, she dropped her shirt to the floor.

He ran his finger in a soft caress along her shoulder, up her neck, to her chin. Circling her plump, quivering lips. She shivered as she closed her eyes. Desire racing through her body, she opened her eyes to look up into his. Passion filled his eyes, burning hotter with each passing moment. He groaned as he pulled her into his arms, and she melted into him.

Slanting his mouth, he took her lips and plundered her mouth. His fiery hands roamed freely over her ribcage and breasts, pinching the peaks until he reached around unhooking her bra. Her breasts fell into his large hands. He trailed his mouth down her neck to capture a rosy crest in his mouth as she moaned deeply. Arching her back to feel more of what his mouth was doing to her senses.

"Lock the door," she breathed.

He lifted his eyes to hers. "You're sure?"

"Yes, I'm sure."

He carried her back and gently laid her on the bed. He hoisted her up and her legs wrapped around his waist as he strode over to the door, flipping the bolt in place. His hands slid over her breasts and down her smooth belly to her jeans. Sliding her jeans off the soft curves of her hips, as his mouth blazed a trail of heat from her lips to her shoulder to pink crested peaks.

Her soft sighs filled him with pleasure as her hands roaming his body. Donall reached over to her nightstand and flipped the radio on.

Hesitant at first, but with a will of their own. Anablue ran her hands over his forearms, then up to his muscular biceps. Hampered by his shirt, she tugged on it. He lifted his shirt so she could feel his chest next to hers, but did not remove it. She slid her hands underneath to explore shoulders and then to his chest, caressing his ribcage.

Inhaling sharply, he quivered at her feather-light touch. Heady with the realization she was affecting him as much as he was affecting her. She continued her exploration of his body while his hands and mouth explored her most secret places. She could not contain her body's response to his touch or slow her wildly beating heart.

She looked into his eyes when he settled himself, and his knee parted her thighs. She felt him pause, and his eyes widened in surprise as he thrust into her. His kisses silenced her cry of pain, and he moved with soft whispers, turning the pain into sighs of pleasure.

---

DONALL PULLED her into his arms, placing soft kisses on her swollen lips. He could feel her body, moist with the sweat of lovemaking, still quivering. He had taken her to the heights of ecstasy, then found his own. All with a woman whose body fit perfectly to his.

He had to admit that it surprised him to find her a virgin. Though, once he realized it, it was far too late to stop. He had assumed after seeing the dog tags she was Brian Baker's widow. He had heard rumors of bridegroom's being whisked away by the military before their wedding night. Maybe the marriage was never consummated?

He felt a twinge of jealousy that she had loved another,

but he pushed it aside. It was possible, in time, that she would love him as well. He knew beyond the shadow of a doubt that he was falling for the woman now curved into his side. He placed a light kiss on top of her head and pulled her closer.

ANABLUE LAY in the curve of Donall's arms. Her breathing and heartbeat slowed to normal.

Contemplating their lovemaking, she blushed at her adventurous behavior, but it had felt so right. This is where I want to be, held in Donall's arms forever. Eyelids heavy, she drifted off, lulled by the music. *Wild horses, indeed.*

DONALL ROUSED from his sleep with Anablue still curled into his body. Her head rested on his chest.

"Are you awake?" his voice, a whispered rumble in his chest.

"Yeah. I'm just laying here listening to the music and enjoying how it feels to wake up in your arms," she whispered.

He moved her, so she lay on top of him. Her breasts pressed enticingly against his chest.

She walked her fingers across his upper chest. "You take canoodling to a whole new level," Anablue murmured.

Donall chuckled as he brushed a tendril of hair from her face. He pulled her in for a soft kiss, his kiss deepened, and she squealed with laughter when he rolled her underneath him.

"Again?" she questioned.

"Oh yes. Again."

---

ANABLUE LAID ON HER STOMACH, her arms wrapped around her pillow as she watched Donall dress. He really was beautiful in an Adonis way. Broad shoulders and long legs, and his fanny was just scrumptious. Though it looked like it had some faded scars going down to the back of his thighs. Giggling, she fought the temptation to reach out and give him a pinch, knowing exactly where that might lead again.

Donall leaned down to place a kiss on her lips. "Were you looking at my ass?"

She bit her lip, giving him a sassy smile. "You looked at mine."

"You have a beautiful ass."

She rolled her eyes. "Whatever."

"How did you get the scars on yours?" she asked.

"Altercation between my dirt bike and a barbed wired fence when I was a kid," Donall replied.

"Ouch. That had to hurt," she said, shuddering.

"It did. But not as much as…" his voice trailed off. "Rest now. I'll be back to see you later on."

She sighed. "I need to take a bath first. I'm a little sore. Kind of like I've been on horseback for three days sore."

"I thought you didn't like horseback riding?"

"I enjoyed straddling you," she said.

He knelt to eye level. "Don't tempt me further."

"You're already dressed," she said coquettishly.

"I… can undress."

She wagged her finger under his nose. "Still sore."

"Okay. Bath. Then rest." with a deep chuckle. "Tomorrow, I will change your oil," he said.

Her eyes sparkled with mischief. "Do you even know how?"

She squealed when he lightly smacked her on the bottom. "Yes. I know how."

"By the way. How did my car get here?" she asked.

"Maude had the keys. I drove it here," Donall said.

"You drove my car? Isn't it groovy?"

"Yeah. That's one powerful car, that engine purrs. Now maybe you understand the expression, "Keep your engines and women purring like kittens."

Anablue's mouth dropped open. "Oh my God."

---

Donall was still chuckling on his way downstairs. He had thoroughly enjoyed his afternoon with Anablue, unplanned as it was. She was passionate, adventurous, and funny. Everything he had ever hoped to find in a woman. He did, however, feel churlish for not taking off his shirt. The scars on his back weren't something he was trying to hide or his time in captivity, but he didn't want to explain it right now, either.

"Three days on a horse." He started laughing again. "God, she's something else."

THE BATHROOM WAS thick with steam as Anablue sank into the bathtub. The lavender scent of the water drifting to delight her senses. She sighed in appreciation. Relaxing, she closed her eyes and leaned back to rest her head on the tub. The bubbles swirled as she sank lower into the tub.

The hot water was easing the ache between her thighs from Donall's lovemaking. She opened one eye and reached for the jars of hot fudge and caramel sitting on a small table. She let the jars sink to the bottom of the tub to warm. After a few minutes, she opened the jar of hot fudge. Taking a spoonful, she licked the warm, gooey treat off the spoon. Another sigh of pleasure. *Heaven. This is heaven.*

Her mind played back her afternoon with Donall. Blushing at what he had done to her body. "Wanton. I'm a Wanton woman eating hot fudge and caramel in the tub, and I love it." She stifled a giggle. *Elyse was right. I never once thought about my feet.*

# CHAPTER 17

Gary reached over and punched Marcus in the arm. "Wake up, asshole. That big dude is here again."

Marcus sat up, leaning forward; he rubbed his eyes. "Tell me again why we are here?"

"I told you before, you dumb fuck. I want to see if I can get Anablue alone. Teach her some respect. Ain't going to let a stupid whore get away with what she did. That, and the old man wants us to watch her," Gary replied.

"Man, if that dude sees us again," Marcus whined.

Parked a block away from Anablue's house. Gary watched the guy walk down the driveway to his motorcycle, rev it up and pull away.

"I've seen him before. Just can't remember where," Gary thoughtfully mused.

"Yeah. Maybe last time, when he launched that rock through your back window," Marcus retorted.

Gary reached over and cuffed him upside the head. "Shut the fuck up and let me think."

An hour later, they still sat watching the house as a car pulled up.

"Look, it's the redhead, and she's got a kid with her. I've got a bone to pick with her too. Holding that knife to my ribs," Marcus said.

"Holy shit. That's it. That's where I saw him before. At Two-Belly's and the diner. He was kissing the redhead and holding a baby. Fucking Anablue is seeing some married guy, and that redhead is his wife, and that's his baby," Gary said, chortling.

"Oh yeah. That's the same guy we saw up at the redhead's house after we followed her home the other night," Marcus replied.

"What we got here is a love triangle. I'm going to enjoy bending that bitch over and giving it to her. All while I tell her that her boyfriend is married, and she's nothing but a home-wrecking slut, fucking her friend's husband," Gary chortled in glee. "Let's get out of here. I've seen enough for one day."

Elyse knocked on the front door. Cooing to Bunker as he fussed in her arms. A tiny Chinese woman opened the door. The woman looked at Elyse, then riveted her eyes to the baby.

She smiled a big smile at Elyse and reached for the baby. Elyse was momentarily stunned; recognizing the kindness in the old woman, she let her take the baby.

"Oh… well, hello. My name is Elyse. I'm here to see Anablue."

The woman waved her in. Elyse followed her into the sitting room as the woman spoke over her shoulder in Chinese to someone in the back of the house. Picking up a few words similar to Vietnamese, she knew the woman asked someone to go get Anablue. An elderly man appeared. Bowing to Elyse before he went up the wide staircase.

Elyse looked around the comfortable room before settling herself on the couch. Her eyes on her son. Mrs. Wang settled into a rocker, rocking and cooing to the baby.

"Anablue speaks highly of you," Mrs. Wang said.

"That's very sweet. She's a wonderful girl, herself," Elyse replied. "I came as soon as I could. I know Donall had been here."

"Donall appears very devoted to her. How do you know him?"

"He's my husband's twin."

"Anablue is a twin, as well," Mrs. Wang said.

"Yes. I know."

"I'm surprised. Anablue never mentioned that Donall was a twin," Mrs. Wang said.

"Well. I'm sure he told her," Elyse replied.

"She grieves very deeply for her brother. She hides it well.

We hope that Donall, and you, will help her come to grips with his loss. And maybe, welcome her father into her life."

"Her father? I thought she was all alone," Elyse said.

"Her father is alive and well. He waits in the shadows."

"Oh my. Where is he?" Elyse asked.

"Elyse."

Elyse looked up to see Anablue, fresh from her bath, standing in the doorway. "Anablue," she cried as she came to her feet. They rushed to each other, hugging and crying.

"Come upstairs. I have so much to tell you," Anablue said.

Elyse looked over to her baby, soothed to sleep by the steady back and forth of the rocking chair. "Well. Um, Bunker."

"Bunker will be fine. Mrs. Wang loves children. She fawns over the neighborhood children. They all love her."

"Mrs. Wang, is that all right with you?" Elyse asked.

Mrs. Wang snorted and waved them away.

They walked to the bottom of the stairs. "She had a son once. He died in a horrible fire. He was about the same age as Bunker," Anablue whispered.

Elyse's eyes teared. "I can't even imagine the grief she must feel losing her child."

"She never talks about him. It was Mr. Wang who told me," Anablue replied.

Elyse looked around Anablue's room in awe. "Wow. Look at these windows. She strolled out to the widow's walk. "Anablue. This is so cool."

Coming back inside, she walked over to the nightstand. Picking up a photograph, she smiled.

"You, your brother, and mom?" Elyse asked.

"Yes. I think we were about two years old then. That was the last time I saw my father."

"I can see someone was cut out of this photo," Elyse ventured.

"My mother cut my father out in a fit of anger."

"Where is your father?"

"I don't know. Out to sea, I suppose. He's in the Navy," Anablue said.

"If you haven't seen him in over twenty-one years, would you even recognize him?"

"No. Brian met him once before he shipped out for Vietnam. He used to talk to him on the phone every once in a while. I never did," Anablue said.

Elyse set the photograph down. Glancing down at the bed, she froze. Virgin's blood on the sheets. Oh, my God. She looked up as Anablue flicked the blankets over the sheets.

"Um. That's what I wanted to talk to you about," Anablue said.

"Donall?" Elyse asked. Anablue nodded.

"Let's go sit outside and talk," Elyse said.

"I think I seduced him."

"You've heard the expression It takes two to tango. Meaning that you both wanted it to happen."

"Does that make me a whore?"

"No, it's human nature. It's society that says it wrong. And that doesn't mean they are right."

"Times are changing. I mean, we are smack dab in the middle of the summer of love," Anablue said. "Or was that in sixty-seven?"

"As the saying goes, sex, drugs, and rock-and-roll. Though, the drugs, that's not my thing," Elyse said.

"Mine either, but sometimes, I wish I could be a hippy," Anablue replied.

"Oh, totally," Elyse said, laughing.

"We should pick out hippy names. I'll be Bambi," Elyse said.

"Let me think, what's a good hippy name? How about Blossom for me? Then we can buy a van, paint flowers on it, and travel the country living off the land," Anablue cried as she dissolved into fits of giggles.

"All five of us together. I can't picture my husband or Donall as hippies," Elyse said, wiping the tears of laughter from her eyes.

"None of that is going to happen. I have my job, and I guess Donall is already getting free love, as well."

"Please tell me he used a condom for protection?" Elyse said, concern in her eyes.

"Protection?"

"So, you don't get pregnant."

"Well. It was my first time. You can't get pregnant your first time," Anablue said.

"Oh, honey. I'm not sure who you heard that from, but it's not true. I conceived Bunker my first time."

"What if it's already too late? What do I do then?" Anablue said.

"I guess that will be something to talk to Donall about. I'm here for you, whatever you need," Elyse replied.

Elyse dug in her purse, handing her condoms. "Here, next time, make him wear one of these. They're extra-large. If he's anything like my husband, you'll need them bigger."

"So, how was it?" Elyse asked with a bit of deviltry in her eye.

Anablue smiled. "It was just like you said it would be."

Elyse smiled and touched the bruise on Anablue's face. "You've got quite a shiner there."

"I know. I'm surprised Donall could even look at me."

"I think I should start training you on some self-defense techniques," sighed Elyse.

"I did smack Gary upside the head with a can of polish," Anablue giggled.

"That's a good start, but you need more," Elyse chuckled. "We both need to be on guard at all times. For now. You're supposed to be resting. Let me throw those sheets in the washer for you. I'm sure you don't want Mrs. Wang to see them."

"No, you're right. Let me get my spare sheets from the closet," Anablue said.

"I'll do it. You sit down," Elyse replied.

Going to the small closet, pushing the neatly hung clothes out of the way, her hand brushed against a small Naval uniform.

Elyse looked at the uniform. *Her brother's? Maybe he was a small man.*

Finding fresh sheets on the back shelf, she pushed the clothes back in place. Elyse stripped the bed, putting the fresh sheets on. Then she took the sheets downstairs to the washer. Once she had Anablue settled, she gave her a hug, and she promised to return soon.

Stopping in the sitting room to collect her baby. Mrs. Wang gave her a small bottle.

"Here, use this for his teething," insisted Mrs. Wang.

"What is it?"

"Bourbon."

Tipping her head to the side. "You want me to give my baby booze?" Elyse asked.

Rolling her eyes, "Of course not. Take a drop and rub it on his gums. It will ease the pain."

Elyse looked at the bottle. *Heh. Who knew?*

## CHAPTER 18

Donall whistled while walking toward his sailboat. Stopping in front of Capt. Jacks had promised to update him on Anablue's condition. Capt. Jack had been worried sick since he had been told of the attack on Anablue. The man wasn't on board his boat. He must be up at Two-Bellies, Donall mused. Figuring he'd take a shower before he went up to the bar to see him, he continued on his way to his boat.

The shower beat down on his back and shoulders. Its soothing pulse melting the ache in his shoulders. He shut the tap off to conserve water while he washed his hair. Wisps of memories of Anablue floated through his mind as he pondered the lazy afternoon in her bed.

He chuckled outright, remembering her look of indignation at being hauled upstairs. When she stood in front of him, angry sparks shooting from those beautiful eyes. Then, those eyes, softening to stormy blue. He had been lost then. Lost to his own needs to hold her in his arms. To kiss those lips, hear her sighs of pleasure and need.

He couldn't wait to see her again. To hear her laughter and silly words. Outside of bed, enjoyable in itself, he truly enjoyed her company.

Finishing his shower, he dried himself off and dressed.

*Maybe I should pick up a pizza and take it over to her for dinner?* Whistling, he left the cabin. He looked up to see two Naval master-at-arms men, MAA's, standing on the dock in front of his boat.

"Shit," Donall muttered.

"Good afternoon, Captain Corrington."

Donall gave them a terse nod. "Good afternoon."

"Sir. Your presence is requested by command."

"I take it, "No" is not an option?" Donall snarled.

"No, sir."

"What's so important they felt the need to send Naval police?" Donall growled.

"We have orders to bring you in. Sir."

Donall looked over to Capt. Jack's boat, *Still gone. I'll write a note for him to give to Anablue.*

"Hold on. I need to leave a note."

Grabbing a pen and paper from inside the cabin, he wrote:

Baby Blue, Called away. Be back to see you ASAP. Donall.

Folding the paper in half, he wrote on the front for Capt.

Jack to give it to Anablue. It was the best he could do under the circumstances.

Jumping up on the dock, he strode down to Capt. Jack's sailboat and slipped the note under the door of the cabin. He followed them to their jeep parked up on the pier.

---

Capt. Jack returned late from closing the bar. A job normally left for his late-night bartender, Jacob. The man had rushed home early, his wife in labor with their first child.

The wind whipped raindrops across the bay, pelting Capt. Jack on the back, seeping down his neck and soaking his collar. He fussed with the key, unlocking the cabin door. The door finally opened just as a gust of wind rushed inside the cabin. Swirling inside the small cabin, it blew the note lying on the floor outside the door to land on the bench outside. The blustering wind recaptured it to fly across the marina to twirl and swirl before, rain-sodden, it settled to float in the bay. Shivering, wet, and cold. Capt. Jack shut the cabin door.

---

Dusk settled over the city as Anablue wrapped herself in a blanket. Padding softly across the floor to sit outside. Confused and fighting back angry tears. She hadn't heard from Donall in over a week. He had just disappeared. She couldn't tell if she was more furious with Donall or herself.

Knowing better. She had fallen for him… hard. Going back and forth between worry and anger. Feeling abandoned and used, she reflected on the past week. The first days had been the hardest. Following the doctor's instructions, she had rested in her room, which was fine with her, considering her foul mood. Eventually, accepting it had all meant nothing to him, wishing he meant nothing to her.

Returning to work earlier that day. Immersing herself in rearranging the window display. Unwilling and unable, she had avoided Maude's probing questions and motherly concern. Gram's voice in her head. She pulled herself up by her bootstraps, determined to learn the lesson of trusting too easily, and giving too much.

The doorbell rang downstairs. A moment later, Mrs. Wang called up to her. "Anablue." her voice echoing up four floors. "Now what?" Anablue grumbled.

"Anablue. There's a telegram for you," Mrs. Wang trilled again from down below.

Rushing down the stairs, she reached the foyer. Mrs. Wang handed her the telegram. Her hands shaking, she opened it and read.

Anablue's face lost all color. "No. They can't do this," she whispered.

"Anablue. What's wrong? What does it say?" Mrs. Wang asked.

"I have forty-eight hours to report… I've been recalled back into the Navy," Anablue said.

CURSING UNDER HIS BREATH. Looking crisp and clean in his service whites, Donall removed his cap. This past week had tested his patience. The endless rounds of interviews, psychological testing, and physical exams with no explanation why was maddening. Left to cool his temper for long periods in between, he wanted it to be over. It was odd that they had pushed this second round of testing before approving his medical discharge. One last appointment today, then he would be free to move on and live his life.

The man gazing out the window turned when he as he stepped into the office.

"Admiral Baker. Captain Corrington to see you," she said.

"Captain. Come in. At ease."

Donall standing at ease, his curiosity piqued. "Admiral Baker. Sir."

"I'm sure you're wondering why you were brought in and subjected to additional testing. We had to determine if your time as a prisoner of war has negatively impacted your psyche and physical capabilities."

"Sir?"

"We have an offer for you. You're a top-notch pilot. Bold and adventurous. Your service record is impeccable, and you come highly recommended. The Navy is partnering with the Air Force here at Edwards Air Force Base. We want to offer you a place in the test pilot training program, with plenty of airtime to test the latest technology. You'll have the best we have to offer with your own crew of engineers, mechanics, and such. It's a dream job for many former combat pilots. However, there is one condition. Sitting right here is your discharge paperwork. All you have to do is say the word, and I'll rip it up. Or, I can sign it, and you're free to go."

Donall nodded. "What is the one condition? Sir."

"You're not to see my daughter, Anablue, in a personal capacity ever again."

*Anablue!* Shock reverberated through Donall. Giving no outward indication that the Admiral's words had affected him. He only had one question.

"Why?" His tone was curt but respectful.

The Admiral leaned over his desk and switched on the intercom. "Please send Petty Officer Baker in."

ANABLUE SMOOTHED out her service skirt and took a deep breath. Her outward calm belied her inner turmoil. Twenty-one years. After so long. She didn't even know what he looked like. She was outraged that her father had personally recalled her back into service. It left her shaking at his cold, calloused show of power.

It was bad enough that she was back to active duty but to do it by telegram. Telegrams usually meant you had lost a loved one. Like the one she received when Brian died. That in itself, was unforgivable.

She opened the door and entered his office. A man stood

at ease in front of the Admiral. When he turned to acknowledge her, Anablue's heart dropped into her stomach. *Donall.*

Staring into his eyes, she watched as his gaze dropped to sweep her body. Her own eyes swept his, rising to read the shock in his eyes she was sure was mirrored in her own. Donall's eyes flickered to cold and hard. *A captain in the Navy.* Furious, Anablue turned to look at the Admiral, her father.

## CHAPTER 19

Donall's mind raced.

The woman he had thought about non-stop over the past few months was standing right next to him in uniform. His mind played over every conversation they had ever had.

She had never given him an inkling of a suspicion that she was serving in the military. Or that her father was an admiral. She had lied to him. She was not who she claimed to be. An officer was never allowed to fraternize with enlisted personnel. And Anablue was an enlisted petty officer.

The Admiral was playing a cruel game, of that he had no doubt. But why? And why dangle forbidden fruit? He was up for the challenge of deciphering the game. He was going to enjoy the added benefit of making Petty Officer Anablue Baker pay for her deception.

THE ADMIRAL calmly assessed the two standing in front of him. If his instincts served him right, neither had been aware that the other was serving. He was delighted with the turn of events.

"The paperwork? Captain," Admiral Baker asked.

"Rip it up. Sir," Donall replied.

"Excellent choice. Captain. I'm sure you both have many questions. But first, I'm giving the two of you fifteen minutes outside to work out your differences and to come to the understanding that you will work closely with each other on a top-secret project over the next few months. Captain, you as the test pilot. Petty Officer Baker, as one of the top aviation machinists in her field, will be at your side."

"Sir," Anablue protested.

Donall nodded and opened the door; Anablue followed him out.

Once out in the bustling hallway, they stopped to glare at each other. Donall grabbed her arm.

"Outside, Baker."

Anablue gritted her teeth and allowed him to lead her outside.

HE LED her to the sidewalk in front of the building. Visibly angry, she yanked her arm out of his grasp. Just as angry, Donall narrowed his eyes. "Explain."

Her voice dripping with barely suppressed anger. "Explain what? You've got some explaining to do yourself, Captain."

"You lied to me."

"I did not," she spat out.

"Were you sent to spy on me? Are you in cahoots with daddy to lure me back?"

"Lure you into what? That you're a Naval fighter pilot is an enormous secret, Captain. A secret that you didn't exactly share with me."

"You have no right to rail on me for secrets. You could have told me your father was an admiral, or that you were in the Navy."

"It wasn't a secret, Donall. I just didn't want to talk about it. I was out. I was out for ten months. You are just as guilty. If I had known you were in the Navy yourself, I wouldn't have had anything to do with you."

"Why?"

"That is none of your business," she cried, poking him in the chest.

"Why are you here?"

"Why am I here? Why don't you go back inside and ask the Admiral?"

"You mean daddy."

"That man is not my daddy. He is my biological father.

Before today, I hadn't seen him since I was two years old. I don't know him. I don't want to know him. He personally recalled me back into active duty. I have nothing to do with this, with him, and after what you did. I want nothing to do with you either."

"What did I do to you?"

"I don't appreciate being another notch on your belt. You used me. You. Sir. Are a lothario."

Towering over her, he snarled. "I didn't use you and I am not a lothario."

"Then what do you call taking off as soon as you got your piece of ass?"

"I left you a note with Capt. Jack."

"You lie. Capt. Jack had no such note for me."

"I don't lie. I'm an officer and a gentleman. How about you stop with your lies? You expect me to believe you. And your husband, Brian. Another little secret you neglected to tell me."

"Brian!" She inhaled sharply. "You've got a lot of nerve throwing Brian in my face," she ground out.

"Who is Brian?" He snarled.

"What are you daft? I have the same last name as my father. I was a virgin, Donall. Married women generally aren't virgins. Brian was not my husband. Brian was my brother, my twin. He's dead and gone. He left me." She flung her arm wide, pointing at the building. "Just like that man inside abandoned me, and just like you did," she said, now pointing at him.

"Your twin? I'm sorry. But, I did not abandon you, Baby

Blue."

"Don't. Don't you dare call me that name. Do you hear me? Never again," she hissed.

His jaw ticking with anger. "Our fifteen minutes are up. You will go back inside and pretend that we worked this out. But, fucking guaranteed. We will continue this discussion. You're under my command now. I expect you will be a team player and follow my orders without question."

"Actually, I'm rather surprised. Most men, especially the pilots, object to my presence. They never think a mere woman can be good enough to work on their aircraft. I proved them all wrong. I'll keep your jet engines in pristine condition. I'll follow your orders, but as far as I'm concerned. This discussion is over." Anablue turned to leave.

"I believe you owe me a salute, Baker."

Anablue narrowed her eyes. "So, I do, Captain Corrington." She saluted him, holding it until it was returned.

BACK INSIDE. They stood in front of Admiral Baker. Anablue assessed the man in front of her. She could see no hint of him in herself. Dark hair, with heavy streaks of gray, five-seven or so, with a paunchy build. She couldn't see him in Brian, either. Brian had been blonde like her, with the same sky-blue eyes, standing six-foot-tall with a stocky build.

Try as she might, she couldn't picture her sweet mother with this heartless man. This man could have passed her on the street, and she would not have recognized him. There were no birthday cards or visits as a child. Other than Brian's limited interactions with the man, she knew of no time that he had made any effort to be a father to her or Brian.

Gram had once told her he was a different sort of man. Ambitious and cold, he had sent his pregnant wife home to live with his mother and cut off contact with all of them.

Everything about this was wrong. It was unnecessary to recall her to active duty. The Admiral was up to no good. She was sure of it. And Donall? His involvement in this cruelty? As soon as she figured a way out of this mess. She'd run as fast and as far away from Captain Donall Corrington as she could.

"CAPTAIN. YOU'RE DISMISSED," the Admiral said. Donall paused as if torn, then nodded and left the office.

"You look like your mother."

"I'll take that as a compliment. Permission to speak freely. Sir," Anablue replied.

"Granted."

"Why did you recall me?"

"Your expertise."

"We both know there are more than enough qualified personnel capable of handling this project."

"Perhaps. You're here because I wished it so."

"Why? Are you trying to re-kindle some kind of relationship with me?"

"No. That's the furthest thing from my mind."

"Then why?"

"I wanted to make sure you knew it was me who put an end to your relationship with Captain Corrington."

"But why?" she cried. "Did you do something like this to Brian as well? When you talked to him on the phone or when you saw him before he shipped out for Vietnam?"

"I've never met or talked to your brother."

"What? I know he talked to you. And he told me he met you in San Francisco."

"No. I didn't."

"Are you punishing me for something?"

He nodded his head. "Sins of the mother. Keep in mind, Anablue, if you fraternize with Captain Corrington. You will both spend a very long time behind bars. And he might still end up there, or worse if you don't toe the line and do as I ordered you to do."

"Do what?"

"You'll find out when the time is right."

"You really are a nasty bastard. Sir."

"So, I've been told. You're dismissed, Baker."

A FEW DAYS LATER, Donall strode through the enlisted mess hall, looking for his crew. The new man, Evans, reporting in this morning, was at his side. He spotted the group. Walker,

Morgan, Wallace, the engineers assigned to the project, and Vaughan, the crew chief, were on break from classroom training. They stood at attention when he approached the table.

"Where's Baker?" Donall demanded. Morgan nodded over his shoulder to the far end of the mess hall. Anablue sat alone in the corner, a stack of books on the table. She was furiously writing in a notebook. She'd stop every so often to stare out the window, then continue writing.

"I'll be damned," Evans said as he looked over at Anablue.

"What?" Donall said.

Evans pointed toward Anablue. "The one and only, "Frosty," Evans replied with a smirk. "I worked with her at Barbers Point on Oahu last year. Before the Red Cross got her out. Frigid. Cold… as… ice." His voice trailed off into a stutter as Donall turned a furious scalding eye on him.

"I never want to hear you disparage a fellow sailor. Whether they're male or female, ice-cold or not. You keep your fucking mouth shut, or I will shut it for you," Donall snarled into Evan's face. "Is that understood, sailor?"

"Sir. Yes, sir."

"I can't hear you."

"Sir. Yes, sir," Evans screamed out.

"Get back to class. All of you." Donall spat out.

They scrambled to grab their things off the table and left the mess hall.

Donall turned his attention to Anablue. Striding toward her, he stopped in front of her table. She jumped to her feet and stood at attention.

"Baker."

"Yes, sir." She stared straight ahead, not looking him in the eye.

His eyes swept her body. From the blue mechanic's one-piece jumpsuit to her tiny boots, back up to her face. He noted the dark circles under her eyes. The pale complexion and her hair. Her hair was scraped close to her scalp, then gathered in a bun.

"You cut your hair," he said, his voice strained and raspy.

Her eyes flew up to meet the pained expression in his. Confused, she looked straight ahead again. "It's a regulation bun. Sir."

"You have dark circles under your eyes? Are you sleeping?"

"No. Sir," she replied.

"Are you eating?"

"I'm trying. Sir."

"Part of your job is to maintain your physical health by eating and sleeping right. What were you doing last night?"

"Taking apart the new jet engine delivered yesterday. Sir."

"After hours?"

"Yes. Sir."

"Why?"

"I need to stay two steps ahead of them. Sir."

Donall nodded his head. "What else keeps you awake at night?"

"It's personal. Sir."

"Why did they call you, Frosty?"

She gave him a half-smile. "Frosty. I refused to date my co-workers. Sir."

"Did that include Evans?"

"Yes, Sir."

"Why don't you date Navy men?" Donall asked.

She looked him in the eye. "My mother warned me not to trust them. Especially, the officers."

His eyes darkened, and he grunted. "Touché."

"Evans has joined the team. Is there going to be problems?" Donall said.

"Not on my end. Sir."

"Let me know if there is."

She shook her head. "Please don't intercede on my behalf. You will make it all that much harder. I have to do it on my own, or they will never respect me. Sir."

Donall thoughtfully nodded his head. "You better get going. You're late for class."

"Yes. Sir."

Grabbing her books off the table, she walked away.

"Baker."

Stopping, she turned to him.

"No more working after eighteen hundred hours."

Anablue nodded. "Yes. Sir."

She turned away again, but not before he saw the deep sadness in her eyes.

He watched her until she disappeared down the busy hallway. Turning away, he stared out the window, willing the ache in his chest to go away.

## CHAPTER 20

Elijah stood staring at the telephone on the wall. Deep in thought. He had just hung up from an hour-long conversation with Donall. Looking out the window at Elyse on the beach as she played with the baby in the surf. Grabbing his car keys, he opened the screen door.

"Elyse. I'm running into town to see my father. I'll be back in an hour."

She gave him a thumbs up and continued pirouetting with the baby, laughing in her arms.

THE PRIVATE JETLINER rolled to a stop, away from prying eyes on the furthest runway on the base. When the clam-shell door opened, NIS Special Agent Max Cohen ran down the steps.

At the bottom of the steps, he shook hands with General Benjamin, the base commander.

"General Benjamin, I'm pleased to meet you."

"Special Agent Cohen. Welcome to Edwards Air Force Base."

"Please, call me Max."

"Max. How can we be of service to NIS?"

"This investigation is to be kept under wraps. I'll be conducting interviews. I've been told that Admiral Baker has returned to San Diego."

"Yes. He left as soon as he installed the Navy test team for an upcoming project."

"I'll need the names and files of every member on that crew. And I'll need some cover."

"You have our full cooperation. Those files will be available within the hour. Just what is it you are looking for?"

"I'm following some leads into the investigation of the death of Ensign Brian Baker."

---

MAX THREW the last file onto the table. Taking a long draw on his cigarette, he contemplated what he had read. Seven members of a crew handpicked by Admiral Baker. Some of the members made perfect sense. Top of their field. Well suited to the project, as he understood it. However, four of them did not. Again, also the cream of the crop, but something was off.

Captain Donall Corrington: Highly decorated, one-hundred and forty-seven successful missions flown over Vietnam. The Viet Cong shot his F-4 jet fighter down in early February. A prisoner of war held for two weeks until he escaped with another prisoner. Found in the jungle by an elite ranger team and repatriated. The oddity there was his medical file. The man should have been discharged on a medical, but he passed a recent physical when his prior physicals showed he didn't have the strength in his shoulders and back. There was no way the man could have rebuilt his strength or muscle mass in his extremities since the last exam in April. The rigors of a test pilot required full physical strength. Corrington didn't have it.

Petty Officer Anablue Baker: Only surviving child of Admiral Baker. Twin sister to Ensign Brian Baker. Honorably discharged ten months ago on a Hardship/Dependency request to take care of an ailing grandmother. Recalled by the Admiral specifically for this project. Again, unusual to recall anyone from a hardship request. Also, the first time he had ever heard of a woman being recalled to active duty. The fact that she was an Aviation Machinist Mate was an unusual job for a woman, but they highly respected her in her field. Also, understandable, they would assign her to this special project. From what he had read in the Admirals file, Anablue and the Admiral were estranged these past twenty-plus years. It wasn't like he was doing her a favor.

Admiral Michael Baker: Father to twins Brian and Anablue Baker. Known for his dedicated but ruthless climb to admiral status. Estranged from his wife, Mary, and children since before their birth. His family had resided with his mother, Margaret, in LaGrange, California. Mary passed away from cancer five years earlier. His mother from natural causes almost nine months ago, followed by Brian two months later, right before Christmas. The Admiral had specifically lobbied the Secretary of the Navy to oversee this project.

Interesting note: On-going litigation with brother, Captain Jackson Baker, Navy (retired) over the mother's last will and testament.

And last, Petty Officer Jamie Evans, Aviation Machinists Mate. Stationed at Barbers Point Naval Base, Oahu, Hawaii, Anablue Baker was stationed there during the same time. Then he transferred to the USS Valley Forge, serving alongside Ensign Brian Baker, deceased in a shipboard accident, currently under investigation. Now Evans was stationed here at Edwards on the same project as Anablue.

Anablue was the common denominator here. Except in the case of Corrington. What was his relationship with Anablue? Drumming his fingers on the table, he reached over and picked up a camera. Photographer for the project. It was a good cover. Hopefully, he remembered all they taught him in his college photography class. It was time to introduce himself to the crew and see if he could find some answers to his many questions.

ANABLUE CRAWLED on all fours on the huge tarp spread out on the floor at the back of the hanger. The tarp, one of seven, was filled with parts of the test jet engine she had spent the last week taking apart. For all that she was still angry at being recalled, she loved the job. The thrill of taking apart an engine just to rebuild it. It gave her a deeper understanding of the aircraft.

A flash of light, and she brought her hand up to shield her eyes. *What the hell.*

Blinking her eyes to remove the bright orbs, blinding her vision. She looked up to see a lanky man with dark curly brown hair smiling down at her.

"Sorry about the flash," he said. "Names, Max. I'm the photographer assigned to document the project. And you are?"

"Petty Officer Anablue Baker," she said as she rose to her feet.

He reached out to shake her hand. She looked at her greasy hands. "Um, I'm a little dirty."

"Oh. Right."

---

HE STARED AT HER. Her picture in her file didn't do her justice. She was a beautiful little thing. The contours of womanly curves visible through the mechanic's jumpsuit. Wisps of blonde tendrils escaped her severe bun. It was her blue eyes and the creamy complexion that had him completely transfixed. She raised a delicate eyebrow at his continuous stare.

"Um. Sorry. Don't think I've ever seen a girl mechanic before."

"Then you haven't looked hard enough," she replied.

"Yeah. You're probably right." He still stared at her.

"Max."

"What?"

"What can I help you with?"

"What. Oh. Photos. I need to take photos. Can you explain to me what you're doing here?"

"Sure." She patiently explained in great detail, each large tarp filled with parts, numbered neatly in order.

"Max. Am I boring you? Your eyes are rolling in the back of your head."

He gave her an endearing grin. "Sorry. Not really my thing."

"I figured that."

"Why do you do this?"

"Well. A man's life hangs in the balance. We can't put a test pilot in the cockpit if we don't completely understand how the aircraft works."

"You do this by yourself?"

"No. I have someone who works with me. Evans."

"Where is Evans now?"

"He went on break."

"Speaking of test pilots. What do you think of Captain Corrington?"

"I'll let you decide for yourself. He's headed this way, and he doesn't look so happy right now," she warned.

Max turned to watch the man as he approached them. *Big man. Looks fit.* His stride was smooth and cat-like.

"He looks like a big cat who hasn't eaten in a while."

"Yeah. He does. I have work to do. Good luck, Max."

Noting the longing in her eyes as she watched Captain Corrington approach. Catching him watching her. Her eyelashes fluttered, her cheeks flushing a delicate shade of pink. She nodded her head and went back to work.

*Hmm. Interesting reaction.*

---

Donall walked up to the man watching Anablue. His irritation with the man's pursual of Anablue grating on his nerves.

"If you 're done ogling my crew member, you can tell me who the fuck you are? And why you're in a restricted area?"

The man turned his inquisitive hazel eyes on Donall. "What? Um. Pardon me. She's lovely, isn't she?"

"Yes, she is. Again, who are you?"

"Captain Corrington, I assume. I'm Max Cohen. Your project photographer. I assure you I have all the proper clearance."

"Okay. Come on. I'll introduce you to the rest of the crew."

Donall made the introductions to the remaining crew. He watched as Max fumbled with the camera before taking some pictures of the crew. *Something's up with this guy.* Max called Anablue over for a picture with the crew.

She stood almost like an outsider on the edge of the group. Donall went over and stood behind her, placing his hands on her shoulders. He pulled her in closer to the men, leaving his hands resting on her tiny shoulders. His hands tingled from touching her. The scent of soft lemon wafted up from her hair to tease and torment him, while his body reacted to her closeness with a mind of its own.

She slightly turned to look up at him over her shoulder. Eyes wide, her pulse beat erratically in her throat. He caught and caressed her gaze with his own before he abruptly broke it off, looking off in the distance while he fought for control of his mind and body. He never should have touched her.

---

Anablue's heart pounded in her chest. She closed her eyes at the pain and anguish of the moment. Her body aching at his touch. She inhaled the fresh scent of him. His warm breath on her neck sending shivers down her spine. All she wanted to do was throw her arms around him and beg his forgiveness. Now it was far too late. They were both stuck in a trap well laid by the Admiral. She inhaled sharply, her heart breaking again as it had so many times in the past few weeks.

"Baker, Captain Corrington. Smile, it's just a photograph, not a torture chamber," Max called out.

*Speak for yourself, Max.*

## CHAPTER 21

*Opening his eyes, he lifted his head. Pain shot through his body. His shoulders were dislocated from hanging so long in the foul pit. A movement in the far corner caught his attention. Another prisoner raised their head. Agony-filled sky-blue eyes stared back at him as his body reeled in shock. Anablue! Arms reached down, yanking her up and out of the pit. Her face contorted in silent scream. "Anablue.... NO....no....no," he cried out. Twisting and thrashing, the rope dug into his bloody wrists as he tried to escape his bonds.*

Donall flung himself out of bed, his heart racing as the adrenaline rushed through him. Crouching on the floor in a fight stance, he looked around his sparse quarters in confusion. Falling to his knees, he leaned his head against the cool metal of the bunk frame. His hands gripping the twisted, sweat-soaked sheets. Slowly, his head cleared, and his raspy breathing returned to normal. Then, with a foul curse, he escaped the confines of his quarters to sit outside in the cool night air of the high desert.

Taking a long draw from his pipe. Anablue. He exhaled, blowing the blue smoke ring into the night. His thoughts were drawn back to her again. She's trapped. Everything in him had wanted to stay in that office after Admiral Baker dismissed him. Intuition told him that the man was no good, and Anablue was in some kind of danger. He was sure of it.

Admitting to himself that he had fallen in love with her. Surprised by the revelation, he smiled. *Sneaks up on you when you least expect it.*

He had been watching her from afar these past few weeks. She was good at her job, damn good. Any test pilot would be assured that the engine of any aircraft that she worked on would be of the highest standards. It was too bad that once the actual test aircraft was delivered next month, he would not be piloting the jet. He had an out but couldn't and wouldn't leave her behind. For now, they were stuck in a situation that forbids any personal contact. He had to hide his feelings for her until he could figure out a way to get them both out.

This entire project was a shit show. Even his part in the project was flawed. Most test planes had the crew assigned to the plane, and the test pilot basically showed up when it was time to test fly the jet. Not him, he was assigned to the plane, and it hadn't even arrived from the manufacturer yet. Thanks to the admiral, he was only here to twiddle his thumbs and show Anablue what she couldn't have. He scowled. Who in San Francisco could have known he was in the Navy or the depth of his feelings for her? Or did it really matter? Would any man who showed interest in her have been used? Nah! The admiral merely took advantage of the situation. So many questions with no obvious answers.

MAX STROLLED along the sidewalk of the barracks. Spotting someone sitting outside, his long legs stretched out in front of him. *Corrington. Perfect.* Strolling over to him, he pulled up a seat.

"Morning, Captain."

"Morning, Max. What brings you out at the crack of dawn?" Donall asked.

Max lit a cigarette, watching the smoke as it rose and mingled with the pipe smoke. "Actually. I'm rather pleased to find you alone. That's quite the car that Baker drives."

"Smooth ride," Donall replied.

"You've driven that beast?"

An awkward silence fell. "Tell me about Anablue Baker," Max whispered.

"Who the fuck are you? I know you're no photographer."

Max sighed deeply. "You're right. Never could figure out those F-stops. I'm a special agent with NIS. I've been told you can be trusted."

"Trusted. By whom? "

"Major Seamus McLoughlin."

"Mac. How do you know Mac?"

"We've worked together a few times. With the help of your father and former Ambassador Booker, your brother Elijah went through General Morgan and got ahold of him. Mac called me, and I got new leads on a cold case.

"Why are you here, Max? And why the questions about Baker?"

Max reached into his jacket and pulled out a flask. Taking a long drink, he handed it to Donall.

"I'm investigating the death of her twin brother, Brian Baker."

"What do you mean, investigating?" Donall barked.

"Ensign Baker died in an accident that was no accident," Max replied.

Donall inhaled sharply. "Does Anablue know?"

"No. Which brings me to my first question. What's your relationship with her?"

"You know as well as I do. I'm an officer, and she's enlisted. There can be no relationship."

"True. Funny thing about WAVES. Made a few phone calls. I can't find any other instance of a woman being recalled into active duty until Anablue. Someone pulled a whole lot of strings to make it happen. But did it in such a way that I can't find a clear path who it was."

"Admiral Baker?"

"Possibly."

"I've never seen a man so cold to his own child," Donall said. "No man should ever have this kind of power."

"They don't. He had to have help. I can guarantee you more than one head will roll," Max said.

"If it is him, I'm not surprised. I've heard he's a real bastard," Donall replied.

"I wanted you to know I'm working on it. Trying to put the puzzle pieces together. You never answered my question. What is Anablue to you?"

Donall looked down at the flask he held in his hand. He drained the flask and handed it back.

"She's the woman I love. We were together up to the moment I was hauled off my sailboat by MAA's and brought here."

"Did the Admiral know you were seeing each other?"

"He must have."

"Then he had to have had someone watching her."

"He seemed delighted when he realized that neither of us knew the other was serving. I had my out that day. There's no fucking way I passed that physical. I could've had him sign my discharge paperwork right then and there, but I stayed in the game because my gut is telling me something is wrong."

"How well do you know Evans?"

"I don't know the man at all. He works side by side with Anablue."

"Evans was with Brian when he died."

Donall jumped to his feet. "Why the fuck didn't you tell me this before?" He growled.

"Sit down, Captain. We have to find out who is behind this."

"You're using her as bait."

"We're watching. We'll keep her safe. What I need from you right now is to keep yourself in check. If you, hamper this investigation. I'll have you thrown in the brig."

Donall gave him a scathing glare.

"I have an informant in San Francisco working another case. I think I'll have him check out that angle and see who was spying on Anablue there and if it leads back to the admiral. I have to cover all the bases. Otherwise, this person, whoever it is, will get off scot-free," Max said.

"This is going to devastate her."

"Yes, it will. Oh, one more thing. Overheard some locals talking when I was in town the other day. They were talking about a pretty girl driving a black "66" Chevelle. She beat the pants off of one of their buddies drag racing outside of town."

"I'm going to fucking kill her."

"Spoken like a man in love," Max chuckled. "Funny thing is. I watched her putt-putting around on the forklift the other day."

Donall laughed a deep belly chuckle. "I saw that too. She looked like a little old lady, all prim and proper, driving that forklift. Yet, she's out there drag racing that demon car." He snorted, "Women."

"You can always take the car keys away."

"No. I'll handle it."

"Does Anablue return your love?"

"She has no idea how I feel. Nor I, her."

"I've seen the way she watches you. She's suffering as much as you are."

"If you can see it, others can as well."

"That's a problem."

"Well, she's going to hate me after I get through with her today."

"I need you to help keep an eye on her. She's getting annoyed with me hanging around. Which reminds me. I need to find a dictionary. Need to look up some of those words she uses."

---

It had started out a rough day when she lost her breakfast behind the hangar. Then Donall moved his workspace into the hangar, and the day quickly went downhill from there. He had practically dragged her outside, her ears still burned from his tongue-lashing over her drag racing with the locals. How he found out was beyond her at the moment. Not that it would stop her. And Max, the photographer, was driving her crazy with his questions.

An argument in the afternoon with Evans about a missing engine part. Then to top it off, long after everyone else was done for the day, having to sweep the entire hangar under Donall's watchful eye as punishment.

She had for-gone dinner after losing her breakfast and lunch that she couldn't keep down, anyway. Instead, Anablue found herself hiding out on the backside of the hangar, sitting on a pile of crates, trying to read. Unable to focus on the book, she looked up to see Donall standing in front of her.

Her patience worn thin; she slammed her book shut. "Now what?" she snapped.

---

Donall raised an elegant eyebrow. Surprised and somewhat amused at her insolence.

"Ten Hut, Baker," he breathed.

She stood at attention. He walked to stand behind her. Leaning down, he whispered into her ear. "Why aren't you at dinner?"

"I… I'm not hungry, sir."

"You're losing weight. I need you to take care of yourself."

"I'm trying," she whispered.

"I need you… to try harder."

He moved to stand in front of her. She looked so small and fragile, full lips quivered. Big blue eyes shimmered with tears. When a lone tear rolled down her cheek, it took everything he had not to pull her into his arms.

"Why are you doing this?" she asked.

"I need you to understand that I am doing everything I can to get you out of this mess."

Donall looked up to see Max rounding the corner of the hangar. "Max is heading this way. Dry your tears and go get something to eat."

She nodded.

"Anablue. I need you to be strong."

"Strong?" she hissed. "I may shed a tear or two, but I am not some shrinking violet. I am far stronger than you give me credit for."

Donall's smile split his face. "There it is. That beautiful spark I've been missing."

"You… are one big kerfuffle."

"What's a kerfuffle?"

"Go look it up," she said as she stomped away.

She stopped and turned around. "I take it, what you said this morning about the three days in the brig on bread and water, was just a threat?"

"No. That's a fact if I catch you drag racing again," he growled.

She glared at him and gave him a big "Hmmmph."

He crossed his arms, watching the swing of her angry hips until Max came up beside him.

"You ever find that dictionary, Max?"

"It's in the hangar. Did she throw one of those silly words at you?"

"Yeah. Always wondered where she gets them from."

"I asked her the other day. She said her mother. Are you ready to go for that drink?" Max said.

"Yeah. More than ready."

Coming from a light meal, Anablue rounded the corner of her quarters. Confusion and questions running rampant through her mind.

*He's trying to get me out. How? Obviously, he wants to stay in. You know the score, Anablue. It's every test pilot's dream job. The chance to eventually be involved in the space program. You cannot risk him losing his dreams for you. You must do everything you can to stay away from him. As much as it hurts, you cannot give your father any excuse to throw him in the brig and ruin his life.*

A hand snaked out and grabbed her by the waist. A man threw her up against the wall. His hand over her mouth to stifle her screams. He leaned into her, pinning her in place. His other hand tightened around her throat.

"Hello, Baker."

*Evans.*

"Got a message for you from daddy. You're to do everything I say as he told you to do." He sniffed at her hair. His foul breath filled her senses. He licked her cheek and neck as she turned her face away in revulsion. He tightened his hold on her neck while she struggled to draw a breath.

"You're to go inside, take a shower and get yourself all pretty for me. We've got a little party planned for you with some boys. I know all about you and the Captain. I've got friends all lined up to testify against him. You do anything but what I say, and Corrington pays the price with jail time or his life. You understand?"

Anablue nodded her head.

"Your daddy wanted you to know it's coming from him. You got an hour to get ready."

He opened the door to her quarters and shoved her inside. She fell to the floor, clutching her throat, gasping for breath.

"One hour." He looked over at Anablue's roommate, Molly, who sat in stunned silence.

"Get her dressed. Find something fitting for a whore."

## CHAPTER 22

Anablue lay on the floor in shock. *This can't be happening.* She rolled to her knees and sobbed. "Oh, my God. This can't be real." She lost her meager dinner on the floor in front of her.

Gentle arms wrapped around her as she looked up into the teary eyes of Molly.

"Oh no. You too," Molly cried. They clung to each other, sobbing.

Wiping the tears off her face. "What did he mean, a party?" Anablue sobbed.

"There were three of them. It's bad, really bad."

"What does he have on you?" Anablue said.

Molly shook her brown hair, her blue eyes teared again. "He caught my boyfriend and me in a compromising situation. I had no choice but to do as he said. It was awful."

Anablue looked at her in horror. "Oh my God. You poor thing."

"And you? What does Evans have on you?"

"Evans is doing what my father told him to do," Anablue replied. "I think this has something to do with my mother."

She felt numb as she showered, then Molly helped her into a slinky dark blue dress with matching heels. Molly applied light makeup, then brushed her hair, so it fell to her shoulders in soft blonde curls.

Anablue grabbed Molly by the wrist.

"I can't do this. You have to help me. I cannot do it."

"What are you going to do? Evans will be here soon," Molly asked. "I'm sure he's probably out front now."

"Anablue looked around their small quarters. "The bathroom window. Help me. Please."

Molly nodded. "I'll help you, but you must hurry."

They went into the bathroom and opened the window, removing the screen. Molly clasped her hands together to boost Anablue up to the window. Anablue scooted through, snagging and tearing the dress as Molly tossed her shoes and purse up to her.

An insistent knock sounded on the front door. Molly looked back to the door. "Damn. Hurry. I'll hold him off as long as I can."

"Thank you, Molly. I won't forget this," Anablue whispered.

Lowering herself to the ground, she put the strap of the purse over her neck. Shoes in hand, she ran toward the officer's quarters. Finding Donall's, she banged on the door. No answer. Giving up before she caused a scene. *I have to get off base.*

Running to the parking lot. Unlocking her car door, she slid into the bucket seat. It was parked on a small hill. Pulling the emergency brake, it rolled down the hill, coasting until just before the guard shack when she popped the clutch and started the car, just like at home.

She drove around the area outside of the base for an hour before stopping in town to gas up the car. She figured she could wait a few more hours before going back to the base and sneaking back to her quarters. Or, if need be, sleep in her car off base. She didn't want to be AWOL, but better that than what her father and Evans had planned for her.

Spying a small bar, a mile or so outside of town, she stopped. *I can get a coke, kill some time, and plot my next steps.*

Donall sat next to Max at the far end of the bar. Facing the door. He watched a steady stream of locals and contractors from the base coming and going from the small bar. Max pulled an envelope from his inner jacket.

"Take a look at these."

Donall took the envelope and opened it. "What is it?"

"Read it," Max replied.

Donall looked at the first paper. "It's Anablue's birth certificate."

"Yup. Keep reading."

"Mother, Mary Elizabeth Baker, age twenty. Father, there's no name listed under father."

"That's right. Michael Baker is not listed as her father. Look at the next one.

"Brian's? The same."

He looked at the third document, "Mary and Michael Baker's marriage certificate."

"Yup. They were married seven months before the twin's birth, but Admiral Baker is not Anablue or Brian's father. Did more digging. Mary Baker filed for a divorce two weeks after the wedding. Admiral Baker denied it, citing his faith, though he's not a religious man. Then he left on a six-month deployment. Meanwhile, Mary left him and went to live with his mother."

"Don't you think it's odd she went to live with his family?" Donall asked. Popping a piece of popcorn into his mouth.

"Mary's parents died in a fire right after the wedding, and Margaret Baker had two sons."

"No shit. So, you think this brother is Anablue's real father?"

"Possibly. Now I just have to find Jackson Cross Baker. Get his story," Max said.

"As wrong as it is, it would explain the admiral's venom."

BOTH MEN LOOKED up as a beautiful woman entered the bar. Donall lifted his glass to his lips and froze. *Anablue!*

Donall's gaze pierced the distance between them, touching her everywhere. The slinky blue dress she wore hugged every curve of her hips and bottom, molding to the swell of breasts, highlighting her cleavage.

She clutched her purse with white knuckles. Small white teeth nervously worried her lower lip in indecision. Determined, she squared her shoulders and walked toward the other end of the bar. Patrons of the bar leaned from their stools to watch the delicate swish of her mid-thigh skirt.

UNAWARE THAT DONALL'S eyes followed her every movement, Anablue chose a table in the far corner. She looked up as an older, heavy-set waitress approached her to take her order.

Placing a napkin on the table. "What will you have, sweetheart?"

"A coke, no ice. Please."

"You okay?"

Deeply shaken by the day's events, she shrugged her shoulders, on the verge of tears. "I don't know anymore," she whispered.

"There, there." the waitress said, patting her arm. "You just sit here and pull yourself together. I'll keep the wolves at bay."

She looked up to see the leering grins of the men in the bar. "I shouldn't have come in here."

"Nonsense. Never let it be said that "Mauri's Bar" isn't a safe haven for a woman in need."

"Where's the lady's room?" Anablue asked.

"Other end of the bar."

"Thank you for everything," she said, as she turned to look out the window, thoughts on Donall.

---

DONALL AND MAX looked at each other in shock.

"What the fuck is she doing in here? Donall growled deep in his throat.

"Something happened," Max replied. "Look at her. Even from here, I can see she is shaking."

The waitress delivered Anablue's order and walked back to the bar. Standing next to Max, she placed an order for another table.

"You ever see her in here before?" Max asked the waitress.

"Never seen her before tonight," she replied.

"What did she order?" Donall barked.

"Just a Coke. Listen, Mister, you leave her alone. In case you didn't notice, her nylons have a run, her dress is torn, and she has bruises on her throat."

Donall's face lost all color as he moved to get up.

"Sit down. She's coming this way," Max said.

ANABLUE MOVED through the bar ignoring the men as best she could. An arm snaked out, and she found herself pulled into the chest of a man. She fought until she heard that one familiar voice a moment ago she was desperate to hear.

"I don't recall giving you permission to be off base, sailor," Donall growled deep in his chest.

She struggled against his chest and pushed herself free.

Donall frowned. "What are you doing here? Dressed like that?"

Spotting the waitress standing there with a tray of tequila shots, she paused, reaching out. She grabbed a shot and downed it. One finger pointed at Donall. She set the empty glass down and grabbed another, downing that one as well. Struggling to breathe for a moment, she looked at Donall and reached for the last shot.

"Anablue. Answer me. What are you doing here?" he thundered.

Seeing what she thought was condemnation on his face, she turned and ran, wrenching the door open. She raced for her car with Donall hot on her heels.

Max looked at the waitress, pulled out his wallet, and placed a ten-dollar bill on the tray.

"She'll be fine." Then he followed them out of the bar.

## CHAPTER 23

"Anablue, stop. Anablue," Donall called out. She was running, fumbling in her purse to find her car keys. He bounded across the parking lot behind her. Each step crunching the gravel underfoot. His breath was hot on her neck as he scooped her up into his arms.

"Nooooo. No. Leave me alone. You don't understand. I'm sorry. I'm sorry, but I could not do it. Even to save you. I love you, but I couldn't do it." She was hysterical now; wild tears streamed down her face. "I can't go through what happened to Molly."

"Save me? Do what? What couldn't you do? Anablue. What happened?" Donall cried.

Anablue dissolved into sob's, clinging to his chest.

"Molly helped me. I climbed out the bathroom window. I went to your quarters; first, you weren't there. Then I left."

"No." she cried, pushing him away. The tequila shots now hampering her reasoning as she rambled on.

"They will lock you up forever, kill your dreams. Or they will kill you. I have to go so they can't use me against you."

She brought her knee up right into his groin as he pulled her back to him. He dropped to his knees in agony as she ran for her car. Backing up in a squeal of tires, flying gravel, and dust clouds, she raced through the parking lot, swerving to avoid Max coming out of the bar.

---

MAX RAN FOR DONALL, pulling him to his feet. Donall leaned over, holding his stomach, trying not to heave.

"Jesus Christ, she's got boney knees." Donall cried.

Max grimaced. The sympathy clear on his face. Max looked out to the main road. He could still see her taillights in the distance on the long country road. "She's got to be going one hundred miles per hour," Max said.

Donall looked at him in panic before he looked to the main road. "One-ten, at least."

They watched as she sped further down the road until the car just stopped.

Max, in his own panic now, pulled Donall along to his car. "Get in."

"Did you see how quickly the tequila hit her?" Max said.

"Light-weight. It doesn't surprise me," Donall replied.

They raced down the road after her. "What did she say?" Max asked.

"It was a kind of rambling. Something about climbing out a window. They're going to lock me up or kill me, and something about Molly, having it happen to her."

"Who's Molly?"

"Her roommate," Donall replied.

Max shook his head. "I'm going to need to talk to Molly."

Pulling up behind Anablue's car at a stop sign. Donall, now recovered, jumped out of the car with Max on his heels.

Donall opened the car door. She was slumped over, passed out at the wheel. He shut the engine off, gently pulled her back, and checked for injuries. "Anablue." She mumbled in response, and Donall breathed a sigh of relief.

They stood next to the car, speaking in hushed tones.

"We have to get her back on base," Max said.

"Okay. How?"

"You can't be seen with her."

Donall cursed. "Everything in me wants to take care of her."

"I know, but we have to be very careful here. I'll drive her car. You take my rental car and meet me back on base. We have to get her back to her quarters unseen and see if this Molly can fill in some blanks."

A sound behind them, and they turned around. Anablue stood swaying next to the car.

"I have to pee," she stated. She pulled down her panties and squatted right where she was.

Donall and Max whipped around, giving her their backs. They caught each other's look of amusement.

"We probably shouldn't mention this to her tomorrow," Donall said.

Max chuckled. "I think you're right."

Hands in their pockets, standing in embarrassed silence, looking everywhere but behind them, they patiently waited. She giggled behind them after flopping over while trying to pull up her panties.

Donall cleared his throat. "Umm… I should go help her."

Max nodded. "Yeah."

Donall sat her down in the driver's seat as he helped her put her panties on. She giggled with his growing frustration with the pantyhose, so he pulled them off of her sleek legs. Throwing them on the side of the road before lifting her out and placing her in the backseat. She wrapped her arms around him, pulling him in on top of her, gripping his waist with her thighs with a strength he didn't know she had. Her hands gripped his head, running her fingers through his hair. She placed a kiss on his lips, dropping her arms to hang around his neck. "I love you, Donall."

He gently pulled her arms from around his neck. "I love you too. Now be a good girl and go back to sleep." She sighed, curled up, and was instantly asleep.

"Max, give me your jacket," Donall said.

Max handed over his jacket, and Donall gently laid the jacket over Anablue's shoulders.

---

MAX DROVE through the gate and pulled into the parking lot. Getting out of the car, he leaned against the hood and lit a cigarette. He had to admit the car was a sweet ride. He hadn't driven a car like this since college. A movement in the shadows told him that someone was watching him. Probably waiting for Anablue. After ten minutes and whomever it was left, he pulled Anablue out of the back seat and hauled her to her quarters.

---

MAX WAITED for the door to be locked behind him before stepping off the porch. Breathing a sigh of relief that Anablue was inside and sleeping soundly in her bed, he walked toward Corrington's quarters. Mulling the conversation with Molly over in his head, he cursed out loud. *As bad as this is, it's not enough.*

He knocked on the door, and Corrington whipped it open.

"What took you so long," Donall snarled. "How's Anablue?"

"She's sleeping. Never woke up. I talked to Molly."

"What did she tell you?" Donall said, pacing back and forth.

"After some gentle persuasion, she told me that Evans blackmailed her and forced her into some sex acts with multiple men. Anablue couldn't do it and escaped out the bathroom window," she said Anablue told her that the admiral ordered Anablue punished in the same way by Evans.

Donall sank into a chair, head in hands. " Punished? Why? Are you telling me the admiral wanted his daughter raped?"

"We've already established that Anablue is not his daughter."

Back on his feet, pacing again, Donall snarled, "To order the rape of any woman is sick and twisted."

"It is."

"At least this bullshit is ending."

"Listen to me, Corrington. As horrifying as this is, it's not enough to nail the admiral or Evans."

Donall stopped his pacing. "What do you mean it's not enough?" he barked.

"We've both heard the horror stories. The women are shamed and blamed for what happened. The perpetrator gets off with a slap on the wrist. This would be more of the same. And I've yet to prove the admiral is working with Evans on anything. That includes Brian's death."

"So. Where do we go from here?"

"Tomorrow, everyone back to work as normal."

"Normal? Are you fucking kidding me?"

"No. Keep a watchful distance from Anablue. Don't talk

about anything that happened here tonight, if it's at all possible. "

"She's going to think I've turned my back on her."

"Possibly. If we're lucky, she won't remember much. Evans mustn't learn that you know about what he tried to do. He'll make another move, eventually. Then we've got him and possibly a confession."

"Give me ten minutes with him. I know a bit about getting a confession."

Max gave him a long look. "I know you do," Max quietly stated. "But justice doesn't work that way. And that's what this is all about. Bringing justice to Brian, Anablue, and Molly. Even you. You were dragged into this nightmare as a form of revenge as well."

"I'm not concerned about myself. As long as she can live her life. Don't get me wrong, I want to live that life with her."

"We're doing everything we can to bring that to fruition."

"I'll expect you at our wedding, Max."

"Doesn't she have to say "Yes" first?"

Donall grinned. "Don't doubt my charm, Max."

"Meanwhile, you're going to have to do what you can to make her angry. To make her hate you. Oh. Here are her car keys."

Donall took the keys and stuffed them in his pocket. "She won't be getting them back anytime soon."

"That's a good start."

Donall grinned. "Yup. But I'm not faking this one."

In the far corner of the parking lot, a lone yellow van sat parked in the shadows, waiting and watching. A man snuck out of the shadows and knocked on the driver's window. The man inside rolled the window down.

"Who's that guy driving Anablue's car?" Gary asked.

"Some photographer," Evan's replied.

"Where's Anablue?"

"No idea. Gary, you need to get the fuck out of here. If they tie you back to me, the admiral will have our balls in a vise."

"You're a fuckup, Evans. All you had to do was arrange a little party, and you let her get away. We could've had the job done and left the slut face-down in a ditch."

"It's not my fault she climbed out the bathroom window."

"It's time for Anablue to have an accident at work. I need that fucking money and my old man off my back," Gary said.

"Where's Marcus?" Evans said.

"I don't know. He had to take a dump."

"As soon as he gets back, get off the base."

"Get the job done, Evans. I don't want to have to come back again."

## CHAPTER 24

The alarm clock blared as Anablue rolled over in bed with a groan. Opening one eye, she scanned the room. With another groan, she pulled the covers up over her head to drown out the noise. Her blind hand reached up, searching for, and found the button to silence the alarm.

Foggy brain aside, used to the noise of Molly getting ready for work. The room was silent. Sitting up in bed, she looked at Molly's bunk. No bedding, and the mattress rolled up. Personal effects were gone, and there was no sign of Molly. *What the hell.*

Her thoughts raced back to the previous night. The horror of the evening hit her like a brick as her heart pounded and a dull throbbing started in her head. Covering her face with her hands, her body shook with the force of her tears of pain and anguish. She spotted an envelope sitting on the table, and she climbed out of bed. Tearing it open, she read:

*Anablue,*

*I've been reassigned to an Air Force base in Georgia. I don't know how you managed it. But thank you from the bottom of my heart. I pray you'll be safe. In case you're wondering, it was Max who brought you back here last night.*

*P.S. Don't worry about the dress. Feel free to burn it.*

*Molly*

ANABLUE LOOKED DOWN. She was still wearing the blue dress and a man's jacket. Max's? She peeled off the jacket and dress and raced for the shower. Standing in the shower, the fog lifted, with nothing but fuzzy memories remaining in her head.

*Drinking shots. Really Anablue!*

*Donall chased you out the door of the bar.*

*Did I tell him about Evans and what he tried to do? No idea…*

*I told him I loved him…Oh my God!*

Kneeing him in the groin. *What kind of woman are you to tell a man you love him, then knee him in the groin? Are you insane?*

And worst of all. He never responded to your drunken declaration of love.

*Obviously, he's disgusted. He didn't even bother to bring you home; Max did. What a fool you are.*

Leaning her forehead against the shower tile. *There's something else, Anablue. Something you've been denying for weeks. Elyse was right. You can get pregnant your first time. What would Gram tell you to do? You're not the first girl to get in trouble. You're pregnant, and soon you'll be out of the Navy. Pull yourself up by your bootstraps and go home. Donall can have his dreams. He doesn't need to know about this. He'll be safe now.*

She huddled in the shower, crying until the water ran cold.

DRESSED and running late for work, Max's jacket slung over her arm. Anablue ran, stopping when an envelope fell out of the jacket, the contents spilling out on the ground. She stooped to pick the documents up, spotting her name; she unfolded the paper with shaky hands.

*My birth certificate, and Brian's as well. My parent's marriage license. No, my mother's marriage license.* Shocked to her core, she stuffed the papers back into the envelope and inside the pocket of Max's jacket. *The admiral is not my father.*

Dawdling the rest of the way to work. Deep in thought, she made it to the hangar one minute late.

*Damn. Now I'm going to get ripped in two for being late. One thing you didn't think about, girl. What are you going to say to Donall about last night?*

*And Evans? Avoid that nasty little prick if you can.*

"Baker."

Anablue paled. *Egads! Already.* Grimacing, she turned around to face Donall.

"Yes, sir."

"Outside. Now."

STEPPING outside of the hangar with Anablue trailing behind him. Donall steeled his resolve, keenly aware that Evans and the other men were watching them from inside the hangar. Evans had to be convinced that he didn't know what happened last night, and that he was angry with Anablue. He abruptly stopped and faced her.

"How did you get off base last night?"

"I told the guard I needed girl stuff, and the PX was closed."

"I don't care if you choose to get dressed up and go play "slap and tickle" with the locals, but you are never to leave this base again without my permission."

Anablue's mouth dropped open. "Slap and tickle? The only "slap and tickle" I recall playing is when I kneed your balls into your brain," she snarled.

"You are speaking to a superior officer, Baker."

"No. I am speaking to Donall Corrington. Don't you ever talk to me like that again?"

"Baker. Your insubordination will land you in the brig."

"Ha. I'm calling your bluff."

"Calling my bluff. Are you out of your fucking mind?"

"No. I am not out of my mind. I am tired. Tired of, Yes Sir, No Sir, Kiss my ass, Sir. Join the Navy. See the world, they said. I call bullshit. I am tired of living in a man's world. I am tired of double standards, tired of working twice as hard to prove myself. I have had to hide in the back of a hangar because the crew chief was embarrassed that he had a female on his crew. It didn't matter that I was the best mechanic he had. I was happy when I got out before. But now I'm back. Back into the same old fucking shit. I did nothing wrong last night, but of course, you blame me. You're not part of the problem. You, Sir, are the problem."

Donall stared at her like she had horns growing out of her head.

"You need to calm down."

"What I need, Captain, is a hot bath and a jar of fudge."

"Baker. I want you to report to the infirmary for a full check-up."

Her fists clenched tightly at her sides. "I have work to do," she ground out.

"Your assigned post for the day is at the infirmary. After that, you are restricted to your quarters, where I expect you to get some sleep."

"I don't want to go to the doctor."

"Now. Baker."

She glared at him and stamped her foot in pure frustration. "Ooooooh. You are a gobshite."

"You made that one up," Donall snarled.

"I did not."

He frowned in consternation as he watched her stomp, grumbling all the way back into the hangar to her locker.

*Swearing and stamping her foot. Now I know she's losing it. What the fuck is a gobshite?*

---

Leaning her head against the cold steel of the locker for a moment before she reached in, grabbing her things out of the locker. She looked up to see Max standing next to her.

"Hey, Anablue."

"Morning, Max."

"You okay?"

"I haven't been okay for a long time."

She handed him his jacket from inside the locker. "You left this behind last night."

"Thank you," Max said.

"The envelope fell out. I saw the papers. Why do you have those?"

Max sighed deeply. "I'll stop by your quarters later to explain. Where are you headed now?"

"The infirmary."

"It's not a bad idea after last night."

She shrugged her shoulders and moved to go around him. "There's nothing wrong with me."

MAX TURNED to see Donall still standing outside of the hangar, looking towards the mountain range in the distance. Donall turned and strode to where Max stood.

"Will you do me a favor? Go catch up to her, walk her over to the infirmary," Donall said.

"Sure."

"Max. What's your rank?"

"I'm a civilian now, but when I was in. I was a Captain, US Army."

"You ever have to deal with an insubordinate female?"

"Can't say I ever had the pleasure."

"Lucky you," Donall replied with a tight smile. "That little shit is the most infuriating woman I have ever met.

"Looks like you did a good job of pissing her off," Max said.

"Too good. Never let it be said that Anablue Baker is any man's doormat."

"She still owes deference to your authority."

"True. Something's up with her. It almost seems like she thinks she's out."

## CHAPTER 25

Anablue stood at the exam room window. Lost in her thoughts, she watched the tumbleweeds tumble and roll down the street. She was lost and alone, just like that tumbleweed, blowing and rolling with no real direction or purpose.

In his condescending and moral high ground tone, Doctor McCarthy had confirmed her pregnancy, blaming her, and her alone, for her predicament. It would take a couple of days for the paperwork to go through, and then she would be free to leave. The military did not allow pregnant women to continue to serve.

The doctor had strongly urged her to place her baby up for adoption. That would not happen under any circumstances. Sighing deeply, she left the office and made her way outside to find Max waiting for her.

"Why are you still here?"

"I figured I'd hang around and make sure you were okay," Max replied.

She gave him a small smile. "I'm fine. You still owe me an explanation on why you have those birth certificates."

"Hmmm. Let's walk while we talk," Max said. "How well do you know your Uncle Jackson?"

"I don't. I've never met him."

"Never?"

"No. Gram used to go visit him once per year. Always in some far-away exotic place."

"Do you know why he never came home to see her?"

"No."

"You speak fondly of your grandmother but never your mother."

"Listen, Max. These are some personal questions to be asking. How do you even know I have an uncle? Who are you?"

"I'm an investigator with NIS."

She stopped in her tracks. "Investigator? What are you investigating?"

Max took a deep breath. "I'm investigating Brian's death and those involved."

"Brian's death?" she whispered. "Did my uncle have something to do with it?"

"No. But I believe your father, the admiral, did. It wasn't an accident."

Anablue felt like she had been sucker-punched. The pain in her heart took her breath away.

She stumbled, and Max reached out to steady her. Finding a bench close by, he sat her down and waited patiently for the tears running down her face and her shaking to stop.

Finding her words, "I believe the birth certificates show he's not our father."

"No, he's not," Max gently replied.

"Sins of the mother. That's what the admiral said to me. That's what he meant by it."

"What else did the admiral tell you?"

"That Donall and I were brought here to torment us because we can't be together here."

"What happened last night?"

"Evans, he's working for my… the admiral. The admiral ordered Evans to force me to go to a party of sorts. With him and his friends."

"Do you know who these friends are?"

"No, but Molly would. Oh, my god. Molly. You're the one who helped Molly."

Max smiled. "She's safe now."

"And her boyfriend? Did he go with her?"

"No. He wanted nothing to do with her after what happened."

"Another reason I climbed out the bathroom window. I couldn't do it to myself or Donall."

"Smart move. You did the right thing."

"They may jail him or kill him."

"Nah. We've got his back."

"Max. Why is the admiral doing this? It seems pretty

stupid for a man to risk his pension and jail time to go after his wife's children for revenge. There's got to be more to it."

"That's the million-dollar question."

"And why kill Brian? If he's willing to kill him, then he's after me too."

"Yes. You sit here for a while, gather your thoughts. I'm sure it's all quite a shock. I'll sit over there and wait for you," Max said as he pointed to another bench.

After an hour, she rose to her feet. "How much of this does Donall know?"

"He knows everything that I know."

" Max, I just thought of something. Before Brian shipped out, he told me he had met our father. I can think of at least three times he spoke to him on the phone as well. The admiral denied it."

"You're sure?"

"Brian would never have lied to me. I can't wait for this to be over. I am done fiddle-farting around with the Navy and the admiral."

Max laughed and pulled out his notebook.

"What are you doing?"

"I started a list of your funny words."

"Whatever. I need some hot fudge."

"Well, let's stroll on over to the PX."

"I'm restricted to my quarters. And I need my purse. It's in my car. Do you have my keys?"

"Umm. No. Captain Corrington has those," Max said,

"He took them after you drove over one hundred miles per hour down a country road."

"I did what? Damn. I'll never get them back. What else did I do?"

Max barked out a short laugh before his face split into a big grin.

"That shit-eating grin on your face is not very comforting, Max."

They had arrived at her quarters. She pulled her key from the chain around her neck to unlock the door, but the door was partially open. Max, looking at Anablue, put his finger to his lips.

"Shhhh." Pulling a handgun from beneath the back of his waistband, he pushed the door open and entered her quarters. After checking if anyone was inside, he came back outside.

"All clear, but your quarters have been ransacked."

"Why? Other than uniforms and a few civilian clothes. As Gram would say, I haven't got a pot to piss in."

"Yes, you do. You have a car."

"You think they were looking for my car keys?"

"Most likely."

"Idiots. There's more than one way to start a car if they're going to steal it."

Max gave her an odd look. "Well, I know how to hot-wire a car," she said.

"Do you have other keys?"

"Well, keys for Gram's house and the post office box, her

safe deposit box at the bank. One for Mrs. Wang's house. I have lots of keys."

"Where are those keys?"

"In my big purse. In the trunk of the car."

"That is why they wanted the car keys. What's in that safety deposit box?" Max asked.

"I have no idea. I haven't gone through Gram's things yet.

"We need to find out what's in that box. Meanwhile, I'll go find the Captain and get your purse for you. And Anablue, you need to rein in that insubordination. He is still your superior officer, and you owe him deference. I won't be able to help you if someone else overhears you, and you end up in the brig. You're too good of a sailor to go out like that."

## CHAPTER 26

Donall and Max walked briskly to the parking lot only to find her car vandalized.

"Jesus. Do you see this? How am I going to tell her about this?" Donall said as he opened the car door. "Look at it. The driver's wing window is broken; the inside of the car ransacked."

"Whoever it was, tried to get into the trunk," Max said as he brushed the glass off the seat with his sleeve and sat in the driver's seat.

"This is no ordinary break-in. Look, the eight-track player is still here. Her eight-tracks," he paused, picking one up before he showed it to Donall, "Christmas music in August. Strangest girl I've ever met."

"I know." Donall chuckled. "Is that her purse open on the floor?"

"This one is little, meant for small things. Lipstick and shit like that," Max replied. "She said it was big and in the trunk."

"Let's look in the trunk," Donall said.

Donall opened the trunk. "Her paint supplies, canvas, all her things to paint on the dock."

Spotting one small painted canvas in particular, his hand shook as he reached for it. "Chrysanthemums. She painted this one the day of our first date."

He lightly stroked the shape of the flower. "It seems like a lifetime ago." Donall put the canvas down and reached for a framed photograph. "Look at this, Max."

A photograph of the smiling tow-headed twins, Anablue and Brian, along with their mother. A man's arm around the mother, but the rest of him was cut out.

Max looked at the photo. "Damn. I'd bet my last buck that this is their real father. Wish he wasn't cut out of the picture. It would've helped so much."

"I kind of don't feel right going through her things," Donall said. "Why isn't this stuff in her quarters?"

"I don't know. Ah, there's her purse," Max said as he hefted it up. "We should bring this to her."

"Yeah."

"What's in it? It weighs a ton." Max handed Donall the purse. "Here."

"I'm not carrying a purse across a fucking Air Force base," Donall growled. "Your case, you carry it."

"No way. Your girlfriend. You carry it." Max snarled back.

Donall glared at Max as he took the purse from him. He

looked down. "Max, what's that puddle of fluid on the ground?"

Max looked down, then underneath the car. "Holy Shit, Corrington. That's brake fluid leaking out. The brake lines have been cut."

"This counts as an attempt on her life. I think it's time to place Evans under arrest," Donall growled.

"I have to brief the brass and my boss first. Let's move her to the other end of the women's building, closer to you. And step up patrol around her quarters and the parking lot, again." Max replied.

---

The sun was peeking over the Sierra Nevada Mountain range as Donall sat looking at the side of the building to Anablue's new quarters. He scowled deeply, remembering her tears and anger when he told her about her car being vandalized. She had pleaded for permission to view and repair the car. Then ranted and raved when he denied her request, reminding her she was still restricted to her quarters.

Deeply troubled, his worry for her safety increased daily. Max had told him about his conversation with her yesterday. His heart ached for her finding out her twin had been murdered. Though he knew Max would have broken it to her gently. Still, he would have liked to have been with her.

A soft click of a door shutting brought him from his thoughts as he looked to the porch in front of her building.

He inhaled sharply, watching the woman of his dreams walk over and sit on the rail. A soft breeze blew through her hair and molded the pale yellow of her nightgown to her curves. She held a straw hat in her hands as she leaned her head against the pole.

His gaze slowly drifted over her face, relishing the opportunity to just sit and look at her. Thick dark eyelashes fluttered as she closed her eyes. Flawless skin and pink parted lips framed by her soft blonde curls hung to her slim shoulders. He lingered over her slim throat as his eyes dropped to the swell of firm breasts, nipples hard and pushing against the fabric. The soft curves of hips and bare thighs brought back the memory of his hands caressing her soft skin. He must have made a sound as her eyes flew open, and she stood up. She looked to where he sat and hesitantly walked to the edge of the porch.

Her hands worried the band of her hat as she peered through the early morning light to see Donall rise from his chair.

"I… I wasn't sure who was watching me," she softly spoke.

Donall padded barefoot down the step to stand fifteen feet in front of her. "I didn't mean to frighten you."

She nodded her head. "Listen, Donall. I-I'm sorry my father, I mean, the admiral, dragged you into this."

Donall protested.

"Please. Let me finish. I'm rather embarrassed and humiliated that he did this to you. It wasn't fair." She fussed with the blue ribbon on her hat. "Brian bought me this hat when I was stationed in Hawaii, and he came to visit me on leave. It's the last thing he ever bought me," she said with a slight smile. "Brian was furious with me when I joined the Navy. He tried to warn me, but I refused to listen. I was proud to serve. It was hard, but I did it, and I did it well. This, whatever this is, that the admiral forced us into, is so wrong, and I'm so sorry."

"I also wanted you to know." she swallowed hard. "That… that I've never lied to you or meant to mislead you. My life in San Francisco is who I am. Just as my life before in the Navy, that is a part of me as well. If that makes sense."

Donall closed the distance between them and stood on the other side of the rail.

"Don't." his voice, a hoarse whisper. "It's not your fault. You are not to blame for anything that happened here. You didn't mislead me. We both know that if circumstances were different, we would have worked out our differences right away."

"I know," she whispered.

Anablue slowly reached out and gently laid her hand on his brow, caressing slowly down to his cheekbone. Then with a whisper, she was gone; the door shutting softly behind her.

Donall leaned his head on his forearms on the wood railing. His heart thudding in his chest.

*Why does it feel like she's saying goodbye?*

SHUTTING THE DOOR BEHIND HER, Anablue leaned against the door. Squeezing her eyes shut to block the burning tears. *Coward. You're a coward, Anablue. It would have been so easy to tell him everything. Instead, you're running away.*

Her stomach heaved. *Again?* And she raced for the bathroom. Afterward, she splashed cold water on her face and washed her hands. Looking in the mirror, she grabbed a towel and patted her skin dry. Confusion filled her as she stared at her reflection. *You cannot make him choose between his dream job and you.*

---

THROWING the pencil down on his desk in disgust, Donall grumbled to himself about the asinine orders Max had moments ago handed him. Another physical. This time he had to travel up to Treasure Island Naval Base in San Francisco. It would take a couple of days, and he worried about leaving Anablue alone. Max would be here to watch over her. Still, he was unsettled about the plan, but Max was insistent that it be done. Since he knew he wouldn't pass the third physical, the only good thing about it would be that it would help cement the case against the admiral, and he would be free. Free to offer his love and comfort to Anablue until this difficult investigation was over. Then they could move on and live their lives. Hopefully, together.

*Fuck, I'd better go pack my things soon and catch that plane to Treasure Island.*

Picking up some paperwork, he peered over the top, watching Anablue as she worked. Clipboard in hand, she went from tarp to tarp, making sure all the engine parts were accounted for and installed. He grinned as a beautiful smile lit her face as she turned to stare up at the jet engine. She seemed to be very proud of her new baby, now resting in a sling hung from a thick cable attached to the biggest hoist he'd ever seen. The Crew Chief Vaughan stopped to chat with her. She pointed out various points of interest on the engine to Vaughan, his muffled comments causing her to laugh with delight. A voice from the other side of the hangar called him away, and Vaughan left, making his way over to the other man.

She looked so tiny, standing underneath the massive engine. She had her hair up in a bun, as usual. He hated that bun. He longed to see her as he did this morning, with her soft lemon curls hanging down to her shoulders. And naked. Naked in his arms, with her legs wrapped around his back. He shifted uncomfortably in his chair, adjusting himself. He was keenly aware of his racy thoughts and responding body. She glanced up, catching his eyes on her. She gave him a saucy smile that he returned with a slow warning grin, and she turned away to refocus on the engine.

A loud crack from above her head, and he looked up in horror to see the hoist give way, bending down from the top. He was over the desk and pounding toward her before she had the chance to look up.

## CHAPTER 27

Anablue glanced up to see Donall sprinting toward her in what seemed like a slow-motion dream. Her vision tunneled as she looked up and froze. Strong arms wrapped around her waist, pulling her close. Pushing her body with inhuman force, they went to the ground, rolling and tumbling along the floor. A huge crash that shook the building sounded behind them. Bits of shrapnel and engine parts flew all around them as they rolled to a stop.

Gripping his shoulders, she dug her nails into him as she opened her eyes. She stared up into Donall's terror-filled eyes in shock.

He lay on top of her, placing his hands on both sides of her face. "Are you all right? Anablue, answer me," he cried.

Placing her hands around his neck, she pulled him closer in a tight hug. "Oh, my God, Donall. Are you crazy? The hoist… it could have killed you." Tears filled her eyes at the thought she could have lost him forever.

"Me? It was you who could have been killed," he said, burying his face in her shoulder. "Thank god you're okay."

She ran her hands over his shoulders and back, then stared in shock at the blood on her hands. "Donall, your back. You're bleeding," Anablue sobbed.

Loud cries and running feet from the other side of the hangar alerted them that help was on its way.

She cried out when he pulled away. "Let me see your back."

Donall sat back on his haunches and stared at her. "There's one thing I haven't told you about. My back…"

"Yeah, it's bleeding," she said. Moving around him, she gently lifted the rip that ran the length of his blood-soaked shirt.

"You have a couple of six-inch cuts. Placing one hand over the cuts to stem the bleeding, she lifted his shirt further. "Sweet Jesus, Donall. What is this?" Ridge after ridge of deep, angry, red scars crisscrossed his back. "What happened to you?"

He quickly turned to face her. "Listen, Anablue," his voice hoarse and pained. He grabbed her wrists. "Listen to me. I did not mean to keep this from you. I would have told you sooner, but this is not the place."

"Tell me what?"

"I have to catch a plane up to TI this afternoon. I'll be

gone for a day, or so, when I get back, we will talk about this, and I promise I will explain everything."

By then, they were surrounded by the crew, and Anablue found herself pushed to the side as they pulled Donall to his feet.

She found herself standing next to Max. "You okay?" Max asked.

Focused on Donall, she responded. "Yeah, I'm fine. Just a bit shook up. He needs stitches."

"He'll be fine. They're taking him to the infirmary now."

"What happened to him?"

"Shrapnel or flying parts."

"No. Before today. His whole back is scarred."

"You don't know?"

"Know what? Max."

"He was a POW. His plane was shot down over South Vietnam. He was held captive for a few weeks."

Her knees went weak as her breath left her with a whoosh. Reaching out to Max, she grabbed his arm to steady herself. "Sweet Jesus," she whispered. "A prisoner of war. Those bastards tortured him, didn't they?" She went to her knees as she covered her mouth with her bloody hands, gulping in deep breaths of air. The tears ran down her face. Donall's words echoing in her head. *I would have told you sooner....*

"Come on. I'll take you to your quarters. You need to clean yourself up. You're covered in blood."

"What I need... is to go to the infirmary with Donall, or

I'll stay here and see what I can clean up with the engine," she said.

"No. They'll take care of the Captain. Besides, I'm locking down this hangar for an investigation into how or why that hoist gave way."

"You think it was Evans?"

"Probably. Evans, like the snake he is, seems to of slithered away."

---

Donall stood at the top of the steps of the military transport plane. Looking around, he'd hoped to see her before he left for the hour-long flight north. Ducking, he went inside. After mumbling a hello to the men on board, he buckled himself in and stared morosely out the window. That was when he spotted Anablue watching from the edge of the airfield. Smiling to himself, he leaned back in his seat as other personnel filtered in and took their seats. He nodded to Dr. McCarthy, who, a few hours earlier, had painstakingly stitched up the gashes on his back. The man was off to a stint at an Air Force Base hospital in Vietnam.

Closing his eyes, he leaned back in his seat, determined to catch a nap.

"It's too bad about that pretty little blonde. Ending her career like that in shame," Dr. McCarthy said, over the roar of the jet engines as the plane was taxiing to the runway.

"I'm sorry. What did you say?" Donall said.

"Your little mechanic. Didn't you get the paperwork I sent over?"

"No. What paperwork?"

"She's out. Got herself into trouble," Dr. McCarthy shouted over the din.

"What kind of trouble?"

"She's pregnant."

"Excuse me, what did you say?"

"A baby. She's going to have a baby."

"Why the fuck didn't you tell me that before?" Donall roared as he unbuckled his seat belt and made to rise.

"Relax, Captain. I'm sure the paperwork will be on your desk when you return. She's probably already gone."

The plane's engines throttled up. The jet raced down the runway and then lifted off, pushing him back into his seat. Donall looked out the window in mind-boggling shock. *Anablue. Gone. And a baby. Holy fucking shit. I've got to find her.*

GLANCING up over the steering column, making sure no one was in sight, Anablue touched the two cables together as the engine on her car roared to life. Revving the engine a few times until she was satisfied it wouldn't stall out, she wrapped some electrical tape to cover the live wires.

Hitting the road, she was on her way north to San Francisco. She still had things she needed at Mrs. Wang's house. From there, she intended to go home. Knowing she couldn't stay there, she had to come up with a plan on where she was going to hide. Life on the run didn't appeal to her, but with the admiral and Evans after her. And Donall? After watching him board that plane, everything in her wanted to stay and wait for his return.

She wiped the tears that rolled down her cheeks. Donall. Just the thought of him brought a dull thud to her chest. It was best this way. She had watched him the day of the Apollo launch, then a few days later, when a man historically walked on the moon.

Even from across the TV room off the mess hall, she had seen the excitement in his eyes. God willing, he would have his dreams and end up in that space program. Confusion filled her as anguish about her decision to leave without telling him about the baby filled her heart and drained her soul. He would never willingly allow her to leave, but she would never know if his sense of duty forced him to stay with her. Foremost in her mind was the child. As far as she knew, Evans was still out there, and Gary too. She had to survive so the baby could live.

THE CELL DOOR SLAMMED SHUT, and Donall glared at the guard on the other side of the door. "Do I get a phone call?" he snarled.

"We'll see," the guard replied.

"What are the charges?"

"I have no idea. Sir. We were ordered to detain you if you showed up on base," he said as he left.

Donall slammed the bars with his hand and went over and flopped on the bunk. After an hour-long flight, he had time to reflect on Anablue. After a few more questions to the doctor during the flight, he had wanted to pound the man into the ground. Shaming her. Advising her to put her child up for adoption. All this while dealing with threats to her life.

She was running scared. Of that, he had no doubt. He loved her; it was plain and simple. And when he found her, he would tell her so.

He wasn't too thrilled when the plane had touched down at Treasure Island, and he had been met by MAA's and thrown in the brig. He intended to jump on another plane and head right back to Edwards. Donall rubbed his brow in frustration. *Max. Call Max. Better yet, Elijah. Elijah can get ahold of Max.*

He was back on his feet, pacing the cell like a caged animal.

*What is the admiral up to now?*

## CHAPTER 28

Max walked into the hangar again, still searching for Anablue. Not here. She wasn't in her quarters. His anxiety rising, he spotted Vaughan talking with the two investigators going over the hoist accident.

"Vaughan, have you seen Baker?"

"Where you been, Max? She's gone."

"Gone. What do you mean?"

"She's out on a medical discharge. I've got a friend over at the infirmary. She said Baker's knocked up."

"When did Baker leave?" Max cried in sheer panic.

"Last night, right before the MP's caught Evans hitchhiking to San Francisco."

"Any idea on where she would have gone?"

"No idea," Vaughan replied.

Max threw his baseball cap on the ground in sheer frustration. Putting his hands on his hips, he turned to look out the hangar door at the mountains. *Corrington is going to kill me.*

Turning back to Vaughan, nodding toward the investigators, "They say anything about the hoist or engine yet?"

"Nah, they're pretty tight-lipped about it."

"I have to go up to San Francisco. I'll check in with their progress before I leave," Max said.

"You're kind of strange, Max. Why would they tell a photographer anything?"

"Oh yeah. Right," Max said.

THE MUSIC BLARED in the ballet studio as Elyse went through her routine. Wearing Elijah's old army green boxers and tee-shirt tied at the waist, spinning and twirling in a pirouette. Closing her eyes, she could picture herself back in Vietnam. The Rolling Stones tune brought vivid memories of the team. She blocked out the horrors she had seen, only allowing herself to think of the good times. Bunker dancing, God, how she missed it.

A small voice called to her, "Elyse."

Elyse opened her eyes to see Anablue standing at the door. "Anablue."

She rushed forward and engulfed her in her arms. "How did you get here? I thought you were still at Edwards."

Anablue burst into tears, and they went down to their

knees together. They clung to each other while Anablue sobbed. "I'm in trouble. Elyse, I'm in trouble."

"Trouble?"

"You were right. You can get pregnant the first time," Anablue cried.

"What does Donall have to say about this? Where is Donall?"

"He took a flight to Treasure Island yesterday. I left the base as soon as I got the discharge paperwork. He doesn't know that I'm pregnant or that I left."

"Oh Honey, tell him," Elyse said.

"I'm can't. I love him, but I can't stand in the way of his dreams. I came to say goodbye."

"No. Anablue. You can't. You're making a mistake. You are his dream."

"Thank you for everything. Your friendship means the world to me," Anablue said.

"Where will you go? What will you do?"

"I don't know. I'm terrified, but I will figure it out."

"Please don't leave. Let me help you. You're not in this alone," Elyse cried.

Shaking her head, Anablue picked her purse up from the floor where she had dropped it. "I have to go now. Goodbye, Elyse."

Pushing the stroller up the sidewalk. Elijah paused at the door to the Ballet studio. He had packed Bunker and his diaper bag in a rush after Donall's frantic phone call. He planned on leaving the baby with Elyse while he went to see if he could get his brother released from the brig.

A young woman was coming out the door. Blonde and petite, her face drained of color when she saw him standing there with the baby in the stroller.

She stared at him, and the baby, then glanced up the stairwell leading to the studio.

"Is Bunker your baby?" she snarled.

Elijah looked around, thinking the woman was deranged. "Yeah, he's my son," he replied.

"And Elyse is your wife?"

Elijah looked at the wild-eyed woman and slowly nodded his head. "Yes."

With that, she hauled off and punched him in the nose.

"What the hell did you do that for?" Elijah bellowed as he cupped his nose.

"You… are a two-bit, two-timing, lower than life… slug. I can't believe you bamboozled me with your bullshit lies. Never mind what you've done to me. How could you do this to a sweet girl like Elyse? You're disgusting. Stay away from me."

She ran across the street to her car. Burning rubber, she pulled away with a squeal of tires, leaving thick black smoke to float in the air.

Elijah parked the stroller in its usual place under the coat rack. Pulling Bunker and the diaper bag out, he climbed the stairs to the studio. He opened the door to find his wife pacing back and forth. She looked up at him with tears in her eyes.

"Oh, Elijah. Thank God. How did you know I needed you?" she cried. "Why is your nose bleeding?"

Elijah set the baby on the floor and watched as he crawled away at a pretty fast clip. "I just got punched in the nose by a pint-sized hell-cat."

"Punched in the nose?" Elyse asked as she pulled the green towel from around her neck to dab at the blood on his face.

"You're lucky it's not broken. Why would a girl punch such a handsome face?"

"I don't know, but she called me a two-bit, two-timing slug."

Elyse's eyes widened. "This woman. What did she look like?"

"Beautiful blonde, big blue eyes. Tiny like you, with a mean right hook," Elijah said.

"Oh, no…no..no..no."

Elijah's eyes narrowed. "Who was that girl?"

"Anablue," Elyse whispered as her eyes went to the baby. He had crawled to the wall and sat babbling at and kissing his reflection in the floor-to-ceiling mirror.

"Please tell me that Donall told Anablue he has a twin."

"He couldn't be that fucking stupid. Maybe, I don't know. What else happened?"

"Oh, Elijah. She's pregnant. Donall doesn't know. She left

and wouldn't tell me where she was going. She's running away," Elyse sobbed.

"It's worse than that. Donall is in the brig at Treasure Island. I couldn't get ahold of Max at Edwards," Elijah said.

"Oh, just wait until I get ahold of this, Max. I don't understand why he's dragging this nightmare out. How is Donall doing?"

"Donall is frantic. He knows she's pregnant and on the run. Do you know where our fathers are today?" Elijah replied.

"Fishing. They're fishing."

"We need to get Donall out of the brig. I'll head over there. You find Pops and Gramps and meet me there. It's an all hands-on deck, four-alarm fire right now."

"I'll ask Mrs. Wang to watch the baby. Maybe Anablue is there."

## CHAPTER 29

Hanging up the phone, Max stepped out of the phone booth. Thoughtfully rubbing his chin, he reflected on his conversation with his informant.

Who the fuck is this Gary, and what does he have to do with the admiral? Corrington should be back at Edwards by now. I'll call him later.

Jumping in his car, he headed over to Treasure Island Naval Base for a meeting to update Navy brass on the investigation.

A few hours later, Max rubbed his brow. His frustration with the brass was growing by the minute after their meeting. Sure, it takes a lot to take down an admiral, but the brass wanted a motive. Why would Admiral Baker want Brian and Anablue Baker dead? Not watching where he was going, he accidentally bumped into a tall, broad-shouldered man.

"Pardon me," Max said, barely glancing up.

"No problem."

Max stopped in his tracks. *Wait,* and he turned to watch the man just as he was approached by two MAA's. *Corrington?* The man was cuffed and taken into custody. Overwhelmed by curiosity, he followed the threesome over to the brig.

SCOWLING at the guard as he slammed the brig door shut on him, Elijah mumbled, "Great. This is just fucking great."

A low rumble of laughter from the cell next door brought Elijah to the bars.

"Now you know the idiots I've been dealing with since yesterday," Donall said.

"Are you telling me those two morons locked me up because they thought I was you?" Elijah growled.

"Yeah. It appears they didn't check their manifest to see they already had me in custody."

"It won't be long now. Elyse was going to find father and bring him and her father here to talk to the brass to get you out. I couldn't get ahold of your friend, Max. They said he was off-base. Why did they send you up here?" Elijah asked.

"I was supposed to get a third physical to prove I should have failed the last one," Donall replied. "Once it's done, I'm out. Then I can be with Anablue."

"Yeah, about Anablue. That little hell-cat has a mean right hook."

"A mean right hook? Explain."

"Well, I ran into her outside of Elyse's ballet studio. She had been up to see Elyse. She saw the baby, thinking I was you. She called me a slug, punched me in the nose, and drove off in a wicked fast car."

Donall growled deep in his throat. "She must have hot-wired the car. I have her car keys."

"Aren't you worried about her thinking you're a two-bit, two-timing slug?"

"Nah. I just have to drag your sorry ass in front of her."

"You have to find her first," Elijah said.

"At least I know she's in town," Donall said with a sigh.

"I have to get the hell out of here. Where the fuck is Max?" Donall said as he slammed his hand on the bars.

---

Pulling out his badge and identifying himself, Max waited patiently for the guard to check his manifest for Donall's name.

"Heh. Here it is. Must be some mistake. He's listed on here twice," the guard said.

"What are the charges?" Max asked.

"None listed on here. Just standing orders to take him into custody if he showed up on base."

"Whose order's?" Max said.

"Admiral Bakers."

"Okay, Sailor. Here's what I want you to do. Call over to

Admiral Barnes office. Explain the situation and that I want Corrington released. Now let me in to see him."

"Yes, Sir."

The door of the brig opened, and Max strode over to the first cell.

"Damn, Corrington. You walked right by me outside." Looking at his worn jeans, tennis shoes, and blue shirt. "Why are you out of uniform?"

Elijah raised an eyebrow as a voice from the next cell called out.

"Max."

Max stopped and leaned to look in the other cell. Leaning back, he looked at Elijah slack-jawed before he leaned back to look at Donall again.

"There's two of you," Max said.

"Max, quit dinking around and get us out of here," Donall snarled. "How did you know I was here?"

"I didn't. I saw your double get arrested outside and followed him here. I have news. Anablue's pregnant. She's left the base. I have no idea where she is."

"I know."

"I met with the brass. We need to talk," Max said.

The door opened, and a beautiful red-headed woman entered the room. Elijah smiled a wide, toothy grin and winked at Max.

"Incoming," he said with a warning smirk on his face.

Max turned to watch the familiar-looking woman as she approached and stopped in front of Elijah.

She smiled a beautiful smile, bit her lower lip, and leaned into the bars. "I'm not sure how you ended up in here. But, just so you know. I'm relishing that I'm on this side of the bars, and you're on that side."

"Careful, Brat, I can still turn you over my knee," Elijah said with a low growl.

"Promise?" she laughingly replied.

Walking around Max she stopped in front of Donall's cell.

"Oh, Donall." Shaking her head, her eyes tearing up. "I don't know what to say other than she loves you, and she's running scared."

Donall looked down, a pained expression on his face. Looking back up to see the confusion still clear on Max's face. "Max Cohen. Meet my twin brother Elijah, and his wife, Elyse."

Elyse narrowed her eyes, hands on her hips; She stalked toward Max. "You're Max? Why aren't you moving heaven and earth to resolve this mess? Donall and Anablue have suffered enough. Why aren't you over there with your hands around the throats of the brass to get my husband and Donall released? Or do I need to go over there and do it myself?"

Max held his hands up as if surrendering. "Good questions. I have some answers."

The door opened again as two more men and the guard entered the room.

One man went and stood in front of Elijah for a second. Passing by Elyse, he tickled her under her chin and then stood in front of Donall.

"Get my boys out of these fucking cells, "Colonel Corrington demanded to the guard."

The guard unlocked the doors, and Donall wrapped his arms around his father. The two men clung to each other, patting each other on the back.

"Come on, son, let's get you home. Then we'll come up with a plan to find your runaway pepper pot."

Donall smiled. "I need to look for her now."

"It's getting dark. You won't find her now. You need to get some sleep and eat something first," Elyse gently chided.

"You're cooking?" Donall asked with trepidation.

"Oh God no," Elyse replied with a roll of her eyes. "We have Romano's pizza delivery. You all go on ahead. I need to go get my baby from Mrs. Wangs first."

"You still need your physical," Max said. "The brass said you never showed."

"I've been in here," Donall replied, his ire rising.

"I can probably get you in to see the Doctor in the morning."

"Okay, I guess I have no choice but to wait. Come on, Max, let's go have some pizza. By the way, meet former Ambassador Arthur Booker, Elyse's father, and my father, Colonel Corrington, USMC, retired," Donall said.

Max shook their hands. Looking at the ambassador. "Booker." He turned and looked at Elyse wide-eyed. "Elyse Booker. Prima Ballerina, the toast of South Vietnam. I saw you dance at An Khe."

"An Khe. Aiden's still at An Khe." Elijah and Donall said at once.

"Perhaps you know my oldest son. Major Aiden Yarusso," The colonel asked.

"Yeah. I know him. He's a good friend of mine," Max replied.

"Wow. Small world," Elyse said. "Alright, let's go, guys."

THE GROUP WALKED out to the parking lot together. Elijah saw his wife to her car.

"Elijah. Do you remember the day I told you Mrs. Wang said Anablue's father waited in the shadows?" Elyse said.

"Yeah, I do."

"I think Max should follow me. He needs to talk to Mrs. Wang and find out what she knows. I'm sorry I didn't remember it until now."

"Are you sure? I can get the baby."

"No, I desperately need to feed him before I burst. I'll be fine. You take Pop's, Gramps, and Donall with you. Don't forget to order the pizza. I'll only be a half-hour behind you."

## CHAPTER 30

Well after dark, key in hand, Anablue fumbled to unlock the door of Gram's house. Once in, she turned on the small lamp sitting on the table next to the door. Looking lovingly around the front room, she spied the silver aluminum Christmas tree still standing in the corner, its lone Christmas gift still unwrapped under the tree. She walked over and plugged the tree in, and watched it spin in its base. A kaleidoscope of color filled the room as she delicately stroked a favorite red bulb. She pulled the sheets off the chairs and unplugged the tree before going into the kitchen.

Room by room, she turned on the lights and pulled sheets from the furniture. Hesitating at her Grandmother's bedroom door, she moved on to Brian's room. Flipping on the switch, she looked about his room. Sports pennants and posters of the Golden Gate bridge decorated the walls.

Football trophies and her grandfather's hand-carved wooden horse sat on the dust-coated dresser. All was the same since the day he left for the Navy. Opening the door to her room, pulling the dusty chenille bedspread off the twin bed, she crawled in. Curling up in a ball, she cried herself to sleep.

---

THE SMELL of burnt toast drifted to his nostrils as he slowly woke up to someone playing with his lips and something licking his toes. Donall opened one eye to stare into curious amethyst eyes and chubby baby cheeks. The baby, sitting in his walker, tried to stick his pacifier into his mouth, all while babbling in baby talk.

"Hey, dude," Donall said as he sat up. Picking the baby up, he lifted him over his head. Looking over to the end of the couch, Soup sat there wagging his tail, a "happy to see you" grin on his puppy face.

Pointing his finger at the dog. "And you, we've had this conversation at Vung Tau about licking my toes."

Tucking the baby under one arm and Soup under the other, he padded into the kitchen to find Elyse knee-deep in chaos, trying to open a window to clear the smoke from the room.

Pointing at the dog, "This one was licking my toes," then indicating the baby. "And this one was sticking his pacifier in my mouth," Donall said as he put the dog down.

"Well, I guess I should be grateful it wasn't the other way

around," Elyse said. "I'm sorry they woke you up. They were both just here underfoot."

Max and Elijah came in the back door, calling out their good mornings to all. Elijah reached over his tiny wife and opened the window, then placed a soft kiss on top of her head.

Elyse took the baby from Donall and put him in his highchair. Donall and Elijah sat on either side of him at the table. Elijah liberally sprinkled a handful of Cheerios on the tray for the baby.

Bunker jammed a Cheerio into his mouth. Gumming the treat, his eyes went back and forth between Donall and his daddy. His little brow furrowed into a frown. He caught his mother's eye, and his lower lip quivered. "Elijah. The baby. Look at his face. He's confused," she cried. Then to Max, "Sit down, Max, we're all family here."

Elijah looked at the baby, pointed to his chest. "Daddy." Then pointed at Donall, "Uncle Donall." Bunker shoved a handful of cereal into his little mouth while giving him a skeptical look.

Elyse set the coffeepot on the table. Returning with a plateful of burnt toast.

Max pulled up a seat and poured himself a cup of coffee. Taking a sip, he choked on the overly potent brew. Elijah shot him a look of sympathy as he pushed the pitcher of cream and sugar bowl toward him. Donall grinned as he eyed the stack of burnt toast and took a sip of his sugar-laden coffee.

"I was going to try my hand at making some eggs," Elyse said, her back to the table.

Three sets of eyes looked up at each other in horror.

"I think I'd rather just have a bowl of cereal," Elijah said as he banged the burnt piece of toast against the plate.

Donall and Max nodded in agreement.

"Suit yourself," Elyse replied, placing the box of cereal, bowls, and a bottle of milk on the table.

"Would you mind scooting down, Elijah? I need to feed Bunker his oatmeal."

Elyse sat in the chair and spooned a mouthful into Bunker's mouth. The baby scrunched up his little face in protest.

"Why do you call him Bunker?" Max asked.

Elyse's cheeks pinkened, biting her lip, trying to contain her smile, as both Elijah and Donall laughed.

"You know we're eventually going to have to call him Andrew," Elyse said with a giggle.

Max looked at the three and nodded his head. "Ah. I get it," he chuckled.

"I wonder how Anablue is doing?" Elyse whispered.

"Yeah. Me too," Donall quietly replied. "Mind if I shower? I need this physical over and done with. Then, I'm going to go find my girl."

"Yeah, bro. Whatever you need," Elijah replied.

Elijah and Donall raced south down the coastal highway. Each on their motorcycle. Donall was grateful that Elijah had driven his bike up to his place. Storing it in the massive garage Elijah had built until he could get back to San Francisco.

It was probably the most beautiful morning he had seen in a while. The rugged coastline, with its waves crashing against the rock-filled beach, flew by as they made their way to Treasure Island.

His thoughts shifted to Anablue. He reflected on what Elyse had told him before they left.

She had told Elyse that she didn't want to stand in his way. *Stand in the way of what?*

---

Admiral Michael Baker uttered a string of profanity-filled with wrath. Evans had failed. Anablue was alive and well, while Evans sat in the brig at Edwards, charged with attempted murder. No matter, he was a powerful man with other minions who could guarantee the man's silence, and others, yet, who could deal with Anablue.

Sitting in the backseat of the car that had picked him up at the airfield at Treasure Island, he thought about the past twenty years. All the scheming that had gone into his plans to secure his future comfort and wealth. Anablue, and his brother Jackson, were the last barriers to securing his dream.

Now that he had finally located Jackson and had Anablue

trapped at Edwards, all he needed to do was ensure they both met with untimely deaths, and Corrington, now held in the brig, remained in custody. All that was left was to convince the other brass that Corrington was trying to flee justice and sign the paperwork to send Corrington to Leavenworth to await his court-martial as a co-conspirator in his dearest daughter's attempted murder. He had no idea why Corrington was really on base, but no matter, it played into his hands.

The car door was opened by the driver, and the Admiral briskly walked into the administration building for a meeting with the commandant.

---

Elijah sat on a bench right outside of the infirmary, waiting for Donall to finish his physical. He looked up to see his brother approaching, flashing him a smile.

"I take it you failed?" Elijah said.

"Never thought I'd be so happy to fail a physical," Donall replied.

"So, you're out now?"

Donall sat down next to Elijah. "Yeah."

"How do you really feel about that?"

"Torn. Don't get me wrong, it was everything to me. I lived to fly. Me, and my fighter jet screaming through the skies, I loved it. But a couple of weeks in a jungle prison camp took that from me. I knew then that it was over, and if I survived, I had to move on. I'll never forget the thrill of being an aviator." Donall sighed deeply. "I've got to go find my Baby Blue."

"Baby Blue?"

"Yeah. Did you see her magnificent eyes? Blue as the sky. I may not be able to fly again, but I will always see the sky in her eyes."

Donall glanced up and froze. "Fuck."

"What is it?" Elijah asked.

"Admiral Baker. He just walked out of the administration building."

Donall and Elijah ducked behind the bench they were sitting on.

"He doesn't look happy," Donall said.

"He probably found out you were released from the brig, and Anablue is gone."

"Let's follow him. See what he's up to," Donall said.

---

GEORGE IRELYNN CROSS adjusted the F-stop on her camera. Pulling her binder from her chestnut-colored hair, she rubbed the achy spot on her scalp. She had been watching a couple of familiar-looking gorgeous men, twins actually, as they followed an admiral across the base. As a war correspondent and photographer, her natural curiosity was piqued. She followed them, snapping photographs of them as they ducked and hid from the admiral's view.

They stood on the side of a building, watching the

admiral as he approached an outdoor row of telephones. She came up behind them. After spending more than a few months in South Vietnam, she knew they were both military men. One was in a Naval uniform, the other in jeans, and they were on a mission.

"He's making a phone call," Donall said.

"Who is he calling that he had to come all the way over here to make the call?" Elijah said.

"I can find out for you," George said.

Both men jumped and turned to look at the feisty brunette.

"Jesus, we're getting rusty if a woman can sneak up behind us like that." Elijah gruffly said.

Donall eyed the beautiful woman from her humor-filled, amber eyes to her blue jeans. An overly large Army issued long-sleeved shirt partially unbuttoned to show a white tee-shirt underneath. She had multiple cameras slung over her tiny shoulders.

"Sure. Why not." Donall replied.

"Do you have a dime? I just flew in from Saigon. All I have is Vietnamese coins."

Digging in his pocket, Elijah handed over the dime, and they watched as the woman nonchalantly headed over to use the payphone next to the general.

She stayed until the general hung up the telephone and walked away. Heading back in the direction he had come from.

The woman walked back to where they stood. "He called the person on the other end of the line, Gary. He was rude, foul-mouthed, and told this Gary person to find her and get the job done," George said. "Sorry. That's all I could get. Now tell me what this is all about? I'd love a new scoop."

Donall shook his head. "No."

"Well. Here's my business card if you change your mind. I have photos if..."

She paused mid-sentence, the shock on her face clear as she reached out an unsteady hand to touch the name tag on Donall's shirt. "Corrington," she whispered. Her eyes flew up to Donall's eyes, then to Elijah's.

"That's why you look familiar. Oh shit. I have to go," she stammered as she snatched the business card from Donall's hand.

"You never saw me," she said, then she stopped. "No. Actually. Give him a message for me. "Catch me if you can." She gave them a saucy smile. Then, racing across the grass way, she was gone.

"Now that was a direct challenge, if I've ever heard one," Elijah said with a wide grin.

"Did you see the shirt she was wearing?" Donall said. "Army, Green Beret, Captain insignia."

"And the name on the shirt?" Elijah asked.

"Corrington," Donall said, chuckling.

"What was the name on her business card?"

"George Cross. Strange. A man's name."

"It's got to be Brendan. She's running like the devil is chasing her," Elijah said.

Donall snorted. "If it is Brendan, the devil is chasing her."

"Let's get out of here. I can only deal with one brother's runaway at a time," Elijah said.

## CHAPTER 31

Spooning the last of her Rocky Road ice cream into her mouth, Elyse savored the delicate treat. "Hmm, this is superb," she said. "I've never had this flavor of ice cream before."

"This flavor was invented right here in San Francisco," Max replied. Throwing his empty paper cup in the trash can. "Let's go over that list of Anablue's hangouts again."

Elyse looked at the list. "We've got the bookstore where she worked, the dock where she painted. She's got friends at the fish market and Mrs. Wangs, of course. This poor girl doesn't get out much."

"I'm hoping someone at one of these places has seen her and would know where she went. "

"Anything on that phone number Mrs. Wang gave you?" Elyse asked.

"Still no answer, but Mrs. Wang was a wealth of information. Some of which I can't share."

"Is it possible she just went home?"

"Possible. I'd like to cover all the bases here before we send Donall off on a wild goose chase." Max replied.

"Donall and Elijah should be back in a couple of hours. They're going to meet us at the dock.

"You know we've discussed the friends she has, but what about enemies? Anyone she didn't care for?" Max said.

"Just Gary and his buddy, umm, what's his name again? Marcus. That's it," Elyse said.

Alarmed now, "Gary? You're sure?" Max cried.

"Yes. Why?"

"I've got an informant who told me about a Gary somehow tied to the admiral. This guy is trying to track her down."

"Gary attacked Anablue at the bookstore on the Fourth of July," Elyse whispered.

"Let's get over to that bookstore and see what we can find out about this, Gary."

---

OPENING THE FRIDGE DOOR, Anablue held her hand over her mouth, trying not to gag.

"Okay, Anablue. Not… a good idea to leave food in the refrigerator for eight months."

Shutting the door, she looked around the kitchen. I'm

going to have to go get food. Pulling a can of peaches from the pantry, she opened the jar and grabbed a fork. Then she took her breakfast, or lunch, since it was past noon, out to the front porch to sit and eat.

Contemplating her situation, she gazed at the mountain range in front of her. From here, you could see the long road. It swerved and curved around the gently rolling hills from the house down to the main road. This was the perfect spot to watch a sunrise, stargaze, or watch company approaching. The porch itself wrapped around the entire house. On the other side of the ranch-style house, from the back porch, past the pole barn and old horse barn. Many a night, she had sat watching magnificent sunsets over hilly grasslands that went all the way to the winding Tuolumne River.

Gram. The house wasn't the same without her. And now that she knew the Admiral wasn't her father, she supposed that meant Gram wasn't her grandmother either. This porch she was sitting on wasn't hers, or even this stupid jar of peaches. The home wasn't home, and she wasn't who she thought she was. A lone tear rolled down her face.

Her mom had property somewhere close by. She knew the old house had burnt down years ago, killing her maternal grandparents before she was even born. Right after her mother had married the admiral. Since she had died, as her husband, it was his anyway.

Anablue couldn't remember how many times Gram, even Brian, had tried sitting her down to get her to listen to them about all the financial stuff. Gram always said she was stubborn and mule-headed. She refused to listen. Preferring instead to bury her head under the hood of a car or her nose in a book and let them worry about such things. None of it mattered anymore; it was never hers to begin with.

One thing was certain. She couldn't continue to squat on someone else's property. She'd have to see how much cash she could scrape up to cover gas and expenses until she could find somewhere to hide, get a job, and face the prospect of raising her baby alone.

Gram had often hidden money in the house. Wrapping a twenty-dollar bill in a newspaper, then taping it to the underside of furniture. If she searched, she might find some cash. She'd pay it back when she could. She still had to pick up her last paycheck from the bookstore, and who knew how she would get the month's pay she earned from the Navy.

Donall. Her mind gently touched on Donall, and a sob escaped her. Wrapping her arms around herself, she rocked in her chair and grieved for lost love and betrayal.

Eventually, she pulled herself together. Finding some old milk crates in the barn. She started packing a few things in her bedroom, determined to put it all behind her.

---

THE CHIMES above the door tinkled as Jane Wagner stepped into the music store. Searching for her little brother, she removed her large round sunglasses. Her long brown hair catching in the hinge of the frames. Pulling her hair free, she looked around. Not seeing any other customers in the store, she called out to him.

"Mike. Are you here?" she said.

Mike came out from the double doors in the back. "Hey, Sis. Long time, no see."

"Hey, Mikey. Gary sent me to see if you have any grass?"

"Gary. When are you going to dump that asshole?"

"Mikey," she pleaded. "You know how hard it is. Where would I go?"

"Look at you. Man, you've got another black eye. You could always come to my pad."

"Please, Mikey. I just need the grass. Besides, we both remember what he did last time I tried to leave. He almost killed both of us."

"Fine. How much?"

"Just a Nickle bag," she replied. Handing him a five-dollar bill, Mike handed her the bag of grass.

"Look," Jane said, excitement lighting up her face. "I got tickets to this big music festival out in New York. I'm hoping this will cheer Gary up." She handed Mike a flyer. "I figure it will take three-four days at most to drive there. We're leaving this afternoon."

"Wow. That's far out, Sis. Woodstock. It says three days of peace and music. Who's playing?"

"Jimi Hendrix, Janis Joplin, Sly, and the Family Stone. Look on the flyer."

The chimes rang again as the door opened and a tiny red-headed woman, along with a tall, dark, curly-haired man, entered the shop. The woman was dressed in a purple mini dress with a gold ring belt spanning her curvy hips. Eyeing the handsome man, she quickly put her sunglasses back on. The man was also snappily dressed in gray dress slacks and a white shirt. Jane looked down, embarrassed at her ragged bell-bottom jeans and green tank top.

The woman approached the register with a smile on her face. "Hi. I'm wondering if you could help me."

"Sure, lady. What do you need?" Mike replied.

"Do you know Anablue Baker? She worked at the bookstore at the end of the block. Have you, by any chance, seen her around?"

Mike looked at Jane in uncomfortable silence. "Anablue. Hot chick. She's been gone for over a month," he replied.

"We mean within the past few days," the man said.

"No. Haven't seen her," Mike said. "Hope she's okay. She's super sweet."

"My name is Elyse. Can you call me if you see her? It's important."

"Sure, leave your name and phone number," Mike said.

"Do you have paper and a pen?"

"Here, just put it on the back of this. He handed her the Woodstock flyer and a pen."

"Woodstock. A music festival that sounds fun," Elyse said. As she wrote her information down. She smiled kindly at the tall, shy woman standing there.

As soon as they were gone, Mike turned to Jane. "Didn't you say before that Gary had been harassing Anablue?"

"Yeah, the jerk seemed to forget he's married to me. His dad's been calling him again. He always gets mean after a call from him."

"Don't know why Gary bothers with that prick. Asshole never even married his mom."

"I know. I'm the one who told you that. He never sees him anyway. The guy only calls when he wants a job done."

"What kind of jobs?" Mike asked.

"I was stupid enough to ask last night, "Jane cried as she pointed at her face. It's a good thing we're leaving. Gary won't know she's back. But keep that phone number, Mikey. You may need it."

---

Elyse and Max walked up the steep incline of the sidewalk toward the car.

"Max. Do you feel they know more than they were letting on?" Elyse said.

"Yeah. They were holding back something. I wish I would have gotten that girl's name," Max said.

"She was cute. Wasn't she?" Elyse playfully teased.

Max raised one eyebrow, a smile touching his eyes. He opened his mouth to reply and snapped it shut.

"Hmm. I thought so. You don't fool me, Max."

Max cleared his throat and looked at his watch. "We need to meet Donall and Elijah at the dock. We can come back after the bookstore opens."

Capt. Jack poured some coffee into a mug and handed it to Elyse. "Here you go, darling."

"Thank you. So, tell me. How often do you take this sailboat out into the bay?" Elyse asked.

"Never have," Capt. Jack replied. "I need a crew."

Elyse rolled her eyes. "You're as bad as Donall."

"Donall's boat might sink to the bottom of the bay," Max said with a chuckle.

"Oh, stop. He's been gone for what, five weeks. I'm sure he'll get it seaworthy in no time at all," Elyse replied.

"Speaking of, here they come," Capt. Jack said.

They looked up to see Donall and Elijah striding down the dock toward them.

Elyse's eyes lit up at the sight of her husband. He never ceased to titillate her senses and send shivers down her spine. Elijah jumped into the boat and pulled her into his arms, kissing her soundly.

"I'm going to go change," Donall said.

He returned a few minutes later dressed in blue jeans, a black tee-shirt, and black boots.

"How about a cup of coffee?" Capt. Jack offered to Donall and Elijah.

"Sure. Got any cream?" Donall asked.

"Elyse. You're closest. Would you mind getting the cream from the fridge and more coffee cups?" Capt. Jack said.

"No problem," she replied. Pushing the door open, she went inside.

Elyse looked around the neat galley kitchen. She spotted the tiny fridge tucked under the cupboard. Opening the fridge, she grabbed the cream and turned around. Some of Anablue's floral paintings graced the small ledge under the window. Next to the paintings, she spotted two framed photographs. One was a black and white headshot of a beautiful blonde woman. The other, Elyse, sucked in her breath. "Sweet Jesus."

Going over to the door, she opened it. Donall was leaning against the wall next to the door. She grabbed him by the arm and yanked him inside.

"I need his help," she stammered to the others.

Once inside, she practically dragged him over to the ledge and pointed at the picture.

Donall looked at the photo she pointed to. "Holy shit," he said. He picked it up, holding it in his hands. Donall and Elyse stared at each other in shock.

## CHAPTER 32

The photograph, the same one they had both previously seen, showed the same beautiful woman with the two tiny tots. The man who had been cut out of Anablue's copy of the photograph was a youthful Capt. Jack.

Donall slowly walked out of the galley with Elyse close behind. Once outside, he stared at Capt. Jack, looking back and forth between the photo and the man. He then handed it to Max, who looked at it and handed it to Elijah.

Capt. Jack, seeing the photo now held by Elijah, held his breath. He stared back into four sets of questioning eyes.

"Who are you?" Donall asked.

Capt. Jack reached out for the picture. Holding it in his hands, he gently stroked the woman with his fingertip.

"My name is Jackson Cross Baker. Her name was Mary,

my one true love. These two little twinkies are our children, Anablue and Brian. I don't know where to start.

"Why don't you start at the beginning," Max said.

"The beginning. I was five years her senior. I watched Mary grow up. She was our closest neighbor. Her parents owned a large ranch south of my parent's ranch, or what was left of it after my mother sold parts of it off to Mary's father after my father died. My brother, Michael, wasn't happy when parts of the ranch were sold. Something I didn't know until years later. Both of us joined the Navy after college. I left behind a little girl and returned on leave to find a beautiful woman grown in her place."

Capt. Jack, tears in his eyes, rose from his chair and turned to look at the bay. "She was perfect. The kind of woman who you could look into her eyes and see the sweetness to her gentle soul. We fell in love and would have married. She ended up pregnant. I was deployed again and didn't know. After a mishap at sea, the navy had me listed as missing in action. My brother swooped in to 'save the day.' Mary's parents forced her into the marriage, even though she didn't love him. They figured any husband was better than none. Her parents died in a fire a week after her wedding.

Michael was never interested in Mary. Come to find out, he only wanted her land. That of her fathers and ours. He never did his research to see that if she died, all the land would go to her children or the church if she had none. It would never be his.

About that time, Mary found out that I was alive and well and that Michael knew it all along. We were both devastated by the turn of events. Michael, in his rage, refused her a divorce. He didn't want her, but he didn't want me to have her, either. We were never close and didn't care for each other to begin with. My mother, of course, was aware of the rift between us. Mary left Michael and came home. This sweet young woman, married to one son, carried the child of her other son. Homeless, with nowhere to go, my mother took her in.

My mother was furious with Michael, and he with her for taking Mary in. They never spoke again after that. She was a very religious woman. I would come home when I could, sent money every month, but the neighbors were talking. I was there when our twins were born. That was a surprise," he said with a slight smile. "I named our daughter. Mary, our son.

After Mary got pregnant again and miscarried, my mother put a stop to my visits home. Mary was another man's wife, and I risked a dishonorable discharge for adultery.

This picture was taken on my last visit home. Mary slowly started slipping from reality, unable to deal with the lot life had cast on her. When Michael found out, as her legal husband, he had her committed to a sanitorium against our wishes. She never recovered. I used to go visit her. She eventually didn't know who I was, but I, I always knew who she was. My visits continued until eventually cancer took her from me.

Meanwhile, Michael was actively trying to buy parcels of

our former land from other ranchers. I started outbidding him. After our mother died, she bequeathed all of her remaining lands to Anablue and Brian.

Michael contested the will, and I'm still fighting to keep the house and seventy-five acres for Anablue. Between Mary's land, my mother's land, and what I own, all of which goes to Anablue. She will own a good portion of the valley, except for a few parcels Michael owns, the town itself, and some smaller ranches to the north. I do not know why Michael wants the land, but it's worth millions."

"Motive," Max whispered.

"Why did you not reach out to Anablue and Brian after Mary's death?" Elyse asked, wiping at the tears running down her face.

"I was able to with Brian. I spoke with him on the phone a few times and met with him before he shipped out. Anablue, thinking I was Michael, refused. My mother and Brian tried to explain everything. But, the stubborn child wouldn't listen," Capt. Jack said.

"Did Anablue ever know any of this?" Max asked.

"From what my son told me, no."

"What's in your mother's safe deposit box?" Max gently pried.

"I assume the usual. Jewelry, stocks, and bonds, deeds for her land," Capt. Jack replied.

Looking at Max, "Who are you in all of this?"

Max exchanged glances with Donall and Elijah. "I'm with

NIS. This is going to come as a shock to you, but we believe your brother Michael, Admiral Baker, is responsible for Brian's death. He's after Anablue, and most likely, he's after you as well."

"I should have put a bullet in him back when he stole my Mary from me," Capt. Jack snarled. "I have spent half my life in the shadows watching my children grow. Unable to claim them as my own. Now he's killed my boy, and he's after my little girl too?"

"Have you seen Anablue in the past few days?" Elyse asked.

"Isn't she at Edwards?" Capt. Jack asked, alarm written all over his face.

"How did you know she was at Edwards?" Max said.

"Mrs. Wang called me after she left. Told me the Navy recalled Anablue and that she had to report to Edwards. She asked me to take care of Bart for her. Asinine that they would recall a woman."

"Your brother, Admiral Baker, recalled her. We believe he's also responsible for attempts on her life."

"Do you know where she might hide?" Elyse asked, gently squeezing Capt. Jack's hand.

"Why wouldn't she come back here?"

Elyse and Donall exchanged looks. "Anablue is running… from me," Donall said.

"Why?"

"Anablue is going to have a baby. She doesn't know that I know. I think she may feel that she was standing in my way. Of what, I have no idea. I was also brought to Edwards. Specifically, to torment her on what she couldn't have.

We're both out now, and we can now be together. If I can find her, and if she'll have me," Donall said.

"She may have gone home," Capt. Jack said.

"She was here. She came to see me, but she wouldn't tell me where she was going," Elyse said.

"Where exactly is home?" Max asked.

"Just a few hours east of here," Capt. Jack replied. "How do you fit into all of this, Elijah?"

"Oh me? I've only met Anablue once. She thought I was Donall, with a wife and baby. Another reason she's running, I'm sure," he said as he massaged his nose.

"How do you know Mrs. Wang?" Max asked.

"Jun Wang is the cousin of our neighbors north of the ranch. A long time ago, she was Mary's nanny. She, and her husband, worked for Mary's parents. They lost their baby boy in the same fire that killed Mary's parents. They moved here afterward to start a new life. Anablue was sent here to Mrs. Wang's by those same neighbors. Just like Mrs. Wang told her to come to this dock to paint. So, we could all keep an eye on her. To keep her safe. Eventually, I planned on telling her who I was."

"I need to find her. She's been through more than...." A lump caught in Donall's throat. "I can't bear it, what's she's been through, thinking she's all alone. I'm going to get on my bike, and I'm going to go see if she went home."

"We'll keep looking for her here," Elijah said, placing his hand on Donall's shoulder. "Check in with us."

---

ANABLUE LOADED the last of her things into her trunk. She had found Brian's extra set of car keys in his room under his mattress, right where he always kept them. With her enormous set of keys in hand, she went inside the old barn looking for a place to hide them. Spotting an old milk jug, she lifted the lid and drop the ring of keys inside. She walked back to the house, wearing a simple blue sundress and her straw hat, her cowboy boots clicking on the creaky old floorboards of the back porch. She roamed the house for one last look. She laid down on her mother's twin bed. Thoughts of happier times with her mother filled her head as she ran her hands lovingly over the white chenille fabric of the bedspread. She glanced over at her matching bed, piled high with throw pillows and Gram's crocheted afghan blankets. Making her way to the hallway, she opened Brian's door, then to Gram's door to peer into the rooms before making her way to the front porch to sit and rock for one last time.

Lost in her memories of Donall, she was brought back to the present by footsteps and creaking floorboards from the side porch. Instantly on alert, she snuck her way around the other side of the house. Silently opening the back door, she slipped inside. Sneaking to the dining room window, she peered outside. Not seeing anything, she moved to the kitchen window. Brushing aside the white swag valance, she saw the moving shadow of a man. Dropping the curtain, she backed up into someone. Turning in terror, she screamed. "Gary."

"Hey, Anablue. How about a kiss?" he said as he grabbed her arms and pulled her in close. He laughed at her struggles as he held a rag soaked in chloroform over her mouth until she went limp in his arms.

## CHAPTER 33

"Marcus, you asshole. Get in here," Gary yelled.

Marcus came through the back door. "Man, what did you do to her?"

"Nothing yet. Here, take her and get her in the van. Tell Jane to use that rope and tie her up in the back. I'm going to look for those keys."

"I don't like this, Gary."

"Do as you're told, you pussy," Gary sneered. Both men looked up at the rumble of a motorcycle coming up the road in the distance. "Get her to the van now. Make sure it's out of sight. I'll be right out."

"It's that big dude, Corrington," Marcus cried as he slung Anablue over his shoulder and rushed out the back door, heading toward the backside of the pole barn.

Gary spotted a baseball bat standing by the back door. Hefting the bat with a smile, he went to hide.

Donall raced up the last stretch of the road, unable to contain his excitement at seeing her car parked in front of a huge pole barn. Parking the bike next to the car, he was off and running toward the house. He stopped on the back porch when he saw the back door wide open. His senses alerted. *Something was wrong.*

Her silly hat laid on the floor of the kitchen, badly crushed, its lone wildflower flattened like a pancake. Alarmed, his eyes darted around as he made his way stealthily through the house. He found her big purse, its contents dumped out on the floor of the front foyer. Room by room, he crept, looking for a sign of Anablue. Coming through the dining room doorway, he didn't see the man with a baseball bat standing off to the side until he felt the bat slam into his head.

Gary stood over the motionless man on the floor. A sneer of satisfaction crossing his face. He dropped the baseball bat to the ground as he stepped over Donall. Knowing his time was limited, he did a rough search for the keys. Not finding anything, he left the house at a run. Climbing into the van, he looked back to see Anablue laying on the old mattress, her arms tied to a bar, and Jane sitting next to her.

"What are we going to do with her?" Marcus asked.

"We're going to have some fun, then find a cornfield somewhere," Gary said.

Gary pulled out from behind the pole barn. "Wait," he said. He got out of the van, yanked the distributor cap from Anablue's car, and slashed the tires with his knife. The last thing he did was to back up and crush Donall's motorcycle before he drove down the long road to hook up with the main road and head east.

"Woodstock, here we come." Gary gleefully cried as he lit a joint and cranked the music up on the radio.

Jane's eyes skimmed the interior of the van. She sat upon an old mattress. Tattered curtains, pulled open, lined the side and back windows. An old cooler filled with beer was tucked in behind the driver's seat. Her small suitcase sat in front of it, next to boxes of camping supplies and another cooler filled with food.

Looking down at the immobile woman lying next to her. *I have to do something.*

A large shard of glass glinted in the sunlight. She glanced up to the hole in the window, then to the rope tied around Anablue's wrists. Brushing the smaller shards off the mattress, she lifted the corner. Her hand brushed over the big rock she had found earlier. She tucked the piece of glass in next to the rock. Grabbing an old blanket, she covered Anablue up.

Glaring at Gary up in the front driver's seat. She had never hated him more than she did right now. Pulling another blanket up to cover herself, she laid down. Determined to protect Anablue in any way she could, knowing damn well she could end up face down in a cornfield right next to her. It was a risk she was willing to take.

---

Donall woke with a groan. His head pounded as he gingerly touched a lump on his head, his hand coming away bloody. Getting to his feet, he stumbled out the back door to the porch. Anablue's car was still out there, the hood up, the tires whistling air. He looked down the long road to see a yellow van turning onto the main road. His vision blurred as he tripped, collapsing on the porch.

Sometime after dawn, his eyes fluttered open. He ran for his bike, only to find it in a mangled heap. He let loose a string of profanity guaranteed to burn the ears off anyone who heard his cursing. Pulling his satchel and flute box from the heap, he ran to the car to see the damage there. Slashed tires, no distributor cap. Pulling open the pole barn doors, he strode inside to see what parts and tools were stored there. Knowing Anablue, he should find something. Searching the shelving, he found a new distributor cap but no spare tires.

Sick to his stomach, *Anablue is in the back of that van. Gary.*

*Bookstore Gary. That little brunette George said the admiral was talking to someone named Gary. I need a telephone, it's in the kitchen.*

Donall ran to the house. Calming his thoughts so he could speak coherently, he dialed Elijah's phone number.

---

Three hours. It would take that long for Elijah and Max to arrive. In a cold, hard rage, he had installed the new distributor cap in less than fifteen minutes. Once inside of the house, he cleaned up his head wound after finding the aspirin. Growing tired of pacing between the front door and the back door while he waited for Elijah, he picked up her silly hat from the kitchen floor. Lovingly pushing it back into shape, he straightened the blue ribbons before setting the hat on the kitchen table. Striding to the front foyer, he picked up her purse and stuffed everything back inside. Shaking his head in disbelief. Books, a bag of old jellybeans, lollypops, tools... really?

Picking up one of the books, recognizing the front cover and title, he chuckled. The same one he had caught her reading in the bookstore. *I've got time to kill. This might be amusing. I need to calm down. It won't do Anablue or me any good if I'm still worked up.*

Going out to the front porch to sit in a rocker where he had a good view of the road, he read. An hour later, he set the book down. "Holy shit!" He sighed and went inside to get a glass of ice water. He looked at his watch. Another hour or so, and they should be here. Sighing deeply, taking a sip, he picked the book up again. *I ought to pour this ice water down my pants.*

Another hour passed, and Donall looked up to see the red of Elijah's Camaro slowly creeping up the road.

Flying off the front porch, he raced to the back of the house to meet them.

---

Elijah cursed again as he watched the steam rising from the hood of his car.

"Elijah. Language. The baby can hear you," Elyse admonished.

"I know, but we just lost the radiator."

They pulled up in front of Donall, who stood with his hands, holding his head in disbelief. Elijah got out of the car and raised the hood.

"Are you fucking kidding me?" Donall said.

"We got hit by a rock just outside of town. It put a hole in the radiator," Elijah said.

"Now we're all stranded here. And Anablue is in the back of some psycho's van, heading God knows where," Donall cried.

"Actually, we know where they're heading," Elijah replied.

"Where?"

Elyse, holding the baby, and Max, with Soup, climbed out

of the car. "We got lucky. Remember Mike at the music store?" Elyse said.

"Not really, but go on," Donall replied.

"Mike's sister is Jane. Jane is married to Gary," Max piped in. "And, Gary is Admiral Baker's son from a prior relationship."

"No shit," Donall exclaimed. "Good to know, but where is this going?"

"I left Mike my phone number in case he saw Anablue. He called me this morning to tell me Jane had called from a gas station. They have Anablue, and this is where they are going," Elyse said as she handed Donall the flyer.

"We stopped to pick up the flyer from Mike," Elijah said.

Donall looked at the flyer. "New York. They're taking her to a music festival in New York?"

"Let's see if we can find a radiator inside the pole barn. Or something to plug that hole," Elijah said. "Donall, can you and Elyse go check that old horse barn?"

Elyse looked over to the barn. "It looks kind of spooky."

"Come on. I'll protect you from ghosts and ghoulies," Donall replied.

"It's more like bats and spiders," Elyse replied, with a slight shudder.

They opened the wide doors and walked into the barn. They looked at each other and smiled.

"Bingo," Donall said.

It was a car. They pulled the tarp off to look at their find. A blue Nineteen-Sixty-Five Volkswagen beetle.

"I knew it. This has to belong to Anablue," Donall said.

"Isn't it cute? It's one of those Lovebugs," Elyse replied. "Look, there are two more cars in here."

They pulled off the other tarps to discover a Ford Model-T, and the other was an old wagon.

"Unbelievable. I think this is a Model-T, one of the first cars ever built," Donall said.

Elyse stepped outside the barn to call Elijah and Max over to see their find. They trotted over to the barn. Stopping in the doorway.

"What did you find?" Elijah asked.

"A Lovebug, a Model-T, and a wagon," Elyse replied.

Donall opened the car door and sat inside, looking for keys, he dropped the visor, and the keys fell into his lap.

"Thank you, Anablue," he whispered as he started the car.

"So, we're going to drive three-thousand miles in that?" Elijah growled.

"Well, we have our choice. It's either this or the Model-T, " Elyse replied, mischief sparkling in her eyes. "Besides, didn't you see Herbie, the Love Bug, in the theatre on the Fourth of July?"

"Three fucking times," Elijah snarled. "You're enjoying this a little too much."

"I am grateful we found a car," Elyse replied.

"I suppose you're right. At least it doesn't have flowers painted all over it," Elijah replied as he opened the trunk.

"Hey Max, look at this. The engine is back here," Elijah said.

Max looked inside. "Heh, the trunk must be up in the front."

"I should go check the house. Make sure it's closed up," Elyse said. "Here. Take the baby. I'll be right back."

"Bring a shoe-horn and a can opener with you when you come back," Donall said.

"Why?" Elyse asked.

"A shoe-horn to jam us all in, and the can opener to get us the fuck out," Elijah replied.

"Oh my God, the two of you. It could be worse. You could both be pulling the wagon."

Crossing the back porch with the dog Soup on her heels, Elyse pushed the back door open. Stepping inside the spacious farm kitchen, Elyse admired the old-fashioned feel of the house. She spied Anablue's purse and hat sitting on the linoleum table. She grabbed them on the way to the hallway that led to the front foyer. Opening the front door, she stepped out onto the porch and fell instantly in love with the breath-taking view of rolling hills leading to the mountain range in the distance.

Spying a book on a side table, she walked over, picking the book up, she rolled her eyes at the title, spotting the glass full of un-melted ice. She bit her lip to contain her giggle. "Oh, this is priceless."

Heading back inside, she locked the front door, giving a

once over to the rest of the house. Pausing at a small writing desk to rip a piece of paper off a notepad. She placed it in the book to mark the page, then stuffed the book into Anablue's purse. She stopped to dump the glass in the sink and placed it on the counter. Pulling the back door shut, she made sure it was locked.

Walking across the yard, a devilish grin lit her face as she stopped in front of Donall.

"I marked your page for you. The book is in Anablue's purse," she whispered, giving him a wink.

A slight blush stained Donall's cheeks as he scowled at her. "Get in the car," he growled.

## CHAPTER 34

Coughing, Anablue opened her eyes. Her head pounded to the beat of the music playing on the radio. She tried to move her arms and looked to see they were tied above her head. Lifting her head, she stared into the swollen face of Jane. Wide-eyed panic filled her as Jane put her finger to her lips, nodding her head toward the front of the van. Pot smoke hung thick in the air as Marcus rolled down the passenger front window, providing some relief as the air in the van somewhat cleared.

Grateful for the fresh air flowing in the window, Anablue tried to clear her scrambled thoughts. *Where am I?* Looking toward the front of the van, she saw Marcus and the back of Gary's head.

*Oh my God! Gary and Marcus.* Memories of looking out the kitchen window then backing into Gary filled her head, and she closed her eyes in terror. Opening her eyes again, she stared into Janes. With a rough sign language, Jane laid her hands against her cheek. Jane was trying to tell her to pretend she still slept.

Slightly nodding her head that she understood, she looked again to her wrists bound tight with rope. Arms ached as she tried to shift slowly to relieve the pain. Closing her eyes in misery, she eventually fell back to sleep.

---

THE CAR SKIDDED to a stop in front of the roadside café. The car doors flung open, and Donall and Elijah practically fell out of the car in their haste to get out. Elijah pulled the seat back, taking the baby from Elyse. He held him a good foot out in front of him.

"Dude. Really?" Elijah said to Bunker. The baby stuck a quivering lower lip out.

"Awww. It's okay, buddy. Daddy's just kidding," Elijah said.

Elyse climbed out of the car, taking the baby from Elijah. "I'll get him cleaned up. You might want to help Max. He appears to be stuck."

Circling the front of the car, he stopped in front of Donall, who was still trying to catch his breath.

"Holy shit. Didn't know kids did that," Donall said.

Elijah chuckled. "Better get used to it. Your time is coming."

He patted Donall on the back. Still laughing, he went to the other side of the car to see Max still trying to unwind his legs and pour himself out of the car. Grabbing his arms, he gave a tug and pulled Max's long, lanky form from the backseat of the car.

Max laid on the ground, looking up at Elijah. "I deserve combat pay for this."

"Got kids, Max?"

"No. After this, I may stay a bachelor."

Elijah chuckled.

"I think I'll go stretch my legs, take your dog for a walk," Max said.

"Thanks. Appreciate it. Put him back in the car when you're done. I'll buy you both a cheeseburger," Elijah said as he pulled Max to his feet.

Donall and Elijah walked into the café. Eyeing the lunch counter and dismissing it, they chose a table in the back with an unobstructed view of the door. A young waitress appeared at the table with two glasses of water. She fluttered her eyelashes and smiled, pointing to the menu placed between the napkin holder and the condiments.

"I bet you two big boys are starving," she said.

Donall smiled at her. "We are. We have two more joining us."

"If we could get a highchair as well," Elijah asked.

She smiled and returned with the highchair. Max walked in and sat down, and Elyse and Bunker soon joined them. Placing the baby in the chair, Elyse eyed the three men.

She crinkled up her nose. "Are all three of you going to sit on that side of the table?"

Max, Donall, and Elijah looked at each other. They had all angled their chairs on the far side of the table, so no one had their back to the door. Max and Elijah rolled their eyes and adjusted their chairs to a more normal angle.

"Let's go over what we know," Max said as he looked at the menu.

"We know where they're heading," Donall said.

Elijah nodded. "We know we are at least a day behind them."

They paused when the waitress brought more water and took their orders.

"I can't stop thinking about Anablue and what she's going through," Elyse said. "I think we need to prepare ourselves to best help her when we find her."

Donall fiddled with his silverware, rising from his seat. "Excuse me," he whispered, leaving the table. He went outside. Elijah rose to go after his brother. Elyse placed a gentle hand on his arm. "Let me go," she said.

---

ELYSE FOUND Donall leaning against the building. Standing with his hands in his pockets, one foot braced against the wall. He looked up as she approached.

"Hey," Elyse said. Leaning against the wall next to him.

"I still can't get past the fact that I could have saved her," Donall said. He turned around and punched the wall.

"If I just would have seen that baseball bat coming."

Elyse flinched. "You can't blame yourself, Donall."

"I failed her. And now. Now, I don't know if she's dead or alive. Or what they've done to her."

"You didn't fail her. You are here, hunting for her, fighting for her. Anablue is strong. A lot stronger than you think."

"I know she is," Donall replied.

"You need to be strong as well. Whatever happens, it will be you who guides her through it."

"If she'll have me. You forget, she ran away from me."

"That's not true. She may have run, but it wasn't from you. She was scared. I've been in her place, pregnant, thinking you're all alone. I can assure you that all she wants is to be held in your arms. I have the utmost faith that she is alive and well. Chin up, Donall. She's waiting for you to find her."

Giving her a slight smile. "Come here and give me a hug."

Elyse sniffled, hugging him. "I'm sure Anablue would have a silly word for this."

Donall chuckled. "Guaranteed. Max started a funny word list. Let's go look at it."

"We need to get back on the road," Elyse grimaced. "The good thing is, it's my turn to drive."

"Oh, joy," Donall smirked.

"What's that supposed to mean?"

"I've heard how you drive."

"In my defense, I only have issues driving tanks," Elyse replied.

Donall rolled his eyes. "How my brother survives you is beyond me."

"I'm sure it's debatable that he's surviving," Elyse replied with a sassy smile.

STEPPING OFF THE CURB, Elyse walked toward the gas pumps where Donall and Max were gassing up the car. A blue van pulled up to the other side of the pumps. The doors opened, and four young people climbed out of the van. Hippies, one and all. Elyse looked them over, admiring the long blue floral skirt and short, frilly white shirt on one of the women. The other woman wore hip-hugger bellbottom jeans with a short pink tank top. Both women's necks were decorated with long chains with a peace sign and flowers in their hair. The men, long, straight, blonde hair draped over their shoulders. One wore blue jeans with a long kaftan shirt. The other, a brightly colored, tie-dyed tee-shirt with gold corduroy pants.

Looking to Donall, Elijah, and Max. All three could never blend in. They all looked a little too clean cut. As the hippies would say. "Square."

"Do you have a picture of Anablue?" she said to Donall as Elijah came up beside her.

"Yeah," Donall said, pulling the picture from his shirt pocket and handed it to her.

Elijah looked down at her feet. "You forgot something, brat."

"Damn. My shoes. I'll be right back," she said, handing the baby to Elijah.

She followed the girls inside to the powder room. Eavesdropping as the two chatted about Woodstock. Stopping the girls, she showed them the photograph. "Have you seen this girl? She's traveling to Woodstock in a yellow van. The van has a broken back window."

The girl wearing the long skirt stepped forward, looking at the picture. "No, haven't seen her. We're on our way there ourselves."

"You're going to have a hard time finding her. There's going to be many people showing up for the festival." The other girl said.

"Okay. Thanks. By the way, I can't help but admire your outfits. Where did you get them?" Elyse asked.

"A free store, you pay what you can. If you can't, it's free. Or, you can try a Goodwill or Salvation army."

Elyse nodded her head. "Thank you." Leaving the powder room, she stopped at the table, grabbed her shoes, and headed out the door. Walking toward her group, she smiled to herself.

*Next stop. Time to do a little shopping. The men are absolutely going to hate it.*

"Lie still. Don't struggle or make a sound," the firm male voice commanded. Anablue opened her eyes; excruciating pain in her arms hit her as she peered up into Marcus' fuzzy face. Jane's face came into view next to his.

"We're trying to help you, Anablue," Jane said.

"I need to go potty," Anablue whispered.

Jane and Marcus looked at each other and then up to the front passenger seat of the van.

"Gary is passed out," Marcus said. "I can carry you to the bushes. Jane will help you relieve yourself."

Anablue nodded, trying to clear her head of the fog. "Okay."

Marcus opened the side door and jumped out. Lifting Anablue into his arms, he carried her to the bushes on the edge of a roadside stop.

Once finished, she leaned heavily on Jane as they made their way, stumbling out to the parking lot.

Marcus lifted her again, carrying her back to the van. Putting her inside, he tied her back up.

"I'm sorry we have to do this. It's for your own protection," he said.

Jane put some pills into her mouth and coaxed her to take a sip of water. "We have to keep you drugged. Gary won't touch you if you're sleeping. Right now, he thinks he over-did it with the chloroform. He wants you awake and screaming," Jane whispered.

Anablue nodded her head. "Thank you… for helping me," she croaked out.

"Sleep now," Marcus said.

Anablue looked up to the stars in the sky through the van window. They twinkled and swirled through the milky way. A lone falling star shot across the night sky, and an old nursery rhyme came to mind.

*Star Light, Star Bright…*

*A sob caught in her throat. The stars, I want to lie under the Milky Way with Donall.*

*If I could only feel his touch again… I wish….*

In her mind's eye, she remembered the feel of lying next to him, her head resting on his broad chest. A lone tear slipped down her face.

She was vaguely aware of Jane laying down next to her, Marcus at her feet. Her eyes grew heavy and fluttered shut as she drifted off to sleep.

## CHAPTER 35

The testosterone hung thick in the air as Elyse faced off with three scowling men.

"We need to blend in," she ventured.

"You want us to go out in public, looking like peacocks," Donall growled.

"You can do this. It's only for a few days."

"Flower pants. You want me to wear fucking flower pants," Elijah snarled.

"If you don't. No one will talk to us, and we will never find Anablue." Elyse pointed at the changing rooms.

"Quit being such big babies. Now get in there and change your clothes."

Donall glared at her. Grimacing, he stomped into a changing room. Elijah and Max grumbled as they followed after Donall. Deep frowns furrowed their handsome brows.

Elyse covered her mouth to stifle her giggles. She looked at the sales clerk standing next to her.

"I saw that you have one of those new Polaroid Instamatic cameras by the cash register," she said.

"Yeah. It shoots the photos out right away," he replied. "It's pretty far-out."

"There's an extra twenty bucks for you if you can get a couple of pictures on the sly."

"You're kind of a little shit, aren't you?" the man replied.

"Absolutely," Elyse replied, flashing him a brilliant smile.

The grumbling from the changing rooms grew louder and was soon replaced by profanity-laced complaints.

"Gentlemen," Elyse said. Looking to Bunker, who played with a necklace at her feet. "The baby can hear you." An eerie quiet descended on the changing rooms.

"Don't be shy. Come on out. All of you."

The doors opened slowly. One by one, the men sullenly came out of the changing rooms. Pointing at each other, all three burst into laughter.

Elijah wore tan-colored pants covered with large orange and yellow flowers, with a brown suede sleeveless vest. Donall had red and white striped American flag pants, the pockets decorated with blue stars. A long, white, flowing shirt finished off his ensemble. Max wore paisley purple, blue, and white pants. His shirt was blue with a long flowing fringe that tapered from wrist to armpit, hanging down to mid-thigh.

Max raised his arms. "I look like a fucking bird with wings."

"Yeah, well, I look like Uncle Sam in a pirate shirt," Donall snarled.

"Better those than a flower power pants," Elijah grated out between clenched teeth.

Elyse bit her lip to keep from laughing out loud. "Hmm. You all look like hippies, but you need something else. Accessories. That's it."

Another sales clerk handed her some brightly colored bead necklaces. Taking one with a dangling peace sign, standing on her tippy toes, she placed it around Elijah's neck.

"Peace out. Baby," she whispered into his ear. "Now, the three of you need to find a hat to cover those military haircuts while I pick out an outfit for myself."

Elijah narrowed his eyes. "Max. Donall. I think it's only fair since she dressed us that we get to choose what she has to wear."

Knowing exactly where his mind went, Elyse's mouth dropped open. "You wouldn't dare."

Elijah smiled a slow, amiable smile. "Watch me," he said.

"I will not strut around a festival half-naked."

---

THE CASH REGISTER ka-chinged as the sales clerk rang up their purchases. Elyse smiled as she looked at her outfit. They had chosen somewhat decent outfits for her and Anablue. Long skirts with matching short tops. Bare-bellied, she self-consciously pulled the bright pink skirt up a bit to cover her barely discernable stretch marks. Elijah called them her love marks, stating she had earned them and should wear them with pride.

Elijah had found what she considered a veritable treasure. A baby backpack. Or, as Elijah called it, a baby rucksack. They could now carry Bunker on their backs. Donall discovered some old camping equipment, including a tent, while Max found a dozen new cloth diapers, a lifesaver as far as she was concerned.

The men carried their new purchases out to the car as she paid for the items, while Max headed down the street to meet someone.

The clerk winked as he slid two Instamatic photographs across the counter toward her. Grinning, she slid an extra twenty-dollar bill to him, tucking the pictures into her purse.

They waited outside while Max met a man on the corner. He had made a phone call at one of their last stops to set up the meeting. The man handed Max an envelope after laughing hysterically at his outfit. Max shot Elyse a glare from where he stood. But smiling, he pounded the man of the back, shook his hand, and walked back to where they waited for him.

Holding the envelope up. "VIP tickets, campsite included. Courtesy of Uncle Sam," Max said.

"I was wondering how we were going to get in," Donall said.

Fifteen miles out from their destination. Cars, converted school buses, and vans teeming with exuberant youth were stuck in bumper to bumper in traffic. A party-like atmosphere permeated the highway as they pulled up next to an old school bus. Billowing clouds of pot smoke poured from the bus, along with legs, feet, and various body parts. All hanging out open windows. One young woman, her bare breasts jiggling over bumps in the road, leaned out the window, catching the eyes of the men as she merrily waved to them.

"Eyes on the road, Elijah," Elyse snapped.

"I'm not driving," he replied, shaking his head with mirth.

"Whatever," Elyse replied, rolling her eyes.

Donall, driving the car, caught Elijah's eye. "Just what kind of festival is this?"

"Three days of peace and music," Max replied from the back seat.

"It's going to be interesting. Keep your eyes open for that yellow van," Donall said.

Three hours later, they pulled into the festival campgrounds. They chose a somewhat private spot within the wooded tree line, close to the lake. Elijah and Max set up the tent while Elyse, with the baby on her back, set up the camp.

Tying Soups' long leash to a tree. "Sorry, dude. You already ran off once. I can't let you run free here," Elyse said as she rubbed his belly. "Such a good boy. You did so well on your first road trip. Well, it's your second."

"When was his first?"

Elyse looked up to see Max standing above her. "Vietnam."

"Hell of a road trip."

Elyse nodded. "Yeah. It was. Except everywhere we went was by chopper, and people were shooting at us."

---

Donall stood at the edge of their campsite. Between him and the stage set up in the distance sat a gyrating sea of humanity. Multiple lighting and sound towers stood next to the stage. On stage, stagehands moved equipment into place for the band up next.

Elyse, Max, and Elijah came up to stand next to him. "Wow. Look at these hippies," Elyse said. "I've never seen so many in one place."

Donall rested his hands on his hips. "There's got to be two-hundred-thousand people here. Maybe more. How am I going to find her with these people?"

"It might be easier to look for the van first," Max said.

"Max and I will start by checking the campsites," Donall said.

"How do we even know they have a campsite?"

"My guess is, they're going to keep her hidden," Max said.

"Elyse and I will get a layout of the land. See where all amenities are located," Elijah said.

THE HORSE BLEW AND SNORTED, stomping his hooves as if anxious to be on his way. Then he softly nickered as Donall pet his neck, speaking low into its ear. Looking up at the mounted policeman, Donall smiled. "Nice animal you have here," he said.

"Thanks. Bart's getting a little excited with all these kids."

"Bart. Nice name. I know another Bart," Donall replied.

"A horse?" The policeman asked.

"Nah. A seal," Donall replied.

The policeman raised his brow in surprise. Max handed the man the picture of Anablue and flashed his badge. "We're looking for this girl. She was kidnapped in California, and we believe brought here by this man." He handed him a picture of Gary. "He is driving a yellow van. He has a dark-haired male accomplice that I couldn't get a photograph of, along with another woman named Jane, tall, with long brown hair who is also in danger."

Another mounted policeman joined them, and the first man handed him the photographs.

"Haven't seen them, but we'll be on the lookout. I don't know, so many hippies here, they're all looking alike," the second policeman said.

Donall stood with his hands on his head. Multiple campsites circling six hundred acres left a lot of ground to cover. He felt a little better knowing they now had law enforcement on the lookout for Anablue and the van. Max had given them the general vicinity of their campsite in case they came up with anything. Watching the horses trot away, he turned to Max.

"Where did you get a photo of Gary?"

"From the same guy who gave me the tickets," Max replied. "I was going to show you earlier, but I didn't want to cause additional alarm." He handed Donall the picture.

Donall sucked in his breath. "A mug shot?"

"Yeah."

"For what?"

"Running heroin from Mexico," Max replied.

"Why is this asshole not in jail?"

"He's on the run."

"If this guy's a pusher. Do you think he's pushing heroin here?"

"Nah. Not that it isn't possible. Mostly, these kids are pretty peaceful. They're more into grass and acid," Max said.

"I know. Been walking through clouds of smoke all day," Donall replied.

"Good thing is, undercover FBI agents could be here looking for heroin. We may have more help than we realize," Max said.

"Why won't they arrest these kids for the marijuana?"

Max rolled his eyes. "Don't think there's a jail big enough for two-hundred thousand hippies."

"Four. There's more pouring into the festival by the hour," Donall replied.

"Look over there. They're climbing the fences. Guess we didn't need tickets," Max chuckled.

"The lack of a ticket would not have stopped me from getting into this festival," Donall growled. "Or keep me from finding Anablue."

---

Averting her eyes for the second time, Elyse turned to Elijah. "They're naked. Not a stitch on some of them."

"Free spirits, my love," Elijah replied. "I guess you could have strutted around half-naked."

"Not funny," Elyse replied.

"How's Bunker doing back there?" Elijah asked, turning his back to Elyse.

Elyse tucked the blanket around the baby. "He's still out cold. He loves this."

"So is Soup. He's thrilled to be out of the car," Elijah said. Nodding to the dog on the leash.

"How are we ever going to find Anablue? This place is enormous. I'm desperately trying to stay positive for Donall, but I'm so frightened for her."

Elijah caressed her face, wiping at the tear rolling down her cheeks. "Have a little faith, my love. We will find her."

A buxom young woman strolled by. Topless, a garland of wildflowers in her hair, her bare breasts gleaming in the warm sunshine. Elijah's eyes widened, watching the woman until Elyse snapped her fingers in his face.

"Hey," Elyse growled.

"Oh. Sorry."

"You're playing with fire, Elijah."

"What. No, she just looked familiar. I think I went to high school with her."

"Ha." Elyse snorted. "She's at least ten years younger than you."

"You never know."

"Fine. Then maybe I went to high school with some of these naked men."

"You had a private tutor at the embassy."

"That doesn't mean some of them weren't in Vietnam."

"You're probably right. I'm betting a good chunk of the men here are vets."

"Better here listening to music with naked girls running around, then over there dodging bullets," Elyse whispered.

Elijah cupped her face. Gently kissing her lips. "You are all I need or want. I'm just not used to naked women running freely through festivals."

CHAPTER 36

Anablue turned her head, spitting the pills to the edge of the mattress. Using her chin, she pushed the pills down into the small but growing pile. Using her teeth, she gripped the blanket to cover up the pills. Understanding Jane and Marcus were trying to protect her, she could never escape if she didn't have a clear head. Looking out the window at the sky, the sun had set, twilight settled over the lush countryside. She could hear the music and voices of many people. After overhearing Jane, Marcus, and Gary talking, she was at a music festival. In New York. How many days have I been out of it? A movement beside her, the little dog was back again. He had been coming to visit from time to time. Curled up next to her knees, the dog gave her a forlorn look. Standing up and stretching. The dog licked her face and jumped out of the van.

Voices approached the outside of the van, recognizing them to be Gary and Marcus. She gave an involuntary shudder. Closing her eyes, she pretended to be asleep.

Gary glanced inside the van. "Why the fuck is that slut still sleeping?"

"You must have given her too much chloroform," Marcus replied.

"That was four days ago. How long does it take to wear off?"

"Who told you to use chloroform? Didn't they tell you how much to use?"

"My old man. Maybe I should try calling him," Gary said. "See what he has to say about it."

"We walked by the lines to use the payphones. They're super long."

"Once that joker shows up to collect his smack, then we can deal with Anablue. If that idiot Evans would have taken care of her at Edwards, I wouldn't have to be dealing with her and the shipment," Gary sneered. "By the time we roll out of here on Monday, the drugs will be delivered, and that slut will be floating face down in the lake."

"There's Jane." Marcus pointed toward Jane, walking into the campsite.

"It's about fucking time. Another stupid slut."

"She's been standing in line for cheeseburgers for hours," Marcus said. "She's got all that cooking stuff in the van. You should have let her cook something instead."

"Only damn thing she's good for. Getting me food and taking care of that other whore," Gary smirked.

---

REELING IN SHOCK. *Gary.... and Evans working together. Oh my God. He means to kill me.* Tipping her head back, Anablue looked out the hole in the back window before looking at the rope tied around her wrists. Scooting herself up a bit, using her teeth, she worked to loosen the knot at her wrists. *If I can get myself untied, Jane said there's a big rock and a piece of glass tucked under the mattress in the corner. Whoever threw that rock through the window... thank you. I may need it.*

---

A GENTLE MISTING rain fell as Donall removed his thrift store cowboy hat. Lifting his face to the heavens, he whispered a prayer. Wiping at his face, he unzipped the tent and climbed inside. Sighing deeply, he rolled himself up in a blanket in front of the doorway. Sometime after two o'clock in the morning, long after the music ended, Donall, unable to clear the worry from his heart, willed himself to sleep.

Donall woke to the camp coming to life. Rolling over, he encountered a warm lump that growled at him. Lifting his arm, Soup was curled up between him and the sleeping baby. The pup, in protective mode, scooted closer to the baby.

Shaking his head at how cute the two were, he covered them both up with the baby's blanket.

He looked around the tent. He couldn't believe they had somehow managed to fit everything here in the car. They had stuffed the trunk on the front of the car. Piling blankets from the thrift store and groceries from the small market in town into every nook and cranny inside the car. Max had called it creative packing. Climbing from the tent, he spotted Elyse sitting on a rock in front of the small bonfire. Catching her eye, he pulled the zipper down. She gave him the thumbs up.

"I don't want them escaping," she whispered.

"They appear to be inseparable," Donall said.

"Soup hasn't willingly left his side since the day Bunker was born. He usually sleeps under the crib at home when at least one of us isn't in the room. We couldn't leave him behind, and there was no way I was staying home. Speaking of sleeping, I put Anablue's purse and hat inside the tent. I caught Soup sleeping inside her hat last night. He smushed it a bit, but I pushed it back into shape."

"He probably smells her scent," Donall said. "Maybe I could use him to find Anablue."

"He's a Chihuahua mix, not a Bloodhound."

"You never know."

"He keeps running off. I caught him this morning dragging Anablue's hat into the woods behind us."

"Where's Elijah and Max?" Donall asked.

"They're searching for water. I wouldn't be surprised if they run out of food and water here. One of us may have to go to town for supplies," Elyse said. Looking up at the fast-moving clouds in the sky. "It's going to rain again. It might be a mud bath later."

"Can't believe so many of these kids slept right where they were sitting in the rain last night."

"They're resilient. And having fun," Elyse replied.

Donall rubbed at the stubble on his face.

"You should get cleaned up and eat before you go back out. I have coffee, eggs, and toast warming by the fire for you," Elyse said.

Donall grimaced.

Elyse rolled her eyes. "Don't worry. Max cooked breakfast. Said he didn't want to be poisoned so far from home."

Donall snorted.

"He's a smart-ass," Elyse said. "But adorable."

Donall chuckled. "Well. You're famous for your dancing, not your cooking."

"I can do it with supervision," Elyse said as she handed him his plate. "Eat up, me hearty."

"Arrrrg," Donall replied with a grin.

"Kind of goes with the pirate shirt," Elyse snickered.

"You picked it out on purpose, didn't you?" Donall growled.

"Absolutely."

Pushing the brush aside, Elijah and Max silently crept through the tall grass at the far edge of a campsite. A tall woman with long brown hair tended a campfire in front of a yellow van. A brown paisley shirt hung down to blue jean cut-offs. Her bare feet sloshed through the mud to lift a cooler lid, pulling a beer from the cooler next to the van. She leaned in, handing the beer inside. She spoke to someone inside the van. Turning around, she tossed a small log onto the fire. The smell of wood smoke and marijuana floated throughout the area. A man climbed from the van, taking the woman by the hand as he led her back to the van.

Elijah signaled to Max that he was going to the other side of the camp for a better look. Moving silently through the brush, he crawled into place. Standing up, he peeked into the side window. The couple and another woman were all locked in a lover's embrace.

Max crawled up to peer in the open door as Elijah came around the front of the van. No one else but the threesome was inside the van. The man looked up to see them standing in the doorway.

"Hey, man. Come on in. The more, the merrier," the man offered.

"Ah, no thanks. Wrong van," Max replied.

"Sorry for the intrusion," Elijah said.

"You're sure. They're both sweet and hot."

"Nah, we're good," Elijah said as they backed away from the door.

Looking at each other, they grinned. "Did we just get invited to an orgy?" Elijah asked.

"Takes free love to another level. Doesn't it?" Max chuckled.

"Yeah."

"Where did we leave the water and milk?" Max asked.

"Over there by those shrubs. Let's get the fuck out of here," Elijah replied with a grin.

PUSHED to the very back of the van. Anablue tried to scoot over. She laid beneath the back window. The incessant drip of rain from the hole in the window had finally stopped, leaving her soaked and shivering. Rolling thunder continued to rumble. The lightning flashed through ominous skies as the rain started again. Huge sheets of rain and tree branches driven by the wind scraped against the van. Anablue pulled the wet blanket further up her body with her teeth. Her body ached from the cold. The music, intermittent in the day's storms, had stopped completely. Stretching her legs, she did some leg lifts to keep the blood flowing. Her legs were strong, her arms not so much.

Jane came in to check on her. Gary loudly berated her from outside the van while pulling a backpack from the spare tire well.

Anablue surprising Jane whispered. "Untie me, Jane. We both know what he has planned for tonight, regardless if I'm awake or not. He's going to kill me. Untie me. Please. I beg you."

"He's leaving with Marcus to meet someone. As soon as they're gone, I'll untie you. I'm sure we can find somewhere to hide. Because he'll kill me too."

---

LIFTING his flute from its case. Dejection seeped through him. They had pounded the pavement today, or as Elyse had accurately predicted, sloshed through a mud bath. Soaking wet, covered in mud. Donall couldn't feel more hopeless. He had a vague memory of Elijah shoving a baloney sandwich and cup of milk into his hand to get him to eat.

Between music sets now. The crowd quiet. Putting his flute to his lips, he played for her; he prayed she heard him and didn't give up hope he would find her… somehow.

---

JANE WORKED to untie the knot. Giving up, she grabbed the chunk of glass, furiously sawing on the rope. She could hear Gary and Marcus loudly arguing as they walked toward the van.

"Hurry, Jane. They're coming," Anablue cried. One hand loose, she held the rope straight for Jane.

Jane cut through the last strand. Free now, Anablue

rubbed her wrists. She rolled to her knees, making for the door as she plowed into Gary.

Gary pushed her back into the van. She landed on her back as he jumped on her. Twisting and fighting to buck him off of her. Her hand felt the rock. Picking it up, she smashed it into his head, pushing him off of her. She made for the door again. Shoving a surprised Marcus out of her way, she ran for the woods. Tripping and stumbling over roots. Branches smacked her in the face as she pushed through the thick brush, falling in the mud.

Then, through the rain and wind, she heard the music of a flute. Moon river… Could it be? Donall…

Stopping where she was, she screamed, "Donall… Donall." Over and over again, turning in circles, she screamed his name.

## CHAPTER 37

Donall stopped. Looking up at Elijah and Max, the shock was written all over their faces. They heard it too. Jumping to his feet, Donall turned. Listening there, again. His name. He pounded through the thick woods right behind their campsite. The more frantic the cries, the faster he moved toward them.

She was on the move again, running through the woods, screaming and crying his name. He spotted her through the trees, running her down. He caught her from behind. Rolling to the ground, she fought him, twisting and turning till she faced him, sitting on his lap. Weak arms pummeled his chest.

"Anablue. It's me," he cried. Pulling her to his chest. It's me, Baby Blue, it's me."

She pulled back, looking up at his face. "Donall? It's you. Sweet Jesus."

He cupped her face. Tears rolled down both their faces. They clung to each other as they cried.

"He was going to kill me," she cried.

"You're safe, sweetheart. You're safe."

---

Running footsteps sounded in front of Donall and Anablue as Elijah and Max flew over the two, taking the man coming up behind them to the ground. Elijah pulled back his fist to pummel the man.

"Hold. Hold on." The man, lying on the ground, held his hands up in surrender. "FBI. Look in my wallet, man."

Max pulled the wallet from the man's back pocket. Looking at the ID. "Jonathan Marcus Sanders. Special agent," Max said.

"We would never let him hurt her," Marcus said.

"We?" Elijah said as he looked up to see two other shadowy figures fade into the trees.

Another movement in the brush, and Elyse stood behind Donall and Anablue. The baby, snug on her back, sound asleep, Soup, next to her. Elijah held out his hand for his wife, and she took it. Watching the couple on the ground, the tears rolled down her cheeks as Elijah gave her hand a little squeeze.

Donall stood, lifting Anablue into his arms. He strode through the woods toward their campsite.

"Maybe we should give them a little privacy," Elyse said.

"I'm sure you have questions. Why don't you come over to our campsite?" Marcus said.

Elijah and Max looked at each other, nodding their heads. Elijah draped his arm around Elyse's waist, careful not to disturb the baby. They followed Marcus.

"That kid of yours, Corrington. He can sleep through anything," Max said.

Elijah chuckled. "Just like his mother used to be."

"What happened?" Max asked.

"I had a baby," Elyse giggled. "Now I wake up if he breathes funny."

Breaking through the woods to the other campsite. Max and Elijah looked around. "Un-fucking-believable," Max said.

"She was right behind us the whole time," Elijah said.

Surrounded by three men, Gary sat on the ground, his hands tied behind his back. His head, bloody with an egg size lump.

Spotting Marcus, he snarled. "A pig. You're a fucking pig."

"We'll take care of this one. We caught his contact with the backpack of heroin right outside the gate."

"He was running drugs?" Max asked.

"Yeah. Drug running, kidnapping, conspiracy to commit murder, amongst other crimes. He's going away for a very long time," Marcus replied.

"And Admiral Baker?" Max asked.

"Along with Evans, he's a co-conspirator. I've been working undercover on this drug case for over a year. We kind of stumbled into this whole thing with Anablue. I tried reaching out to you down at Edwards, but you were off base."

"So, you're the secret informant. I'm sure our two agencies can work together to combine our cases," Max said.

"Let me get this dirt ball out of here. I'd rather keep this festival peaceful. I don't want five-hundred-thousand hippies freaking out over a drug bust. Though, I am disappointed that I'll be missing Jimi Hendrix," Marcus said. "Oh. Jane's over there. She's a bit shaken up."

"Peace out, man. I'll be in touch, Max." Marcus gave them the peace sign, pulling Gary to his feet. The five men disappeared into the night.

---

ELYSE TURNED to look at the young woman sitting on the ground. Her arms wrapped around her knees, shaking with cold.

"The poor thing," Elyse exclaimed. Going over to her, she sat next to her and wrapped her arms around the woman, who laid her head on her shoulder and cried.

"It's alright. It's over," Elyse whispered to her.

After a few minutes, Jane raised her head. "How's Anablue?"

"She's with Donall now."

"We kept Gary away from her. I still can't believe Marcus was a cop."

"We are all grateful for what you both did for her," Elyse said.

The campfire sputtered, and Bunker raised his little head. Giving Jane a curious stare, his face split into a grin.

"Your baby is awake."

Pulling the pack off her back. "This is Bunker. Bunker, this is Jane."

"And who is this?" Jane asked. Petting the little dog who had climbed into her lap.

"That's Soup. Bunker's partner in crime."

"He's been coming to visit Anablue every day we've been here."

"Say what?"

"Your dog. He's been over here a few times a day."

Elyse looked at the dog. "You could have told me."

---

STIRRING THE COALS, Donall added more wood to the campfire. Holding her close, she shivered uncontrollably.

"I need to get you out of these wet clothes," Donall said.

He set her down to sit on the rock. Opening the tent, he pulled a blanket out. Draping it around her shoulders, he went to pull her dress off over her head. Her cries of pain stopped him.

"What? What hurts?"

"My arms, shoulders."

He knelt in front of her. "Let's try pulling it off this way.

Stand up." He slid the straps off her shoulders and shimmied them down over her breasts and waist, over her curvy hips. "Lean into me. Don't use your arms, just lean."

She stood and leaned into him. "Yes, sir," she whispered.

"No. I'm not your superior anymore. It's just Donall," he said, flinging her dress away.

"With two L's?"

He inhaled sharply, pulling her in to wrap his arms around her. "With as many L's as you want." He squeezed his eyes shut to stop the burning tears.

She pulled away. "I love you," she said, as she lovingly stroked his cheek.

"I love you too."

"How did you know where I was?"

"I followed you from your ranch," Donall said. "I would follow you through the heavens above to save you. You are my pilot, co-pilot, best friend, and lover. You are everything to me. I want to build a life with you. I want you as my wife. And our baby."

The tears rolled down her face. "You know about our little bean?"

"Bean?" Donall said.

"It's the size of a bean."

Donall chuckled, pulling her closer. "Then Bean it is."

"Wait. You're flying? What about your dreams?" she asked.

"Since the day I met you. You have been my dream. Marry me, Anablue."

"You're sure? I'm a dork. I have two left feet. I listen to Christmas music year-round. I love roller derby and fast cars. I'm a bit of a flibbertigibbet."

"That's codswallop. I love you, no matter what."

"Codswallop," she giggled. "You got it right. The answer is.... yes."

His lips descended on hers. Soft, then urgent, he plied her mouth like a man long denied.

Eventually, she pulled away. "Not to put a damper on this moment, but I stink. I don't know how long it's been since I've had a bath.

Donall looked around. "Hmm. The air is a little chilly, but the water should be warm."

Reaching inside the tent, he grabbed the soap and shampoo. Taking her by the hand, he led her the short distance to the lake.

A COOL CLEANSING breeze blew through her hair as Anablue stood on the shoreline, looking at the lake. Tightly gripping the blanket around her shoulders, she questioned her sanity.

"The water is black. How are we going to see what's swimming around us?" she asked.

"It's freshwater. Just little fishes."

"You're sure about this? Remember, I can't swim."

"I'll be right there with you," Donall said, stripping off his shirt and pants.

Reaching out his hand to her, she dropped the blanket and trustingly placed her hand in his. Together they entered the lake.

Chest deep in the chilly water, she clung to him.

"Lean back and get your hair wet," Donall instructed.

Leaning backward, she wet her hair. "Now turn around," he said.

Shivering with cold, clutching the bottle of shampoo and bar of soap to her breast, she closed her eyes to feel the sensation of him lathering her hair. Her body came alive at his touch. Forgetting the cold, a deep burning need warmed her, engulfing her senses.

"Rinse your hair," he groaned in her ear, sending shivers of delight coursing through her body. She obeyed.

Taking the washcloth and soap from her hands, he unhooked her bra, letting it float away. Washing her back, her neck, the washcloth slipped around the front. She leaned into him, his ragged breath in her ear. His erection was hard and throbbing against her backside. Washcloth abandoned. His hands roamed her breasts and smooth belly. She snatched up the washcloth before it floated away.

Pulling away from him. "My turn," she said breathlessly. "Turn around."

She plied the soapy washcloth to his back. Feeling the ridges and scars, her hand brushed against his stitches.

"You still have the stitches in."

"I completely forgot about them," he replied, turning to capture her in his arms again.

She waved a finger under his nose. "Still my turn." She washed his chest, lightly placing kisses as his hands roamed her hips and backside. Gripping her hips, he pulled her in hard against him.

The whoop, whoop, whoop sound of a chopper filled the night as they looked up to see an Army helicopter flying in. Its spotlight shining on the lake, then directly on them where it paused. Then the light pointed toward the shoreline, shining brightly on numerous couples spread along the shoreline locked in lovers embraces.

Eyes wide and scandalized, clutching the washcloth to her chest to cover herself.

"Where the hell are we?"

Donall chuckled. "Welcome to Woodstock."

As Janice Joplin took the stage, thankful for the cover of darkness, they stumbled from the lake, laughing the whole way. He had brought her back to the tent, rolled her up like a burrito in a new blanket. Her eyelids were already heavy as he curled up by her side, pulling her into his arms. She drifted off to sleep.

ELIJAH AND MAX, lounging in front of Jane's campfire, both stood up at the familiar sound of the Huey helicopter flying low across the lake. Rigid, lost in their memories, they stared into the night sky. Elyse stood up, turning to look at the lake. Her memories triggered. She turned back to look at the men.

Both had the echo of battles won and lost, playing across their faces. She walked around the campfire, placing her hand in Elijah's. He looked down at her. She stared into his eyes until he pulled her into his arms. He sighed deeply, holding her tightly until his racing heart returned to normal. Elyse reached out to Max, still lost in his thoughts, and took his hand. Shaking himself, Max looked at Elyse and Elijah.

"Funny how you never forget the sound of a Huey," Max said.

"It fills my nightmares," Elijah replied.

"Yeah. Mine too," Max said.

"What's it doing here?" Elyse asked.

"Looks like a dust-off. Medi-vac chopper," Elijah replied.

Elijah tossed another chunk of wood on the fire. Looking over to Bunker, sound asleep in Jane's arms. "Elyse, we're going back to the tent in fifteen minutes."

"I guess I'll be sleeping in the car," Max chuckled.

"You can sleep in the van with me. There's plenty of room," Jane replied, her voice trailing off in embarrassment. "I mean, not together. You can sleep on one side, and I'll sleep on the other."

## CHAPTER 38

Opening her eyes, Anablue stared into Donall's face. Sound asleep, a lock of dark hair dangled over his forehead. She was tempted to brush it off his face, but didn't want to wake him.

A sound from the other side of her, and she rolled over. Donall again? Confusion filled her. When the man laying behind her hand touched her, softly stroking her belly before settling to rest on her hip, she inhaled sharply. Brushing the hand off, she sat up.

She looked to the right to the Donall she woke up to, then to the left, another Donall. Turning, she scooted on her bum to the front of the tent, clutching the blanket around her. Both Donall's sat up and looked at her. Looking back and forth between the two, she was speechless.

"Anablue. It's alright," the real Donall said.

Elyse sat up then, holding the baby close. Anablue looked at Elyse, the baby, and between the identical men.

"Holy shit," Anablue cried. Reaching behind her, she fumbled for the zipper. Pulling it up, she scrambled from the tent in sheer panic.

---

"Damn," Donall said.

"I take it you never told her you had a twin?" Elijah said.

"Evidently, not," Donall replied.

Climbing from the tent, Donall looked around. She stood staring at the smoldering fire pit, lost in thought.

"What kind of a woman am I, Donall? That I forgot that I thought I was in love with another woman's husband. My best friend's husband, at that. Even last night in the lake, I was so happy that you found me. I completely spaced it," she whispered.

"The fault is mine that I didn't tell you I had a twin. I'm sorry," Donall said. "I could have saved you a lot of pain and anguish."

"So, whose nose did I bloody?"

"Elijah's."

"Elijah, that's his name? Elyse is his wife? And Bunker is theirs?"

"Yes."

She turned to face him as the tears ran down her face. "Oh, God. I'm so relieved. Will, you hold me… please?"

He strode over to her; she opened the blanket for him. Wrapping her in his embrace, he held her tight.

Placing soft kisses on the top of her head. "You okay?"

"I am now," came her soft reply.

Donall glanced up as Elijah climbed from the tent. Elyse handed him out the baby and climbed out herself with a helping hand.

Donall tried to pull away from Anablue. She squirmed and held on tighter.

"Don't you dare move! I'm practically naked under this blanket, and you are poking my belly with your..." Anablue said.

Donall's eyes danced with amusement as he caught Elijah's eye. Nodding his head as if to say, "please leave."

"Let's see if Max is up and go find some breakfast?" Elijah said, pointing behind the tent toward the other campsite.

"I put some clean clothes out for you, Anablue," Elyse giggled. "Not that you're going to need them for a while."

Donall scooped Anablue up to squeals of laughter and carried her into the tent.

---

Elyse bit her lip in amusement as a moment later, Donall handed Soup out the door. Taking the pup from his hands, she followed Elijah through the woods to the other campsite.

Coming through the tree line, she found Jane and Max glaring at each other in a stand-off on either side of the fire pit. Jane pointed her spoon at Max. Whatever she was going to say died on her lips when she spotted them.

Looking between the two combatants, Elyse caught Elijah's eye. He shrugged in response to her unspoken questions.

"Good morning," Elyse said.

"What's so good about it?" Jane and Max both snarled.

Elyse, wide-eyed, looked at Elijah. "Oh, um. Well then, how about just morning, and well forget the good part?"

"What happened?" Elijah asked.

"What happened. I'll tell you what happened," Max cried. "She rolled into me in the middle of the night. I woke up to a warm woman snuggled into me."

"Ha!" Jane said, her voice dripping with sarcasm.

"I already told you. I'm sorry. But, you rolled into me, not vice versa. I didn't touch you," Max said.

"What do you call that poking me in the backside?" Jane hissed.

"I'm a man. It was a perfectly normal reaction to a beautiful woman. Besides, I don't go after married women."

"I'll be taking care of that once I get back to San Francisco. Find a job and a new place to live. Then I'm filing for a divorce," Jane said.

"No kidding?" Max said, a smile playing across his face. Max took a drag of his cigarette. Jane used her spoon to wave the cloud of smoke away. "Get rid of that nasty thing."

"Fine." He threw his cigarette in the firepit. "I planned on quitting, anyway."

Elyse and Elijah made to rise. "Maybe we should go for a walk," Elijah said.

"Sit down," Jane commanded.

"We made breakfast," Max growled, handing them their plates.

"Ah. The thrill of the chase," Elijah murmured under his breath. Winking at Elyse, he ate.

Taking a bite, she rolled her eyes in appreciation. "This is yummy. What is it?"

"Fried potatoes," Elijah said. "Where did you get the potatoes?"

"Up at the information booth. The town folk are donating food to help feed everyone," Max said.

"We got some milk, eggs, the potatoes, and a few other supplies," Jane said. "Enough for me to make some good meals."

"You like to cook? And you like kids?" Elyse ventured, giving a sideways glance to Elijah.

"I love both," Jane said, taking Bunker from Elijah. "Come on, sweetie, I made something special for you."

Elyse and Elijah exchanged looks. "She loves kids," Elyse whispered.

"She loves to cook," Elijah replied."

"She needs a job," Elyse said.

"Where's Donall and Anablue?" Max asked.

Amusement danced in her eyes. "Umm. They're busy," Elyse replied.

Sitting on her knees, Anablue watched as Donall handed the dog outside of the tent. "Whose little dog is that?"

"Elyse's," Donall replied.

"He came to visit me a few times," she said.

"He did? I guess we should have been paying attention to what Soup was trying to tell us all along," Donall said. "Enough of the dog. Come here."

Anablue walked on her knees, stopping in front of him. Her eyes held his, and she dropped her blanket. His gaze dropped to her body, and she felt his eyes caressing and roaming over each curve and valley. He reached out to touch her hair, fingering the soft shoulder-length curls. Running his finger down her jawline, his thumb traced the outline of her full, pink lips.

Eyelashes fluttered as she leaned her head back to feel his finger softly trace her neck. A soft sigh escaped her when his fingers stopped at her frantically beating pulse.

"I have dreamt of this moment, over and over. To touch you again, your lips and hair," he said, his voice a velvety murmur as he placed light kisses on her neck, then buried his face in her shoulder. He grasped her tightly to him. She ran her fingers through his hair, across his wide shoulders, then pulling back to gently cup his face.

She planted soft, fluttery kisses on his jawline while his hands left a trail of shivers down her back. He gripped her bottom, lifting and pulling her up tight against his erection.

His lips found hers, plundering her mouth in a fiery frenzy. Gently easing her back on the pile of blankets, her thighs trembled as he pushed them apart with his thighs. Finding a taut pink peak, his tongue flicked and teased as she arched her back to feel more. Running her hands up and down his muscular arms, her fingers lightly trailed across his chest and down to stroke lower on his furry belly.

One swift tug and her panties fell away, his boxers soon followed. His mouth covered hers when her cries of passion filled the tent.

Laying on her tummy, Donall ran his hand down her back to gently squeeze her bum. She opened one eye to look at him.

"You make me feel so loved," she breathed.

Donall smiled. Placing a light kiss on her shoulder. "What's not to love."

"I'm starving. I don't know when I last had something to eat," she whispered.

"You are? Well, let's go take care of that," Donall said, brushing her hair from her eyes. "I could eat a horse myself."

Bunker squealed in delight as Elijah held him up over his head, blowing raspberries against his round belly. He looked over to see Donall standing in the tree line. Standing slightly behind him was Anablue. Elijah's gaze swept the tiny woman, understanding his brother's attraction to the woman. She was beautiful. Soft blonde curls fell to her shoulders, porcelain skin, full pink lips, and the bluest eyes he'd ever seen. She wore a white mid-riff shirt. Bare-bellied, her red peasant skirt hugged her curvy hips. The flounce of the skirt fell mid-calf, barefoot. She was the perfect picture of a flower child. He caught Donall's eye and nodded his approval.

Donall looked down at the woman at his side. Squeezing her hand, he led her to the firepit, where Jane had strewn a blanket on the grass. Urging her to sit. He put a finger to his lips. Sneaking up behind Elyse, he scooped her up and tossed her up into the air while swinging her around, eliciting a small scream from her.

"Donall, you big lug. Put me down," she demanded. He put her down, and she hugged him. Looking past him to Anablue on the blanket.

"Anablue." Elyse rushed to her side, enfolding her in an embrace. The women alternated between crying and laughing. Anablue looked up and called Jane over, and the three clung together, laughing and all talking at once.

Donall, Elijah, and Max stood watching the women.

"Aunt Meg would have killed me for saying this, but it's like a fucking hen house," Elijah said.

The three women rose together. Still chatting, they headed for the woods.

"Where are you ladies going?" Donall called out.

"The biffy," Anablue said.

Max grinned, reaching for his shirt pocket. He grimaced, not finding a pocket, then reached into his pants pocket as he pulled out his notebook and pen.

"You still keeping a list?" Donall asked.

"Yeah. Now someone tell me why chicks always go to the bathroom together. I mean, what do they do? Chat while they pee?" Max asked.

"No idea. Did no one ever tell you two that women don't come with SOP's" Elijah said, "And neither do these?" Swinging Bunker up to throw him a foot up into the air, the baby squealed in delight. "But, your mama is the best. She drives me crazy. She's a perfect wife and mother, a brilliant ballerina, who can still kick ass... she just can't cook." Nuzzling the baby's belly. "That's your mama, alright."

"Speaking of. Anablue is starving. I'd also like to know what happened last night with Gary and Marcus," Donall said.

"Gary is on his way to life in prison. Marcus and a few of his friends hauled him away. Marcus was an undercover FBI agent." Max said.

"No shit," Donall replied.

## CHAPTER 39

The calm of the lake was in direct conflict with Anablue's inner turmoil. Standing on the shore, she played back in her mind everything that Donall and Max had patiently told her. It was funny in a way that they knew more about who she was than she did. Capt. Jack? Never in her wildest dreams would she have thought he was her true father. And her mother? A sob tore through her. Understanding now, her slip from sanity. Picking up a smooth flat rock, she skipped it along the water, watching in satisfaction as it bounced eight times before sinking in the lake. *Ha! Beat that one, Brian.* It had been Brian who taught her to skips rocks. She missed those lazy summer days when he had coaxed her out from under the hood of a car to spend time down on the river in open competition.

Sinking to her knees, the water gently lapping around her. She wrapped her arms around herself, and she grieved. For the first time, not for herself, but for her mother, love lost, driving her to madness, for Gram, unable to have her sons reconcile and know the joy of her whole family surrounding her. For Brian, taken in the spring of his youth, he would never grow old. Even Capt. Jack and Donall had suffered.

Her guilt weighed heavy that she had been stubborn, not giving them the time to listen. Understanding now what they were trying to tell her and that life dealt harsh lessons. No longer feeling alone, she had Donall, little bean, and now, Capt. Jack. Not to forget, Donall's family, Elyse, and the many friends who had helped along the way. Rinsing her face with the cool lake water, she rose to her feet. Turning, Donall was up on the hill, watching and giving her time to sort it all out. She knew it wasn't going to happen in a day or an hour, but she had hope. Placing her hand on her belly,

"We're going to be okay, Bean," she whispered.

CHUCKING HIS APPLE CORE, Donall had an unobstructed view of Anablue down by the lake. His heart aching. He could feel her grief from here. He wanted nothing more than to hold her in his arms, but she needed to be alone. Picking a blade of grass, he put it to his lips and blew, making a funny horn sound. *Shit. I haven't done that since I was a kid.* He had more to tell her. It didn't seem fair to dump it on her all at once. He looked over as Elijah sat down.

"How's she doing?" Elijah asked.

"I'm not sure. It was a lot of information to process," Donall replied.

"How old is she?"

"Twenty-three," Donall said.

"So young. Do you remember us at that age?" Elijah asked.

"Shit. I barely remember how old we are now. Let alone what we were up to at twenty-three."

After a moment's thought, Elijah said. "I think the end of this week we'll be twenty-eight. Elyse's birthday as well. But I digress. Keep your line of communication open. Tell her what you can about your time in Nam. I know for myself, even with Elyse being there for a good chunk of it. I've never told her all, and I never will. Every man deals with it differently. Where you might have it easier is that she's a Navy vet. Though, truthfully, I can't picture that tiny pepper pot working on jet engines."

"She's amazing. Never thought I'd fall so hard," Donall replied. "Especially for a mechanic."

"None of us do," Elijah replied. "Oh. Check yourself and Anablue for wood ticks. I had to chase Elyse down and pick one off of her ass," Elijah chuckled. "She's still traumatized."

---

Lifting her wet skirt above her knees, Anablue eyed the hill leading up from the lake. Spotting Donall near the top, she started the climb. Halfway up, she paused for a breath. Her legs ached from the effort, assuming it was from lack of use for five days. Rubbing the ache out, she continued the climb. Thoughts of Capt. Jack. entered her mind. *What am I supposed to call him?* Joe Cocker crooned from the stage as the wind picked up, blowing her hair. A light rain fell from the ominous, rolling dark clouds above. The wind picked up, whipping her hair and skirt, and the sky opened up, pelting her with sheets of rain blocking her vision.

Donall's arm wrapped around her waist, pulling her close, guiding her the remaining distance up the hill. Gaining the top of the hill, people dashed by on their way to whatever shelter they could find. Thunder crashed around them while lightning lit the dark afternoon sky.

Anablue stopped to look at the sea of humanity spread out before them. Some sat right through the rain, taking what cover they could under blankets and tarps. Watching the bustle of activity from the stage as stagehands rushed to cover equipment from the rain, amidst the announcers call for people to get down and move away from the towers.

Turning to Donall, she reached up on her tippy toes and pulled him in for a kiss. Rolling thunder clapped above them, and Donall grabbed her hand, pulling her along. They ran until they reached the campsite.

---

ELIJAH AND MAX had moved the tent next to Jane's van. Combining the two campsites to the more private location earlier that day. The van's side door was opened with all inside seeking protection from the torrential downpour. Music played from Elyse's transistor radio while Max, up in the passenger seat, sat with his long legs stretched out over the center console. Elijah, Elyse, and Jane were comfortably lounging in the back of the van, the baby with his toys spread out around him, lay on his back gnawing on a favorite toy.

Donall made to lift Anablue into the van, spotting the rope dangling from the bar. She pulled back as panic overtook her.

"No. I can't. No, please."

She clung to him, burying her face in his chest. Cupping her chin, he looked into her wild eyes. "Anablue. It's alright. You don't have to go in."

Pulling her tightly to him, he held her trembling body. Donall looked up to see what was inside the van that frightened her so much. Spotting the rope, he made eye contact with Elijah, nodding to the rope. Elijah yanked the rope off the bar and tossed it out the driver's side window.

Holding her close, he had to think of some way to distract her from her fear. The music from the van floated ever so gently to surround them. *Love is Blue, perfect.*

"Dance with me," Donall whispered.

"In the rain?" she whispered back.

Slowly moving, he guided her through the steps of the dance, his hand firm on her back.

"Do you remember, Baby Blue? On the dock, our first date. We danced."

"Grilled cheese," she replied.

"And dill pickles," he said, spinning her around.

"And Bart."

"Our first kiss," he said, lightly trailing kisses on her lips. "Each kiss is as sweet as the first."

"Now, it's you, and me….and Bean."

Donall chuckled, "Yes, and Bean. I love you, Anablue, and our little Bean."

The song ended, and another started. Donall called out to the others in the van.

"Get out here. Dance with us."

With a glance at the now sleeping baby, Elijah grabbed Elyse's hand and pulled her from the van to dance. Jane jumped out, opened the passenger front door, and yanked a surprised Max out. They danced through the rain, spinning around the sputtering campfire.

Once the rain stopped, they packed up the baby and headed over to people watch and enjoy the last night of the festival.

Elyse and Anablue spread a blanket out on a grassy spot to avoid the mud and puddles. Behind them ran a river of mud, the masses passing through compounded the mess, and before their eyes, it became a mud fest. People slipping and sliding, some falling on the slight incline until it became a game of who could slide the furthest. Hooten and hollering, they stood on the sidelines cheering on each competitor.

Donall turned to Elijah. "Come on. Let's go. You and me, bro."

"I've never been one to back down from a challenge," Elijah said. "Alright, bro. You're on."

Both pulled their shirts and boots off. Donall handed his shirt to Anablue.

"Hold this while I kick my brother's ass."

Anablue rolled her eyes. "You know, you're both crazy."

Anablue watched as Donall and Elijah stood in line, waiting their turn. Up next, they flexed their muscles, pumping themselves up. Then they'd lean on each other and those around them, laughing hysterically. All around them floated clouds of smoke from people smoking grass.

"They're acting kind of strange. They're almost giggly," Anablue said.

"Oh shit. I think they've been waiting their turn for too long," Elyse replied.

"You mean, they're stoned?" Anablue said with a laugh.

"This should be interesting," Max chuckled.

"They're up now," Anablue said as a man slid by.

Elijah and Donall stood at the top, both ready. The signal was given, and they pounded down the hill, jumping. They landed on their stomachs and slid, neck in neck, down the slippery slope. Mud and rainwater sloshed as they slid faster and faster, coming to a halt in a mud pit. Standing up, they whooped, pounding on their chests. They wrestled, twisting and landing to roll in the mud, each trying to gain the advantage over the other.

"What are they doing?" Elyse said, handing the baby to Jane.

"We have to stop them," Anablue cried, rushing out to stop the wrestling match. Elyse, right behind her.

"Donall. Elijah. Stop." Both men were covered in a thick coating of mud, unable to tell the two apart. Anablue tugged on an arm, trying to pull them apart. Another arm reached out, gripping her ankle they gave a small yank. She fell on her bum with a woof of breath escaping her. She heard a screech from Elyse as she met the same fate. A grinning mud monster rose to his knees and crawled toward her. A squeal escaped her as she scooted backward.

Pointing her finger at him. "No," Anablue cried, slipping and sliding. She made to escape. Donall lunged at her and brought down flat on her back, and they rolled in the mud till she lay on top. Sitting up, she gently cleared the mud from his lips as she noticed his eyes went right to her breasts. The mud clung to her, accentuating every curve and valley, her nipples, hard buds against her shirt. A toothy, white grin lit up his face.

"Damn, woman. You tempt me to fuck you right here."

Anablue's mouth dropped open, wagging her finger under his nose. "I am not canoodling with you in a mud pit for all to see."

"No?"

"No," she firmly replied.

"I thought canoodling was just hugs and kisses?"

"It's so much more with you, Donall."

Chuckling, he rose to his feet. Picking her up, he threw her over his shoulder. "To the lake," he declared.

Elijah, with his own sweet temptation thrown over his shoulder, mirrored. "To the lake."

Off they trotted with their prizes, heading to the lake. They waded out to their waists, their bundles squirming and squealing in protest, and dropped them into the lake.

Max stood on the shoreline holding the baby while Jane ran to the campsite and back to the lake.

When the two men, arm in arm, singing and laughing, made to leave the lake. Jane tossed a bar of soap to them.

"Wash. Now," she said.

"She's bossy," Donall said.

"Ha. Soon to be an ex-employee," Elijah threatened.

"I'm not your employee," Jane replied.

"Consider yourself hired," Elijah said. "Nanny and cook, room and board provided."

"Didn't you just fire me?"

"Did I? Forget that," Elijah snorted. "Can't fire someone who I haven't hired yet."

Jane rolled her eyes. "Wash." Glancing out to where Anablue and Elyse stood in the lake. Bare-breasted, their backs to the shoreline, furiously trying to wash the mud out of their shirts. Glancing over their shoulders from time to time, making sure the men were distracted long enough to finish the job.

Donall glanced back at the women, noting the bare backs and curvy hips. He tapped Elijah on the arm.

"Looks like we have a couple of half-naked mermaids," he said, pointing to the women.

Elijah turned to look. Looking back at Jane, he gave her a devilish grin, flipped her the soap, and dove into the water, swimming in powerful strokes after his wife.

Elyse and Anablue squealed, and the chase was on. Elyse swam further out into the lake. Anablue, unable to swim, ran sideways through the water, pulling her shirt on as she went, with Donall chasing after her.

Jane sighed deeply. Turning to face a grinning Max. "Don't go getting any ideas."

Max perused her long, lithe body. "You're not ready yet," he replied. "But soon."

"Hmmmph." She replied. Taking the baby from his arms.

"I need to make dinner. They're going to have the munchies," she said over her shoulder.

## CHAPTER 40

Lounging on a blanket. Donall looked around the campsite. Elijah was spread out on his blanket. The baby sleeping on his chest was comforted to sleep by the rise and fall of his father's breathing. The women cleaned up after the meal Jane provided. In his defense, he offered to help, but was shooed away by Jane. The band Ten Years After had taken the stage, the crowd cheered, whistled, and clapped as they played the final song in their set. I'm Going Home. Tapping his foot in time to the music, he looked at Max sitting nearby doing the same. He had to admit, other than the nightmare of getting here and finding Anablue, he had enjoyed the festival and the music. He was amazed it really was three days of peace and music. A good bunch of kids, half a million strong, to be sure.

Drawn from his thoughts by Elyse and Anablue, laughing hysterically.

"What's so funny?" Donall asked.

"We had forgotten all about it."

"A few months ago, we had talked about being hippies and living off the land," Anablue laughed.

"We picked hippy names," Elyse said.

"Bambi, for Elyse," Anablue giggled.

Elijah rolled his eyes. Bambi? He mouthed, shaking with laughter, while trying not to disturb the baby.

"And what's yours?" Donall asked.

"Blossom," Anablue replied with a giggle.

Donall jumped to his feet, coming to stand in front of Anablue. Reaching out to touch her hair.

"You're more of a Chrysanthemum to me," he said.

"Blue or yellow?" she breathed.

"Blue," Donall replied.

---

Monday morning, Elijah, Max, and Jane were finishing up packing up the van.

Anablue sat behind Donall, painstakingly removing the stitches in his back. Elyse, next to them, nursed her son. Soup, sleeping on his back, was out cold next to her.

"These should have come out days ago. There, all done." Anablue said, sitting back on her haunches to admire her work.

Elyse yelped, pulling her son off her breast. "He bit me,"

she exclaimed. Checking his mouth. "Look, Elijah, he has a tooth."

They fawned over the baby and his new tooth while Donall pulled Anablue into his lap.

Max rolled his eyes. "I'm going to go get the other car," he stated. "No sense hauling the rest of this stuff through the woods."

Donall tossed him the keys.

Ten minutes later, Max pulled Anablue's love bug into the campsite. Anablue jumped to her feet.

"Betsy?" She turned to Donall and Elijah. "You drove Betsy here? Why?"

"I blew the radiator on my car. It's parked in your pole barn," Elijah said.

"Where's Brian's car?" Anablue asked.

"Also, in the pole barn. Gary slashed the tires," Donall replied.

"He slashed my tires?" Anablue said. "So, the four of you, a baby, a dog, and your stuff, jammed into Betsy and drove three thousand miles," Anablue laughed.

"That is the last time I will ever sit with my knees shoved up my nose," Elijah growled. "We're riding with Jane in the van home."

Anablue laughed, "So why didn't you just switch out the tires?"

Donall and Elijah looked at each other. "Mother fucker," they said at once. Anablue bit her lip, trying to hold back her grin.

"Well, I guess you did it for me. By the way, Elijah. I never apologized for popping you in the nose," Anablue said. "I am sorry."

"Your apology is accepted," Elijah said. "You need to figure out how to tell us apart."

"How do I do that? I mean, what if I walk up and kiss the wrong man?"

"Here's a hint for you. If you get kissed back, it's Donall. If you don't, it's me."

Anablue glared at him. "That's not too helpful. I tell you what. I have a tube of red lipstick in my purse. I vote to paint numbers on your foreheads." Elyse, standing nearby, covered her mouth to stifle her giggles.

Elijah scowled at her. "Just what I need, another troublemaker."

"Don't get your knickers in a twist. It's really pink lipstick," Anablue said.

"All this from a hell-cat who wiggles in her sleep like a squirrel trapped in a bag of nuts," Elijah retorted.

Anablue grinned. "Thank you for confirming you're all nuts."

Elyse snorted out loud.

Turning to Elyse. "Keep laughing, Bambi. I'll haul your sweet ass out to the woods and bend you over a log," Elijah threatened.

"Is that supposed to be a punishment?" Elyse coquettishly replied. Taking Anablue by the arm, the two walked away, snickering.

Elijah looked at Donall. "What the fuck are knickers?"

"Your boxers," Donall replied with a grin.

Max rolled on the ground, howling with laughter. "Holy shit…jammed into Betsy…lipstick…twisted knickers…nuts...then…then….bend her over a log." Wiping at his tears. "Damn. My stomach hurts. You Corrington's, are crazy."

"So, I've been told," Elijah replied.

---

MOST OF THE crowd had left by the time they were packed up and ready to leave.

"We really should go listen to Jimi Hendrix," Donall said.

"We'll never get another chance like this," replied Max. "He's the all-time greatest guitar player. My favorite."

They walked over to the field, spreading a blanket to sit and listen to the music.

Leaning into Donall's chest, his arms curled around her, Anablue sighed in contentment. Happy for the moment to just sit in his arms. There were decisions to make once they made it home.

"Donall."

"Yes, my love."

"Where exactly is home? Where are we going to live?" she asked.

"Where do you want to live?"

"I don't know. There's the ranch, and Mrs. Wangs, Your sailboat."

"I have an apartment above Two-Belly's as well. We can only stay on the sailboat a few nights a week," Donall said.

"We will not be able to live together yet."

"We have Bean to think about as well. We should get married as soon as possible."

"What kind of wedding are you two thinking about?" Elyse asked.

Anablue looked over her shoulder to Donall. "Small," they both said.

"Small. I have a ton of ideas," Elyse said.

"Well, let's hear them," Anablue said, coming to her feet. She pulled Jane to her feet.

Elyse getting to her feet, as well. The three grabbed their purses and walked away.

"Where are you going?" Donall asked.

"The biffy," Anablue said.

"Again?" Elijah said.

The women chattering away stopped and looked back. "Well, I am pregnant," Anablue said.

"Me…." Elyse paused. "Never mind, we have to go."

HOOKING THEIR ARMS TOGETHER, they walked away, giggling.

"Are you pregnant?" Anablue whispered.

"I'm two weeks late," Elyse whispered back. "It seems like no matter how careful we are, all Elijah has to do is give me a steamy look and bang… I'm pregnant."

"Yeah. Bang," Jane giggled.

Elyse glanced over her shoulder to see Elijah standing up. "Elyse," he bellowed. "Are you pregnant?"

Elyse turned, smiled, and curtsied.

Elijah's mouth dropped open. Running his hands through his hair. "Sweet Jesus. We're going to have another baby," he groaned. He trotted after Elyse. Scooping her up, he swung her in circles. "Brat. I swear, all I have to do is look at you and…"

"Bang," Anablue and Jane said.

Elijah laughed. "Yeah, bang. How long do we have?"

"Eight months or so," Elyse replied.

"Plenty of time to finish the new house," Elijah said.

"I'm going to need a raise," Jane smirked.

"Didn't you say she was sweet and shy? Elijah said.

"I guess she found her voice," Elyse replied.

"With salty old Marines, I find I need it," Jane said sweetly.

"I am neither old nor salty," Elijah snarled.

"Ah, but you are a Marine," Jane said.

"Once a Marine, always a Marine.

"Well, there you go," Jane said.

Elijah opened his mouth and snapped it shut. Elyse grabbed Jane and Anablue's hands. "Let's go before we dig a deeper hole."

Scowling deeply, Elijah watched the women walk away. He walked back to his brother and Max. "Women," he muttered. Bending down, he scooped Bunker up into his arms. Looking into his son's amethyst eyes, "You're going to have a baby, brother."

"How do you know it's a boy?" Max asked.

"Mine's a boy too," Donall replied.

"It's all we Corrington's have, boys," Elijah said.

Bunker grabbed Elijah by the ears and gave him a sloppy, open-mouthed kiss.

Jimi Hendrix went into his rendition of the Star-Spangled Banner, and the men jumped to their feet, clapping and whistling.

The set was over by the time the women returned. Piling into the vehicles. Anablue in the driver's seat of her car, Donall by her side. Everyone else was in the van.

"No matter what the circumstances, at least we can always say we were at Woodstock," Anablue said.

## CHAPTER 41

Out on the open road, the miles whizzed by. Making their way westward, the long highway disappeared into the horizon. Donall was driving, clapping his hand on his knee in time to beat the song playing on the radio. The heat of the long, hot, August day wearing on her. Desperate for cool air, Anablue rolled the crank down on her window. Hot air hit her in the face, and she exhaled.

"I swear my next car is going to have air conditioning."

"It will cool off once the sunsets. Next time we stop, we'll look for local campgrounds for the night," Donall said.

"I love campfires," Anablue replied. "I would love to toast some marshmallows."

"With graham crackers and chocolate bars," Donall replied. "Haven't had s'mores in years. My Aunt Meg used to take us camping as kids."

"What about your dad?"

"He was usually on deployment. But would join us when he could. It was my aunt who taught me to fish for trout."

"I tried fishing a couple of times. It didn't go well," Anablue said. "I always felt sorry for the worm. What else did you do as a kid?"

"The usual stuff. Band, Boy Scouts, and... an Alter boy for a short time."

"What did you do?" Anablue asked.

"Well. Elijah and I must have been about eleven or twelve or so. We came up with the brilliant idea to put a dozen Alka-Seltzer tablets in the Baptismal Font right before our priest baptized a Colonel's baby. It was epic. The font, frothing like hell's cauldron, Father Andrews, waving the bubbles away. My father and Aunt Meg, mouths hanging open, sitting in the front pew. My three older brothers could barely hold it together. The Colonel, my father's superior officer, was red-faced and apoplectic. The baby screaming, the mother crying. Needless to say, never mess with a Marine Chaplain. It must have taken us a month to clean that chapel with a toothbrush and much longer before we could sit down."

Anablue shook with laughter. "Oh my God. You're both going to hell in a hand-basket."

"That's exactly what Father Andrews said." Donall chuckled. "It was epic."

Pulling into the campgrounds, they parked next to the van. Anablue jumped out of the car, happy to stretch her legs. She came face-to-face with Elijah. "I heard you were quite the Alter boy," Anablue said.

Elijah grinned. "One of our best pranks."

"There's more?"

Both Donall and Elijah laughed. "Yeah. Lots more," Donall said.

"It sounds like you were juvenile delinquents," Anablue said.

"Not really. We were excellent students," Elijah said.

"Great musicians," Donall said. "Just pranksters."

"More so, when Mac came into the picture," Elijah said.

"Knit a lot of scarves that the first year," Donall chuckled.

Scanning the campsite, Elijah's eyes came to rest on Elyse, Bunker fussing on her hip.

"It's going to come back to haunt us tenfold, isn't it?" Elijah said.

"Yeah," Donall replied.

"Wait. You both knit?" Anablue asked.

"Doesn't everyone?" Donall chuckled.

"I'm all thumbs to go along with my two left feet, so no," Anablue replied.

"I can teach you," Donall said.

"No, that's okay. I'll stick with cars."

"Let's get that tent up before night falls," Elijah said. "Elyse is tired. The baby has been a handful today."

"I'll go help Max pick firewood," Anablue said.

"You should be resting as well," Donall said.

Rolling her eyes. "I'm more than capable of..." Anablue replied.

"Taking care of yourself," Donall and Elijah replied.

"That works, but I was just going to pick up sticks," Anablue laughed.

Three brightly colored peasant skirts lay drying in the morning sun next to the babbling stream. Fresh sparkling water rolled over the rocks surrounding a clear waist-deep pool as Anablue eased herself into the water.

"It's chilly but refreshing," Elyse said as Jane handed her the baby before climbing in herself.

"Gram would say it's colder than a witch's tit," Anablue said. Fully dunking her body in the pool, leaning back, she wet her hair before applying shampoo.

"It's a little cold for Bunker," Elyse said. Dipping the baby's toes in, he squealed in delight, bending in her arms to splash the water.

Jane poured shampoo into her hand, lathering her hair. "I hope this soap doesn't bother the fish."

"It should dissipate," Anablue said. "Elyse. Let me hold Bunker while you wash your hair."

Elyse held up the bottle of Prell shampoo, eyeing the pearl inside. "I've always wondered how they got the pearl in there?"

"It's smaller than it looks," Jane replied.

"I'm looking forward to a real hot bath or shower. Seriously, my mimsy is freezing," Anablue said.

"What's a mimsy?" Jane and Elyse asked.

Blushing profusely. "You know," Anablue said. "Down there."

"Oh. You mean your Hoo-hoo." Jane said, laughing as she climbed out of the pool.

Elyse giggled, "When I was little, I called mine a front butt." Taking the baby from Anablue, she handed him up to Jane.

"I'm sure Donall would be more than willing to warm up your mimsy," Elyse said

"Are you kidding? All I have to do is look at him, and it's warm."

The bushes next to the stream shook, and the women fell silent. Eyes wide with fear. "Wild animals?" Jane whispered.

"Maybe a bear," Anablue whispered back. Climbing out of the pool, she reached out a hand to help Elyse out.

Hearing growling noises coming from the bushes, abandoning skirts and supplies, they ran to the safety of the campsite.

Climbing into the van, Elyse turned to Anablue. "Are you okay with being in here?"

"If it's a bear out there. It seems the lesser of two evils."

Shivering with cold, their wet blouses and panties hugging their curves, they peeked out the windows of the van.

"I don't see anything," Jane said.

"Where are the men and the dog?" Anablue asked.

"They were sleeping when we left," Elyse said. "They're not here now."

"I hope they don't run into anything wild. I heard something outside of the tent last night," Anablue said.

"Me too, but Elijah said it was probably raccoons," Elyse said.

---

THE BUILDING HOUSING both men's and women's showers were not more than five minutes down the road from the campsite. Fresh from their showers, Donall, Elijah, and Max strode down the dirt road. Nodding to an elderly couple out for a morning hike. The couple scanned their hippy attire, giving them a terse nod. They hurried on their way.

"Did you see that?" Max said. "I want my real pants back."

"What's the matter? You don't enjoy looking like a peacock?" Elijah chuckled.

"Not really," Max grumbled. "I get it for Woodstock but, we're on our way home now."

"Where is home for you?" Donall asked.

"D.C. but I'm requesting a transfer to San Francisco," Max replied.

"Is that because of a certain long-legged beauty?" Donall asked.

"Maybe, did you see her at the stream? Hot damn!" Max said.

"Not sure what was funnier, you, silently laughing so hard the bushes shook, or the three of us growling like animals to cover your ass," Donall said.

"Like you, both weren't laughing. And whose idea was it to spy on them?" Max retorted.

"We only went to the stream to tell them about the showers down the road," Elijah said.

"Not sure I'll get past knowing women name their lady parts," Max laughed.

Walking into the campsite, they stopped. "Where are the girls?" Elijah asked.

Frowning, Donall scanned the site. Spotting a pair of blue eyes peeking out at him from the front passenger window of the van.

"In the van." Striding over to the van, he waited patiently while Anablue rolled down the window.

"You okay? Why are you in the van?" Donall asked.

"There are bears out there," Anablue replied, her lower lip quivering.

"I see chipmunks but no bears," Donall replied.

"Not here. Down by the stream."

Sticking his head in the window. "You can get out of the van now," Elijah said.

"We've been hiding in here for twenty minutes. Will you please go get our clothes and things? We left them at the stream," Anablue said.

Donall and Elijah looked at each other. "Sure," they replied.

※

Stomping through the woods, Donall turned to Elijah and Max. "I feel like an ass, scaring them like that."

"Me too. As long as they don't find out it was us, we should survive," Elijah replied.

"What do you mean… survive?" Max asked.

"Put it this way, be prepared to write your epithet for your tombstone if they find out," Donall stated.

They came upon the stream, spotting the skirts lying on the rocks. Donall picked them up while Elijah and Max went for the bath supplies, stuffing them into a small bag.

Soup was nosing along in the bushes on the shoreline, following the scent trail of an animal. A low growl, and the dog, startled, jumped back and started barking. Elijah threw the bag to Max as a massive black bear stood up on its hind legs, roaring at the little pup.

Elijah jumped to scoop the dog up.

"Run," he yelled.

Not needing any further prodding, Donall and Max took off like the hounds of hell were after them.

Tucking the dog under his arm like a football, Elijah thrashed through the woods after Donall and Max, the bear in hot pursuit.

"Elyse… Anablue… Jane. Get back in the van," the men screamed.

---

Wrapped in blankets to keep the morning chill out while they waited for the return of their clothes. Anablue stoked the fire while Jane prepared breakfast. Elyse had spread a blanket out, placing the baby in the center.

Anablue paused, "Is that Donall yelling? What's he saying?"

Jane stopped what she was doing to listen. "Get back in the van." The women looked at each other as Donall and Max burst into the clearing.

Donall grabbed the baby while Max started tossing women into the van. Once the women were inside, they jumped in as Elijah cleared the tree line. Launching himself head-first into the van, Donall pulled the door shut with a slam. The bear seconds behind slammed into the side of the van with a roar.

The bear stood up on his hind legs and roared again, banging and pushing on the van before dropping to sniff the food spread out on the picnic table.

Elijah held up Soup. "You okay, buddy?" The shaking pup licked his face. "Good boy."

Donall and Elijah looked at each other before turning to look at the terrified women and baby huddled in the back.

"Everyone okay?" Donall asked. The women nodded.

Anablue crawled to Donall. "I don't know about all of you, but I've had enough of this living off the land shenanigans. I just want to go home," she said.

"We'll be back at your ranch by early afternoon," Donall replied.

They watched out the window as the bear rummaged through the campsite, eating everything it could find. After an hour or so, it sauntered away.

"It looks like we'll be having breakfast on the road," Jane said.

THE WAITRESS SET a stack of plate-sized pancakes in front of Anablue. She patiently waited until everyone was served before slathering her pancakes with butter. Pouring the warm maple syrup over the mouth-watering stack before handing it to Jane. Elyse stirred a small bowl of oatmeal, blowing gently to cool it off, before spooning a mouthful into the baby's mouth.

Max enthusiastically cut into his steak and eggs as condiments were passed amongst the chattering group.

Donall leaned into Anablue, whispering in her ear.

"I can't wait to warm up your mimsy,"

Anablue, eyes wide, turned to look at him.

"Oh fuck," Donall said.

Donall, Elijah, and Max crammed into Anablue's little car, followed the van on the open road.

Elijah in the backseat, knees to his nose. "You just had to open your fucking mouth," he snarled.

Looking in the rear-view mirror at his twin, Donall scowled deeply.

## CHAPTER 42

Turning onto the long road that led to the Anablue's house, Jane looked into the rear-view mirror to make sure the men made the correct turn. "I kind of feel sorry for them," she said.

"If they would have come clean in the beginning, the bear incident would never have happened," Elyse called from the back as she sat nursing the baby, the dog curled up next to her.

Anablue in the front passenger seat. "At least we're home, or I am. I do not know what I'm going to do with a ranch, let alone an entire valley, someday."

"I'm sure Capt. Jack and Donall will help you work it out," Elyse said.

"Donall would make a hot cowboy," Jane said.

"Wearing nothing but chaps and a cowboy hat," Anablue giggled.

Elyse laughing behind them, "We're as bad as they are."

"They are still in the doghouse," Anablue replied.

"Poor Donall, I bet it's his first time," Jane said.

"We had some spats at Edwards," Anablue replied. "But those were different. If I argued, I could go to jail."

"That is not cool," Jane replied.

"As much as he was an ass, in the beginning, he kept telling me to be strong," Anablue said. "He saw the light at the end of the tunnel but couldn't tell me." Her lower lip quivered as she looked in the side mirror at the car behind them. They pulled up in front of the pole barn as the men parked behind them. Anablue was out of the van and racing toward the car. Stopping in confusion in front of the car to look between the identical men sitting in the front seats. The driver pointed to his passenger, and Anablue went to the passenger side. Donall jumped out of the car, and Anablue flew into his arms, wrapping her legs around him as he carried her away.

Elijah got out of the car as Elyse with the baby came into his arms. Max climbed out of the backseat, seeing Jane standing there alone. He opened his arms wide. Jane rolled her eyes and flipped him the bird.

"That's my long-legged wench," Max said.

"Wench? Have you been sniffing fumes, Max?" Jane replied.

"No. I found Anablue's smut book in the backseat. I've been reading these last two hundred miles."

"Did you learn anything?" Jane asked.

"Plenty," Max replied with a wicked grin. "But most of it, I already knew."

Jane grunted in response. "Where you headed, Max?"

"Back to San Francisco. I have some loose ends to tie up before I file my report with the brass. Where are you going?"

"I'm going back to my dump of an apartment to pack my stuff and move up north to Elyse and Elijah's."

"So, you're taking the job?"

"Yeah. After Gary, I think it will be good for me. Fresh air, the beach. Bunker is a sweet baby, and I adore Elyse. Elijah is a nice guy too." She looked Max in the eye. "I need time to heal. To find myself again."

"I know," Max replied.

Jane smiled. "Do you want a ride?"

Max nodded his head. "That would be nice."

---

WAVING AS THE VAN LEFT, Anablue turned to Donall. " We're all alone. What shall we do?"

Donall pulled her into his arms. "Everything we've ever dreamt of doing. I'm going to make love to you under the sun and stars. I'm going to cook fabulous meals for you. Then, I'm going to start all over again."

"That's a lot of food and sex," Anablue laughed.

"We only have three days before they come back. We'd

better get started." Donall laughed as he scooped her up in his arms, running to the house.

"Donall," she squealed. "Put me down. Your shoulder's?"

"I can carry you. I can't, however, deal with G-forces," Donall replied.

He set her down to open the back door. Anablue escaped his arms, taunting him; she pulled off her shirt, flinging it to the floor. She ran through the kitchen and down the hallway, leaving a trail of clothes. He followed her, dropping his clothing. Catching her outside her bedroom door, he pinned her against the wall. Gripping her hips, he hoisted her up, burying himself deep inside of her. His lips plundered hers, tasting and teasing. He opened her bedroom door, carrying her inside. He kicked the door shut.

---

"Hmm," she sighed as Donall lightly massaged her back. "I'm hungry. Unless we can survive off of canned peaches, we have to go to town for food."

"I could eat a horse," Donall replied, burying his face to nibble at her neck.

"You'd have to steal one, and they might still hang horse thieves out here," she giggled.

"I guess that rules that out. How about rustling cattle?"

"Nope, they'll hang you for that too."

"Then I guess we have no choice but to shower and go to town to get a steak," Donall chuckled.

"The best there is," Anablue replied.

DONALL WAS AMAZED at the number of people who stopped by the local café to say hello to Anablue. Some offered their condolences, since she had left town right after Brian's funeral. The waitress, a handsome woman in her mid-forties, set two glasses of water on the table.

"Give us a hug, Anablue. How are you, sweetie? I told Walter you'd be back soon enough."

The woman turned and yelled into the kitchen. "Walter. Anablue is back."

"I'm fine, and you?" Anablue said.

"Never mind me. We've all been worried about you, losing your Gram and Brian like that. And who's this big hunk of handsome with you?"

Donall looked up into Margaret's animated eyes. He gave her a brilliant smile. "Donall Corrington. Anablue's fiancé'."

"Fiancé', there's going to be a wedding? Oh, Lord! Where is Walter? What will you have, handsome? I already know what Anablue wants. Since she was little, the poor girl still orders the same thing every time."

"Steak, rare, French fries, and a double hot fudge malt, make that two malts," Donall said.

Anablue barked out a laugh. "How did you know about the malt?"

"I've seen all the jars of hot fudge in your cub board," Donall replied.

"Well, it's about time your home. We haven't had a decent mechanic in town since you left for the Navy," Margaret said as she left to place their order.

"So, what is it you've been eating since you were little?"

"Open-faced hot turkey sandwich, with mashed potatoes and cranberries. Along with a double hot fudge malt, both my favorites."

Donall reached out to stroke her soft cheek. "You are a small-town girl, aren't you?"

"Also, part of who I am. They're going to be sad when they find out I'm not staying more than a few days."

"Well, we still have to decide where we want to raise Bean," Donall replied.

"What about you? What do you want?"

"I'm a Marine brat. I got used to moving around. I'll be happy wherever you are."

"What about sailing the seven seas?"

"Did Elyse tell you that?"

"Yes. I guess I'm your pirate wench."

"Yeah, you are. The sailboat is going to take a long time to get seaworthy."

Anablue giggled. "A pirate, a wench, and a bean. What if we have more beans?"

"How many do you want?"

"A few."

"Thank God. I was afraid you were going to say at least a dozen."

"You'd need a bigger boat."

Their dinner was delivered by none other than Walter, the cook. A small, grizzled, black man with salt and pepper hair. He enveloped Anablue in a bear hug.

"Glad you're home, little girl. We've missed you."

Anablue made the introductions, and Walter disappeared back to his kitchen.

"You've got a lot of people who love you. Both here and in San Francisco," Donall said.

"I guess I'm not as alone as I thought I was," Anablue said. "And best of all, I have you. Now eat your steak. It's mooing at you."

THEY STROLLED THE BOARDWALK, hand in hand. Stopping in front of the auto-parts store.

"This is it, my favorite store in town," Anablue said.

"Not a bookstore?"

"I have lots of favorites," Anablue replied. "But here, there is no bookstore, and the library is two towns over."

"Whoo-hoo. Anablue," A shrill woman's voice trilled behind them. Anablue turned around to see a young woman coming up the walk toward them.

"Damn," Anablue said under her breath.

The woman rushed up to them. "I heard you're back and had to come to say hello."

"Hello, Becky."

"And who's this?" Becky asked. Her eyes insolently sweeping Donall.

"This is my fiancé, Donall."

"Fiancé? Now I am surprised. Here I thought you'd be an old maid with your head stuck under a car hood forever, or God forbid, stay in the Navy. Which my Pa said is no place for a woman. What were you thinking, Anablue? Oh, and look, here you are, right in front of your favorite grease-monkey store. I am sorry about Brian. We had a thing going on in high school, you know. I used to write to him." Her hand fluttered to her heart. "I would have waited for him," Becky said.

"I'm sure Brian appreciated hearing news from home," Anablue replied.

Donall's head spun from the woman's shrill chatter. He could feel Anablue's grip tighten on his hand as she politely nodded.

"Oh, look at the time," Donall said, looking at his watch." We need to get going, sweetheart, before it gets too late."

"Yes. So nice to see you again, Becky," Anablue said.

"I expect to see a wedding invite in my mailbox," Becky said sweetly.

"Well, we're getting married in San Francisco," Anablue replied.

Donall pulled the door open, and they both escaped into the store.

"You can sheath your claws now," Donall said.

"I counted at least five insults out of that simpering flibbertigibbet's mouth. And Brian. Brian would have burnt any letter he got from her," Anablue growled.

"So, we're getting married in San Francisco?"

"Sorry. Split-second decision. I hope you don't mind. It's not all sunshine and rainbow's here."

"Not at all. I'm quite pleased," Donall replied.

"Anablue Baker." A tall blonde man called out as he rounded the endcap. Swooping in to pick her up and swing her around.

"Johnny. You're such a dork. Put me down."

Donall's eyes narrowed at the man's familiarity with Anablue.

"Donall. This is Johnny Miller. Brian's best friend," Anablue said. "They enlisted together. Are you out now, Johnny?"

'Yeah. Got married last month to Lizzie Taylor too. We saved an empty spot at the wedding table for Brian. Kind of an honorary best man thing," Johnny said.

"Congratulations on your wedding. I'm sure Brian would have loved it," Anablue said as her eyes teared up.

"Enough of that. There's a drag race this weekend if you're interested."

Anablue's eyes widened as she caught Donall's frown.

"Saw a little county jailhouse down the street," Donall said. "Perfect for three days in the brig."

Anablue laughed, "No thanks, Johnny. We'll be leaving town by then."

"You're coming back, right?" Johnny said.

"Eventually. Right now, I need tires and a radiator."

Johnny frowned. "For the Black Beast?"

"The tires for the Beast, the radiator for a sixty-nine Camaro," Anablue said.

"The Black Beast?" Donall asked.

"Brian's car," Anablue said.

"I'll have to order the radiator. I can bring it all out to the ranch if you want." Johnny said.

"That would be cool," Anablue replied.

"I sure miss those days when your Gram would drive the old Model-T to town for Bridge night," Johnny said.

Anablue rolled her eyes.

"Bridge night?" Donall asked.

"Don't be fooled. Gram had a wild streak. They played poker, not bridge, and snuck whiskey in their tea," Anablue laughed. "Since we were twelve, Brian and I took turns driving the Model-T home from her monthly Bridge night. She had a blast with her friends, and that was all that mattered to us. She worked hard on the ranch."

Donall gave her a grin. "Wild streak, huh? Now I know where yours come from."

TWILIGHT FELL as they rested on the front porch, a full day of working on cars behind them. Donall had thought his motorcycle was a lost cause, but Anablue had someone who could make the repairs to get it back on the road. They had helped load it on an old pickup truck and watched as it was hauled away.

Pouring olive oil into her hand, she slid her hands up his back to his shoulders. She worked the oil into his scars and aching muscles.

"We should do this every day," Anablue said. Sprinkling light kisses along his back.

Donall spread out on his stomach, his head resting on his forearms. "Hmm. I couldn't agree more," he replied.

"Seriously, it's good for your scars."

"What it seems to be good for is making me rock hard. I'm about to burst through the porch floor," Donall chuckled.

"Now, how would I explain Linkie Pinkie holes in the porch?"

Donall roared with laughter. Rolling, so she lay under him. He buried his face between her breasts. His laughter muffled, lifting his head, he grinned. "You. Are too much. I refuse. Refuse... to call my cock a Linkie Pinkie."

Chuckling, she ran her hands through his hair, cupping his face. "No?"

"Absolutely not."

Crinkling her nose at him. "Fine. Cock holes."

"I'm not sure what delights me more. Your funny words, or that you're so matter of fact about them."

Lifting her arms, he pulled her shirt off.

Much later Anablue nestled into his warm body as they lay star-gazing on the hood of the car.

"When I was a little girl looking up into the sky. I used to think the planes were spiders in the sky," Anablue murmured.

"Donall chuckled. "I was the opposite. I used to think spiders on the ceiling were planes. It's all I thought about as a kid. Being a fighter pilot."

"Tell me about the sky," Anablue said.

"The sky?"

"Yes. What's it like to fly?"

"You've never flown before?"

"Well, I did fly in a military transport plane to Hawaii and back. No windows. Couldn't see a thing. Truthfully, I had the collywobbles the whole trip. I'm sure it's nothing like being the pilot."

"Hmmm. It's freedom. And exhilarating. Sometimes, the sky is so blue, like your eyes. Other times, I've seen rainbows of color above the cloud deck that took my breath away. Of course, when you're sitting in the cockpit of an F-4 in the middle of dog fight with a MiG, you're not looking at the beauty around you."

"What was your callsign?"

Donall gave her a sheepish grin. "Dark Adonis."

Anablue's mouth dropped open.

## CHAPTER 43

Max followed Anablue and Donall up the street. After driving Elijah here to collect his car, he had one more meeting here before he completed his report and turned it over to the brass. Then they could arrest and start the proceedings against the admiral. The history of the old Gold rush town fascinated him. Nestled in the Sierra Nevada foothills. He could imagine gold miners with their donkeys, laden with tools of the trade, coming to town to barter their gold for supplies with the French settlers. The buildings, many of them built in the eighteen-hundreds, had lots of charm.

"A penny for your thoughts, Max," Anablue said.

Lost in his thoughts, he didn't realize they had stopped in front of the bank. "Hmm. Oh, here we are. I imagined what this town looked like during the gold rush days."

"We're very proud of our history," Anablue replied.

"Are you ready? Do you have the key to the safe deposit box?" Donall asked.

Anablue held up the keyring, shaking the key. "Right here."

With a deep breath, Anablue steeled her jittery nerves as Donall pulled the door open.

---

The long metal box sat on a high table in the middle of the vault.

Donall and Max stood on the other side, watching. Lifting the lid open, peeking inside, Anablue stopped.

Looking up into Donall's eyes. "This is not exactly what I expected to see," Anablue whispered. Flipping the lid open, they all leaned to peer inside.

"What are those?" Donall asked.

"S & H Green stamps," Anablue replied. Her confusion clear, she chewed her lower lip. She looked at the man standing in the far corner of the room. She pulled one of the booklets out and flipped through it.

Howard Long, Gram's attorney, stepped forward to peer into the box. Pencil thin, with gray hair and bushy eyebrows, the elderly man chuckled. "That's all that's inside?" he said.

"There's got to be thirty booklets in here," Donall said.

"What are those for?" Max asked.

"Well, she got them from the market. When you buy so

much in groceries and gas, you get the stamps. Then you can trade them in to get stuff from the catalog," Anablue said.

"So why keep them here at the bank?" Max asked.

Anablue shrugged her shoulders. "It's Gram. I mean, I know they were valuable to her, but you would think that there would be important papers in here."

"Well, they're part of her estate. Once the will is resolved in probate court, we'll know more. As Margaret's sole surviving beneficiary, Anablue, we need to sit down and go over her assets at some point." Howard said. "Your grandmother lived comfortably off the proceeds of the sales of her property after your grandfather died, but she was not a wealthy woman."

"Well, it's all a mystery to me. Why was the admiral so desperate to get into this box?" Anablue cried.

"Anablue. I saw on your key ring that you have another key for another safe deposit box. Whose box is that?" Donall gently pried.

"Brian's," Anablue said. Her eyes lit up. "I wonder what's in Brian's box?"

"When did you get Brian's key?" Max asked.

"It was in Brian's things that were returned to me from the Navy."

Max called the bank manager into the room, and Brian's safe deposit box was unlocked and placed on the table.

"Brian, I swear, if this is full of stamps, I'm going to kick your ass when I get to heaven."

She opened the box. Looking inside, she looked up to the three men in front of her. "Bingo."

War bonds, a black velvet bag with heirloom jewelry, the deed for the ranch, a title for the car, and birth certificates for Michael and Jackson Baker.

Max perused the birth certificates. "I think we have an answer here. The admiral has different parents. The mother is listed as Josephine, his father, Zeke Baker."

"Michael and Jackson are not brothers," Howard said. "Michael's parents must have died."

"And your grandmother raised Michael as her own," Max replied. "I don't see any adoption papers."

"Michael did not want anyone to find out that he was not your Grandparent's son. He would have no standing in court to contest the will, leaving everything to her direct descendants, Anablue and Brian," Howard said.

"But why contest the will. Wouldn't he have inherited everything anyway as a distant relative if everyone else was dead?"

"It's possible. He didn't want anyone to know," Max replied. "Also, possible that he was covering all of his bases."

"My head is spinning here. Howard, you were Gram's lawyer. Why didn't she tell you any of this?" Anablue said.

"I'm sure she had her reasons, but I'm representing you in this matter," Howard replied. "It appears to me that other than the ranch, everything in this box was signed over to Brian before her death. Anablue, you're named as Brian's beneficiary in his will. All of this is yours."

"There's another key," Donall said, pulling the key out of the box. "And an envelope addressed to you, Anablue."

"What's with all of the safety deposit boxes?" Anablue grumbled.

Once the box was opened, "This one is yours," Howard said. "It's more of the same. It looks like she split everything up into equal shares."

"If I had given Gram and Brian the time of day, I would have known all of this before," Anablue cried, the tears running down her face.

"You can't keep beating yourself up over this. It is what it is," Donall said, pulling her into his arms. He lightly kissed the top of her head. "You okay?" She sighed deeply. "Yeah."

"Howard, what do you need for the trustee?" Anablue asked as she wiped her tears away.

"The deed to the ranch, the birth certificates. The S & H Green stamps should stay in the box, but I'll take your grandmother's key. Max already gave me copies of everything he had. Including a notarized letter from Captain Jackson Baker claiming you are his true and legal daughter. I will present all of it to the trustee tomorrow. This should be resolved shortly."

"Why do you suppose Gram never told Captain Jack about Michael not being a true brother?" Anablue asked.

"Remember they were raised as brothers. Maybe she hoped they would someday reconcile," Howard replied.

"I can't speak for Capt. Jack, but I'm sure after everything that has happened, it's unlikely," Anablue replied. "If we're done here, I want to go home. I'll take that envelope now."

Her hand shook as she reached for the envelope. "It's from Brian," she whispered. "I'll read it later."

"There's one more thing," Howard said. "I sit on the town board. There's been talk of the government wanting to build another base in this area."

"He only wanted the land to sell it," Anablue whispered.

DONALL WALKED through the kitchen to sit on the back porch. Anablue sat in the distance on a little bench on a hill overlooking a breathtaking view of the valley. It had been a rough day. His mind drifted back to their last stop after the bank. The cemetery.

*Her eyes shimmering with tears, wildflowers in one hand, the other hand squeezing his hand, they stopped at the family plot. First at her Grandfathers, then moving to her Grandmother's grave. Next to her was her mother, then Brian's grave. She placed a handful of flowers on each grave. Dropping to her knee's she pulled weeds and straightened up the area.*

*"It's not fair, you know. Brian never had the chance to live his life. Robbed of the chance to know the love of a woman, to be a father to children, to grow old. He was proud to serve his country, proud to be a sailor in the best Navy in the world. The admiral stole all of it from him. And for what? Money."*

*She inhaled sharply, and Donall dropped to his knees next to her.*

*"I don't know if I have it in me to forgive the admiral. I don't know," she cried.*

*Donall pulled her into his arm, and she sobbed against his chest.*

*"It takes time, my love," Donall said. "You'll find forgiveness for him if, and when, you're ready."*

*"Time," she whispered. Do we really have time?"*

*"A wise man once told me that tomorrow is not promised, but we have here and now. We live on, Anablue, as survivors. We can't mourn the past or bring back the dead. We have a duty to live the fullest lives we can. And when it's our time to go, we go, knowing we gave it our best," Donall replied.*

*"You stole the words right out of my mouth. I was going to give you the same speech about Vietnam," she said.*

*"You were? No."*

*"Yeah, I was," she said. "I know you don't talk about what happened when you were a prisoner, but I'm here for you."*

*"I know you are, and that means the world to me," Donall replied.*

*"By the way. I have a creepy secret for you."*

*"What is it?"*

*"The three plots next to Brian. One is for Capt. Jack, one is mine, the other is for my spouse."*

*"You're right. That's creepy."*

*Rising to their feet. "Oh, one more thing," Donall said. Reaching into his pocket, he pulled out a dime. Placing it on Brian's headstone. We may not have served on the same ship sailor, but we sailed the same ocean in the same fleet. Proud to have served with you. Rest in peace, mate. Know that I'll take care of her.*

Donall looked up from his musings to see Anablue on her way back to the house. The wind lightly blew at her hair, molding her dress to her lush curves. So young to have so much tragedy in her life. But one of the strongest women he knew. His heart swelled with love. He couldn't wait to start their life together.

She stopped in front of him and handed him Brian's letter.

"You want me to read it?" Donall asked.

Anablue nodded her head, her eyes shimmering with tears. Donall pulled the letter from the envelope.

> Boo,
>
> If you're reading this that means I didn't make it home. I want you to move on, don't grieve for me. Live the best life you can.
> You can still have it all. Buy that gas station, paint bridges for me, along with the flowers. Most of all, find a special man and have babies.
> Once you're out of the Navy, I want you to go to San Francisco and look up Jackson Baker, he's our real father. Not our uncle. Mom was supposed to marry him, but it didn't work out.
> Anyway, he owns a bar called Two-Belly Jacks. Get ahold of him, he can explain it all. He's a pretty cool guy. Above all, stay away from Admiral Baker. The guy's a scallywag and no good.

Be careful with the Black Beast. I always tell
> my buddies "I've got the best mechanic for
> a twin sister and she's pretty cool too."

Be yourself, never change who you are.
I miss that gigglemug of yours.

All my love,

Brian

Donall smiled. "He called you Boo?"
Anablue nodded. "Since we could talk."
"Come here." He pulled her into his arms. She wrapped her arms around his waist as they walked back to the house together.

## CHAPTER 44

Newspaper in hand, Capt. Jack took a sip of his coffee. A slight breeze blew across the bay, and he pulled the collar of his jacket up around his neck to ward off the chill. Not yet noon. It promised to be a glorious day. He glanced up to the wharf, spotting Donall, his eyes riveted to the woman excitedly pulling him along. Her straw hat with its blue ribbons sat upon her head. Capt. Jack inhaled sharply. Anablue looked so much like Mary. It brought an ache to his chest. With tears in his eyes, he climbed out of the boat and stood on the dock, watching their approach. He had waited a lifetime for this moment. He opened his arms.

She paused at the dock. Spotting Capt. Jack standing in front of his boat. She pulled her hat off and nervously played with the brim. Their eyes met, and she chewed at her lower lip as twin tears ran down her face. He opened his arms wider.

Then she was racing down the dock, flying into his arms. She wrapped her arms around his neck, and they cried together.

※

CAUGHT IN THE MOMENT, Donall looked out to the bay, blinking back the burning in his eyes. Their reunion brought him happiness and joy for both of them. He prayed that the healing could begin. Turning around, he spotted Max standing behind him.

Striding toward him, he reached out and shook his hand. "Thank you, my friend."

"You're welcome. Just one more loose end to tie up," Max replied.

"What's that?"

"The admiral is AWOL. They went to arrest him this morning. He was gone."

"They're both still in danger until he's caught," Donall growled. He watched as Anablue and Capt. Jack walked arm in arm to the end of the dock.

"I need a drink," Donall said. "Let's see what he's got in the galley."

"Roger that," Max replied. "It's four o'clock somewhere."

Stepping inside the galley, Donall and Max opened cub boards in search of liquor. Hearing another voice right off the starboard side of the boat. Donall lifted the curtain to see who it was, crouching down. "It's the admiral. He's got a gun."

Max ducked down, and they crept to peek out the door.

Max pulled his gun from his pants, and they crawled on their bellies out the door, climbing over the port side of the sailboat and down into the frigid water.

Swimming under the dock to the other side, Max held his gun above his head. Soundlessly swimming from boat to boat, communicating with hand signals, they made their way to the end of the dock. Stopping on either side of where the admiral stood on the dock, pointing his gun at Anablue and Capt. Jack.

DEEP IN CONVERSATION, Anablue held hands with Capt. Jack as they leaned on the white wood railing.

"I can't believe it. You've been here with me this whole time," Anablue said, "Why didn't you tell me who you were?"

"I'm a bit of a chicken. I was grateful I had a few hours every morning to watch you paint. I was afraid that if you knew…"

"Well, well. What do we have here? A father-daughter reunion."

Anablue and Capt. Jack both stiffened. Looking at each other in horror, they turned around. Anablue gripped Capt. Jack's hand and arm as she stared at the gun in the admiral's hand. She glanced around. *Where is Donall?*

Capt. Jack moved to pull Anablue behind him.

"What are you doing here, Mike?" Capt. Jack said.

"Now, Jack, is that any way to greet your brother?" the Admiral said.

"You're no brother of mine."

"Funny, how true that statement is," the Admiral replied.

"And this is how you repay mom and dad? After they took you in, raising you as their own," Capt. Jack said.

"Your parents made it clear, they may have raised me, but I had no claim to the land. It would all go to you as their true son. Of course, then mom got sneaky, bypassing you to give it all to Brian and Anablue. Don't get me wrong, they provided for me. But it was not what I wanted. So, I set out to take what was due to me. I took your girl, your children, and now I'll take your land."

"You never wanted Mary," Capt. Jack stated.

"No, I didn't. But I didn't want you to have her either. She was far too frail and timid for a man like me. Lucky for me, her parents were more than happy to cover up her shame. Too bad they died in such a horrendous fire."

"You started that fire. Didn't you?"

"Maybe."

Anablue listened in horror to their conversation. Glancing down, she caught sight of Donall in the water.

He put his finger to his lips. Shhhhhh.

"You're a monster," Anablue said.

"Ah, Anablue. So, like your mother. I used to visit Mary at the sanitorium. I would whisper in her ear details of the torment I planned for her children. She became quite distressed. What little sanity she had slipped away, and I had her lobotomized."

"I hope you burn in hell," Anablue gritted out.

"Perhaps, but for now. Who's first?" The admiral said, pointing his gun at Capt. Jack, then at Anablue.

"Eight bells, Anablue," Capt. Jack whispered.

"End of watch, how fitting," replied the Admiral.

Anablue's eyes widened in understanding as Bart flung himself out of the water, knocking the admiral off the dock as a gunshot rang out. Capt. Jack, in a knee-jerk reaction, flung his arm wide, knocking Anablue into the bay.

Screaming as she fell, hitting the water hard, her arms flayed in panic as she sank to the bottom.

DONALL WRAPPED his arms around her, pulling her close. He rose to the surface. Setting her on the dock, he closed his eyes to feel her touch when she reached out to push a wet strand of hair off his forehead. She moved to where Capt. Jack sat on his knees, staring into the bay. Max reached down to help him to his feet.

"Where's the admiral?" Anablue said.

Donall pointed to where the admiral floated face down in the bay. The water around him red with blood.

"We should get him out before the sharks find him," Max said.

Bart, seeing Donall point, jumped into the water, swam

out to where the man floated. The seal gently pushed him to the dock. Max and Donall pulled him out of the water, laying the man on the dock. He checked his pulse.

"He's dead," Donall said.

"It's over?" Anablue asked.

"Yes," Capt. Jack replied. "He can't hurt us anymore."

Donall retrieved a blanket from his sailboat and covered the dead man.

Donall pulled her into his arms. "How do you feel?"

Anablue shuddered in his arms. "I feel nothing but pity for him. He wasted his whole life on vengeance. Gram loved him."

Donall looked at Max. "Did you shoot him?"

"No. His gun must have discharged when the sea lion hit him."

"Bart is a seal," Anablue said.

"No, he's a sea lion. You can tell by the ears and flippers. Actually, he's a very special sea lion," Max said.

"How so?" asked Donall.

"Do you see the tag on his flipper? What we have here is U.S. Navy property. He's part of the Navy-Marine Mammal Program. I had heard one escaped during a training exercise in San Diego last year. I'm betting this is him."

"Bart. Are you AWOL?" Anablue chided.

The sea lion had jumped back on the dock, barked, and clapped his fins in response to Anablue.

"I'm sorry. I don't have any fish for you," Anablue said.

"I've got some in the cooler. Spoiled bastard. Now he comes back for dinner every night," Capt. Jack grumbled.

"I'm going to go make some phone calls. Police and such," Max said. "How am I going to explain that a sea lion killed the admiral with his own gun? This is the icing on the cake to the craziest case I've ever worked."

## CHAPTER 45

Late August.

Pulling the dresses on the rack apart, Anablue stuck her head through. Spotting Elyse on the other side.

"Have you seen the amount of fabric on some of these wedding gowns? Donall would be searching through yards of lace and silk to find me," Anablue said.

Elyse rolled her eyes. "Search? He'd tear through it to stroke soft skin."

"You're probably right."

"Of course, he's going to have to find you first," Elyse laughed. Pulling out a dress."Oooooh. Look at this one."

Anablue came around the other side of the dress rack. "That's beautiful. What do you mean, find me?" Anablue said as her fingers stroked the delicate lace.

"Well. They have this tradition where they steal the bride.

Elijah and his brothers, and I suppose Mac, will be here. They will do everything they can to delay your wedding night."

"Did they do this to you?"

"Yes. Only for a couple of hours, but that was in Vietnam."

"I'm a little befuddled why," Anablue said.

"It's a brother thing. Just go with the flow."

"Did you look at any of the bridesmaid dresses?"

"I peeked at them. Most seem to have puffy sleeves and clouds of pink taffeta," Elyse replied.

"Hmm. I think we should look at a pale blue for you," Anablue said.

"You know, if I had time, I would have made them myself."

Anablue pulled out a dress. Holding it up next to her. "This is it."

"Oh, Anablue," Elyse said, wiping at her tears. "It's breathtaking. Try it on."

They left the shop after an hour of the seamstress poking and prodding as she took measurements. Elyse, as the matron of honor, also found a similar cut dress was also fitted.

Arm in arm, they walked out of the shop into crowds of people, as a peaceful protest march was in progress.

"What are they protesting?" Elyse asked.

Her eyes were bright with excitement. "Look at the signs. Women's Liberation movement! We refuse to stay silent! This is a women's rights march," Anablue said.

"It's so cool," Elyse said. "I've always wanted to march in a protest."

Caught up in the moment, they followed along on the sidewalk until bystanders pushed them into the street. Walking with the protesters. Women of all shapes and sizes had turned out to give voice to their oppression.

Someone shoved a sign into Anablue's hand, and they ended up at the forefront of the protest.

A barrel was plunked down in the middle of the intersection. Circling the burning barrel, the women sang and cheered as a young brunette tossed her bra into the barrel.

Anablue. a mischievous smile on her face. "Should we?"

"Oh, hell yes," Elyse said.

Laughing, they unhooked their bras, pulling the straps down over their arms. They made a great show of pulling their bras off while maintaining their modesty. Stepping up to the barrel together, they held them up to wild cheering and tossed them in the barrel.

Facing the crowd, Anablue shouted. "Free your titties, ladies. Down with male chauvinism."

"Woman power," Elyse cried out. "We want equal rights and birth control."

"Birth control? Too late," Anablue said. "Gram would say we were brazen hussies. Bra-less and demanding birth control."

"Not," they both said. Giggling, they left the protest, making their way to meet Elijah and Donall.

The taxicab pulled up in front of Elijah's address. A tall, dark-haired soldier stepped from the cab and handed the driver a ten-dollar bill. Walking up the path to a white picket fence, he opened the gate. Dumping his duffel bag at the gate, he was immediately confronted by the small, growling dog. Leaning down, "Hey Soup, remember me?" as he offered his hand to smell. Soup wagged his tail and rolled on his back for a belly rub. "Where is everybody?"

The dog jumped to his feet and led the way to a massive garage.

The garage doors were open, the hood on a car was up. He spied two sets of shapely female legs sticking out from underneath. He raised an eyebrow and continued down the path to peer in a kitchen window of the tiny house. He could see his twin brothers inside preparing a meal. Shaking his head, he headed back to the garage.

Standing above the women, he reached down, grabbed ahold of an ankle of each woman, and gave a tug, pulling them out from under the car.

"Has the world gone fucking insane?" he said.

Startled, Elyse cried out, "Brendan."

"Happy Birthday, Beautiful," Brendan said. Eyeing the striking blonde with grease on her face. "And who do we have here?"

"Down, boy. This is your future sister-in-law, Anablue Baker," Elyse said as an impish grin split her face.

"Donall's girl?"

"Anablue. This is Brendan. Donall and Elijah's brother," Elyse said.

"Hello," Anablue shyly replied.

Staring into her blue eyes. "Some guys have all the luck," Brendan said. "What are you doing under a car?"

"Anablue is teaching me how to change my oil and to change a tire. In case my car breaks down on the way home some night."

"I suppose Donall is trying to teach Elijah to cook? I'm surprised they haven't come to blows yet," Brendan said.

Elyse rolled her eyes. "Give them time."

"I come home from Nam to find women in the garage and men in the kitchen. I can't believe this much would change in a year," Brendan said.

The screen door slammed behind them, and Brendan turned to see his brothers. Crossing the distance, he wrapped them in his embrace.

"Welcome home, Brendan," Elijah said.

"That's much better than the reception I got at the airport," Brendan replied as he flicked tomato seeds from his lapel.

"Someone should have warned you about the war protesters," Donall said.

"Well, one punk who threw tomatoes is nursing a black eye right about now. Where's father?"

"He's down at the beach with the others and the baby," Elijah said.

"Bunker, I haven't seen him since he was minutes old," Brendan replied. "He's probably as big as Elyse by now."

Elijah chuckled. "Damn near."

"He is not, though he is a big boy," Elyse said, rolling her eyes.

Donall clapped Brendan on the back. "You're just in time. We've got steaks and crab legs to grill."

"Don't forget birthday cake, too," Jane called out. Cake in hand, she made her way down the steps from her apartment above the garage, followed by Max.

Brendan looked up to see the long-legged beauty coming down the steps. "Damn, it's good to be home. I'm surrounded by beautiful women." Looking at his brothers. "And your ugly mugs too. By the way, Happy Birthday."

They walked down to the beach. Brendan took in the beauty of the ocean, the waves rolling in and out, the sandy beach with the sun high in the sky. Two men sitting at a picnic table played chess, as another man, with the baby in his lap, looked on. He placed one hand on his father's shoulder, reaching over, taking the knight. He moved it in front of the queen. "Checkmate," he whispered.

The colonel's eyes teared as he reached to place his hand over the one on resting on his shoulder. Wiping at his eyes.

"Good Lord. It does an old man good to hear your voice again." Standing up, he yanked Brendan into his embrace. "Now, if I could get the rest of my boys home, I'd be a happy man."

Brendan reached over and plucked Bunker from Capt. Jack. "Hey, there, little fella. You've got your mama's eyes."

Bunker gave him a look of pure skepticism. Then spotting the chain around his neck, he pulled until he had the dog tags in hand. Before he could put them in his mouth, "Let's not eat Uncle Brendan's dog tags," Elyse said.

She reached for the baby, then remembered her greasy hands. "Jane, would you mind taking him? I need to clean up, and he's due for a diaper change."

Jane set the birthday cake down on the table. Pointing her finger at the men. "No one touches this chocolate cake, or I swear, I will tear you limb from limb."

"Yeah, I need to wash up as well," Anablue said as Donall pulled her into his arms, placing a light kiss on her lips.

The afternoon passed at a leisurely pace. A delicious dinner and birthday cake was consumed with relish, followed by a gift opening. Elyse, Elijah, and Donall each opened their presents from each other to see the same gift.

Anablue laughed and shrugged. "It's not like I could tell any of you that you all bought the same book."

Elyse handed Donall a gift. "This is actually for both you and Anablue."

Donall opened the gift and looked up at Elyse. "You're such a little shit." He pulled out a black pirate bandana replete with a Jolly Roger and a gold earring. He clipped the earring on one ear and tied the scarf around his head. "Argh," he growled.

"Keep going," Elyse said.

Donall lifted another sheet of tissue paper, and he chuckled. Pulling out a pale white corset, laying it on his chest, he shimmied his shoulders to whistles and catcalls. Anablue turned a bright shade of pink as Elyse handed her the book, A Pirates Plunder.

"Here's your book back. We've all read it now. It's quite scandalous," Elyse giggled.

"Oh, my God. I will get you for this," Anablue laughed.

---

Sundown brought the group to a bonfire built to ward off the night chill. The men enjoyed a beer from the nearby cooler while the women had gone inside to change into warmer clothing.

Max pulled a pint of whisky from his pocket, taking a swig. He passed it along.

"So, what are your plans, Brendan?" The colonel asked.

"Not sure. Find a job, a place to live," Brendan said.

Donall and Elijah exchanged glances. "Do those plans include a certain beautiful brunette?" Elijah asked.

"Yeah, with amazing amber eyes?" Donall said.

Brendan narrowed his eyes at his brothers. "Possibly."

"We have a message for you," Donall said. "A challenge, so to speak."

"Yeah, what was her name?" Elijah said.

"George," Donall replied. "Strange name for a pretty girl."

"Cut the shit. What's the message?" Brendan growled.

"Catch me if you can," Elijah said.

"What are you going to do about it?" Donall asked, passing him the bottle.

Brendan took a long swig from the bottle. Staring into the fire, he chuckled.

"I... am going to get my shirt back."

Grinning at Elijah, he passed him the bottle.

"Hmm. I'm sure there's a wild story behind that comment," Donall snickered.

"Oh. You know damn well there is," Brendan replied.

ELIJAH WOKE EARLY the next morning. Strolling down the pathway to the gate, he picked up the morning newspaper. He opened the paper and did a double-take. Front and center, a photograph that was taken at the women's march two days earlier.

Two beautiful, well-endowed, young women holding their bras up in front of a burning barrel.

"Elyse," he bellowed.

## CHAPTER 46

Slamming the cash register shut, Renaldo scowled at the man who had entered the bookstore. He had returned from his eight-week recovery from an appendectomy to find chaos. Anablue had been kidnapped, Gary in jail, Marcus was a cop.

*Crazy, they're all crazy.*

"That dark Adonis. I'm going to give him a piece of my mind. Leading that sweet girl on like that. And to think there's a wedding planned. He's already married," he muttered to himself. He pivoted to the wall to place some books on the shelf. The chimes on the door rang again, and he turned around. Oh, for Pete's sake, there he is again.

His mind made up, he stomped over to the first aisle.

Approaching the man. "I'm just going to say my peace. I think it's terrible what you're doing to Anablue. You ought to be..." The man, listening intently, looked up and grinned at someone behind him, and Renaldo turned around.

"Oh, dear gawd, there's two of you," Renaldo said.

The man behind him held out his hand. "I'm Donall Corrington. You must be Renaldo. Anablue speaks fondly of you. This is my brother, Elijah. We hope to see you at the wedding next weekend."

"You were saying?" Elijah said.

Renaldo's hands fluttered to his chest. "Oh, I'm so embarrassed."

"You should have seen Anablue. She thought the same thing. Punched me in the nose," Elijah said.

"She did? Oh, good for her, standing up for herself. I mean, well, never mind." Renaldo said. "What can I do for you?"

"I need to exchange this book. My wife and I bought the same book for each other," Elijah said.

"What is it they say? Great minds think alike," Renaldo quipped.

Helping Elijah exchange books, he waved goodbye as they left. Winking at them, "I'll see you, boys, at the wedding."

Sighing deeply, he turned around to see Maude standing behind him. "They're both just so gorgeous."

"And both spoken for," Maude replied.

"More's the pity," Renaldo sighed.

STANDING OUTSIDE OF THE BOOKSTORE. Elijah and Donall exchanged glances.

"That was weird," Donall said.

"Maybe Anablue is right, and we should paint numbers on our foreheads," Elijah said. "If you would quit wearing the same color shirt as me every day, people could tell us apart."

"You've been saying that since fourth grade when Rose Swanson kissed me by mistake," Donall replied.

"You engineered that one," Elijah growled.

Donall chuckled. "Maybe. Come on, let's go pick up the tuxedos and the rings. Then I'll buy you a beer."

---

ANABLUE GRIMACED AS AGNES, the seamstress, pulled up on the bodice of her wedding dress.

"My boobs got bigger," Anablue said.

"I'll let the bodice out a bit. You should be good till the wedding," Agnes replied.

"I need to buy more bras," Anablue said. "Bigger cups."

Elyse snorted, "I guess we shouldn't have burnt our bras."

"Not sure what I was thinking, burning my favorite," Anablue said.

"It seemed the right thing to do," Elyse said.

"Elijah still mad?"

"No. He understands the protest. He was more miffed by my nipples showing through in the photo."

"Donall wasn't too happy either. He seemed to think that

since I carry everything else in my purse, I'd have a spare bra as well."

Elyse laughed, "It defeats the purpose of burning your bra."

"They'll get over it," Anablue said.

Agnes pulled the pins out of her mouth. "You ladies need to know that the way to equality is to keep your husbands fed, happy in bed, a clean house and children, but most important of all. Keep your independence, take care of yourselves. Most men, but not all, respect that a woman has her own dreams too. If you're lucky, you'll have a man like my Frank, who isn't afraid to run the vacuum cleaner or put a roast in the oven to help out. There's your equality."

"Except for putting a roast in the oven. I have that now," Elyse said.

"It sounds more like a partnership," Anablue said.

"It is. Keep in mind, you're going to fight. Sometimes over the stupidest stuff. Just last week, we fought over baloney, of all things. I guess he's sick of it. I bought more baloney, and he wanted peanut butter. I had to explain that I don't know what peanut butter looks like, so I couldn't buy it," Elyse said.

Anablue's mouth dropped open. "You don't know what peanut butter is?"

"I grew up in Vietnam. My nanny wouldn't have known, and neither did I," Elyse said.

"So, what happened with Elijah?"

"He took me to the market in town, and we bought peanut butter and grape jelly. Then we had a romantic candlelight dinner with our sandwiches. It was perfect. Oh, and olives. He bought me a jar of green olives with those little red things inside. So good. Now, I carry a jar with me everywhere."

"Pimentos. Olives sound good," Anablue said.

Elyse pulled the jar from her purse and offered it to Anablue.

"The dress comes off first," Agnes said with a smile.

"It would be just my luck, mess up my dress with a week to go," Anablue said. "It's almost time to go meet the guys, and we still have a few more things to pick up."

---

Giving a glass a final wipe, Capt. Jack placed the glass on the shelf. He looked up as the door opened and two men entered the bar. Both in uniform, one an Army soldier, the other a Marine. Pausing inside the door, their eyes adjusting to the dim light, they dropped their duffel bags and moved to the bar and pulled up a seat.

"Afternoon, boys. What can I get for you?" Capt. Jack said.

"Beer." They both replied.

Capt. Jack nodded. Filling two mugs, he set them down in front of the men. They picked up the ice-cold mugs and toasted.

"To a perfectly poured ice-cold beer," said one man.

"Can't get that in Nam," replied the other.

They drained their glasses and pushed them to the edge of the bar to be refilled.

"You Corrington boys all have a certain look about you. I'd know any one of you anywhere," Capt. Jack said.

"And you are?"

"Capt. Jack."

"Aiden Yarusso."

"Collin Corrington." Reaching out to shake his hand.

"I take it you're here for the wedding?" Capt. Jack asked.

"Yes, we are," Collin said.

"Do you know the bride?" Aiden asked.

"Yes. You could say so," Capt. Jack replied.

"So, what's the scoop on this chick? I'm curious to see what kind of woman Donall fell for," Aiden said.

"I got a letter from Elyse not too long ago. She said this girl was a Navy mechanic," Collin said.

"No shit. God. She's big and burly. Isn't she?" Aiden said.

Capt. Jack chuckled.

"I'm betting tall and leggy, with big tits," Aiden said.

"Five bucks say medium height with brown hair," Collin replied.

"So, what say you, Capt. Jack? Does she have big tits, tall or short? What color are her hair and eyes?" Aiden said.

A voice came from behind them. "She's blonde, with big blue eyes." Both men turned around in surprise.

"Brendan!" They both exclaimed as they jumped from their stools. After hugs and pats on the back, the three sat with Collin scooting over so Brendan could sit in the middle.

"Where the fuck did you come from, anyway?" Collin asked.

"Donall's apartment is upstairs. I came down the back steps," Brendan replied, as Capt. Jack set a cold beer in front of him.

"Well. We've established that this girl…" Aiden said.

"Anablue," Capt. Jack said.

"This Anablue is a blonde, blue-eyed, navy mechanic. I've got five bucks riding on whether she's tall with a rack," Aiden said. "And possibly, big and burly."

"Nope, I'm guessing she's about five-six," Collin said.

Brendan exchanged amused glances with Capt. Jack.

"I'm just going to sit here and let the two of you dig a deeper hole." Brendan chuckled.

"How so?" Aiden asked.

"Capt. Jack here… is Anablue's father," Brendan said, laughing in his beer.

Aden and Collin looked at each other. "Sorry, sir," they both said.

"It's alright, boys, but to answer your question. She's not much bigger than Elyse. Everything else, you'll have to judge for yourselves," Capt. Jack chuckled.

"She's a pee-wee," Aiden stated.

"Where's Donall and Elijah?" Collin asked.

"Wedding shopping," Brendan snickered.

"It'll be a cold day in hell before I get caught in that snare," Aiden said. "What about you, Brendan?"

Brendan grunted. "Yeah. I'm taking it all in stride"

The door of the bar opened, and Donall and Elijah made their entrance. Settling into their seats after more greetings and black slapping.

Capt. Jack eyed the five men. "You boys always sit alphabetically?"

The five started laughing. "Since we were kids," Donall said. "Goes with maintaining order in a Marine household."

"Whiskey all around. We need to toast the groom," Aiden called out.

LATE, as usual, Elyse went to pull open the door to the bar. Anablue paused, looking up to the sky in fear.

"What's wrong?" Elyse whispered.

"Gram always said I'd get stuck by lightning if I entered a bar," Anablue replied.

Elyse giggled. "And you believed her?"

"Of course."

"This is your father's bar. You should be good."

"True. I survived going into that bar off-base at Edwards."

"Well, there you go."

Pulling the door open, raucous music, laughter, and the lingering smell of pizza hit them as they stepped inside.

Elyse looked around, spying six empty pizza boxes neatly stacked at the end of the bar and the men.

"Sweet Jesus. All five of them, and they're all shit-faced."

"At least they ate something," Anablue said.

Pulling Anablue along by the arm, they stood behind the men.

Aiden turned and spotted Elyse, his eyes riveted to Anablue. "Women," he shouted. He picked Anablue up by the waist and set her to sit on the bar. Then he set Elyse up there as well.

Aiden's eyes narrowed as he looked at Anablue. "You don't look like a mechanic."

"How exactly are mechanics supposed to look?" Anablue said.

He gave her an endearing grin. They had Brendan and Collin's attention now. "Big and burly," Collin replied.

"All greasy, smelling like sweat and motor oil," Brendan said.

"Ewww!" Anablue replied.

"So, if I sent you to the auto-parts store to get some blinker fluid, you'd know what to buy?" Aiden said.

"That's gobbledygook. There's no such thing," Anablue replied.

"Elijah said you have a mean right hook," Brendan said.

"I caught him by surprise," Anablue replied.

"Oh, good grief. Don't pay them any mind," Elyse said as she looked over to Elijah and Donall, both laughing in their beer.

"I can see that we're going to need some backup here."

Anablue looked at all the drunken men around her and turned to Capt. Jack. Leaning over to place a kiss on his cheek.

"Hi, Dad, can you call the colonel?"

"Already did, darling. They'll be here soon," Capt. Jack replied.

Elyse jumped down from the bar, strolling down to Elijah. She wrapped her arms around his waist. "Hello, handsome."

"Hello, brat," Elijah said. Pulling her in for a kiss, his hand snaked down and cupped her bottom.

Slapping his hand away, "Behave," Elyse said.

"I have a surprise for you," Elijah said.

"What is it?"

"If I tell you, it's not a surprise," he chuckled. He reached over the bar and pulled up a pizza box.

"Pizza?"

"Open it," Elijah replied.

She looked inside. "Pepperoni and... green olive. This looks amazing... I will reward you."

"I'm sure Capt. Jack has a broom closet in the back," Elijah whispered in her ear.

Elyse giggled, slipping from his grasp. "Wait until we get home."

Taking the pizza box, she held it up so Anablue could see it. Giving Elijah a saucy smile, she walked to a table near the pool table and sat down.

Anablue jumped down from the bar. Giving the men a brilliant smile. "Never stand in the way of a pregnant woman and food." Pausing to kiss Donall as she passed him by, she made her way to the table.

The men watched her walk to the back of the bar. "Miniskirts. Damn, it's good to be home," Aiden said.

"I'll drink to that," Brendan said.

"What about you, Collin? Where's your wife?" Donall asked.

"Belinda." He paused. "She can't make it this time. But she'll be home… eventually," Collin replied.

The door opened again, and The Colonel and the Ambassador made their entrance to shouts of greeting.

## CHAPTER 47

A few nights later, sitting in the car parked in Mrs. Wang's driveway, Donall pulled Anablue into his arms, his lips claiming hers in a heated exchange that left them both panting with need.

Donall growled in frustration. "This is crazy. We have nowhere to go for privacy." Placing a searing kiss on her neck.

Anablue giggled. "You have to admit it's kind of funny that Mr. Wang trimmed the branches after he caught you climbing the tree to get to my room."

"I've got Aiden, Brendan, and Collin staying at my place, Capt. Jack covering my boat. That old nosey neighbor of Elijah's is watching my beach property."

He growled. "I'm on fire."

"The cops let us off easy for parking up at Lover's Crossing. And let's not forget tonight's Drive-In theatre fiasco."

Donall chuckled in her ear. "Nothing deflates the libido more than cops with flashlights banging on the window or cars full of little kids parked on either side.

"The movie was good," Anablue said. "Mrs. Wang is flashing the outside light."

"What are we, sixteen again? I swear they all made a pact to keep us apart. I'm sure Elijah is rubbing his hands in glee."

"The wedding is the day after tomorrow, my love."

"We should have rented a room," Donall said.

"At this point, we'll have to wait until our wedding night to be together."

"About our wedding night, I think I should warn you. My brothers may try to kidnap you. I have a plan to stop them."

"Elyse told me whatever happens, just go with the flow," Anablue said.

Donall's brow dropped into a worried frown. "Yeah. Sounds about right."

---

THE ALARM CLOCK went off with an incessant ringing. Anablue reached out, fumbling to shut off the annoying noise.

*Whoever invented the alarm clock should be shot.* Burying her head under the pillows, she groaned. Up late the previous night, seeing to last-minute details, she had fallen into bed exhausted.

*Thank God for Mrs. Wang's eye for detail. And Elyse, I'd be a basket-case without them.*

The doorbell rang downstairs. Groaning, Anablue buried herself deeper into the blankets. Mumbling to herself. "I've got a few minutes before Elyse bursts through that door all morning person cheery and bubbly. Ugh!"

Five minutes later, a knock on the door and Elyse stuck her head inside. "Wakey, wakey, eggs, and bakey."

"No, go away," Anablue grumbled.

Elyse giggled, "Rise and shine. The early bird gets the worm."

"And the second mouse gets the cheese. Enough of the idioms," Anablue mumbled from under the covers.

"Oh, that's nasty," Elyse replied. "Get up, you slug. It's your wedding day."

Anablue opened her eyes and smiled. *It's our wedding day.* Flipping the covers up, she sat up.

"I wonder how Donall is doing?"

"I dropped Elijah and Max off at his apartment. They're all going out for breakfast later. Donall probably has butterflies in his stomach, just like you."

"I don't have butterflies."

"That's good. Mrs. Wang is making breakfast. Then, a hot bath for you. Then we're off and running. Before you know it, you'll be walking down the aisle."

Anablue rolled her eyes, flung the covers back over her head, and laid back down.

"Now, I have butterflies."

A knock on the door and Mrs. Wang entered bearing a tray overflowing with food. The aroma of fresh croissants and strawberries drifted to Anablue, and her stomach rumbled with hunger. Throwing the blankets off, Anablue crawled to the end of the bed to grab a croissant. Holding the treat between her teeth, she slipped her arms into the bathrobe Elyse held up for her.

"I'll be spoiled after this." Between bites of the croissant, she popped a strawberry into her mouth.

"Heavenly."

Climbing off the bed, she poured herself a cup of tea. Strolling out to the balcony, she leaned on the railing, basking in the warm sunshine while sipping her tea.

A florist van drove up the street and pulled into the driveway. "The flowers are here," Anablue called into the room.

Elyse stepped onto the balcony. "It's so sweet that Donall wanted to surprise you with the flowers."

"Very romantic."

Mrs. Wang, who had been fussing with the wedding dress. "I'll go down and see to the flowers, then help Jane with the baby."

"Thank you for everything, Mrs. Wang," Anablue said.

Teary-eyed, Mrs. Wang stopped to caress her cheek. "You're like a daughter to us, Anablue. We are proud to help you on your special day."

"Elyse wiped the tears from her own eyes. "Where was I? Oh, he knew exactly what he wanted for you."

"It's a small and elegant wedding. Short of a white bikini on the beach type wedding, this is exactly what we wanted."

"You could've had whatever you wanted," Elyse replied.

"I know. The beach party tomorrow suffices, then we leave for our honeymoon."

"Any idea on where you're going?"

"He won't tell me. It's a surprise. I don't know where we are staying tonight either," Anablue said.

"Okay, girl, you have exactly one hour for a bath," Elyse said, piling towels and bath supplies into Anablue's arms. Placing a jar of hot fudge on top of the load. "Open your mouth." Placing a spoon in her mouth and she pushed her out the door.

"One hour."

THANKFUL TO BE out of the crowded apartment, Donall jogged up the street. Each pounding step sending the blood coursing through his body as he inhaled and exhaled. Covered in sweat, reaching his destination. Hoping for a glimpse of his bride, he hid behind a tree. The florist van was parked in the driveway. The house, a beehive of activity.

Stooping to pretend to tie his shoe as a car drove by, he looked up to the tower room. He frowned when he looked over at the newly trimmed tree out front. He watched the neighbor's cat across the front lawn. Sniffing at the tree in disdain, the cat walked to the other side of the house. When the cat appeared up on Anablue's balcony a minute later, Donall smiled.

Slinking around the backside of the house, he spied

another tree with enough sturdy branches to support his weight.

Intent on the climb, he paused outside an open window on the third floor. Glancing in, he spied Anablue in the steaming bathtub. The tantalizing aroma of soft lavender assaulted his senses as he watched her bathe.

Anablue sat up with a squeal as he slid through the window into the room. Her face lit up in delight. "Donall, what are you doing here?"

He held his finger to his lips. "Shhhh. I came for a kiss."

"You're not supposed to see me before the wedding," she whispered.

His hungry eyes touched on her breasts. Tiny bubbles clung to soft pink peaks, her pale skin glowing from the heat of the bath. Checking the lock, he kicked off his tennis, pulled off his shirt, and he dropped his shorts. "Maybe more than just a kiss," he said.

She slid forward so he could climb in the tub. Once he was settled, he pulled her on top of him. Straddling his waist, she plied his chest with a soft sponge. Gazing into his eyes, she held him breathless in her love. "Happy wedding day, my love," she said.

"Happy wedding day, Baby blue," he replied as he cupped her face and pulled her in for a soft, lingering kiss.

Twenty minutes later, Mrs. Wang knocked on the door. "Anablue. Did you fall asleep in there?"

Donall and Anablue bolted upright, scrambling from the tub in a panic. "I'm almost finished. I'll be right out," Anablue called. Donall grabbed a towel and quickly dried off. Pulling his clothes and shoes on, he pulled her to him for one last kiss. "I'll see you in a few hours."

"I'll be there with bells on," Anablue whispered.

Donall climbed out the window, launching himself into the tree. The old tree's brittle branches didn't hold, and Donall fell, hitting a few branches on the way down. Miraculously, he was saved from hitting the ground by a branch stuck through his shorts and boxers. Dangling five feet off the ground, he found himself face to face with Mr. Wang. Mr. Wang, with no expression on his face, looked up to the bathroom window. Donall, still dangling, looked into the kitchen window to see Elyse standing there, watching with her mouth hanging open.

Taking the ten-foot pole tree pruner he held in his hands, Mr. Wang reached up and snipped Donall's shorts and boxers.

"No. Wait… wait, wait," Donall cried out. He fell to the ground naked. Rolling to his feet, he caught the grin on Mr. Wang's face as he walked away. Turning to look at Elyse, he pulled his shirt down to cover himself. Elyse's eyes followed his shorts and boxers, fluttering to the ground. Elyse's eyes crinkled up as she shook with laughter. Donall reached down and grabbed his shorts, wrapping them around his waist like a skirt.

Muttering to himself, "Old bastard, could've cut the fucking branch." Scowling at Elyse, he stomped out of the yard with as much dignity as he could muster.

## CHAPTER 48

Staring into the mirror, Anablue bit her lip. "I feel like a princess," she whispered.

"You look like a princess," Elyse whispered back.

Anablue caught Mrs. Wang's and Elyse's teary-eyed smiles in the full-length mirror.

"Are you ready to see the flowers?" Mrs. Wang asked.

"Oh yes," Anablue smiled.

Elyse handed her the bouquet. "You can't cry."

Anablue's breath caught in her throat. Pale blue Chrysanthemums interspersed with bright Baby Blue Eyes and clouds of Baby's breath.

"Oh…" she breathed. "How lovely."

"Donall told me the story of your first and second dates. He went to his beach property yesterday and picked the Baby

Blue Eyes himself, then delivered them to the florist. He wanted you to know that he re-seeded the area," Elyse said.

She put her hand to her mouth, blinking back the tears. "Oh my God, these are perfect." Anablue cried as she fanned her eyes.

"To help avoid twin confusion, since they're all wearing black tuxedos. Donall's boutonniere is a blue Chrysanthemum with the Baby Blue Eyes. Elijah's and everyone else's flowers are yellow, with Baby's breath," Elyse said.

Anablue nodded.

"Are you ready? Your father is waiting," Mrs. Wang said.

"I'll go get him," Elyse said.

---

Elyse walked into the chapel vestibule, her blue gown whispering as it swished around her legs and her high heels clicked in a staccato beat on high polished marble floors. She stopped to help pin Capt. Jack's boutonniere on his lapel. "You can go into the bridal room now," she sweetly murmured. Moving down the line of brothers, she straightened lapels, pinning flowers, her melodic voice, softly whispering words of encouragement.

Stopping at the colonel, she straightened his bow tie.

"You look very dashing, dad."

"Spoken like a true Sargent overseeing the troops," the colonel replied.

Elyse snorted. "You forget I've seen Sargent's at work. They don't exactly dish out compliments."

"So, you have," he grinned.

Elijah was next in line. She brushed a piece of lint from his shoulders. He grabbed her waist and pulled her in for a soft kiss.

"You're taller today," he whispered in her ear.

"I'm wearing four-inch heels," Elyse replied.

"I give you an hour, tops, before you lose those shoes," he said. "You look divine in that dress."

"Thank you. I look forward to you removing it later," she coyly whispered.

Moving to Donall, she pinned his blue boutonniere on as well. With a grin on her face, she looked up into his eyes biting her lip to hold back her laughter. "So, we're even now," Elyse said.

Looking down at her, he narrowed his eyes. "How so?"

"I'll never mention your… um… fall from grace this morning. If you never mention that back massage," Elyse said.

"That's blackmail. You truly are a little shit," Donall growled.

"I'll take that as a compliment," she retorted. "Seriously, I'm so happy for you and Anablue. May all your dreams come true."

Donall grinned. "They already have. I'm marrying my best friend today, and she carries our child."

Teary-eyed, she kissed his cheek. Stepping back, she eyed

the men. "You all pass muster. You can take your places now. The ceremony starts in five minutes."

---

Capt. Jack knocked on the door, which was opened by Mrs. Wang. "There you are, Jack. She's ready," Mrs. Wang said. As she stepped outside the room, pulling the door shut.

"Hello Jun. You look lovely today. I'd like to thank you for all that you have done for my little girl." Capt. Jack said.

"Anything for you, Jack, and in Mary's memory," Mrs. Wang replied.

"We have much to celebrate," Mrs. Wang said. "Tonight. I intend to dance and drink a glass of champagne."

Capt. Jack chuckled. "Save a dance for me, Jun."

Knocking again, Capt. Jack entered the bridal room. Closing the door softly behind him, his breath caught in his throat at the sheer beauty of his daughter in her wedding finery.

His eyes teared up. "It seems unfair that I have to turn you over to another man after so recently finding you," he said.

Anablue rolled her eyes, "That's codswapple. You'll always have me as a daughter. Besides, we're going to be living right next door."

"It's codswallop."

"Oh, ninny muffins! I said it wrong. I must be more nervous than I thought," Anablue replied.

"You're nervous? I had this whole speech worked out in

my head. Now I find I can't remember what I was going to say," Capt. Jack said. "Though I do know. Your mother, grandmother, and Brian would all be so proud of you. Just like I am."

"I like to think they're watching over us," Anablue said.

"They truly are. It's time. Are you ready?"

Anablue nodded. "My father is walking me down the aisle, and I get to marry the man I love. I'm more than ready for the happiest day of my life."

THE FIVE BROTHERS, standing in line at the front of the pews, shifted uncomfortably, exchanged glances, and looked to their father in the front pew, his grin a mile wide. They looked again to the officiating priest who had just entered. Their boyhood priest, Marine chaplain, Father Andrews grinned back. "Afternoon, boys. Beautiful day for a wedding." Each man grinned as the memories of many pranks gone awry filled their heads.

The harpist started a lovely melody as a hush fell over the small gathering. All eyes glittered with anticipation as they turned to the back of the tiny chapel. Elyse, a vision in pale blue as she moved down the aisle. Her glorious red hair fell in soft ringlets topped with a crown of yellow chrysanthemums and blue ribbons, matching the small bouquet she held in her hands. Taking her place next to Father Andrews, a minute passed, and Anablue appeared on her father's arm at the entrance to the chapel. Teary-eyed guests stood to honor the bride.

---

Inhaling sharply, Donall blinked back the mist in his eyes. His gaze caressed his bride from the tiny braids circling her head like nature's crown. They shimmered through the sheer veil attached at the back with a tiny blue flower clip. The remaining hair falling in soft natural curls to brush her shoulders.

The dress was beautiful. Champagne colored. It hugged her bodice and waist. It was sleeveless with delicate scalloped lace edging the straps. Tiny blue seed pearls were embroidered across the bodice and curve of her hips. The a-line skirt fell in pleated folds to sweep the floor. He looked at the delicate flowers he had picked for her, clasped in one hand. The other hand lightly resting on Capt. Jack's arm trembled ever so slightly.

She was perfection.

Donall stepped forward as she turned to kiss her father's cheek. She turned back to him, and her smile radiated across her face as he gazed deep into her eyes. Taking her by the hand, he led her the remaining distance to stand in front of the priest.

A simple ceremony, and soon over, Donall pulled her into his arms for their first kiss as husband and wife. Gentle, sweet, and raw, he poured everything he had ever felt for her into his kiss. That she returned it tenfold made his heart swell. He didn't stop until Father Andrews cleared his throat. She smiled, and laughing, he smiled right back.

---

Walking back down the aisle, they beamed at their guests on either side of the aisle. Anablue glanced over in surprise at the hobo sitting in the back of the chapel. The man dressed in rags, with shocking red hair matching his long bushy beard. His bright green eyes sparkled, and he winked at her.

Looking at Donall. "Who's that man?" she asked.

"What man, My Love?" Donall said.

She turned back to the man, and he was gone. "Oh. He's gone now."

---

Standing in the vestibule, Donall rolled his eyes as his brothers stepped forward to offer their congratulations. He had expected this. He supposed he had it coming, remembering Collin and Elijah's weddings. Each brother pulled Anablue into their arms and kissed her. They let her up for air, and the next one took over.

"Are you assholes done yet?" Donall growled.

"Let the Army show the Navy and the Marine Corps how it's done," replied Aiden, as he bent Anablue in his arms and thoroughly kissed her.

"I'll second that," replied Brendan.

"You don't get seconds," Donall snarled.

"Holy shenanigans," Anablue said, "I wasn't expecting all that."

Elyse stepped forward to hug her. "It's all in good fun. It's kind of ongoing thing they have."

"That's it, though. Right?" Anablue said.

Elyse snorted, her laughter bubbling through. "That's it. Here's Jane and Max."

Donall reached out and shook Max's hand. "Didn't I tell you, Max?"

"So, you did," Max replied.

"Tell him what?" Anablue asked.

"I told Max not to doubt my charm, and he'd be at our wedding."

Max laughed. "That was back at Edwards."

"It seems like so much has happened since then," Anablue said.

---

Sitting at the table facing the small group of twenty-five guests. Anablue counted her blessings. They filled each of the tables with friends and family. Stomachs replete from the delicious dinner, they lingered over coffee and wedding cake. Elyse stood in front of the four-piece string quartet, softly swaying to the music. Bunker, with his head laying on her shoulder, exhausted from the day's festivities, fought to keep his eyes open. Jane and Max would soon take him to Mrs. Wang's house, a neighborhood teenage babysitter would keep an eye on him and Soup for the evening.

Anablue watched Elijah, his loving gaze on his wife and son. "She's quite beautiful. The way she dances with him," Anablue said.

"She dances him to sleep every night," Elijah said. "Tonight will be the first time he'll be gone overnight with a sitter. We're both nervous."

"He'll be in excellent hands with Mrs. Wang," Donall replied. "Where are you staying tonight?"

"Elyse booked us a room at some swanky hotel downtown. I don't know where. Sometimes, I just go where I'm told," Elijah chuckled.

"Where are you staying at?" Elijah asked.

Donall snorted. "Like I'd tell you."

"Worried?"

Donall gave him a long, cool look. "Not a bit."

"You should be," Elijah said.

---

THE PHOTOGRAPHER, at Donall's request, wanted additional pictures taken at the marina. Strolling the dock with his new bride, Donall felt like the luckiest man alive. The entire wedding party, along with the colonel and Capt. Jack were posted at various spots along the picturesque dock. White sailboats with their festive sails and motorized boats passed by the wedding party, blowing their horns and shouting their congratulations to the happy couple.

Lifting his wife in his arms, Donall posed in his sailboat to the good-natured teasing by his brothers, wondering if the old rust bucket was going to sink to the bottom of the marina.

The photographer, a young blonde-haired man named Joe, prompted all the men to stand at the end of the dock. Aiden, Brendan, Collin, Elijah, the Colonel, Ambassador Booker, Capt. Jack and Father Andrews all waited somewhat impatiently for Donall standing behind Joe to tear himself away from Anablue's delectable lips to join them for the photograph. Donall looked up to see Max, Jane, and Elyse standing behind them.

"Go jump in that line-up Max," Donall prompted.

The men posed for pictures while Donall dawdled a bit. Looking at his watch, he grinned. "Eight bells," he whispered to himself.

Anablue looked at him in confusion. Then her eyes widened. " Bart," she whispered back. She turned to yell a warning as Donall's hand slipped over her mouth.

Bart launched himself out of the water and onto the dock. Like a bowling ball hitting the pins, every man there went sailing into the drink. Donall grabbed Anablue's hand. "Run," he yelled.

Behind them, loud cursing guaranteed to burn the ears off of anyone who heard them filled the air. The loudest, Father Andrews. Bart barked for his supper as the younger men climbed out of the water, and the chase was on.

Donall pulled Anablue along as they ran down the dock and up to the wharf. Spotting cable car, they ran after it until it stopped. Jumping on the back, Donall spotted his brothers and Max half a block back, giving chase.

Pulling Anablue into his arms. "Epic," he whispered, as his lips descending onto hers. When their kiss finally ended, he lifted his head to see that they were no longer moving away from his brothers. With a dawning sense of dread, he realized instead the cable car had hit a turnabout and was headed right back down to where his brothers and Max stood grinning.

"Oh, poppycock," Anablue said.

## CHAPTER 49

Elijah grinned while walking along the dock. Every so often, he dropped a piece of his twin's clothing on the dock. Tucking a piece of a treasure map in the jacket pocket before he dropped it. With one last glance back to Donall to make sure he was alright and everything was in order. Elijah's face lit up in a devilish grin as he climbed into the back of the black limousine they had hired for the evening.

SETTING THE CHOKE AND THROTTLE, Jane pulled the rope to start the outboard motor as Elyse pointed to the dingy anchored not too far out in the bay.

Pulling up next to the dingy, Jane and Elyse exchanged glances. "Oh boy," Jane said.

Donall was duct-taped, arms at his sides, wearing nothing but his boxer shorts to the mast. Hiking her gown up, Elyse climbed into the dingy.

"Seriously, Donall. You and your brothers take these wedding night pranks too far," Elyse said.

Donall, with duct tape over his mouth, rolled his eyes.

Pulling her knife from the pocket of her gown. "Well. We have to start somewhere," Elyse said, pulling the duct tape from his mouth.

"Where's my father? Why are the two of you out here?" Donall snarled.

"We weren't sure exactly which of the two marinas you were at. They went to the other one. So, you're stuck with us," Elyse said.

"Let's start with your legs."

Donall yelped in pain as Elyse pulled a piece of duct tape from his legs.

"I hate to tell you this, but you're going to be bald in some spots by the time we're done," Jane said.

"Just make it quick," Donall growled.

Elyse slipped the knife between the mast and cut the tape. "Okay. Your belly and forearms are next. One, two…."

"Don't. No counting. Just do it," Donall snarled.

"You know, I've heard of hair removal similar to this for women before," Elyse said. "I read about it in a magazine article."

"No kidding," Jane replied.

"Yeah. It's called waxing. It goes back to the Egyptians. I guess Hollywood starlets do it," Elyse giggled.

Jane yanked the duct tape from his sensitive belly as Donall gritted his teeth.

"I think the Egyptian's didn't leave any body hair," Elyse said.

Her eyes widened in shock. "You mean everywhere?" Jane asked.

"Everywhere," Elyse whispered.

Looking skyward, "Oh for the love of God," Donall thundered. "Could the two of you quit with the chatter and get on with it?"

Looking at the duct tape right at his underwear line, Elyse giggled. "Be grateful you're wearing boxers," she said as she gave the tape a hard yank.

GUIDING the motorboat to the dock, Donall jumped out. Offering a hand, he helped Elyse and Jane out of the boat.

"I'm going to kill them. You know that, right?" Donall said.

"No, you're not. You're going to look at this as a prank and start planning revenge for Aiden and Brendan's weddings. You were never in danger. In case you didn't notice the three sailboats floating nearby. All at ready, in case you needed help, or if we didn't find you by a certain time. Go find Anablue. She's in excellent hands." Elyse said.

Donall nodded and took off at a trot down the dock. First, he found his pants, pulling them on at a run. Then his shirt, socks, and shoes, one at a time. Finding his dinner jacket, he slipped it on and found the map to the first bar in the pocket.

Running up the street, he hailed a taxi.

---

GRIMACING as another round of drinks was served. Anablue glared at her captors. "I'm going to float away if I drink any more water," Anablue said. "I mean, this is the fifth bar we've been to. I'm a little flummoxed at how Donall is going to find me."

"Hold on. I've heard that one before," Max said as he pulled out his funny word list. "Flummoxed, here it is. Perplexed," he translated.

Anablue raised her eyebrows. "Really? You keep a list?"

"Doesn't everybody?" Max said.

"No, they're all kind of used to me," Anablue replied.

"This is it, then we take you back," Elijah said.

"We've been leaving pieces of the map with the bartender at every bar. He has to drink a shot, and then they'll give him the map. He'll eventually wind up back at the reception to claim his bride," Collin said.

The men all laughed as they toasted her again. Downing their drinks, they paid the tab.

"The five of you are sloshed." Sighing deeply, "I need to find the biffy," Anablue said.

"Again?" Brendan said.

"You pee a lot when you're pregnant," Anablue said.

The waiter directed her to the ladies-room outside of the bar. In the attached hotel, right off the front lobby, past the elevators. The five men escorted her out to the lobby.

"The limo is parked out the front door. We'll wait for you outside," Aiden said.

---

Twenty floors up, five brides waited for an elevator. Already running late, they impatiently argued with each other.

"If you wouldn't have taken so long with your make-up, Frank, we wouldn't be running behind schedule," Mark whined.

"Don't blame me if we're late, Mark. Blame that Diva bitch, Annabelle, two floors up. Too damn good to have his room by us," Frank said.

"Please, I'm in costume. Call me by my stage name, Shontell," Mark replied.

"Have any of you met Annabelle before?" Clyde asked.

"No, but I've heard he's quite the bitch, though very good," James replied. "With George sick, we were lucky to find a replacement. Especially, the queen of the queens."

"Well, let's pray he knows the routine, or we're screwed. We'll never get another gig again," Frank replied.

Fluttering his hands in front of his eyes. "Don't make me cry. I'll ruin my make-up," Mark cried.

"Thank Gawd. Here's the elevator," John said.

"I hope they have champagne in the limo," Mark said.

---

THE HOTEL NIGHT MANAGER, Jacob, wrung his hands. Standing in the lobby, he waited for the bridal troupe to appear. He had been told that the famous troupe, though wildly popular, was to be ushered quickly through the hotel and out a side door. He breathed a sigh of relief as the elevator doors opened and brides filled the lobby. Quickly moving the chattering group through the lobby and out to their limo parked at the side entrance.

"Wait, honey, Annabelle isn't here yet," Frank said.

"I'll go inside and get her," Jacob replied.

---

APPLING her lipstick and straightened her veil. Anablue checked her look one more time.

"Just go with the flow," she whispered to her reflection.

Picking up her bouquet from the counter, she walked out the restroom door. Pausing for a minute to get her bearings, the hotel manager rushed up to her.

"Oh, there you are, Annabelle. They're waiting for you in the limo."

"It's Anablue," she replied.

"Whatever. You know. You all do such a remarkable job. I

mean, you actually look like a woman. Your tits are perfect. They look real."

Anablue gave him an incredulous look. "I would hope so."

"Well, never mind. You're going to be late," Jacob said as he rushed her out the side door. The doorman opened the car door, and she climbed inside, and the limo took off into the night.

PACING outside the front of the hotel, Elijah checked his watch again. He had promised Elyse that their prank would last only a couple of hours before they returned Anablue to the reception.

Aiden, who leaned against the car with Collin, Brendan, and Max, called out. "What's taking her so long?"

"I'm not sure," Elijah replied. "Why don't one of you go in and check."

"I'll go," Collin said, as he sauntered inside the hotel. Coming back out a moment later. "Jacob, the manager said he'd bring her out as soon as he spots her leaving the restroom."

LEROY CROSTAN, also known as Annabelle, smoothed out his hoop skirt. Looking in the mirror in the men's room, "You are a gorgeous bride," he said to himself. Giving his long blonde wig one last pat, he pinched his cheeks, grabbed his frilly white parasol from the counter, and left the men's room. Standing in the lobby, he made eye contact with Jacob.

"Oh, there you are. They're waiting for you by the limo," Jacob said. Taking her by the arm, he guided her out the front doors to the men waiting outside.

"Here you go. I found your bride," Jacob said.

Breathing a sigh of relief, Elijah turned around. He looked from Jacob to the bride, who stood at six-foot-four in heels. "Are you fucking kidding me?"

"Brendan, who stood next to Elijah. "Uh, this gargantuan is not our bride," he said. Turning to Annabelle,

"No insult intended."

"It's alright," Came Annabelle's reply in a deep male voice.

"Where… is Anablue?" Elijah demanded.

"Well, what does she look like?" Jacob asked.

"Tiny little blonde, big blue eyes," Collin piped up. "In a wedding gown."

"Oh… Oh shit… I… well…," Flinging his arm wide toward the side street. "I put the little bride in the other limo."

"You did what?" Elijah growled.

Elijah and his brothers exchanged looks of horror.

"How the hell are we going to explain we lost her?" Aiden said.

A taxicab came to a squealing stop in front of them. Out hopped a visibly pissed-off Donall. Handing the driver forty bucks. "Thanks, Mike," he said calmly. Turning to his brothers and Max. "Where is she?"

"Oh fuck," Elijah said.

"Who's that? Jacob said. "He doesn't look happy."

"That... is the actual bride's husband," Brendan said.

"Jesus, Mary, and Joseph. He's going to kill me, isn't he?" Jacob cried.

"Possibly," replied Aiden. "We'll do our best to keep you alive." Chuckling at the absurdity of the situation. Aiden looked over to Max and Collin leaning against the car, laughing their asses off.

"Where is Anablue?" Donall asked, looking between his brothers. He did a double-take, looking at Annabelle.

"There was a slight misunderstanding," Jacob said. "I put the real bride in the limo with the other drag queens."

"Drag queens? Donall bellowed. "You can't tell the difference between a real woman and a six-foot-four bride with Adam's apple?"

Turning to Annabelle, "No offense meant."

"None was taken," Annabelle replied.

"In my defense, they're all quite beautiful," Jacob said. "It's hard to tell. I mean, I complimented the little bride on her beautiful breasts."

Donall's eyebrows dropped in a thunderous glare.

"Thank you, honey," Annabelle said. Poking Donall with his parasol. "If you hot heads would calm down. I know where they're going."

"Okay, let's get out of here," Elijah said. They all climbed into the limo. After pushing the hoop and yards of taffeta with lace inside the car, Elijah rolled his eyes, climbed in, and pulled the car door shut with a slam.

"Scoot over sugar, unless you want me sitting on your lap. "Annabelle said to Donall. "There's one of those new-fangled car telephones in here, you can use if you want to make a call. Otherwise, champagne, anyone?" holding up the bottle.

"Sure, why not," Donall glumly replied. "I could use a drink right about now."

## CHAPTER 50

Staring out the tinted windows, the lights of the city whizzed by. Anablue watched the full moon rising over the Golden Gate bridge. The bay, smooth, silvery, and calming. She inhaled sharply.

*Jiminy Crickets! That's it. That's what I need to paint for Brian.*

Anablue had the oddest sensation that something was wrong. The men were unusually quiet. Hearing the soft rustle of silk, the hair on the back of her neck stood up, and she shivered.

"Can someone turn on the light, please?" Anablue said.

They flipped on the switch, and Anablue looked in wide-eyed wonder at the other occupants of the limo.

"What a nincompoop I am. I'm in the wrong limo," she breathed. Flipping around, she stared out the back window.

Her anxiety rose, and she leaned over and knocked on the window between the driver and the occupants.

"Hey. Hey, take me back," Anablue cried.

"He can't hear you, honey. That window is soundproof, and the button to lower it is broken," came a deep voice from the bride sitting next to her.

She turned in shock to stare at them. Her gaze swept all of them, looking from the bouffant wigs to long fake eyelashes. Heavy eye make-up, and the overly rouged cheeks, bright red lipstick, back to the bridal gowns. Up and down, her eyes swept them before coming back up to rest on their pretty faces.

"I'm a little flummoxed here. Who are you, people?'"

"Oh, Annabelle. Don't be such a drama queen," the bride sitting directly across from her said.

"It's Anablue," she whispered. "You're a man." She firmly stated.

"We all are, honey."

She blinked. "Pardon my ignorance. But why are you wearing bridal gowns if you're men?"

The brides gave each other uneasy looks.

"Are you, or are you not, Annabelle, the queen of the drag queens?" the bride across from her asked.

"No. What's a drag queen?" Anablue said.

The inside of the limo erupted into warbling chaos as they all spoke at once.

"Everyone, relax. We're performers. We're men who dress as women for a song and dance show."

"Well, you had me fooled at first. You're all quite beautiful," Anablue said.

"We flew in from Vegas last night for tonight's performance at the Roaring Twenties Club. By the way, I'm Frank. This is Mark, Clyde, James, and John."

"Obviously, we've taken the wrong bride. Annabelle must be back at the hotel," James said.

"Annabelle is a sharp cookie. She'll find her way to the club," Frank said.

Anablue teared up. "How is my husband going to find me? It's supposed to be my wedding night."

"There, there, Honey. We'll work this out as soon as we get to the club," Frank said as he patted her hand.

"Here. Have some champagne," John said as he shoved a glass into her other hand.

"Is champagne is good for the baby?" Anablue asked.

"Oh, give me that. Haven't you heard? No drinking or smoking when you're pregnant," Frank said. "It's in all the magazines."

"Here we are at the club," Clyde trilled.

---

THE CHAUFFEUR OPENED the car door, and the brides were rushed into a side entrance. The club manager quietly admonished them for their tardiness. Pushed into the dressing room with the others, Anablue stood watching them amidst the hubbub of activity as they touched up their make-up and wigs in front of vanity tables with tall mirrors surrounded by bright lights. Wig stands, perfume bottles, and jars of make-up brushes cluttered the tops of each vanity. The bride's bright chatter changed tones to higher womanly pitches.

A man came up to her. "What's your name, darling?"

"Anablue."

"I'm Ralph, the stage manager. You're just the one I was looking for. Are you ready to go?"

"I'm more than ready," Anablue replied.

"Good. Quickly. Follow me."

Anablue followed him outside of the dressing room. Stepping over electrical cables and up a short flight of stairs. Coming upon a small throne held by cables.

"Your throne awaits. Have a seat. It won't belong. Remember, hang on tight," Ralph said before he disappeared into a rising fog.

"Hey. Wait. Don't leave me here. And why do I have to hang on tight?" She called out after him. Anablue squealed, hanging on for dear life; her stomach twisted in knots as the chair rose off the floor, lifting her higher and higher into the rigging.

"I guess he wasn't taking me out front to call a taxi," Anablue muttered. Looking out, heavy red velvet curtains hung to the floor. Forcing herself to look down, the brides were taking their places below while stagehands slid wooden set designs into place on the foggy stage.

"Bumfuzzle. What is this, Moulin rouge?"

One of the brides looked up at her. Shock written plainly

on her face as she pointed toward Anablue. Another much taller bride joined the group, twittering, holding their hands over their mouths. That must be Annabelle. Anablue shrugged her shoulders in a silent response as the curtains rose and the brides began an improvised routine.

PULLING to a screeching stop in front of the club, Elijah and Donall jumped out from each side of the limo. Reaching a hand in to help Annabelle out, Elijah grinned as Annabelle cursed loudly, trying to get her tangled hoopskirt out of the car. Once she was out, she flounced into the club, swearing the whole way.

The rest of the men came around to Elijah's side.

"Nice enough, guy. Not sure I can un-see some things I've seen tonight," Brendan said.

"Brace yourself. I'm sure there's more to come," Collin chuckled.

"Aiden looked up at the flashing pink and purple neon marquee lights. Then to the searchlights swaying through the night sky from the roof of the nightclub. "What kind of club is this?"

"No idea. But we're about to find out," Max replied.

Elijah rolled his eyes as they followed a determined Donall into the Nightclub.

STRIDING INTO THE SMALL LOBBY, Donall stopped, his path forward blocked by three large bouncers.

"Ten bucks to get in," said the host standing at a podium. The man's gaze swept Elijah and Donall. "Oooh! double trouble."

"Did a limo full of brides arrive?" Donall snarled, his patience worn thin.

"I'm sure they did. The show starts in five minutes."

"Did they come through here? Was there a small blonde bride with them?"

"No idea. Other than the tall one who just came through here, the others would have entered through the side entrance. They would have gone straight to their dressing room."

"How do I get to the dressing room to speak to them?"

"You don't. The closest you can get are the tables in front. And, they're full."

The man held out his hand. Donall growled deep in his throat. Pulling out his wallet, he started placing twenty-dollar bills in the man's hand.

"You know. I think a table just opened up. Right this way, gentlemen."

FRONT AND CENTER of the stage, Donall stood, hands on his hips. His eyes scanned the large club. Tables filled quickly with patrons, anxious for the show to begin. Wait staff dressed as flappers from the roaring twenties, balanced trays filled with all manners of festive cocktails. Their short, tiered fringe dresses swinging to and fro as they took care of the needs of the thirsty crowd.

Feeling dejected at not seeing that one sweet face he sought in the crowd. He looked to the table his brothers and Max sat at. Spotting the familiar faces at the table next to them. Father, Elyse, Capt. Jack, the Ambassador, Renaldo, Maude, and Jane. After some shuffling around, they pulled tables together and sat as one group.

Elyse rose from the table, approaching Donall. "I checked the powder room and the coatroom. Capt. Jack and your father already circled the club twice. She's probably backstage."

"How did you get here so fast?" Donall asked.

"We were closer to the club than you, and Renaldo knew exactly where it was. Don't you think it's cool that Elijah was able to call us from the limo?" Elyse said.

"Yeah," Donall replied.

"I'm sure she's fine."

"But the question is. Is she here?"

The lights of the club dimmed, and a hush fell over the crowd as the curtain rose.

"Sit down, Donall. There's nothing we can do until the show is over."

Donall had to admit they were quite good. Their lip-syncing was right on. Six brides moved to the tune Chapel of love. A white and gold throne decorated with floral garland began its descent down from the rafters.

Donall's eyebrows shot straight up as the throne came into view. The seated bride appeared to be praying. Eyes closed, she clung to the cables. The crowd clapped and cheered. Donall exchanged shocked glances with his family. They burst into laughter and clapped along with the crowd.

The six brides and two men dressed in tuxedos flanked the chair. A smile lit Donall's face as he watched with barely contained mirth as the tiny bride was coaxed off the throne and into a dance routine with the men. They took turns swirling and twirling her until she was in a line across the front of the stage with the other brides. They would turn right, and she would turn left. Blushing profusely until she got the hang of the fancy footwork.

Donall stood and strode to the stage. Crooking his finger at his bride. Relief flooded her features, and she practically flung herself off the stage into his arms.

"There you are, Baby blue," Donall whispered.

His lips descended onto hers in a passionate kiss. The crowd rose to their feet, roaring their approval as Donall strode from the room, his bride in his arms.

## CHAPTER 51

The limo pulled up in front of the hotel. The doorman opened the door, and Donall hopped out. Pulling Anablue out, he lifted her into his arms and strode into the lobby. Going up to the front desk, he waited for the night manager to look up.

"Good evening, sir. I'll be right with you." Looking up. "Oh, good Lord, you're back," Jacob said. "I see with the correct bride."

Anablue giggled in his arms. "If I would have known this is where we were spending the night, I would've stayed put."

"Your key to the bridal suite, Mr. and Mrs. Corrington. Your luggage was received and is in your suite. Again, we apologize for the misunderstanding earlier," Jacob said.

Twenty minutes later, Jacob looked up again. Eyeing the

red-head, a man held in his arms. "Mr. Corrington, just how many wives do you have?"

Elijah grinned and chuckled. "One is more than enough, Jacob. I take it my twin and his bride are here?"

"They're in the bridal suite," Jacob replied.

"Elijah, you get that look of the devil off your face. We are going to leave them alone," Elyse said.

Setting Elyse down. "Send a bottle of champagne, orange juice, and a plate of chocolate-covered strawberries to Mr. and Mrs. Donall Corrington in the bridal suite." Elijah wrote a quick note for Donall. Taking his key from Jacob, he scooped his wife back up in his arms to her squeals of laughter and strode to the elevator.

A KNOCK SOUNDED at the door. Donall opened the door to see a steward with a cart. "A gift for you and your bride," said the steward as he wheeled the cart into the room. He handed Donall the note. Donall placed a five-dollar bill in the man's hand and pushed him out the door.

Opening the note, he read:

*Bro,*

*All tomfoolery aside. Have a blessed life with your beautiful bride.*

*Much love,*

*Elijah.*

*P.S. Don't fight over baloney. Life's too short.*

Donall grinned and lifted the silver plate cover. "Yum." Popping the cork on the champagne, he poured two glasses, one with orange juice. Hearing a whisper of silk, he looked up to see Anablue standing in the doorway.

His eyes sinfully kissed every inch of her, from her blonde hair brushing her silky shoulders. Her pale pink nightgown hugged every curve and valley of her lush body. Down her shapely legs, to her pale pink toenails, and back up again. He paused at the pink panties peeking through the black lace trim of her nightie.

"You're so beautiful," he breathed. "Come here."

She moved to stand in front of him. "I've never been with a married man before. It's kind of hot."

Handing her a glass of orange juice. "Feeling decadent, are we?" Donall asked.

Taking a sip before she set her glass down, she slid her hands up his forearm to his biceps. She lightly caressed his shoulder before moving behind him to run her fingers lightly across his back. He shivered with need as she came back around him. Running her fingers along his neck, down to his partially unbuttoned shirt.

"Absolutely wanton." Tracing her finger down his chest, she unbuttoned the rest of his shirt, placing feather-light kisses on his chest.

Shrugging his shirt off, he tossed it onto a chair before pulling her into his arms. Nuzzling her neck, he breathed in the scent of her.

"You still smell like lavender from this morning's bath," he whispered in her ear. Suckling on her earlobe, his mouth moved to her neck. Teasing and flicking, he made his way down to one shoulder. Pushing the silken strap down her arm, his lips made a trail across her chest to the other side. Pushing the other strap down, her nightgown dangled precariously off of pale pink crests.

His mouth greedily pushed the fabric off her breast and captured a nipple. Her nightgown slid to pool at her feet, and he hoisted her up, his hands roaming, cupping, and squeezing her round bottom.

He carried her to the bed, laying her down. He made quick work of removing his remaining clothes before crawling up the bed.

Picking up a silken limb, ever so slowly, he placed small kisses up her leg. Watchful for her reaction, he gazed into her stormy eyes.

"I think you've got something there. It is hot kissing the thighs of a married woman," Donall whispered.

"Get up here," Anablue whispered back.

"No, I saved something special for you tonight." He gave her a roguish grin, bending his head to remove her panties with his teeth.

A minute later, she gripped his head as she bucked her hips. "Oh, bumfuzzle. Whatever you are doing is wicked. So good, but oh so wicked."

DANGLING a chocolate-covered strawberry above his mouth, Anablue giggled when Donall reached up and captured a bite. Licking at the strawberry juice that dribbled down his chin. "Delicious. Who would have thought strawberries and chocolate would be so sexy," Anablue said.

"It's right up there with eating a jar of hot fudge in the tub," Donall replied.

"When I'm feeling really naughty, I have a jar of caramel too."

Anablue bit into a strawberry. Trailing the juice down his chest. "What happened to the hair on your chest and belly?"

Donall grimaced, then chuckled. "I've been assured it will grow back."

"I need a shower. I'm covered in chocolate and strawberries." She rolled from the bed, taking the sheet with her. Wrapping it around herself, she giggled as he growled at her.

Pointing her finger at him. "No. I cannot survive on strawberries and sex alone. We need breakfast." She squealed when he leaped from the bed. Wiggling out of his reach, leaving him holding the sheet, she ran for the bathroom. Stepping into a large walk-in shower, she looked around in awe. *Wow. What a cool shower.* She turned the water on. Donall came up behind her, cupping her breasts with his large hands. Then turning her around, he hoisted her up, leaning into the shower wall.

Wrapping her arms around his neck. She stared deep into his eyes. "I love you. I can't say it enough, on how happy I am, knowing that I get to wake up by your side every day for the rest of my life."

"I love you too, Baby blue."

LATER AT BREAKFAST, pushing her plate away. "Holy Moly. I can't eat another bite. I'm stuffed," Anablue said.

Donall chuckled. "You ate that entire stack of pancakes."

"I know. I'm blaming this whole hungry all the time thing on Bean."

Anablue glanced over to the table next to them. Six men sat at the table, enjoying a hearty breakfast. Her eyes widened, nudging Donall with her elbow. He glanced over as well. The men turned to them, lifting their glasses, winking. They blew kisses their way.

"The brides," Anablue whispered as she and Donall lifted their glasses of orange juice in a silent toast.

Shaking her head. "Well, you have to admit. Our wedding day was memorable."

Donall snorted. "I'll never forget it. Not only my beautiful bride walking down the aisle. But that throne," he chuckled. "Just the sight of you sitting on that throne."

Rolling her eyes. "All I needed was to be top-less with a feather boa."

Donall laughed as he rose from his seat, pulling her chair out, taking her by the hand. They left the restaurant.

"Like Moulin Rouge," Donall laughed.

"That's exactly what I was thinking at the time," Anablue replied.

"So, were you a cabaret singer or courtesan?"

"At the real Moulin Rouge in Paris, some were both. But I can't sing or dance, so you're stuck with a courtesan."

Donall stopped, pulling her into his arms. "Hmm, both wife and courtesan. How lucky can a man get?"

"No more canoodling. We have to check out by eleven. Besides, courtesans were prostitutes."

"Okay, let's stick with wife with courtesan skills," Donall said.

Anablue laughed out loud. "You're incorrigible."

---

LATE IN THE AFTERNOON, Anablue pulled into Elijah's driveway. The beach party was well under way. Aiden, Brendan, Collin, and Elijah, Max, along with Capt. Jack, the Colonel, and the Ambassador all stood in the garage. Bunker sat in his highchair, gnawing on a teething biscuit, his little face and hands covered in cookie goo. Soup ran back and forth between the women at the beach and the men, making sure all was in order in his happy little world.

Climbing out of the car, Donall grinned at his family. Reaching down, he gave Soup a belly rub before placing a kiss on top of Bunker's head. Bunker babbled at him before offering his biscuit. "No thanks, little dude. You eat your cookie," Donall said.

"Nice ride. When did you get the muscle car?" Aiden said.

"It's not mine. It's Anablue's," Donall replied.

"No shit," Collin said.

Brendan, Aiden, and Collin circled the car. Looking at Anablue, who stood smiling, holding a box of bakery goods.

"You drive this?" Brendan asked.

Anablue rolled her eyes. "Here we go again."

"What's under the hood?" Aiden asked.

"A 396," Anablue replied. "Go ahead, look."

Aiden opened the hood. Whistling, "Pristine."

"Can you even see over the steering wheel?" Brendan laughed.

"I have phone books to sit on."

"Can you reach the pedals?" Aiden asked.

Giving him a look of pure exasperation. "Only if I tie wooden blocks to my feet," Anablue sarcastically but sweetly replied.

"How fast does she go?" Collin asked.

Glancing at Donall as he scowled. "I pegged her at 125," Anablue whispered.

"Two words," Donall said. "Bread and water."

"That's three," Anablue replied.

"Oh, for Pete's sake. Are they harassing you about the car?" Elyse said, coming upon them. Hooking her arm through Anablue's.

"Ooooh. What did you bring?" Elyse said.

Anablue lifted the box lid. "Thick and gooey frosted brownies."

"Those look amazing. We should sample them," Elyse giggled. "You know, to make sure they're okay for everyone else."

"My thoughts exactly," Anablue replied.

Elyse led the group down the path to the beach.

Bunker watched as everyone left. Leaning over the side of his highchair, he offered Soup, stretching up on two legs, a lick of his biscuit.

Ten seconds later, Elijah returned at a trot. Picking up the baby, highchair, and all. "Do not tell your mama I forgot you." He trotted back down to the beach with the baby.

The afternoon passed at a lazy pace. The Colonel took charge of the grill, cooking burgers and hot dogs on the grill. Jane made a fabulous potato salad and homemade beans, followed by fresh brownies from the bakery. Anablue and Donall opened their wedding gifts.

Capt. Jack handed Anablue and Donall a present. "This was your mother's and mine. Use it wisely."

Anablue glanced at Donall; he nodded his head. "Open it."

Pulling the pretty paper off the small box, she opened the lid.

An eighteen-eighty silver dollar rested on a bed of purple velvet.

"When you disagree, this will keep your arguments fair,"

Capt. Jack said. "It's the same coin we tossed when you were named."

Giving Capt. Jack, a hug. Anablue wiped the tears from her eyes. Handing the silver dollar to Donall. "You'd better hang on to it. It will get lost in my purse."

---

Beneath the shade of an umbrella, Elyse adjusted Bunker's hat, Elijah's head in her lap. They laughed in delight, watching Bunker camel crawl, his bum up in the air, across the sand to climb up to stand next to Donall sitting in a chair.

"What's the matter dude, don't want your knees in the sand?" Donall said. Picking the baby up to sit in his lap.

Anablue and Capt. Jack, hand in hand, strolled further down the beach.

"She's showing," Elyse murmured.

"I know. She's got a cute little bubble," Donall replied.

"Hmmm. Before you know it, she'll be looking like she's going to explode," Elyse giggled.

Her attention turned to Max and Jane, tossing a Frisbee back and forth. "And look at those two."

"They're going slow," Elijah said.

"They spend a lot of time together," Elyse replied.

"Which is funny, considering how much they argue," Donall said.

"Oh, they're not really arguing. It's more like verbal sparring. It's quite funny when you listen to them," Elyse said.

"It's like two peas in a pod." Elijah laughed.

"And these two?" Elijah said, pointing to the Colonel and Ambassador. Both side by side in lounge chairs, snoozing away under the shade of another umbrella.

Donall laughed. "Pops and Gramps. I'm thoroughly convinced neither remember who's who anymore."

"We thought the same thing," Elyse said.

"Mac never showed," Elijah said.

"I could have sworn I saw him at the chapel yesterday. It turned out to be a bum," Elyse said.

Donall and Elijah exchanged glances. Grinning, Elijah reached out and stroked her chin.

"Same red hair, same build," Elyse paused. "It was him, wasn't it? Is he working undercover?"

A shout from the shoreline and their attention were drawn to Aiden, Brendan, and Collin. All three were fishing from the shore.

"Looks like Aiden caught something," Elijah said, watching Aiden reel a fish in.

"Whatever happened with Aiden and Brie?" Elyse asked.

"Not sure. She got out a few months back," Elijah replied. Taking a sip of his beer.

"What about Collin and Belinda?" Elyse asked.

"Something's up with those two, but he's tight-lipped about it," Donall replied.

"And Brendan?" Elyse asked. "We have to find a girl for Brendan."

Donall and Elijah exchanged grins.

"That we will have to wait and see," Elijah replied.

Elyse snorted. "Oh, the two of you. How am I going to make sure everyone is happy if you won't tell me anything?"

"Always the matchmaker," Elijah said, pulling her down for a soft kiss.

"By the way, both of our fathers have been dating women in town," Elyse said.

Donall and Elijah looked at each other. "No shit," Donall said.

Pushing Elijah off her lap, she stood up, taking her sleepy baby from Donall's arms. She took him over and laid him in the playpen. Pulling his pacifier from inside her swim top, she stuck it in his mouth. Covering him with a light blanket, she covered the top of the playpen with a fitted crib sheet to keep the sun off of him.

Elijah laughed. "She still carries everything in her bra."

"You give her those names of that chopper crew yet?" Donall asked.

"No, I wanted her to get past the wedding festivities first. It will be hard on her. She still carries a lot of guilt," Elijah said.

"We all do," Donall replied.

"The best thing we can do is live life to its fullest," Elijah said. "What about you?"

"We're going to stay in town for a while. Eventually, we'll

settle down at the ranch. Maybe buy some cattle. We'll see," Donall said.

"A cowboy, huh?"

Donall snorted. "Yeehaw."

"What are your plans for your honeymoon?"

"We rented a beach house for a week. I am going to teach my bride how to swim. We'll be leaving shortly. We have one pit stop to make before we head down there."

---

AFTER HUGS AND KISSES GOODBYE, Anablue and Donall were finally on their way to San Francisco.

Parking on a side street, they walked down the pier to the dock.

Arms full of painting supplies and her painting stool. Donall carried it all to the end of the dock.

"You've got a little time before the sun sets," Donall said.

"It should be enough time to get at least an outline. The full moon rising is what I want to see," Anablue replied. "I can memorize the colors."

"You're sure ready for this?"

"Yes, when I saw the full moon over the Golden Gate Bridge last night, I knew it was what Brian wanted me to paint. It's his way of telling me to let him go." A single tear streamed down her cheek.

He cupped her face, using his thumbs to wipe at her tears. "You know you have to."

"I know, but it's so hard."

"Come here," Donall said, pulling her into his arms. She sobbed against his chest.

"You know Brian would want you to move on. Live a good life, have babies, and grow old just like his letter said."

"All of that with you. He would have liked you," Anablue whispered, hugging him tightly.

"You'd better start before you lose the light. I'll be right here sitting in my sailboat."

A few hours later, Anablue was finished with what she could get done. Packing up her things, Donall came up behind her, wrapping his arms around her as she leaned into him.

"I'm proud of you, Baby Blue."

"Look at the moon Donall, it's so beautiful."

"It is. You ready to go?"

"Yes. I have like, seven bikinis to show you this week."

"Why seven? You're going to be naked most of the time, anyway."

Walking to the car, they placed the canvas and paint supplies in the trunk. Looking at each other, glaring, they narrowed their eyes.

"It's a fun car to drive," Donall said.

"Fine," Anablue grumbled.

Donall pulled the silver dollar out of his pocket. "Call it."

"Heads," Anablue replied.

Flipping the coin. "Ha! Tails it is," Donall laughed with glee."

Anablue made a face and handed him the car keys. Donall tossed the phone books in the back seat. Once inside, all scrunched up, he found the lever to pull the driver's seat-back. Anablue climbed in the car, resting her head on Donall's shoulder. He reached out to stroke her cheek, then he pulled away from the curb.

The End

# EPILOGUE

Brendan climbed onto his motorcycle. Looking at his family.

"I'll be back," he said.

"Where are you off to?" Aiden asked.

"I told you. I'm going to get my shirt back."

"What's so important about an old army shirt?" Collin said.

Brendan grinned. "It's more about who's wearing it," he replied.

Elyse looked at him in confusion. "So, who is wearing your shirt?"

He looked out to the ocean. Brendan grinned again. "My wife," he said.

His family's jaws dropped open at the bombshell news, and he pulled away, chuckling to himself.

George Irelynn Cross walked up the path to the shiny red door. Ringing the doorbell, she turned to admire the quaint neighborhood. The door open and she turned back around.

"Hello Mrs. Wang. I'm Irelynn. We spoke on the phone earlier. I'm here about the room for rent."

# MAX'S FUNNY WORDS LIST

**Biffy** - Ladies room

**Bamboozled** - Fool or cheat someone

**Bumfuzzle** - Flustered

**Canoodle** -Kiss, cuddle, fondle

**Codswallop** -Nonsense

**Collywobbles** -Upset stomach

**Farklempt** -Choked up

**Flibbertigibbet** -Frivolous, flighty or talkative person

**Fiddle farting** -To play, or mess around when one is supposed to be doing something more productive.

**Flummoxed** -Bewildered or perplexed

**Gobshite** -One who engages in nonsensical chatter

**Gigglemug** -Smiling face

**Gobbledygook** -Meaningless nonsense

**Gollygoops** -Gibberish

**Kerfuffle** -Commotion or fuss caused by conflicting views

**Nincomepoop** -A foolish or stupid person.

**Poppycock** -Nonsense

**Scallywag** -A disreputable person

**Shenanigans** -Secret or dishonest activity or maneuvering

# GLOSSARY

**Bird Farm** - Aircraft Carrier

**SOP** - Standard Operating Procedures

**Wizzo** - Weapons Systems Officer. The second man in an F-4 fighter jet

**Callsign** - Nickname. They are usually based on how badly you've screwed something up, a play on your name, your personality or just the whims of the of other squadron pilots.

ALSO BY LEESA WRIGHT

Book One of the Corrington Series

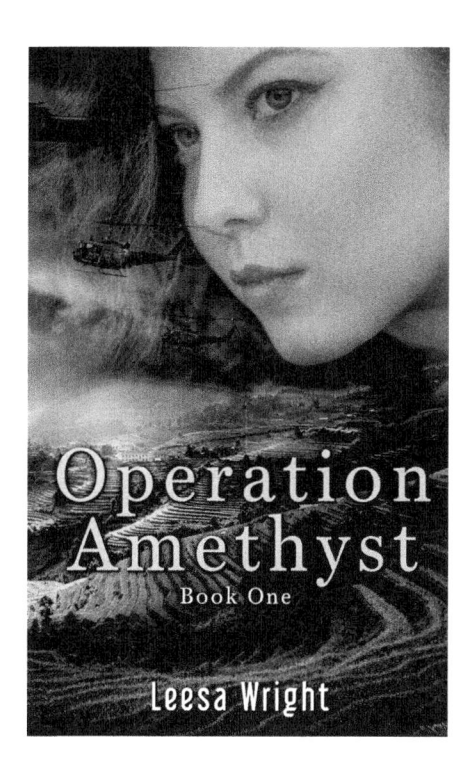

Find the 1st Chapter on the next page!

## OPERATION AMETHYST 1ST CHAPTER

South Vietnam, Mid-January 1968.

ELYSE BOOKER FELT the chopper shudder from the heavy spray of gunfire as the crew chief and gunner returned fire. Bullets whizzed by, some striking the windshield and other parts of the aircraft. The pilot and copilot fought to maintain control of the helicopter in what was supposed to be a quick trip from Huế City to the Khe Sanh military base.

After a bullet hit the engine, it began to go down in heavy jungle, churning out of control. Elyse hung on to the bars of the chopper for dear life. The chatter from the pilots and gunners screamed through her head along with her own screams of terror. The crew chief took a bullet and his lifeless body slumped over his weapon. One more spin threw her to the doorway of the chopper. In a selfless act of desperation, the gunner used his foot to push her out the door before the chopper hit the ground. The thick jungle foliage cushioned her body as she rolled away. The chopper crashed on its side in the sickening grind of metal meeting metal as it continued to roll and spin before bursting into flames.

An hour or so later, Elyse opened her eyes. She laid on the ground looking up at the sky. Curious formations of white, fluffy clouds floated by, mixed with the fading plumes of thick, black smoke as a pounding headache started just behind her eyes.

*Oh my God. My head.* She rolled to her knees as confusion took over. *Where am I? What happened?* Confusion was soon replaced by the terrifying memories of the chopper and it's sickening spin. Elyse spotted the burned shell of the chopper about two hundred feet away from where she sat on her knees. All on board were dead, and a sob caught in her throat. *Those poor men. The gunner… his eyes…* his beautiful eyes had mirrored the terror she had experienced as he pushed her out the door.

Excited voices speaking in Vietnamese filtered through the jungle to where she knelt. They were too far away for her to make out the words but close enough to warn her that danger was approaching. Elyse was not ignorant of the war; it was one of her father's main concerns when calling her home. She knew how dangerous it would be if the North Vietnamese Army (NVA) or the guerilla forces, Viet Cong (VC), caught her. Run.

The foliage was thick, lush and so tall it blocked her view of the sun at times. Since she was using the sun as her compass, she was frustrated by the thick growth both on the ground and overhead. The sounds of insects, monkeys, and birds calling to each other added to the exotic hum of the jungle. She did not know exactly where she was, but she knew to move eastward toward the South China Sea.

Elyse did not know how far or how long she had walked. She had survived two long, hot days and two terrifying, sleepless nights filled with bugs, the pitch blackness of the jungle, and the sounds of night creatures. She was exhausted again, and it would soon be time to stop and rest, but first she searched for water and food. Finding large curled leaves of jungle foliage with small pools of water in the center, she drank the water. After many attempts, she mastered her technique so not a drop was wasted. She had found berries the day before, but they were bitter and left a foul taste in her mouth as she spit them out. Not that hungry, she halfheartedly searched for something to eat and found some small green berries. She had seen these before in the outdoor markets of Huế City. There weren't many on the bush, but she ate them savoring their exotic flavor.

She played back the last telephone conversation with her father in her mind, the argument that ensued as he told her to notify the South Vietnamese Royal Ballet of an emergency at home, pack all of her things as a chopper was already on the way to pick her up from the American compound where she lived in Huế City.

"Daddy, Why? Why do I need to come home? What's going on?"

"Elyse, please don't argue with me. There is no time to explain. I need you home as soon as possible."

"I have responsibilities here. I have two performances next week."

"I'm sorry, you need to do as I say."

"Why are you always ordering me about? I'm a grown woman." The call was breaking up, and soon, all she heard was the crackle of static on the line.

"You're," more static, "danger," then the dial tone as the call disconnected.

It was not a good way to end her last conversation with her father and Elyse was racked with guilt, wondering if she had heard him correctly. *Did he say danger?*

The afternoon heat was oppressive, and the humidity hung thick in the air as she stopped to pin her hair back up again. She looked down at her bare feet for the hundredth time, unsure if she had lost her shoes during the crash or in the jungle. Her simple, orange muslin mini dress was torn and ragged from the jungle, and her feet bloody, dirty. She was hot, sweaty, thirsty, and miserable. Slapping at another blood-thirsty mosquito, she sighed and moved on, determined to make it as far east as she could before nightfall.

Leaning against a tree to rest, Elyse brushed the hair from her eyes and adjusted a bobby pin to secure her bun. Noticing the bark of the tree, she thought, *that looks like banana bark*. She looked up. *Bananas, sweet.* The tree was immense, tall and thick. *No Problem.* Pulling her dress up to her waist, she began the climb, scooting herself up inch by inch, foot by foot until she reached the very top of the tree. The large leaves drooped over the fruit as she reached out to brush them away.

A small brown hand reached out from the leaves and slapped at her. Screeching, Elyse almost lost her hold on the tree, but her thighs held firm, gripping the tree. A small monkey pushed its way through the leaves and bared its teeth at her, daring her to touch the forbidden fruit.

"Come on, I just want one," Elyse said, as she reached again for the bananas. The monkey screamed and slapped at her hand again, then it leaped at her causing her to lose her hand grip as she fell backwards.

Elyse dangled upside down high above the jungle floor, her legs firmly wrapped around the tree. The monkey hung from her hand screeching in terror. That's when she saw them, VC, creeping through the jungle below her.

Cold dread filled her as she almost lost her grip on the squirming monkey. If the animal fell, the VC below would see her. She swung it so it landed on the tree, and it scooted back up to hide within the large leaves. Gracefully and silently, she pulled herself up so she was again hugging the tree with both arms.

Watching the VC guerillas now directly below her, she counted eight of them. She held her breath, heart pounding in her chest, as they stopped to rest and quench their thirst, their voices quiet and muffled.

The monkey again bared its teeth and handed her half an

unpeeled banana before it jumped from the tree with a screech to land in another tree. Elyse gripped the tree, hanging on for dear life, all the while, praying that the men didn't look up. Eventually, they moved on and she stayed in the tree for another ten minutes watching for movement in the jungle below. Stuffing the banana in her mouth, she chewed the fruit before she scooted herself down and headed east through the jungle away from the VC guerillas.

She came upon a small village and watched from the jungle for a few minutes. Children played, and women weeded the small vegetable gardens, but there were no men. Stepping out from the jungle vegetation, she slowly walked up the pathway into the village. The huts with their grass roofs, the chickens and ducks waddled aimlessly about, the goats and other livestock in their neat little pens, all spoke of a poor but functioning village.

The children spotted her first, chattering amongst themselves. The women stopped their work to stare at her as she made her way to the center of the village. Women with infants in their arms and children gathered around her as a small boy of nine or so reached out to touch her hair, exclaiming in awe at her hair of fire. Smiling at him, she paused and waited for the elders in respect of their customs and culture. An old man, bent with age and years of hard labor, walked toward her as the crowd of women and children parted to let him pass. Elyse, having been raised in Vietnam and fluent in the language, addressed the old man with respect as she asked for water to quench her thirst. He signaled to an old woman, who Elyse assumed was his wife, and the woman brought a cup of water to Elyse.

"Are you American?" he asked.

"Yes."

"We are a peaceful village. We do not want trouble with the Americans or the VC."

"I do not mean to bring trouble to you. I am lost and need to find my way home."

"Do the Americans search for you?"

"I do not know."

"You are not safe here. The VC come through here to take our food to feed their men. We will feed you and point you in the right direction to find the Americans, but you must leave."

"I understand. I am grateful for whatever help you can give me."

Elyse sat on a stool outside, near the center of the village, as the children gathered around her, touching her hair and skin, pointing at her amethyst eyes, and asking a thousand questions. She patiently answered each one. A gaunt young woman with a babe at her breast handed her a bowl of rice. Elyse was hesitant to accept the food and take what little they had, but the woman urged Elyse to take it and eat. A girl of three with big eyes and a body too tiny for her age watched as Elyse took a small handful of rice. Unable to eat in front of the hungry tot, she put the handful of rice into the toddler's hands. The little girl called her "Toc chay," fire hair, as she stuffed the rice into her tiny mouth. Elyse smiled and stroked her head. The other children asked for some, and she split the remaining rice between them.

A young boy came running into the village, shouting that he had spotted VC heading toward the village. Elyse jumped to her feet, dropping the bowl.

The old man turned to Elyse. "You must hide, there is no time for escape." He took Elyse inside a hut and moved aside some weaved mats hiding a trap door in the floor.

"Quickly, inside. Stay silent, do not come out until I tell you so."

Elyse climbed down the shaky ladder into the pit. She squeezed her eyes shut as she felt a moment's panic when the trap door was shut and the mats replaced. She steadied her breathing. Calming herself as she could see daylight through the cracks in the floorboards left uncovered by the mats. She heard voices of men when the VC entered the village. Coming closer and closer to the hut where she hid. Her panic rose again, and she covered her mouth with her hands. Sheer horror at her predicament rose as Elyse realized that she may have been tricked. There was a strong possibility the elder might turn her over to the VC to save his village, and Elyse cursed her own gullibility.

Soldiers stood directly above her now, arguing about weapons placed in the pit a week ago. The elder argued that other VC guerillas had removed the weapons a few days earlier, but the other man screamed at the elder, demanding to know who took his cache of weapons.

Elyse scooted her back to the wall of the pit, searching for the weapons as her eyes adjusted to the darkness of the pit. Biting her lip, she could see nothing but the beady red eyes that watched her from the far corner. *Rats.* The hair on her arms stood straight up, and she broke out in goosebumps as the rats advanced.

Her eyes swung back up to the floorboards as the argument intensified, and the VC guerilla repeatedly struck the elder, knocking him to the floor of the hut. The old woman screamed and cried as the soldier refused her entry to the hut to see to her husband and forced her out to the center of the village, ordering her and the other women to prepare food for his hungry men.

The elder laid on the floor above Elyse for a while, and she worried that he was seriously injured or dead. He stirred, and Elyse breathed a sigh of relief as she wiped at the tears that threatened to spill from her eyes while she kicked at an encroaching rat.

Eventually the sounds of the women's screams and children crying quieted as the VC left the village. After what seemed like an eternity, the mats were removed, and the trap door opened. Elyse climbed up and out of the pit and followed the frail elder outside. She stopped to thank him, looking into his frightened eyes.

"I'm so sorry he hurt you. Thank you for saving my life."

He nodded his head in response. "You must go now." Pointing east, he said, "Go that way. You will find American soldiers."

Thanking him, she left the village at a run.

She slipped through the jungle for a time. An hour or so away from the village, the sound of a burbling stream reached her ears. She gave a small giggle of delight as she found the small stream. Climbing down the shallow incline, she sat on the bank of the stream, soaking her feet, washing the blood and filth of the jungle off her soles, and massaging her arches. She ripped a strip of cloth from her dress to use as a washcloth on her face and neck. Then, she stripped off her dress and entered a shallow pool to rinse the grime from the rest of her body and wash her dress. The cooling water lifted her spirits. She had a momentary concern about bathing in her orange panties and bra, and then she laughed out loud. *It's like a bikini, and there is no one here to see me anyway.*

Elyse cupped the water to her lips and giggled as the water trickled down her bosom. Sighing, feeling a moment's regret that she would have to move on. She hoped to find Americans as the village elder said she would. Silently praying that she would find help.

Climbing back up the bank of the stream, she stood, wringing out her dress when she heard the snap of a branch. She froze, a million thoughts racing through her head. *Animal, human, friend, or foe?*

Elyse heard whispers. *Vietnamese, VC. Run.*

Dropping her dress in her panic, she stumbled through the thick undergrowth. *The sun. Where is the sun?* Elyse was turned around and could not get her sense of direction. *Just keep running.*

Elyse heard them as she stumbled onto an overgrown

path. They were hot and fast on the trail behind her. They must have followed her from the village. Her heart raced, pounding in her chest as she ran through the jungle. She eventually came to a small clearing.

*Where to hide? Think. Look for somewhere to hide.* She backed up to the tree line, looking for somewhere—anywhere. Their chattering closed in behind her. *Oh God help me.*

Turning to run, she tripped and fell, partially catching herself in the shrubbery as she felt her bra catch on a branch just as someone grabbed her from behind.

## ACKNOWLEDGMENTS

**To Mary:**

Your laughter and pain at those long-ago memories moved me to tears. Thank you for sharing.

**To Anna and Trista:**

My rock-solid sounding boards. Thank you.

**To Mia:**

Thank you for your patience with me. You're awesome.

## ABOUT THE AUTHOR

Leesa makes her home in Twin Cities metro area in Minnesota with her husband and their two dogs Rosie and Jax. When she isn't writing, she enjoys gardening, painting, and reading romance novels. She and her husband also enjoy movies, traveling, and entertaining their two grown children, along with their spouses, and seven beautiful grandchildren. Leesa's favorite romance authors are Kathleen Woodwiss, Christine Feehan, and Johanna Lindsey.

The book's inspiration came one night from a dream about the characters, a song, and the story around them. Please leave a review and let me know you enjoyed my story—

Connect with me and join my email list!
www.leesawrites.com

facebook.com/Leesa-Wright-Author
twitter.com/Leesaauthor
instagram.com/Leesawright.author
goodreads.com/0381892.Leesa_Wright

Printed in Great Britain
by Amazon